W9-CUH-410

Advance praise for Lee Killough's *Killer Karma*

"Sat down with the book last Monday night, gonna fill in the commercials during Monday Night Football, and suddenly realized it was 3:00 in the morning. A first-class supernatural police procedural that I just couldn't put down. I loved every minute of it."—Glen Cook, author of the Garrett Files fantasy detective series & Black Company military fantasies

"How do you solve your own Murder? In *Killer Karma*, dead cop Cole Dunavan learns to control his ghostly body in an effort to clear his name and bring his wife some peace. Through frustrating trial and error, Dunavan communicates with his fellow cops, goads his murderer, and learns more about the world than he ever imagined. In a book that's sometimes poignant and sometimes funny, Lee Killough gives us a tutorial on what it's like to be incorporeal and mightily pissed off."—Charlaine Harris, NYT bestselling author of *Dead to the World*

"I know of nothing comparable either living or dead. After all, Cole is a ghost, and his current job description now starts with 'haunt.' Killough writes 'COP' like a seasoned flatfoot, with plenty of humor, ghastly violence, and paranormal takes on how the dead get even."—Detective Ryan Runyan, Riley County Police

And here's a blurb from cop-turned-mystery author Robin Burcell, prefaced in her note with the comment: "I very much enjoyed it, surprisingly so, as I never would've picked up a book of this nature had you not expanded my horizons."

"This book caught me on the first page and didn't let go. Cole Dunavan is a most unusual investigator, one I won't soon forget."—Robin Burcell, Anthony Winner for *Deadly Legacy*

KILLER
KARMA

LEE KILLOUGH

Meisha Merlin Publishing, Inc.
Atlanta, GA

Killer Karma

Published by Meisha Merlin Publishing, Inc.
PO Box 7
Decatur, GA   30031

Editing by Stephen Pagel
Copyediting and Proofreading by Josepha Sherman
Interior layout by Lynn Swetz
Cover art by Hoang
Cover design by Kevin Murphy

ISBN: Hard Cover 1-59222-006-1

http://www.MeishaMerlin.com
First MM Publishing edition: July 2005

Printed in the United States of America
0 9 8 7 6 5 4 3 2 1

For DENNY
very significant other, cheer leader, first reader

Many thanks to Alan Beatts and Jude Seldman at Borderlands Books in San Francisco, also to Claudius Reich, for their assistance in checking and tracking down San Francisco city details; to former detective Jeff Stratton for contributing, albeit unknowingly, to the character of Cole Dunavan. And a very special thanks to Marie Loughin and former RCPD sergeant Stan Conkwright for their technical input and helpful critiques.

KILLER KARMA

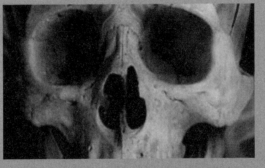

LEE KILLOUGH

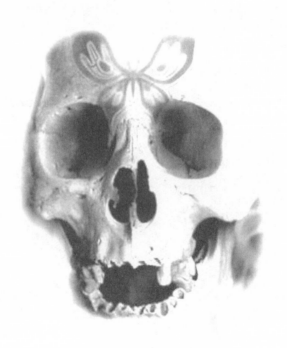

— 1 —

HE FOUND HIMSELF standing in a parking garage with no memory except of his murder. Those final sensations felt seared into his brain: the hard pressure of a gun muzzle behind his right ear; his body stiffened by surprise, horror, and anger; a cry of *No, wait!* rising in his throat...but all vanishing the next second in an explosion of pain that hurled him into darkness.

As he recoiled from the memory, however, reason overrode terror. Those could hardly be final sensations if he were able to remember them.

"Way to go, numbnuts," he said.

The sound of his voice reassured him of his reality, too. So did feeling the back of his head. His exploring fingers found just short hair...no stickiness indicative of fresh blood, no matting indicative of dried blood. Certainly no bullet hole.

"You just had a bad dream."

But if that were the case, how did he explain the amnesia?

He fought the panic threatening him again. Maybe he had been mugged and received a concussion. Except how could he be on his feet if he had been hit hard enough to lose all memory, and even awareness of what city he was in? Tan lines on his wrist and ring finger attested to a missing watch and ring. A quick examination of his clothes—grey suit, pinstriped shirt, tie striped in yellow, maroon, and grey—found no blood or other signs of attack. Nor did running his hands over his body—a lanky one better than six feet tall—locate any injuries. His chin felt smooth, free of abrasions. Except for his tie being loosened and shirt unbuttoned at the collar, he seemed ready to walk into a business meeting.

Meeting! The thought sent him reeling backward, staggered by a rush of anger, guilt, leaden foreboding, a pounding sense of urgency, and—insanely—images of...*butterflies?* He shook his head to clear it. Butterflies. That was crazy. The rest, though, seemed to indicate he was scheduled for an unpleasant but critically important meeting. Life or death important. But where was it? How could he find out?

The answer hit him a moment later. Duh. "Use your phone, stupid." People at the numbers in it would know him.

He reached into his coat but to his dismay found no phone. Not only no phone. Checking the rest of his pockets one by one found them all empty. No billfold, no business cards, no keys, no loose change. Not even a handkerchief.

He ran for the exit arrow at the end of the row. The garage entrance would have an attendant who could help him. But running, panic rose in him. His feet seemed to make no sound. Nor could he smell the exhaust of an SUV that passed him trailing blue smoke. His brain had been royally screwed up.

He was fighting hysteria by the time he reached the exit and charged up to the booth. "Help me!" he yelled at to the middle-aged woman inside. "Call 911! I need a doctor!"

The attendant never looked up from her book.

He waved his arms frantically. "Hey!" But when she still did not respond, fear turned to fury. "Damn it...are you frigging *deaf?*" He slammed the glass with both fists.

Anger vanished in a blast of icy fear. Like his feet, his fists made no sound...and despite the force he put into the blow, he felt as if he was hitting a layer of foam rubber. Whatever happened had turned him into a total wack job. Unless he was not crazy but...

He cut off the thought. No! That was even crazier. He stumbled back from the booth. Fine. Forget the attendant. At least some of the buildings around the garage must have a security force. One of those officers could help him.

He turned and charged up the ramp. Where he came face to face with a Lexus on its way in. He leaped sideways, but not fast enough. The left front headlight and fender caught him head-on...and passed *through* him.

He stared down at himself, clutching his chest and abdomen, chaos roaring in him. But what he did *not* feel engulfed him in terror. His heart should be thundering. But he felt nothing beneath the hand on his chest. No heartbeat, no frightened gasp for breath. He felt only the remembered pressure of the gun muzzle against his skull.

"No!"

Thrusting away the memory, he bolted from the garage and along the sidewalk outside. What he thought had just happened could not have. It was impossible...a hallucination! It had to be. He halted at the corner. Look at him! He was real. Holding up a hand to the afternoon sky blocked the light. When he socked one arm with the other hand, his body felt solid.

Down the block two women came out of the building and up the hill toward him.

He ran to meet them. "Ladies! Can you help me?"

They kept moving without missing a beat of their conversation.

"Please!" Desperate, he reached for the arm of the nearest woman. "Look at me! You see me, don't you?"

The arm slid through his grasp as though greased. He started to grab for her again...and froze, staring at the reflection in the glass doors. It mirrored the women and the street, and the building across the street. But not him.

Cold, cold ice filled him. That gun, the explosion, the darkness swallowing him...not a nightmare, he thought in despair. Not a hallucination. Memories. It happened. And he died.

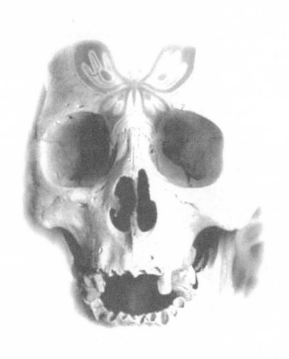

— 2 —

HE TURNED HIS back on the reflection. It helped relieve the shock. Though shock did not so much fade as disappear under the sense of foreboding and urgency. He gladly focused on that in place of his terrible final moment of existence. Spirits supposedly hung around because they had unfinished business, right? Judging by the pressure in him, he had some major loose ends to tie up. Logically, he would think it involved settling with whoever killed him, or the circumstances that had earned him a bullet. But that idea brought no resonance in him. The foreboding shouted *danger*. With him beyond danger, it meant someone else was the target. Because of him, maybe. That would account for the guilt. The urgency indicated he had no time to waste removing the danger.

He scowled skyward. "But how the hell am I supposed to do that with no frigging idea what the danger is and who's involved?" Trying to dig that out of the Black Hole in his mind, all he came up with was the stupid butterfly image. And that just made his gut lurch with another kick of guilt.

Being a ghost needed to come with a guidebook, he reflected irritably. But since it did not, he'd better start figuring things out for himself. Beginning with who he was. *Where* was fortunately no longer a question—up the hill rose a pyramidal skyscraper that could only be the Transamerica building, which made this San Francisco. Hopefully he could identify himself as easily. Once he had, he should know who he had to save and from what.

Since he had been murdered, might there be a story about it in the newspapers?

He turned to the doors behind him. Now he recognized them as the entrance to Two Embarcadero Center. The stores in the shopping arcade included a newsstand. He reached for the door handle. But when he pulled, it slipped through his fingers. Just as that woman's arm had. Shit. Did that mean—

He ended the thought, shaking his head at his own stupidity. Duh. "You're a ghost, numbnuts. You have no material substance. So how can you hold anything material?" But being a ghost, he also had no need to *open* the door. He could walk through it.

A thought that lasted until he tried that...and crashed into the glass.

He staggered backward in disbelief. Hitting the door had the same foam rubber sensation as pounding the attendant's booth but...what blocked him? If people and door handles moved through him, the reverse should be true. He tried again, this time holding his hands out in front of him as he walked forward. His hands met the surface and...stopped. He tried more force, slamming his shoulder into the door. In vain. He just smashed against it again...the glass withstanding him painlessly and soundlessly, but stubbornly impenetrable.

Alarm flared in him. Unless he could go where he wanted to, how was he going to do what he needed to do?

At the edge of the Black Hole, something stirred. He froze, afraid to move for fear of losing it. It had something to do with going through a wall. Gingerly, he teased the memory out where he could see it...and found an image of someone named Harry Potter...trying to reach platform nine and three-quarters. Except Harry got through by running at the wall and the forceful approach had already failed here. Wait. When Harry thought he was about to crash, he closed his eyes.

Okay...try that. Closing his eyes, he walked forward, counting strides. Two...three...four. On *five* he opened his eyes and grinned. Yes! He was in!

Wasting no more time, he hurried through the mall to the newsstand in 1EC.

But once there, to his disappointment, neither the *Chronicle* nor the *Examiner* had anything above the fold about a recent murder that might be his.

"Damn!"

All the papers gave him was the date: Sunday, August 29. Which was no use even for telling how long he had been dead, since the date of his last conscious memory still lay buried in the Black Hole.

He stalked away from the newsstand. Terrific. No way to check the papers. And since no one appeared to see or hear him, that ruled out asking about himself. He ran both hands back through his hair. Now what?

His fingers met a ridge of scar under the hair above his left ear. As they did, a tingle shot through him. Slowly he traced back over the scar. Touching it brought a lightning series of sensations and images. The deafening noise of combined music and voices. Standing with his back to a bar thinking that the saving grace of being stuck at Fort Riley when you were twenty and single was Aggieville, Kansas State University's campus village, full of bars and coeds. Two men angrily facing each other, one a preppy type with a big wet spot on the front of his trousers and the other with a military burr haircut and an empty beer mug in his raised hand. He remembered himself stepping between the two...and stars exploding in his head.

When they'd cleared, he had found himself on a stretcher, with a paramedic asking how many fingers she held in front of his face. *"Your buddy clobbered you with his beer mug,"* she'd said.

His wry thought had been that as an MP, *he* was usually the one breaking heads.

Memory of the incident broke off abruptly as a buzz like a low grade electric current spreading through him, followed by a startled yelp and a head of corn-rowed brunette hair leaping from beneath his chin.

He jumped backward. "Jesus!"

In front of him, a blonde girl stared at her brunette friend. "What's the matter?"

The brunette grimaced. "There was this, like, icy cold spot." She pointed to where he had been standing. "And I got an electric shock." She rubbed her arms. "Like, you know, from a doorknob when you've rubbed your feet across the carpet? It was totally weird." Shuddering, she hurried off down the concourse.

"I didn't, you know, like it either," he called after her, and though the sensation had been more disconcerting than uncomfortable, he moved over by a planter to think back over the recovered memory.

At the same time, he tried watching around himself to avoid another walk-through. With a start, he found himself able to look in all directions at the same time. Vision no longer depended on what direction his eyes pointed. It was, to quote the brunette, totally weird. It also made him dizzy and would not turn off now that he had discovered it.

After several excruciating minutes of vertigo, he managed to focus forward and shut out the rest except as a kind of extended peripheral vision. Then he returned to the bar memory. While it did not give him his name, it did suggest the way to learn more about himself: check his body for other scars.

Invisibility theoretically gave him the freedom to strip down right here, but he cringed at the idea. While it would sure be one way to discover if anyone could see him, it smacked too much of a naked-in-public dream. No…the men's room upstairs was a better idea.

Outside its door minutes later, he paused long enough to close his eyes, then walked forward. Would the trick take him through this door, too?

It did. He felt no barrier, and opening his eyes after a few steps, he found himself inside.

To keep clear of anyone else using the facilities, he moved to the far end of the basin row. A glance in the mirror as he shrugged out of his coat halted him for a moment. Like the store window, the mirror did not reflect him. The indisputable proof of his nonexistence chilled him again. As soon as he'd stripped to his boxers and laid his clothes across a basin, he turned away from the mirror.

"Cross your antennas for luck, butterflies."

Nothing on his chest triggered any memories, just told him he had black hair. But a peculiar set of scars on his right wrist and hand caught his attention. An arc of four, each about a quarter inch long, on the inside just below the base of his thumb and an arc of similar scars on the upper side.

He ran his other thumb across them. What would do that?

The answer came abruptly: teeth. Remembered pain shot up his arm. Along with it came memory of kneeling on a man's back, yelling: "*Let go! Quit resisting!*" as he struggled to free his wrist from the man's mouth and wrestle the douchebag's arm back for cuffing.

Cuffing? Of course. He was a cop. He had been one for nearly sixteen years, since finishing his hitch in the Army. Was that why he'd been killed? But if so, why had being shot surprised him?

No answer came. Nor did his name.

In growing frustration he identified other scars: healed fractures in his left hand and right forearm, scars from knife cuts, other scars from burns caused by deflecting a thrown cigarette and from a tail pipe while wrestling a suspect from beneath a car. But all they told him was what *kind* of cop he was…one who hated losing foot chases and who hung onto suspects he caught no matter what.

Then a surgical scar running the length of his left thigh brought up another memory…of hanging on the door of a suspect's car and being dragged under the wheels…ending up on a stretcher again.

This time the face of his sergeant glared down at him. "*Dunavan, why the hell do you have to be a fucking John Wayne?*"

Relief and elation swept him. Finally! His name was Dunavan. Coleman Douglas Dunavan.

He waited for the Black Hole to release the rest of his memory.

Nothing happened.

Frustration and despair boiled up in him. "No! Damn it...*no!*"

Cole slammed a fist into the towel dispenser, then each of the stall doors...though the sensation of punching marshmallow only added to his frustration. Shit, shit, *shit!* He had to know why he was here! A life could depend on it! What was holding back the memories? What the hell did it *take* to release them!

After the last stall door, he clenched his jaw. Okay, if he had to keep fighting the Black Hole...fine. After all, hanging on and plugging away was what had earned him the nickname Bulldog.

He wheeled back toward the basins to dress...and stopped short. His clothes were gone! "For the love of..." This just kept getting better and better! Now he was supposed to run around half naked while—

Belatedly, he realized he wore the missing items. He stared down himself, shaking his head. Son of a bitch. Weird, weird, weird.

He headed for the door. If death limited him to one outfit, he mused, it was a good thing he'd died decently dressed, not been blown away in his sleep so that he spent ghosthood in bare feet and whatever he wore to bed. Or worse, whacked during sex. He could be taking care of his unfinished business with it all hanging out. That image made him cringe and laugh at the same time.

Which ended abruptly as he crashed into the door.

Way to go, numbnuts. Closing his eyes, Cole decided maybe he was glad no one saw him.

Outside the men's room, he peered around at the concourse, considering what to do now. There must be an investigation into his death. Maybe seeing what they had in the way of evidence and suspects would help him learn what held him here. So he needed to visit Homicide.

As he started for the escalator, though, a dismaying thought struck him. Could he leave Embarcadero Center? Ghost stories always had them haunting specific places. A scene from some old movie played in his head...the ghosts of airmen who hadcrashed in the African desert trying to walk away from their plane, only to find themselves circling back to it.

Downstairs, he approached the Sacramento Street exit with caution. To his relief, nothing blocked his way, nor pulled him back when he dodged across the street. He appeared to be free to go where he wanted.

Now it was just a question of reaching the Hall of Justice. Take the bus? He could ride free. But on a bus he would have other passengers not only walking through him but standing or sitting in the same space he occupied. Cole grimaced. What about flying? He was a ghost, after all.

Except, he had no idea how to go about flying. Flap his arms? That sounded ridiculous, even with no one seeing him. He would walk. The Hall was only about two miles away.

After a few blocks, though, impatience to arrive turned the walk to a jog, then a lope. Zig-zagging through the South of Market, Cole noticed he maintained the pace without effort, and on reaching the Hall's front steps, he was astonished to realize he felt no trace of fatigue. He was ready to run another two miles. Or a marathon. So...no matter how many trips across town he might have to make, he could keep going? That was good to know.

Inside, Cole paused at the elevator, but then walked on and passed through the stair door. Pushing buttons had to be as impossible as picking things up. Taking the steps two at a time, he raced up to the Investigation Bureau on the fourth floor. It felt bizarre not hearing his footsteps. The bare concrete walls and un-cased windows of the stairwell usually made every little sound echo.

He paused in mid-step. Usually? How often had he come up these stairs?

Continuing to climb, he decided it must have been often. This felt so familiar. When he reached it, the Bureau corridor and its walls hung with photographs of SFPD officers on the job felt familiar, too. Then as Cole passed Burglary's door on the way to Homicide, he realized why. He was a detective. He had been one for almost seven years, assigned to Burglary there, working the cases in the Mission District.

He stopped short, visualizing his desk inside...case folders stacked on it and the deep window sill beside it. So why was he killed? Burglars were not usually violent individuals. Still...

Cole closed his eyes and stepped through Burglary's door. Past the counter and in the main office, he headed for his desk. Stan Fontaine and Gail Harris sat at their desks, typing reports. He waved. "Hi, guys."

Neither looked up.

No surprise there, but if only someone *would* see him. When the identity of his killer and an explanation for this foreboding and urgency might be in one of his case folders, not being able to pick things up *sucked*! Since association seemed to be triggering memory recovery, he had to hope that just seeing or touching the right folder—

A photograph by the telephone interrupted the thought. Four children, a brindle dog, and a woman with a Dolly Parton bustline and a kinky mane of bright red hair sitting on the steps of a Victorian. His family.

Guilt stabbed him. How could he remember he was a cop before remembering Sherrie and the kids? He and Sherrie had been married longer than he carried a badge. His family meant much more to him than the job. After growing up with his cop father an absentee dad, he'd worked hard at not inflicting that on his own kids. He made a point of being there to help them learn to ride bikes and shoot hoops, for birthdays, Travis's school wrestling matches, and Renee's music recitals. But especially, how could he remember that Aggieville brawl without remembering that Sherrie Trask had been the nurse waking him every hour to take his blood pressure and shine a light in his eyes?

Cole ran his fingers across the photograph. God, he wanted to go home and see them. If only it were less urgent that he find out what brought him back.

Reverberation in him squeezed his chest and brought an icy wave of realization. Oh, shit. Sherrie and the kids were part of what brought him back. Whatever caused his guilt and foreboding also threatened them.

He bolted for the door.

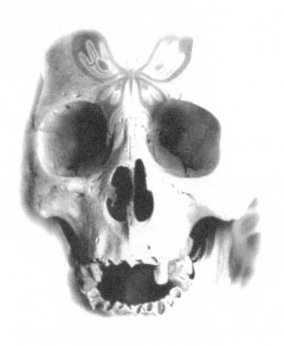

— 3 —

URGENCY POUNDED IN Cole as he rushed out of the Hall and across the front terrace to the steps. How long would it take him to run to Noe Valley? Too long. But even a car would take longer than he liked. If only he could fly. He wanted to be home *now*.

With which thought he hit the newel post at the bottom of their hall stairs.

Cole gaped around him and through the archway into the livingroom. What happened? Was he really here? He ran his fingers along the crack in the cap of the newel post filled with wood putty, one of his first repairs when they moved in. From upstairs came furiously-paced violin music…"Summer," from Vivaldi's *Four Seasons*. Hearing the female half of their twins play brought her image to mind…all gangly arms and legs, seemingly taller every day, so intent on the music that Renee looked almost angry, and older than nearly fifteen. This was real, but…how had he gotten here?

A voice coming up the hall from the kitchen said, "Talk to me, Sherrie."

Joanna Trask, Sherrie's mother. He headed down the hall. Did her presence mean he'd died recently? She made sure to be here when Sherrie needed her. Though living in Oakland let her visit almost any time.

In the kitchen Joanna sat on a stool at the island—an older version of Sherrie but with plain, tame hair—watching Sherrie fill a plastic bucket at the sink.

Cole focused on Sherrie, too. Despite the weight of fore-boding and urgency, seeing her brought the usual surge of warmth. Even after sixteen years, nothing welcomed him home like wrapping his arms around her and burying his face in the kinky mass of her hair...today tied back. The thought of her body against his and her breasts in his hands still had the power to arouse him.

Then she turned. The strain in her face kicked him in the gut.

Joanna frowned with concern. "I know that phone call upset you."

Sherrie said nothing, just carried the bucket to the stove. He saw she wore rubber gloves, and instead of adding water to the big simmering soup pot, she opened the oven door. Sherrie scrubbed savagely at the glass in the oven door.

A chill ran through Cole. Silent and scouring the kitchen? Something had seriously pissed her off. The same thing that caused his guilt?

Joanna continued, "What did Sergeant Leach say to you?"

Cole grimaced in dismay. *Management Control* was involved in his murder investigation? What the hell had he been *doing*? And of all the internal affairs officers that could be on his case, what bad karma picked Norman Leach? He doubted Leach had forgotten the fake bullet holes put on his new Corvette when they worked together in the Northern District...and maybe still brooded over the suspicion that Cole Dunavan and Kevin Rasgorshek were responsible.

His old partner's name brought a mental dope slap. Damn! Razor was someone else he should have remembered right away. Since becoming partners on patrol in the Northern District, they had been like brothers. All the time they spent running around together off duty resulted in endless ribbing and lewd comments when Sherrie and Razor's second wife Lauren turned up pregnant at the same time and delivered Kyle and Holly within a week of each other. Razor could tell him what had been going on...if only there were a way to ask.

"Did the sergeant have something more to say about that woman?" Joanna asked.

Cole abruptly forgot Razor. What woman?

Sherrie silently rinsed her sponge in the bucket.

"Does he still think Cole went off with her?"

What! Anger and horror sent heat and ice through Cole. Leach was accusing him of an affair!

"Sherrie, no!" He ran to the stove and dropped to his knees, coming to her eye level. If only he could turn her to look at him. "Don't believe Leach. I wouldn't do that to you!"

Not when it was one of her biggest nightmares and he knew the cost of screwing around. Goodbye Sherrie. She made it clear when he convinced her to marry him—after growing up with a father whose zipper automatically dropped for anyone female, she had zero tolerance for infidelity.

If she believed he cheated on her, that would explain this cleaning mania. And without memory, how could he be sure what had happened? He felt guilty about something. Heartsick, Cole watched her wipe under the oven's lower heating element. "Sherrie, no matter what, I'd never *leave* you."

Suddenly, the real meaning of Leach's assumption hit Cole. No one knew he was *dead!* He jumped to his feet. Shit! He had to find a way to tell them.

Joanna sighed. "Listen to me. If anyone knows the signs of an affair, I do, and one phone call means nothing."

Cole groped for memory of a phone call...or a name or face. Anything. In vain.

"Not just *one* call." The words came in brittle syllables. Sherrie scrubbed at the oven. "Now Leach says there were three. She called Cole twice Wednesday evening before he made that call to her. When he phoned *me* to say he had 'something to do' before coming home, it was the second time in three days he'd done that." She dunked the sponge and wrung it out with a savage twist. "Cole was on edge since Monday. A case bugging him, he said...but those make him distracted, not jumpy. How would *you* call it?"

Cole winced. Damn! Was there another explanation for why he acted that way? "Sherrie, help me remember. Mention a name."

Joanna said, "At least guilt would indicate it's probably the first—" She broke off as Sherrie shot her a withering stare. A moment later, she frowned. "Aren't people supposed to be innocent until proven guilty...even husbands?"

Sherrie scrubbed savagely at the glass-in oven door. "I'm *not* letting him turn on the charm and blind me with bullshit until I'm alone in ICU with a dying child while he's off—"

Joanna choked.

Immediately, horror filled Sherrie's eyes. She choked, too, and rushed to throw her arms around her mother. "I'm sorry! Please forgive me. I wasn't thinking."

While they clung together, the front door began beeping. Someone was punching the keypad. Mother and daughter looked at each other, pulled apart, and took deep breaths. By the time the front door banged open and the thump of dumped objects came down the hall, they had put on calm faces.

"Mom, we're home!" Kyle's voice yelled.

Sherrie stripped off her gloves. "We're in the kitchen!"

Cole moved to the far end of the island, away from the danger of walk-throughs.

Feet ran their direction, accompanied by the scrabble of claws on wood. Tiger bounded into the kitchen first and threw his square body at Sherrie, tongue lolling, stubby tail a frantic metronome.

Kyle and his virtual twin Holly arrived seconds later. Even at ten Kyle had the Dunavan lankiness...topped by his mother's hair. "Have they found Dad?" he asked eagerly.

"Not yet." Sherrie reached down to pat the dog's blunt head. "How was sailing?"

That would be on the *Chimera*, the sloop Razor co-owned with his sister Denise.

The light died from Kyle's face. He shrugged.

"We had a delightful time," Holly said. "We went north as far as San Quentin. Daddy let Kyle take the helm all the way back and he was splendid. No one fell overboard, not even Tiger when gulls dive-bombed him." Then her pixie face lit with mischief. "And Travis thinks Denise's new girlfriend is a real babe."

Joanna's mouth tightened. Sherrie sent her a sharp *Don't say a word!* glance.

Tiger spun from Sherrie and ran down the island to dance in front of Cole, his eyes and tail declaring: *Fearless leader, you would have been proud of me! I chased a bizillion killer seagulls and watercraft away from the boat!*

Cole stared. The dog *saw* him?

Travis, the male half of the twins, came through the doorway...the Dunavan coloring his only similarity to Renee...built like a middleweight wrestler, and winner of high school trophies proving it. "What's with Tiger?"

Cole said, "Tiger, freeze. Get on the ground."

The dog dropped to a sphinx position on the floor.

Razor followed Travis, and stopped in the doorway to polish his glasses on the tail of his 49ers sweat shirt. He should have been the one nicknamed Bulldog. When they were all out somewhere together, his stocky build sometimes made strangers mistake Travis for his son.

"You've all probably worked up an appetite," Sherrie said. "Please stay for supper. We have enough of my famous Italian soup to feed a battalion. Or do you have to get Holly back to Lauren?"

Cole came on alert. That was her I-want-to-talk voice.

"No." Razor shook his head. "I have her for the night."

Cole pumped a fist. Yes! Now maybe he would learn some answers.

Sure enough, Sherrie said, "Mother, will you see if Hannah's finished her nap? The rest of you, pick up your stuff in the hall and put away Tiger's life jacket. Then go wash up. Except you, Razor."

Travis wheeled from checking out the soup. "Have you heard something about Dad?"

Cole grinned. Travis had cop instincts...watching everything around him, a natural at reading body language and hearing what lay behind the words people said.

Which Sherrie well knew. The shake of her head signaled *ask me later.*

Joanna's frown said she wanted to stay, too, but after a sharp look from Sherrie, she slid off her stool and followed the kids out. Sherrie took it over. Razor straddled another stool, resting his arms on the back. Cole leaned on the island where he could see both their faces. He expected Tiger to follow the boys, but the dog stayed, sitting against Sherrie's legs.

She leaned down and rubbed his head until footsteps faded up the hall. "Is there anything about Cole's disappearance you aren't telling me?"

Behind his glasses, Razor's eyes narrowed. "No. Why?"

"Leach called earlier. He asked if Cole loses his temper with the kids and me and has ever been physically abusive."

Cole stiffened. What!

Sherrie straightened from petting the dog. "Can you find out what's going on?"

"From Leach?" Razor grimaced. "I doubt it. But..." He pulled his cell phone off his belt. "...there's someone else I'll try." He looked up a number and punched it in.

Sherrie released the clip on her hair, letting the kinky mass spring loose. "See if they'll give you any details about this Benay woman."

Benay! The name hit Cole like a physical blow. The Black Hole collapsed, spewing a tidal wave of memory. He reeled before it, remembering everything...about his murder, and about his relationship with Sara Benay. In horror, he realized that Benay was the unfinished business that brought him back...that the majority of the foreboding and urgency arose from danger that he had brought on her. But for all he had to feel guilty about, at least none of it came from an affair.

"Sherrie," he said in relief, "she was just an informant! Nothing happened between us."

How did he make Sherrie hear, so that she knew he had not turned into Eddie Trask?

He came around the island to their stools. "Can you tell at all that I'm here?" Tiger whined and he bent to scratch the dog's ears. What let Tiger see him when they did not? "Razor, do *you* hear me?"

Apparently not. Razor stared into space as he talked into the phone. "Jer, you're the man who'll know. I hear there's been a development in finding Cole Dunavan."

As Razor listened to the answer, Cole noticed a rhythmic thumping. It sounded like a heartbeat. Moments later he tracked the source and realized it *was* a heartbeat. Razor's. And in the last few seconds the rate had gone up. If ghost hearing was sharp enough to hear hearts, Cole wondered, could he also listen to the other end of Razor's conversation? He leaned toward the phone.

Just in time for Razor to disconnect.

"Well?" Sherrie stared at him expectantly.

Razor slowly folded the phone and returned it to his belt before answering. "They found the car this afternoon...at the San Jose airport. It's being brought back for processing."

Sherrie's breath caught. Cole heard her heart jump.

Razor shook his head. "No, Cole wasn't in it. But..." He hesitated. "...there's blood on the passenger side and Homicide is taking over the investigation."

Which explained the question about physical abuse. Leach obviously thought a lover's quarrel had turned violent. Cole had to admit that in Leach's place, he would, too.

Color drained out of Sherrie's face. "Leach thinks Cole killed that woman, doesn't he?"

"But he's wrong!" If only he could take her in his arms. Cole settled for touching her hair. "The lab will find it's my blood." Unless Benay also had AB positive. But determining *he* was the victim did not clear him about having an affair. He had to come up with more to do that. "I'm sorry, babe...for getting myself killed and putting you through this. If I hadn't been so damned obsessed with—"

Joanna's voice interrupted, calling from the hall, "Guess who's awake from her nap."

Hannah burst into the kitchen, red curls bouncing and her t-shirt warning: *Watch Out! I'm Two!* She started toward Sherrie, but halted, wheeled Cole's direction, and squealed in delight. "Daddy!"

Cole started. She saw him, too?

"Daddy!" At his feet, she held up her arms. "Play airplane!"

Cole's throat closed. Shit. "I can't, pumpkin. I'm sorry. I can't pick you up."

The adults stared at her. "Hannah," Sherrie called. "Come here."

Hannah frowned. "Play airplane!" She reached out to tug at his slacks...stared in bafflement when the grab failed to connect with anything. She broke into an angry wail.

He smiled wryly. "I know how you feel, kiddo."

Sherrie slid off the stool and scooped Hannah up. "Daddy isn't here."

Hannah twisted, reaching toward him. "Daddy!" Her wail rose like a siren.

Cole ruffled her hair...without a curl moving. "We Dunavans do fixate on things, don't we?"

A thought that brought him back to Sara Benay. He needed to find her and save her from the mess he'd landed her in. Which included, he suddenly realized, becoming the chief suspect in his murder! Once the blood was established as his, the two of them would change places in the lover's quarrel scenario. Threat and urgency beat at him. He just hated to leave here. What if he was never able to come back...never saw Sherrie and the kids again?

So what are you thinking? a voice in him sneered. *Hang out here forever? Ignore why you're still around...blow off cleaning up the mess you made and getting straight with everyone? You don't mind Sherrie being afraid the man she thought you were is a lie?*

He sighed mentally. No, he could not do that to Sherrie, and he had to deal with screwing up. He brushed Sherrie's hair. "If I never see you again, remember I love you."

Cuddling and soothing Hannah, she still showed no sign of hearing him.

He forced his feet toward the hall.

— 4 —

GOING DOWN HIS porch steps, Cole eyed the twilight sky, considering where to start looking for Benay. The Flaxx Enterprises office in Embarcadero Center where she worked, or her apartment? The office, he decided. She had been there when he called her…and the garage under 2EC where they arranged to meet was where he had died.

He started to loosen his tie some more for the run, then wondered, *did* he have to run to Embarcadero Center? He glanced back at the house. Coming here had been incredible …in front of the Hall one minute, in his own hall the next. Instant travel was the way to go. He just needed to figure out how he did it. All he remembered was feeling desperate to be home…then here he was.

Was a desperate desire to be at a particular destination what it took to instant travel? He had no trouble with the desperation part…just focus on the urgency in himself. Let it overwhelm him. Benay disappeared…when? Maybe Wednesday? He had a cold trail going colder by the minute!

"I have to get to the Flaxx office!" He pictured the reception area in his head. "I have to get there *now*!"

Nothing happened. He remained on the sidewalk in front of his house. So…it took something more. He had been tearing out of the Hall before. Maybe he needed to be in motion? He launched into a run, then tried again.

Still no luck.

Cole set his jaw. What happened once should work again. But until it did, he kept moving. Every block or so he made another attempt…ramping up emotion to near frenzy and picturing different sections of the Flaxx office where he had been…reception, Bookkeeping, Flaxx's personal office.

None of it kicked in the instant travel.

Along Castro, the number of pedestrians out enjoying the evening forced him to pay more attention around him to avoid walk-throughs. The dogs being walked avoided *him*. A few breezed by with just a sidestep around him. More slowed long enough to eye him or lift their heads for a sniff...and the sniffers either looked baffled, or they bristled and growled.

"What do you see, boy?" those owners asked. Except one woman, who smiled down at her Lab and ruffled his fur. "Oooh, are you seeing ghosts?"

Despite her light tone, it sparked hope in Cole. Might she believe in the possibility and be persuaded to see him? It was worth a try. He stepped in front of her. "As a matter of fact, he is seeing a ghost. *Me*. You try to see me, too."

She just tugged at the dog's leash and walked on, forcing him to jump out of her way.

"*I* see you," said a voice off to his side.

Cole whirled in search of the speaker, and found a rail-thin fiftyish woman lounging in a canvas chair behind the grille of a doorway alcove. He grinned at her. "Those have to be the sweetest words I've heard in my li—heard today." And since she saw him...could he make use of that to contact ...Razor probably, to report the details of his murder? "My name is—"

"How'd you die?"

Her interruption and childlike abruptness set off a warning bell. Was she just short on social skills or did he have a problem here? "Ah...I was shot in the head."

She leaned forward and peered at him. "I don't see any bullet hole. Are you sure you're a ghost? Princess Di glows."

The warning bell turned into a sinking feeling. "You've seen Princess Di's ghost, too?"

She sighed. "Not as much since I started medication."

Shit. She was a nut case. He fought disappointment to keep his tone polite. "And did you happen to skip your meds today?"

The woman glanced behind her toward the door, then gave him a conspiratorial smile. "Don't tell my daughter. I never take them on Sunday. I don't want to miss seeing Jesus if He comes by."

Terrific, Cole reflected, leaving her. He was visible to dogs, a toddler, and a wacko. Why were they the only ones? Frustration pushed him into an even harder run. What made them different from everyone else?

Half a block later the answer hit him. No reality check. They had nothing in them declaring this or that as imaginary. So did it take someone with their reality detector missing or out of whack to see him? Hopefully not. He could just imagine trying to find Benay and straighten things out with Sherrie using, say, the Princess Fan as an intermediary. Would Razor even listen to her claim of having information the ghost of Cole Dunavan had asked her to pass on? The chances with one of those so-called psychics who purported to commune with the dead were just as bad. Even if he found a genuine one, Cole doubted Razor would consider her or him any more credible. He better find out if anyone of sound mind could see him.

He slowed to a jog and began hailing people he met, greeting them like old friends. Going on the theory that even without recognizing someone, people respond to an individual who appears to know them. If they saw him. "Hi there. It's been a while. Yo, dude, it's good to see you again."

After a block and a half, only a dog had reacted, wagging its tail, but Cole kept waving. Before worrying, he needed what the statisticians called a significant sampling.

Then the back of a woman jogging down the block ahead of him wiped out all thought of statistics. Excitement leaped in him. It looked like Benay! Right height, right build, blonde...and the portion of her shoulder bared by her tank top revealed a butterfly tattoo.

"Sara! Sara Benay!" Cole charged after her. Not bothering to dodge people now...running through them. Leaving them, rear vision showed him, staring around themselves in startled bewilderment. "Sorry," he called back, then yelled at the woman again. "Hey, Sara, wait up!"

She did not respond, and as he came up behind her, expectation turned into wrenching disappointment. It was not Benay. Close up, even the tattoo was different.

Swerving around the jogger, Cole raced on down Castro and reflected wryly, no wonder he saw butterflies even when he remembered nothing else. Benay had them everywhere in her apartment. Ceramic figurines and sun-catchers, on candles, sofa pillows, lamps, and switchplates. And on *her*. Not just the one on her shoulder…a flock, each in a different style, fluttering down across her breasts and flat belly to an elaborate Art Deco one perched on her blonde pubic thatch.

He shook his head in anger at himself. He might not have slept with Benay, but he still had plenty of reason for guilt. He had known why she'd invited him to the apartment for coffee. He had still gone, thinking he could back out before things went too far. Yeah, right! It took the skin show, which should not have caught him by surprise, to jolt him into retreat. Being so hot for the information Benay had access to made him stupid, stupid, *stupid!*

Not telling Sherrie was just as stupid. What kept him from it? Reluctance to admit being a jerk? Or alarm at how close he'd come to the point of no retreat, and fear that Sherrie might doubt he managed a retreat. She thought he was jumpy? More like sweating blood, worrying if a justifiably furious Benay was pissed off enough to file a complaint against him…or drop a note to Sherrie. He had wanted nothing more than to never hear from her again.

If only.

For her sake as well as his.

He reached Market and while his body headed for the Financial District, his mind went back to Wednesday night.

Leaving the Hall after working late on reports, he turned on his phone and found two voice mail messages.

"Call back as soon as you can." the first began. *"This is Sara."*
The sound of her voice hit his gut like lead.

"Surprised? Me, too. I was really steamed at being turned down that way. But after I cooled down I realized you weren't any more manipulative than I was. Then I got to thinking. You obviously believe that both the burglaries and fires the company's had are inside jobs. I checked the Chronicle's *web site for stories on the fires and—I never realized the firefighter killed in the Woodworks fire was a woman with a new baby at home! That's terrible! So I decided to go ahead and do what we never talked about in that conversation we never had. Because of the firefighter and her baby. And I think I've found proof you're right. Of course, if solving your case makes gratitude overwhelm your scruples about extra-marital recreation, I certainly won't complain."*

Exultation swept away his discomfort at hearing from her. This was what he had been waiting for! Finally...after six years long years...hard evidence against her boss, Donald Flaxx. Proof Flaxx shored up sagging bottom lines, first by having his own stores burglarized, then by torching six others of his last month. The insurance money plus what Flaxx collected from selling off the "lost" goods added up to a tidy sum. But until now there had been only Cole's gut feeling and circumstantial evidence...burglaries in a number out of proportion to the law of averages and owners of neighboring businesses saying the victim stores had seemed to be doing poorly. Despite the profits showing in the superficial look at the books Flaxx allowed without a warrant. And most of all there was Donald Flaxx's attitude, so cocksure, sneering behind a mask of politeness.

It was a case he had no luck making with Lieutenant Lafferty. She just pointed out that an average had extremes on either side, that Flaxx Enterprises owned dozens of little stores, and that the burglaries were committed with a variety of MO's. Meaning multiple perpetrators.

As for the fires...the Arson Task Force had a suspect—now Homicide's, since arson made the firefighter's death murder—a supposed fired employee named Luther Thomas

Kijurian. But Cole did not believe in Kijurian any more than he did in Flaxx as an unfortunate favorite target of burglars. Now he would have something solid to show everyone!

Then the second message played. It froze him halfway into the car.

The words slurred. Benay sounded drunk. But that did not diminish the fury and fear in her voice. *"Damn it; why don't you have your phone on! I need you. That bitch caught me leaving the other message for you and tortured me into telling her everything. She held my—"* Then in the background a door clicked open, and the line went dead.

Alarms screamed in Cole. He hurriedly punched in number shown on caller ID. Would she answer? She had been tortured, she said. What happened after that disconnect? Whatever happened, it was his fault for encouraging her to pry in those files.

Three rings went unanswered. Cold ran down his spine. *Come on, woman, come on*! It rang for the fourth time.

"Hello?"

He let his breath out in relief. "I got your messages. Are you all right?"

"I was afraid I wasn't going to reach you." She sounded in tears. "I'm sorry I let myself get caught. Now you probably can't use any of the information."

No, but…"Never mind that. What's important is that you're all right." He *hoped* she was. "Who tortured you? What did they do?"

"Didn't I say before?" She caught a ragged breath. "This is like a nightmare. It was Mrs. Gao."

Cole blinked in disbelief. "Gao?" Doris Gao, second in command of Bookkeeping, was an officious bitch, yes, but…a torturer? She came barely to his armpits. And Benay never sounded afraid of her before.

"Please." The word had the whimper of a frightened child. "Can you come and get me?"

He started the engine. "Where are you?"

"Hiding in the men's room. I'm hoping it's the last place she'll look for a woman."

"Give me fifteen minutes then head for the reception room. I'll meet you there at the front door."

"No!" The fear in her voice rose. "They're locked. I can't get out before she catches me. I'll sneak down the emergency stairs. Just park on the upper level if you can and stand by your car so I can see where you are. Please hurry!"

"I'm on my way."

But he got in the way of a bullet instead. And now he wondered, as he had no chance to do at the time...had he been set up?

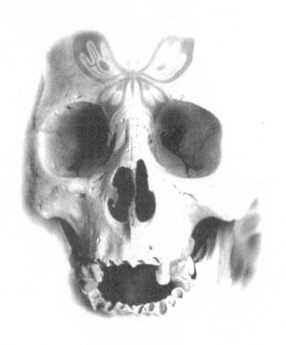

— 5 —

WHEN HE REACHED Embarcadero Center, Cole eyed the office tower's elevator, then, grimacing, looked for some emergency stairs. While climbing them to the Flaxx floor was no more tiring than the run from home, having to use them irked him. The elevator would be so much faster. Instant travel, better yet. He tried for it again, telling himself that he needed to be in the office right now. Benay sounded in fear when he'd talked to her. He needed to look for evidence that Gao had assaulted her. Or that Benay had played some role in his death. It was urgent to determine which. Critical!

Apparently not critical enough. Five attempts at instant travel all failed.

Swearing, Cole finished the climb two steps at a time and exited the stairwell to find himself in the architectural firm that used the majority of the floor.

But while Flaxx Enterprises occupied much less space than the architects or the financial consultants also on this floor, the reception area inside Flaxx's big glass doors pretended otherwise....presenting visitors with thick carpet, chrome-and-leather chairs, current slick magazines on the side tables, and a forest of greenery. Cole liked the reception desk best, a big modernistic glass slab that perfectly displayed their eye candy receptionist, Gina Galechas

Cole eyed the desk as he passed it and circled the rubber plants partially screening the hallway beyond. Since Donald Flaxx liked to think that leaving the dumb flatfoot cooling his heels up front demonstrated lack of fear—i.e., a clear conscience—and how busy he was, Cole had had plenty of opportunity to appreciate Gina in the four years she worked there. A mistake on Flaxx's part, because rather than just stare at Gina's legs, Cole had used the time to chat her up and lead her into office gossip.

Which was how he had learned about the three women from Bookkeeping, one of them Benay, who always ate lunch together. A piece of information he'd dusted off last month and put to use. It had been a simple matter arranging "chance" encounters with the trio over the course of a week, until they'd finally invited him to join them. There, amid entertaining them with war stories, he had pumped them for information on Bookkeeping's operations.

Bookkeeping was the whole key to getting away with the burglaries and arson. Flaxx's head of Bookkeeping, faithful minion Earl Lamper, cooked the books to make the stores look profitable so there appeared to be no motive for faking burglaries. But how had he prevented other members of the staff from noticing the alterations? Cole did not see the entire Bookkeeping department engaging in a conspiracy. That could not have lasted six years without a leak. He learned nothing from Benay and her two coworkers, however, who proved more careful than Gina about what they said. He had written the operation off as a failure...until Benay had called him at work on Monday.

"I'd like to talk to you about some of the store accounts I happen to be working on right now. They're ones you mentioned the day you had lunch with us. Can you meet me after work?"

His pulse had raced. Maybe he had the break he was looking for! *"Pick a place."*

Remembering his elation, Cole grimaced at a new stab of guilt. Because he agreed to the meeting, Benay maybe had a target on her. And might be wrongly branded a cop killer. Even if it turned out she had a part in his death, the whole fatal chain of events had begun that evening, and he'd started it.

He worked his way through the offices along the central hall. The Security office had just a small bank of monitors, but they covered the reception area, central hallway, break room, a supply room, and their one emergency exit. That had to be how Benay had planned to escape.

Bookkeeping sat quiet and tidy today. Looking from Mrs. Gao's desk by the door to Benay's desk on down the room, he wondered how such a small woman had tortured Benay into talking. Maybe she had a black belt in one of the martial arts disciplines. If so, none of the photos and nicknacks on the shelf by her desk reflected that.

They all had some shelves for personal items. He checked Benay's. If Leach thought the two of them took off together, Benay must be missing. Maybe something here hinted where she would run. A photograph showed her with her two friends here, Kenisha Hayes and Joy Quon...taken at an office Christmas party. A small stand-up calendar had this Friday, Saturday, Sunday, and tomorrow circled in red, then X'd out, as was the notation *Baja*. The missed cruise she'd mentioned during their Monday meeting. Too bad she had not noted the name of the yacht. It could be a lead to her. He eyed the drawers in her desk with frustration, then turned away from the desks and moved into Lamper's glassed-in office. Nothing interesting sat out on Lamper's desk, but the man had been out sick all week, the reason Benay had access to the files she'd called him about.

She'd claimed to be hiding in the men's room. He went and checked both restrooms without really expecting to find any sign of her. Anything she might have left in either place would have been removed by the cleaning crew that Gina told him came in every Saturday.

Finally he reached the end of the hallway and the desk of Flaxx's secretary, Katherine Maldonado...positioned to be his gatekeeper. He eyed the door of Flaxx's office but decided not to bother going in. He already knew what it looked like.

Flaxx furnished his office as though he headed a major corporation. An acre of desk dominated the room, accompanied by a summit-sized conference table, gentleman's club leather chairs, and wood-paneled walls hung with large color photographs of Flaxx—health-club buff, smile news-anchor-white, beachboy highlights in hair restored to youthful thickness by implants—opening various stores, playing golf with his father and celebrities, shaking hands with several California governors and a Vice President. A door in one side wall led to Flaxx's private washroom. Paneling on down the same wall opened to reveal a bar.

The exit sign above the narrow side hallway across from Maldonado's desk interested Cole more. That was the way Benay had left on Wednesday.

He followed the hall to the emergency stair door, and to his surprise, passed an office. The name plate on its door read: *I. L. Carrasco, Asset Management*. Whoever occupied that office must feel like a stepchild, stuck back there across from a storeroom and custodial closet. Even Security rated an office on the main hallway.

Cole descended the stairs slowly. A reason for Benay failing to meet him might be that she had been caught in here, and the stairwell might not be cleaned often enough to remove evidence left on Wednesday. But although he carefully examined each flight for blood or marks on the walls that might have been left by a head or kicking feet striking it, he found nothing.

From the retail levels he made his way down to the garage and through it to where he remembered parking that night. Where he had died. Without surprise, he saw it was the same slot where he'd found himself this afternoon. He felt his terror hanging over the row like fog.

Cole started to back away, then halted. Maybe examining the memory would tell him something about the shooting that he'd lacked the opportunity and presence of mind to appreciate at the time. A Neon parked in his stall now. He sat against its trunk, as he had sat against that of his Taurus, and put himself back in the place of his living self.

Checking his watch, Cole saw he had been here ten minutes. Added to the time it took him to drive over, Benay should have had time to be down here by now. Unless she showed up soon, he was going to go after—

Footsteps interrupted the thought. But not the footsteps of a woman in heels. Softer soles made them. Moments later their maker appeared, an adolescent boy in Nike's, jeans, and a jacket that would have looked baggy even on someone twice his weight. He sauntered down the parking row, shoulders and head bobbing in time to something playing through his earphones.

The retail stores had been closed for almost an hour and the boy looked too young to drive...maybe fifteen. Automatically, Cole noted the rest of his descriptors...about five-six, a hundred ten pounds; Caucasian, or possibly Hispanic since dark hair hung around his face; a Giant's baseball cap worn backward; carrying a plastic shopping bag.

After a furtive look around, the boy turned in on the passenger side of an SUV several spaces down. Cole headed that way to see what the kid was up to.

Suddenly the kid jumped back into the drive. Cole froze. He now wore a plastic Elvis Presley mask and had the shopping bag pulled up over his left forearm...pointed straight ahead and held in place by the kid's elbow pressed against his side. The plastic conformed to the shape of a gun muzzle inside. Now the bobbing of the kid's head and shoulders looked like the twitches of a junkie.

After a glance around, the kid slid the bag down his arm far enough to display the butt of a compact semiautomatic ...with the hammer cocked and his fingers gripping the weapon so tightly they were white. "Trick or treat." He pulled the bag up again.

Cole spread his arms away from his body, and made his voice casual. "Are you sure you want to be doing this, partner?"

"Oh, shit!" The reedy voice cracked. "You're a cop!"

A quick glance down showed Cole that his suit coat hung open far enough to reveal the star still clipped on his belt. Two thoughts raced through his head simultaneously: that he had to prevent the kid from wigging out, and get rid of him before Benay showed up.

Keeping his tone soothing, Cole said, "This doesn't have to be a problem. Nothing's happened yet. You can just put down the gun and walk away."

"Oh, sure." The hand in the bag twitched.

Cole forced himself not to wince.

"And then you'll tackle me."

"No. But if you're worried, don't turn away. Back off until you feel it's a safe distance." *Just go, you little bastard; get the hell out of here.*

The tweaker shifted from foot to foot. "And as soon as I run, you'll be on your radio. No...I gotta have a better edge than that." His free right arm reached up to wrap across the top of his head, then dropped to rub at his left shoulder and fiddle with the edge of the Elvis mask.

Cole waited for a glimpse of the face beneath, but the mask stayed in place.

As though driven by a will of its own, the arm flopped back across the top of the tweaker's head. "I know. Go get in your car, the passenger side, and toss your gun in the back seat. And move easy."

Cole moved as though carrying nitroglycerine. "You don't have to do this."

The tweaker followed, halting to the rear of the open door, where he stood shifting from foot to foot. His voice slid up a register, cracking. "I been in juvie once. I ain't goin' back." Granite determination rang in the words. "Handcuff yourself behind your ankles."

Cole breathed slowly. Their positions hid his hands from view, giving him the chance to use a technique he and Razor had practiced for just such situations. As he closed the first cuff around his left wrist, he deflected the rachet section so the blade slid along the outside of the cuff and the pieces overlapped instead of engaging. At the same time he squeezed the other cuff with his left hand, creating sound of a closing cuff. So far, so good.

As Cole started to run the chain behind his ankles, the tweaker said, "No, no...wait...wait. I got a better idea. Before you put on the other one, loop it through the adjustment bar down there in front of the seat."

Cole complied, cuffing his other wrist normally. As soon as the tweaker left, he would pop the rigged cuff open and be home free.

The tweaker giggled. "I like that. It's like the bar on the bench in Booking." In Cole's peripheral vision his whole body twitched. "It's gonna be real embarrassing when you're found and have to tell the other cops what happened. Oh...wait ...wait." He giggled again. "I got an even better idea."

Peripheral vision caught the tweaker reaching into the car. The next second Cole felt the gun muzzle behind his ear. Surprise, anger, and terror collided in his head in screaming pandemonium. He wrenched desperately at the rigged cuff. *No, wait*! But before the cry could leave his throat, explosive pain hurled him into blackness.

Cole's head snapped forward, staggering him. A spin and lurch against the Neon kept him on his feet. He clung to the spoiler while chaos echoed in his head and sent shivers through the rest of him. Shit. He never expected to *relive* the damned memory! Had it given him anything except a bad trip?

When the shivers subsided and all but the terror in the air around him faded, Cole realized it had given him more. The Elvis mask hid the shooter's face but not his ears. They had no lobes, a distinctive enough feature to help identify him. And while the shooter might well be a kid—there were plenty these days capable of cold-blooded murder—he was no tweaker. Now Cole could see it had all been an act...designed to maneuver him into position for an easy kill. The proof was finding the Taurus. A real junkie would have sold it to a chop shop for drug money, not driven to San Jose and dumped it. Cole also doubted a junkie would bother hauling the body away.

So it was a hit. He *had* been set up.

The location and timing pointed toward Donald Flaxx arranging it. While the tweaker act seemed a complicated way to make a hit when a drive-by would do the job, it did keep things tidy. The car caught all the blood.

Cole knelt down to peer under the Neon and neighboring vehicles, searching the garage floor. Sure enough, the area looked clean. No stains that might be blood. No spent casing, either. With his body removed, nothing indicated a murder had taken place here. An important point considering the garage's proximity to the Flaxx offices.

The trouble was, as much as he liked Flaxx for the hit, Flaxx had no motive. Flaxx could sneer at anything Benay found in the files. Criminally greedy pond scum he might be, but not stupid. Part of his arrogance included showing off how familiar he was with the search and seizure rules. So when Benay admitted she and Inspector Dunavan discussed searching the company books, Flaxx would realize it was an illegal search. Which made all her discoveries fruit of the poisoned tree...evidence inadmissible in court.

Cole climbed to his feet and started dusting off his knees before realizing what he was doing. Catching himself, he shook his head—reflexes!—and considered one other problem with Flaxx ordering the hit on him. How could it have been set up in the time between the call to Benay and when the shooter appeared?

Benay, on the other hand, had had two days if she wanted him dead. His gut said *no*...something threatened her and he was here to stop it. Yet the old saw about the fury of a woman scorned ran through Cole's head. He leaned against the Neon, drumming his fingers on the spoiler, and considered the possibility Benay'd set him up. Killing him because of Monday night seemed extreme, and even two days was not very long to find a hired gun. But a psycho might lurk behind those butterflies and, being someone who spelled "weekend" P-A-R-T-Y, she could have connections.

But...he would swear the fear in her calls was real. Even in memory it felt palpable, as intense as his terror swirling around here.

Or *was* this his? He had been assuming so because he died here. But now something about it…Cole closed his eyes to concentrate…and found disbelief mixed in the terror, rather than his anger and surprise. This terror was someone else's. Whose?

"Miss Benay? Sara? Was it you?"

What were the odds of an unrelated incident generating terror in this same spot? What created her terror, though?

Possibilities ran through his head. She came looking for him and arrived in time to witness him being forced into the car and killed. Then paralyzed by shock, she stood there instead of running…and the shooter caught and shot her, too. Or she came looking for him and the shooter lay in wait to eliminate her. Her disbelief could come from being shot by a kid.

Guilt dragged at Cole's gut, cold and leaden. If either scenario happened, his obsession with nailing Flaxx had killed her. And her death was his fault even in the case of a third possibility. That she'd set up the hit, only to find that when she came to gloat over the body and pay the shooter, he decided to leave no witnesses. That could account for the disbelief. It did not account for removing the bodies, however. Cole saw no reason for that shooter to care if they were found.

There was just one problem with all the scenarios. Where would Sara have been killed? Not in the car. Razor said nothing about blood anywhere other than the front passenger area. Both the rear seat and trunk must have been checked. And Cole saw no blood on the floor here.

Examining it again, just to be sure, he still found no evidence of blood. No visible blood anyway. Nor any wipe marks to indicate a clean-up. Maybe extreme emotion could leave a psychic impression without the person dying and Sara had managed to escape.

The urgency in him cranked higher. He had to see if she'd made it home.

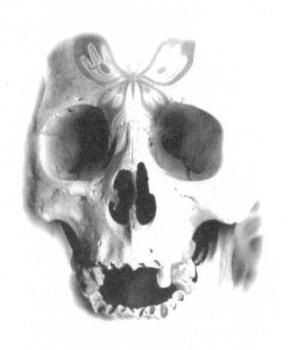

— 6 —

RACING FOR THE garage exit, Cole tried to think of the fastest route to her apartment. Instant travel would be nice. If not to her apartment, at least somewhere close. He knew the Marina. It had been part of his old patrol territory and Razor lived there with his first wife, Jessica. Razor and Denise moored the *Chimera* in the Small Craft Harbor. So he could walk mentally down every street, even the one outside Sara's apartment building.

Suddenly the garage blurred...and became a Marina street. Sara's street. Her building lay just ahead of him, wrapped in fog.

Cole blinked. Son of a bitch. Nothing happened when he willed it, yet here he had made no real effort and...

He shook away his frustration. Puzzle over that later. Right now, think about Sara. He hurried into her building

Up on the third floor, her livingroom and little kitchen looked no different than they had Monday night. They still had all the butterflies he remembered. A file sorter sat at the back of a small desk. He frowned at the envelopes and papers visible in its slots. What a drag that he could not look through them, or open and operate the laptop lying in the middle of the desk. This was one search where the restriction to what lay in plain sight could not be fudged.

He grimaced in frustration. Nothing here indicated whether Sara made it home.

Until he walked into the bedroom. There he stopped cold. The closet door stood ajar and two dresser drawers hung partially open. Plastic hangers lay scattered on the bed. Where she had butterflies even on her comforter and pillow-cases, Cole saw. Peering into the closet, he noted empty slots in the double-decker shoe rack running the length of the floor. The bathroom had an empty toothbrush holder. A plastic caddy like the one Sherrie used for cosmetics, brush, and comb sat empty and askew in the middle of the counter.

Cole returned to the bedroom and eyed the hangers. So she did make it home…but packed and left again in a hurry. The state of the room screamed panic and flight.

But where did she run to? Kenisha Hayes and Joy Quon probably had ideas. Except that he had no way to ask them. He had to find a way to communicate!

His fingers itched for the tools in his basement workshop at home. The endless repairs the house needed not only gave him the satisfaction of finite tasks with visible results, the physical activity helped him think. Lacking the workshop, Cole walked back out to the livingroom and paced around it.

On his second circuit, the lamp on one of the couch's end tables brought back a memory. Coming in Monday night, Sara turned it on by tapping the base. The girl who walked through him at the mall remarked she felt zapped. That implied the presence of some energy charge in him.

He touched for the lamp. And grinned when it came on. "Call me Electric Man."

Two more touches brightened the light. A third turned the lamp off.

He ran it through its cycle three more times for the plea-sure of being able to affect *something*. The question was how to use this ability. Turning lights on and off was a nice ghost trick but not much good for communication. SOS being as much Morse Code as he knew.

Then the laptop on Sara's desk caught his attention. Might affecting current let him operate a computer? That would be great. Then he could worry less about being seen, just talk to Razor with something like instant messaging.

Cole left the apartment and headed east toward Russian Hill. He probably had a while before Razor came home…time enough to play with Razor's computer. If that worked, he would write up a message and have it waiting.

The fog in the street had thickened still more, turning car lights into fuzzy glows and pedestrians into figures as ghostly as himself. A couple down the block moved to the outside of the sidewalk as they approached.

He blinked. Did they see him?

As they came closer, the male gave a surprised frown, then returned to the middle of the sidewalk. Cole stepped to the curb to let them pass.

"What was that about?" the woman asked.

The man shrugged. "For a minute I thought I saw someone coming toward us."

Cole wheeled after the couple. If the man glimpsed him, maybe he could hear, too. "Excuse me, sir," he called.

"I didn't see anyone," the woman said.

"It was probably just a spot where the fog was thinner."

Mulling over the encounter, Cole continued on toward Razor's apartment. The fog let him appear as a negative density? Since the guy had almost seen him, might he have heard if spoken to while still thinking someone was there?

Cole tried that approach with other pedestrians he met, calling, "Excuse me, what bus goes to North Beach?"

Like the male half of the first couple, one woman seemed to notice him at a distance. Then as they neared each other, her gaze shifted from looking at him to through him.

A man answered, "What did you say?"...tilting his head to hear better. Only to grimace as he came closer and give a furtive glance around that said: *Did anyone see me making a fool of myself?*

No one else reacted. But two responses out of maybe a dozen tries were enough to give Cole hope that a rational individual might see and hear him. An encouraging thought to take to Razor's place with him.

Which would be a faster trip if he could figure out that instant travel thing. Why had he jumped home and to Sara's apartment building, but not the Flaxx offices? As far as he could remember, he did the same thing each time...picturing somewhere he wanted to go and wanting to go there right now. But if it took familiarity with the destination, then Razor's apartment ought to be reachable.

Cole stopped by a light pole and, shutting off all his vision, pulled up a mental image of Razor's front room. But when he opened his eyes, he remained on the street.

Crap. The successful trips had to be more than a fluke. So, where else should he try? Burglary came to mind. He certainly knew it thoroughly enough.

He carefully pictured the office…crowded with desks, half of them unoccupied…the big poster for the Kurt Russell movie *Tombstone* tacked above Stan Fontaine's desk on the wall separating them from Fencing…his own desk with one end against the outside wall and a map of his Mission District taped beside his window. He tried to feel himself standing at the door.

The street blurred and…he *was* in the office.

Cole shot his hands toward the ceiling in triumph. Score! And this time he had paid attention to what he was doing. A clear picture of his destination seemed more important than the strength of his desire to be there. So now maybe he could make it to Razor's place. And find a better name than the instant travel thing. Ziptrip?

He pulled up an image of Razor's front room again, this time concentrating on details…the kitchen nook at one end; the bookcase at the other—one he built for Razor and Lauren's wedding, to replace the boards-on-cinder blocks Razor had been using until then—the big futon that folded down for Razor's bed when Holly stayed overnight. He pictured himself at the front door.

But he remained standing inside Burglary's door. No ziptrip, just zip. Setting his jaw, Cole started to try again…then noticed that across the room, Phil Braff's laptop sat open and running. Braff himself was nowhere in sight. Why not try communicating with him? Braff could pass information on to Homicide, too…such as where the shooting took place, a description of the shooter, and the likelihood of Sara being a witness.

Cole made his way to the desk. There, taking a mental breath, he ran a finger across the notebook's touchpad.

The screen saver cleared! Cole grinned. Feeling like a kid with a new toy, he zig-zagged his finger around the touchpad and watched the arrow cursor trace the same pattern across the screen. When he dragged his finger down the scroll side of the touchpad, the page obediently rolled up or down. Presently he noted the image on the screen, a hand-drawn room diagram with accompanying scrawled notes, and remembered how proud Braff was that his laptop could also be used as a PC tablet, letting him draw or write directly on the screen. Cole felt a prickle of excitement. Could he work the screen, too?

He scrolled clear of Braff's notes and drew his finger across the screen. A corresponding line appeared. All right! Below the line he wrote: *Please pass the following information to Homicide.* Writing with his finger was clumsy. That sentence took two lines. Still, it worked!

But that was just on Braff's computer. For Razor's he would have to use the keys. Could he?

He ran the arrow up to File and left tapped to pull down the menu. Nothing happened. He tapped the button harder. Still no menu. His heart sinking, he leaned on the button as hard as he could...without results. Frustration sparked in him. No! This had to work.

Keys rattled outside the door. Cole glanced toward the sound. Braff?

Yes...Braff. He came in and re-locked the door.

A faint tickle running up Cole's finger pulled his attention back to the computer. He found the end of the finger sunk in the key. And on the screen the File menu had opened.

He stared at it. How did that happen? The finger part he understood. Like everything else material, the keys felt solid only as long as he looked at them. But what did going *through* do? Cole pulled back the hand and rubbed the finger with his thumb. That tickle...He must have made contact with the relay or whatever under the key.

Behind him, Braff grunted.

Cole grimaced. Rear vision caught Braff almost on top of him, eyeing at the laptop. Damn. He had forgotten to keep track around himself.

Braff came closer to the laptop. "Where did that come from?"

Cole sidestepped enough to avoid physical contact but leave his finger still in contact with the screen. *The blood in Dunavan's car—*

He lost contact with the screen as Braff, gaping, turned the laptop. "What the *hell?*" Then Braff's eyes narrowed. He glanced around the office. "Okay, very cute. Who's doing this? Fontaine? Sekulovich?"

Cole groaned. Braff thought it was some kind of practical joke. Son of a bitch.

Braff tried the door connecting to Fencing, looked into the interview room, and even unlocked the front door to check behind the clerk's counter in the outer office.

Was there any way to make Braff take this seriously and pay attention to *what* was being written? Cole tried, scrawling: *No stunt! This is for real!*

Before Cole had time for more, Braff closed the laptop …right through Cole's hand. "I don't know where you are or how you're doing this, guys," he called, "but the game's over. I'm too tired to play." He sat down and turned his chair toward his typewriter. Cole left him rolling a form into the typewriter.

— 7 —

WELL, THAT WAS a bust, Cole reflected. Except now he knew to be careful how he relayed information. He hoped that with the home computer, Razor would be less likely to assume someone was playing a joke. Before heading to Razor's place, though, it would be smart to run Gao through the computer. And Sara. Check whether either of them was in the system, with criminal connections that put them in a position to set up the hit on him. He also wanted to give Razor as much information as possible, to avoid him running into a bullet, too.

In the Southern Station downstairs, the computers outside the holding cells were busy. One in the sergeants' office was on and idle, however…with a chair conveniently at the keyboard and the office empty.

Okay, now to see what he could do with a regular computer.

Eyes closed, he wiggled his finger around on the Escape key until he felt the tickle. Opening his eyes, he found the screen saver gone. So far, okay. Could he open and operate the search program without using the mouse, just the keys?

To his relief, he could. But it was excruciatingly tedious. Finding the contact point did not always work the first time, and since he had to close his eyes to find the contact, his hand could drift to another letter. Then he had a mistake to correct. He hoped the sergeant stayed busy elsewhere for a long time. He needed every minute.

The search on Gao came up negative. Cole exited, and gritting his teeth, slogged through entering Sara's name for a new search. Damn it! If only he could type while *looking* at the keys.

"Dunavan, what's this frigging hangup about surfaces you *see?* Get past—"

He broke off. The computer had a hit on Sara's name. Shit.

Reading the entry, he was relieved to find nothing serious. Two and a half years ago she had been among a number of guests detained when Narco raided a house party, but she was released without being charged with anything.

Still...drugs. Thinking of the fake tweaker, Cole made himself run the house party's host. That revealed Mr. Antonio Novello had been charged with narcotics violations several times, though never prosecuted. The Nob Hill address suggested why. Money had not saved him from being blown away by his girlfriend six months ago, however.

Cole exited the search and slumped in the chair, feeling wrung out. If a little record search gave him this much trouble, how was he going to carry on a conversation with Razor via computer. Start things off with the computer, yes. Use it to alert Razor to his presence. But then the two of them had to *talk* to one another. Somehow.

And was alerting Razor going to be enough? In Razor's place, he would need evidence a ghost was present. Sara's lamp came to mind. Maybe he could play with the lights. Give Razor a message like: *To show you I'm for real, I'll turn the lamp in the corner on and off five times.* Except Razor had no touch-on lamps.

A desk lamp sat on one of the sergeants' desks. Cole swivelled and scooted over to see if he could affect it. But groping around in the base and switch had no effect. The lamp remained off. He drummed soundlessly on the desk. If Razor had a lamp already on, interfering with current might turn it *off*. And maybe not. What else could he do? A walk-through?

A key in the door lock brought him to his feet. Time to go.

But turning toward the door, he halted, staring at the chair in front of the computer. What was it doing there? He had scooted—Cole slapped his forehead. Duh. Of course the chair remained at the computer. He had apparently scooted across the room and played with the lamp while sitting on thin air...like the cartoon characters who walked off cliffs and kept going until they noticed the ground had disappeared from under them.

As the door opened, Cole passed through the wall into the hall and headed for the rear entrance. Once out on the north terrace, he concentrated on visualizing Razor's apartment and himself in it. An additional detail came to him. The big window behind the futon was flanked by Razor's framed collection of police patches and a watercolor of the *Chimera* that one of Denise's artist friends had painted.

He waited expectantly, but remained standing on the north terrace. Another try failed, too. In disgust, he gave up.

"Okay, have it your way," he told the sky, and broke into a lope. "I'll leg it."

For the first several blocks he brooded over the inconsistency of ziptripping, analyzing every attempt, comparing the successful trips to the failures. But to his frustration, whatever made the difference eluded him.

Then crossing Market, a chair tied to the top of a passing car made him think of the chair he had not been sitting in. It had *felt* like a chair, though. This must be the flip side of what-I-see-feels-solid...imagining surfaces where none existed. More mental stuff.

Could he *choose* to imagine a solid surface, Cole wondered. Say a walkway about eight feet up so he could quit having to dodge people. He halted and pictured a stairway. Then he put one foot on the bottom step and carefully brought up his other foot beside it. They remained where he put them and he stood eight inches off the sidewalk.

Gingerly, he started up the rest of the stairs...just in case the illusion failed. When he caught his thinking, Cole laughed at himself. Even if gravity could affect him, what was he afraid of, a fall killing him? He ran up the rest of the virtual steps to a height he liked, then pictured his walkway and stepped out on it. Seeing nothing under him remained a little unnerving but, yes, he decided, it felt cool, too...loping over the heads of the other pedestrians. If such an ordinary word

as pedestrians applied to the prostitutes, gangbangers, drug dealers, junkies, and winos populating the streets of the Tenderloin.

After a couple of blocks, he noticed that now and then,
someone glanced up and appeared to see him. Remembering
the Princess Fan, however, he looked them over before
letting himself feel hope. It saved him disappointment.
Observation identified most as winos. One almost toppled
over backward gaping up at him. This could be a new sobri-
ety test, Cole reflected wryly. *If you can see me, you're under the
influence.* The one non-wino had a looking-at-other stare that
signaled disconnection from reality.

As he started to doubt that any rational adult would
ever see him, he noticed three prostitutes outside the mouth
of an alley down the block. They stood off to the side of
the alley, peering fearfully into it around the corner of the
building. Moments later Cole heard a choked-off cry and a
snarling male voice.

"Bitch! I warned you not to hold out on me!"

Reflex kicked in. Cole raced down the block and into the
alley. Below him, a burly male had both hands around the
neck of a woman wearing a lacey camisole and panties under
a hip-length faux fur jacket. Clearly a prostitute and her pimp,
but anger still boiled up in him. He despised men who beat up
women, no matter what woman and for what reason. "Get
your hands off her!"

"Baby, no, I swear," she choked out. "Business just isn't—"

"Then you're not trying hard enough!" The pimp slammed
her head into the wall behind her.

Cole tried to drop on top of the pimp. Only to remain
suspended. He grimaced. Of course. No gravity, no drop.
He charged down virtual stairs. By which time the pimp had
slammed the hooker's head into the wall again. And Cole
remembered he had no way to intervene.

Or did he?

He lunged through the pimp from shoulder to shoulder. "I
said, get your hands off her, dogshit!"

The pimp yelped and jumped back, releasing the hooker's neck. A moment later he reddened in fury. "Now you've done it, you stupid cunt! You're dead! Give me that stun gun!"

She gaped in bewilderment. "What stun—"

The pimp pulled back his fist. Cole went through him again, this time slowly. Maybe his anger helped. He barely felt the buzz. But the pimp felt it. He jumped back another step

Cole followed, and this time instead of walking through, kept in the pimp's space. As the pimp backed away, Cole stayed with him. Through the buzz, Cole felt faint heat flowing into him. From the pimp?

Apparently. The pimp started shivering. Seconds later he retreated toward the alley entrance. "I'll let it go this time…but you get out there and hump, bitch!" he snarled, and wheeling, stalked away.

Gaping after him, the hooker stumbled out of the alley.

The other prostitutes crowded around her. "Are you all right, honey? God, look at your neck. You're gonna have huge fucking bruises. You ought to go home—"

She shrugged them off. "I gotta go back to work or Danny'll get *really* mad. I'll be all right."

"No, Dannyboy is the kind who'll kill you sooner or later," Cole said. Maybe the next time he beat her, which was likely to be twice as vicious anyway. Rescuing her did her no favor in the long run. "You need to drop a dime on him and find yourself a different job—"

The sentence died in his throat. One of the prostitutes, a tall red-head in red leather hot pants and a matching waist-length jacket, had glanced at him. A second later she turned away, but excitement leaped in Cole. She saw him. He was sure of it! And she looked sober and rational.

The prostitutes spread out along the block. Cole followed the one in red to her corner. His corner, really. Despite a good job of battening down his willie and a nice manicure with long false nails, those unmistakably male wrists gave away "her" sex. "Looking for a date, Red?"

She dug a cigarette out of her bag and lit it. "Not with you, baby."

She *did* see him! "Why not?"

One brow arched. "I've resurrected dead dicks in my time, but the body has to be at least breathing. You don't qualify."

Cole felt his jaw drop and snapped it closed. "You know I'm a ghost?" And accepted that without batting an eye? "How can you tell?"

"Well let's see." She dragged on her cigarette and blew the smoke at him. "Maybe because...you *look* like a ghost?"

"And how's that? I look like myself to me."

The brow went up again. "Yeah? To me you look like those tapes of old TV shows...kinda faded, and fuzzy on the edges. Except you're colored instead of black and white."

That described bad security tapes, too. Terrific. *I'm not live; I'm worn-out Memorex.* "Is that how other ghosts will look to me?" He should check whether the horror in the garage had a ghost attached to it. And hope it did not.

Red sniffed. "You ain't gonna see other ghosts. You're around because you got business to finish with *living* people."

"That's hard to do when you're the only non-wacko adult who sees me." Cole grimaced. "Why *do* you see me?"

She shrugged. "I been seeing spirits all my life...just like my mama and gran." After a last puff, she dropped the cigarette on the sidewalk and ground the butt under one platform heel. "You're the first to give me the third degree, though. It must come from being a cop."

Cole ignored the jibe. "You can tell that, too?"

She rolled her eyes. "Well, *yeah.* Even the ghost of a cop still looks like a cop."

"Can I make someone else see me? When they're rational and sober, I mean."

"Do I look like a fortune teller?" She dug into her bag for another cigarette. "The odds ain't good. Most people normally won't, and some never will, no matter what."

Normally? The word reverberated in him. "You mean it *is* possible to see me? When and how?"

She took a deep drag, then watched the smoke as she blew it out. "I don't have a clue." Her eyes focused past him, searching the street. "Look...I know you're trying to figure yourself out and you seem like you were a decent guy. I appreciate what you did for Vicky and I hope you froze that prick Danny's balls off. But...enough already. I'm trying to make a living here and I can't fucking do it talking to you."

Cole's heart sank. Damn...he was losing her...and he had no official leverage to keep her talking. But the let's-continue-this-downtown line had always been his last resort anyway. He put on a smile and slid his voice into a Jimmy Stewart impression that had served him well in the past for dealing with nervous or reluctant witnesses. "Honey, I-I can't believe that with all the ghosts you've seen and-and the power of observation you've got in-in your job, you haven't made *some* guesses about other people seeing ghosts."

She snorted. "I bet you were a first class bullshitter." Then after several seconds she sighed. "Okay...for what it's worth, if someone wants to see you, they can usually learn. And there's a way to make yourself visible to almost everyone...for a few minutes anyway. This ghost back home does it. But don't ask me how. I just know the room gets cold as hell when she shows up, like a deep freeze." Her eyes focused past him again...on a car pulling up at the curb. "Now get lost." Flipping away her cigarette, she slapped on a professional smile, then sauntered through him toward the john.

That definitely ended the conversation.

Cole trotted back up to his walkway and on toward Razor's place. He noted the activity on the street below him—hookers and crack dealers doing business...homeless men and women settling into doorways for the night...officers confronting three young men about drinking in public, making them pour their beers into the gutter—but his thoughts were on Red's information. If someone wanted to see him, they could learn.

Razor ought to want to see him…once convinced he was there to be seen. Considering the walk-through's effect on Danny the Prick, it and a computer message should be convincing enough. But…was wanting to see him enough to make it happen? Red did say "learn". Expecting to see someone was not enough to make him visible close up to those people who glimpsed or heard him in the fog. Yet the Princess Fan and winos who saw him went through no learning process that he could see.

He halted and stared down at the scene below. Maybe that was the way to go…let Razor know he was around and then have Razor turn off his reality check. Except, he doubted Razor would agree to drink that heavily with Holly there. Was there any other way?

Yes, Cole realized, looking down at a homeless man asleep in a doorway. Everyone's reality check shut off in dreams. So maybe he just needed to convince Razor he was dreaming in order to make Razor see him. He probably needed to start with Razor asleep, though Razor never went to bed this early. He had been a night owl long before he started working Night Investigations.

Which, Cole reflected, did not prevent seeing whether a dream visit worked on someone else. He eyed the sleeping man as he walked back down to ground level, then decided against using him. This needed someone he could be confident would not normally see him. Say, a clerk in one of the area's cheap hotels.

Clerks at the first four hotels all proved awake…reading, knitting, watching TV…but stepping into the glorified hallway that served as the lobby of the fifth hotel, he heard gentle snoring. Behind the desk's protective wire mesh, the clerk, a dwarf, dozed over a crossword puzzle. An ink blot spread out from where his pen point rested off to the side of the puzzle. Cole studied him. First challenge: He needed to wake the man. But then he had to make the clerk think he was still asleep.

"Hey, man," Cole called.

The clerk did not stir.

So it took more than talking to reach him. Closing his eyes, Cole stepped into the desk.

Opening his eyes again, he found he had cleared the desk but stood up to his knees in a set of steps that let the clerk reach the desk. However, the mental hangup about solid surface did not appear to affect him once inside the object. He moved forward without restriction.

The steps gave him an idea. The answer to convincing people they were still asleep might be making them think: *That's impossible; I have to be dreaming.*

He laid a hand on the back of the clerk's neck. Cold ought to rouse the man. "Hey! How's it going, dude?"

As the clerk reached for his neck and lifted his head, Cole backed into the steps and crossed mental fingers.

The clerk blinked up at him. "Huh?"

At him. Seeing him. Yes! Cole grinned.

Now for challenge number two. The clerk's eyes were widening, registering the fact that Cole was on this side of the desk. "Hey...what—"

"What am I doing in here with you? It's a dream. See?" Cole pointed down at his legs.

The clerk looked down and blinked. Still seeing him. To keep the fantastic going, Cole climbed virtual stairs until his feet were at the clerk's eye level and circled around behind him to the clerk's other side.

"A dream?" the clerk muttered. But he craned his neck to follow the motion.

Cole cheered silently. This was working! "Are you having trouble with the crossword? Maybe I can help. I'm the puzzle fairy." He stepped back down to floor level and leaned over the clerk's shoulder. "Let's see. Thirty-eight down, six letter word for a trip and a treat. Try *junket.* That'll make fifty-three across, Potter villain?, *Snape.*"

"Puzzle fairy?" The clerk's eyes narrowed. "You look more like a cop to me."

Cole shrugged. "I can be that if you want. It's your dream."

The clerk snorted. "Why would I want a cop in my dream? Give me a long-legged blonde riding my lap smothering me in her D-cup hooters." He wiggled his brows.

Cole grinned. There was nothing small about the guy's libido. "Sorry...I don't do sex changes. Even with D-cup hooters, I make a lousy-looking woman. So I'm out of here." He walked away through the desk. "Good luck with the rest of the puzzle."

He hummed to himself all the way to the door and onto the street. This would work.

And not just for Razor, he realized. This would let him talk to Sherrie! Explain all about Sara Benay and reassure her about their marriage and his love for her. Even if the full force of that red-haired temper laid into him for Monday night, no problem. He welcomed it. Anything to get straight with her.

— 8 —

WAS HIS ZIPTRIP ticket good to go home again? Cole pictured it and concentrated.

The Tenderloin blurred…and—success!—turned into the front hall.

The house lay dark and silent, but that did not surprise him. Here at home Sherrie rarely managed to stay awake past ten or eleven…even waiting up for him when he worked night shifts. He always came in to find her dead to the world on the sofa, bathed in the glow from the television screen. With school tomorrow and Joanna being a day person, too, everyone in the house should be settled for the night by now.

He started up the stairs, only to stop at a whine coming from the livingroom. He turned and saw Tiger on the sofa, looking toward him. A pale shape lay beyond Tiger. Cole's chest tightened. Sherrie?

Yes. Going into the livingroom, he found her in a cocoon of blankets with Tiger at her feet.

Tiger's tail stub worked like a slow metronome. Cole scratched his ears, then sat down on the coffee table and reached up to run his fingers across Sherrie's hair. His chest tightened still more. "I'm sorry, babe. I won't make it home this time."

Never again slip in the door, tickle her awake, and lead her up to bed. When they were first married, he'd liked waking her by undressing her enough to make love right there. After the twins came along, he carried her to the privacy of their bedroom. Moving here ended the Rhett Butler stunt, too. The narrowness and pitch of the stairs made it impractical, not to mention life threatening, and for some reason she found the alternative carry, being slung across his shoulder like a sack of grain, unromantic.

Tiger whined again.

"Shhh," Cole whispered. "Settle." Sounds Tiger or the kids made always snapped her awake. He wanted to wake her slowly.

Too late. Sherrie sat bolt upright, eyes flying open. "Cole?"

He choked at the desperate hope in her voice. It sparked hope in him. Maybe it would make her see him. "Yeah, it's me...sort of."

"Cole?" She twisted, peering around her...looking straight through him.

Hope crashed. The disappointment felt like being stabbed.

"Tiger, what did you hear?" she asked.

The dog stared Cole's direction and whined again.

She reached down to pet him. He kept whining. Sighing, she moved the pillow to where her feet had been and rolled up in the blankets again with her arm stretched out so her hand rested on the dog's neck. Her eyes closed.

Tiger propped his chin on the other side of the pillow and watched Cole with questioning eyes.

Cole shrugged. "We'll let her go back to sleep, then make another try." Hopefully without pushing her alarm buttons this time.

In minutes her breathing settled into a regular rhythm once more. He gave her another minute, then covered the hand on Tiger's neck with his hand. "Nurse. Nurse Trask. Help me." A name she had not been called for years ought to seem dream material.

She pulled her arm back under the blanket.

He leaned down to her ear. "You have to help me. Some naked little bastard shot me in the heart with a red arrow and I'm mortally wounded." It had been a corny thing to say to her way back then, but it had amused her, even while she came back dryly, *"All bleeding stops eventually."*

Now she smiled, too, but remained asleep.

Shit. Cole cocked a brow at Tiger. "What do you think, boy? Do we need a little more irritating piece of the past to wake her?" Like the incident at their wedding when her father tried to hit on his mother. He laid his hand against her cheek. "Uh...honey...if I tell you something, will you promise to keep your cool?" Which she had not, then. "*Give me the cake knife so I can cut off his nuts!*" "My father's cop buddies have hand-cuffed Eddie to the steering wheel of his rental—"

He broke off as Sherrie frowned and burrowed deeper under the blanket, away from his hand.

Dismay spread through him. Red said there would be people who never saw him, but...not even in dreams? And how could Sherrie be one of them? He raised his voice. "Sherrie! Come on. Please. Let me tell you about Sara Benay. Wake up a little."

Instead, she fell more deeply asleep, breath slowing to a regular rhythm and heart beating steadily on.

Pain wrenched his chest as though to tear it apart. "Sherrie..." But he could only whisper. If she would never see him, how could he explain things to her?

After a last touch on her hair and pat on Tiger's head, Cole backed out of the livingroom and headed upstairs. He could not leave for Razor's place without looking in on the kids.

Near the top of the stairs, a thought dropped into his gut like lead. What if Razor turned out to be blind to him, too?

He tried shrugging off the possibility. *Think positively.* Even if the dream ploy also failed with Razor, he was just back to using the computer, right? But now he could not help wondering if computer messages *would* work. Might he have to find a way to help Sara all on his own?

At Hannah's door, he shoved the questions aside. Right now, only his family mattered.

Joanna slept on the futon in Hannah's room. In her own bed, Hannah lay rosy-cheeked and curled with her head almost against the safety rails. He kissed her forehead and stood watching her for several minutes, listening to her breathing and heartbeat, remembering the baby smell of her, before moving on to Kyle's room.

There a faint glow coming through the comforter betrayed that number two son was still awake...reading under the covers by his book light.

Cole slapped the hump marking Kyle's butt. "Lights out, sport. I know Horatio Hornblower is great stuff, but tomorrow you've got school."

Kyle read on, oblivious to him.

Up in the attic where Travis and Renee had their rooms, Travis was asleep. A tear stain crossed his check. Cole's throat closed. He had visions of Travis keeping a brave front while Sherrie told them about the car, then giving way to tears in the privacy of his room.

Cole ran his fingers across the rumpled hair before leaving. "Hey, partner, you don't have to try to be so tough, you know."

Renee's room was dark, too, but without surprise he found her awake. Another night owl. She sat in front of her beloved peacock window, wrapped in her bathrobe, violin tucked under her chin. By day, the fan of panes she had colored with glass paint cast a rainbow across the floor. Now only light from the street lights silhouetted her as she played quietly.

Even at a whisper, he recognized the piece, Barber's *Adagio For Strings*. The melancholy music always reminded him of the Omaha Novembers of his childhood...overcast skies, bare trees, and the ground carpeted with dank leaves. Was it one of the choices for her upcoming recital?

A recital he had to miss.

Thinking about that, Cole realized in despair how much else he had to miss. He would never know if Renee made it to the concert stage. He would never walk her or Hannah down the aisle, see his sons turn into men, or know his grandchildren. He and Sherrie would never do the things they had planned for retirement. The strains of the *Adagio* wrapped around him ...tonight sounding even bleaker, sighing of unutterable loss.

Grief and searing anger boiled up in him. He might be here to pull Sara out of the mess she landed in, but that son of a bitch in the Elvis mask was unfinished business, too. Before he left, he would hunt down the bastard and ruin *his* life.

— 9 —

THE ANGER AT his killer fueled Cole's resentment at walking to Razor's place. Damn it, he ought to be able to ziptrip! Standing in the hall outside Renee's room, still hearing the *Adagio*, he tried again...picturing the apartment...straining to remember every detail as he imagined himself in the apartment. Did he need to take into account that at this time of night the drapes would be closed? Or maybe open just a crack, enough to admit light from the street and from the ground floor shoe store's sign...and from the right angle, give a glimpse of the Coit Tower to the east.

The hallway blurred...turned into Razor's front room. Cole stood behind the futon, at the window. Triumph at making it here mixed with bafflement. What was different this time? Yes, he thought about the view from the window, but could that detail really be what did the trick? Shaking his head, he turned away from the window.

Razor had the futon made out into a bed and wore sleep shorts and a t-shirt, but he still looked wide awake. Propped against pillows, he watched a movie on TV with the sound muted and closed captioning on.

Checking out the movie, Cole grimaced. He knew this one and it had barely begun. "Come on, amigo...you don't need to watch this again. You know Seagal whips Tommy Lee Jones's ass and keeps Honolulu from being nuked. Turn it off and go to bed." He moved behind Razor and dropped his voice to a drone. "Your eyelids are feeling heavy. Heavy ...heavy. You're getting sleepy...very sleepy."

Razor remained wide awake.

Scratch suggestion as a solution. The TV remote Razor held gave Cole an idea, though. It should not be much different from a computer, right?

He reached down across Razor's shoulder, put a finger on the power button, and closed his eyes. "Time to go to sleep." He fished around until he felt the tickle, and heard the click of the TV shutting off.

Razor muttered. Cole opened his eyes to see Razor pushing the power button.

Well of course Razor would turn it back on. Cole turned it off.

Muttering, Razor hit the power again, this time with a hard punch of his thumb…and kept the thumb resting on the button.

Though that did not block his access to it, Cole decided to change tactics. He went for Mute. The closed captions disappeared and the sound came on.

The mutter became an expletive. Razor re-muted the sound.

Cole found himself enjoying the game. He went to the channel buttons and switched up one. When Razor changed back, Cole dropped down a channel.

With expletives turning into a longer curse, Razor returned to the movie channel. Cole hit the Menu button. Razor cleared that off the screen…back to a short expletive he never used around Holly.

Cole grinned. Now what could he do? Oh, yes. There was that time at home when Hannah played with the remote. He punched DVD.

The screen went blank except for the message VID, replaced moments later by: "Unusable Signal". And as *he* had after Hannah's monkeying, Razor began trying every button on the remote to restore normal TV function. His disgust and frustration grew visibly with each failure. Even turning the TV off and on did not restore the picture. Finally Razor happened to punch WHO-Input. Cole was ready, poised over the power button. As the movie came back, he turned off the TV.

That did it. Swearing in a tone which suggested that only supreme self control let him keep it under his breath, Razor hurled the remote away from him. Fortunately, into the easy chair, not through the TV screen. He set his glasses on the end table, switched off the lamp, and flung himself flat on the futon.

Cole watched in satisfaction. They should be in business any time now.

Razor took several deep breaths and let them out slowly. His whole body relaxed and Cole heard his heart rate drop. In less than a minute, Razor's breathing stabilized.

Asleep, just like that. Razor had done it in their patrol unit, too. Cole shook his head. It still amazed him. But Razor woke just as abruptly. When their call number came over the radio, he went from dead to the world to fully alert, snatching up the mike for a reply. Despite that, once wakened, he had to be convinced that he was still asleep.

Cole considered the possibilities. He could wade through the futon, or sit on an invisible chair. That should be freaky enough for a dream.

He gave the chair a try. It worked fine, except it seemed …blah. Maybe make it a lounger? He lifted both legs and leaned back with his hands behind his head. It gave him the position of someone in a lounger, and felt like a lounger. But it still lacked the craziness a dream ought to have.

Staring at the ceiling, he suddenly remembered coming home after one late shift to find some old movie playing on the TV and Fred Astaire or Gene Kelly dancing up the wall. He should be able to do that, too…and better.

Behind him, Razor sighed and rolled over. Cole turned. Tension cranked tight in him. Time to see if he could pull this off. "I hope to hell you're not ghost blind, amigo." He stepped between the futon and drapes, grabbed one of Razor's ears to give him a shot of cold, and hissed, "Sergeant coming."

Razor sat bolt upright, eyes snapping open.

He heard! Would he launch into one of his start-in-the-middle conversations that made it sound to a sergeant as if he had been awake all along? It had been worth crying wolf once in a while just to see what came out of Razor's mouth.

"I don't know if there's any good answer," Razor said. "The Quakers thought their concept for Eastern State Prison was…" About which time he registered where he was and fell back on the pillow. "Sheesh. You're starting to lose it, Kev."

Cole laughed. "I don't know. Your reflexes look as fast as ever to me."

Razor jerked back upright and reached for the lamp. "Cole? Where the hell have you been?"

"No, don't turn the light on! You'll wake yourself up."

Razor twisted toward him…and blinked. "What the hell? What's with the glow-in-the-dark getup?"

Cole looked down at himself. Glow? Well, maybe a faint one. The important thing was…Razor saw him. Maybe they could skip the dream scam and just talk. Except, he realized, what happened when he came to the revelation that he was dead? No, better stick to the plan. "You're dreaming."

"No." Razor squinted at him. "You look like those moon and stars we put up on Holly and Kyle's bedroom ceilings."

"I mean this is a dream." Time to prove it. Cole imagined a curved surface reaching to the ceiling and trotted up it while Razor's jaw dropped. Weird. The room appeared to revolve while he walked in place. "And, shhh." He doubted Holly would hear him but he lowered his voice to encourage Razor to do so. "Just in case you're talking in your sleep, you don't want to wake Holly." It felt like a dream…standing here with the furniture hanging overhead and Razor gaping down at him.

Then Razor felt himself and the bed around him, and squeezing his eyes shut, shook his head.

Shit! "Razor, no…don't wake yourself up!" Cole dashed back down to the floor, mind racing ahead of him. "You need to keep dreaming. There…there are issues for you to work out, and this is the way to do it."

Razor opened his eyes. "Issues?"

"The blood in the car for one. It's mine and I'm dead. In your heart of hearts, you suspect that. Which is why you're dreaming of me as a ghost." He waded into the futon and sat down. "You know that even if I killed Sara Benay and decided run for it, I'd have contacted you and Sherrie."

Razor stared at Cole's legs disappearing into the futon.

Cole punched his shoulder. "Pay attention. The other issue, the most important one, is Sara Benay."

Razor expression went baffled. "Benay? Why is she an issue?"

"She's in some kind of danger because of me."

"Danger?" Razor sounded skeptical.

Cole leaned toward him. "I don't know whether it's from witnessing my murder and recognizing the killer, or being caught searching the Flaxx company books for evidence against Donald Flaxx, but there's this cloud of terror in the 2EC garage that I think is hers. From her apartment it's obvious she blew out of there in one hell of—"

Razor blinked. "What? Wait. How did she happen to be searching the Flaxx books?"

Cole winced. But he had to tell Razor. "Sara works in Flaxx's Bookkeeping department. She's the informant I met Monday evening. On Wednesday she left me a phone message saying she'd found—"

"Did you put her up to it?" Razor reached for his glasses and peered at Cole through them.

Cole cleared his throat. "Not exactly."

Razor frowned. "Not exactly? What the hell does—" He broke off, sighing. "What am I doing? You'd think I'm really talking to you."

Cole heard rising disbelief in that tone. He tried to keep Razor involved. "It's your subconscious trying to work things out. Checking the books was her idea."

Razor eyed him skeptically. "Her idea."

"Basically." He told Razor about the surprise call from Sara on Monday. "And we arranged to meet at Bon Vivre, where—"

"Wait." Razor frowned. "If she called Wednesday to tell you she'd found something, then the meeting Monday was for what...other than sending you to the men's room to call in the cavalry?"

"Which didn't come," Cole said. "I had to rescue myself."

Razor grunted. "I got tied up. I've already apologized for that. What happened at Bon Vivre?"

Across the table in the back booth she chose, Sara had shed her shoes and rubbed her feet, then downed nearly half the brandy and soda he'd ordered for her. "Here's to Earl Lamper's health. Preserve me from ever having Mao Tse Gao as my boss full time."

Some interviewees had to circle a while before coming to what they wanted to talk about. Cole sat back to wait on Sara. "Lamper's sick?"

"He had an emergency appendectomy last night." She took another slug of her drink. "He's such a sweetie to work for. Carries a share of the load; doesn't give someone grief if they can't make it in because their baby-sitter didn't show up that morning; doesn't care if we come in late or play games on our work stations...as long as the work's done and accurate. And he brings us flowers on our birthdays. But General Gao..." She grimaced. "If she'd divided Earl's accounts among all of us, there wouldn't be that much extra work for anyone."

Cole sat up. His ears pricked. Lamper's accounts?

"But she split them just between Joy and me—you remember Joy from lunch that day."

Joy Quon, yes. A plain face but keenly intelligent eyes. She referred to accounting as having "elegant symmetry." Kenisha Hayes, the third member of the trio, had personal elegance...tall and regal as her Masai ancestors.

Sara swirled the ice in her glass. "So I ended up with half of Earl's accounts on top of my own. And of course Genghis Gao wanted *everything* updated before Joy and I left today."

The skin prickled down Cole's spine. So the books for the individual stores were divided up among the bookkeeping staff. *That* was how Earl Lamper altered figures without anyone else being aware of it...take over the books for target stores! He fought to keep his voice casual. "Is it some of Lamper's accounts you wanted to talk about?"

Sara swung her legs under the table and sat up. "I'm starved. Have you eaten? They have great sandwiches here, especially the Reuben and the Philly beef."

They were still circling. Cole bit back his impatience and waved down a waitress. After waiting six years for a break in the Flaxx burglaries, he was not about to blow it by rushing things. Sherrie had been warned that he would be late.

As the waitress left, Sara leaned over the table toward him. The open top buttons of her blouse gave him a view down her cleavage and a cloisonne butterfly pendant dangling into it. "You come around to see Earl every time we have a burglary. Office gossip says you think the company is involved."

He gave her a bland smile. "An inside job is always something we have to consider. You've had detectives from Homicide visit, too."

"Yes, but they were asking for more information on that Kijurian character who was throwing firebombs into our stores. I didn't think Homicide investigated arson."

"A firefighter died in the Woodworks fire. Any death occurring in the course of a felony is a homicide."

She stared at him for several moments, then ran her finger around the rim of her glass. "What does bookkeeping have to do with any of it?"

He took a sip of his beer, and pushed it aside. It had gone flat and warm while he nursed it at the bar, waiting for Sara. "Which of the stores I mentioned at lunch is Lamper doing the books for?"

Sara hesitated, then named five...two that had been burglarized and three that were torched, including Woodworks. "He also has stores that I remember being robbed other years. Two I used to do the books for, Glass And Brass and Wild 'N Whimsey."

Excitement jumped in Cole. Glass And Brass was hit last year, Wild 'N Whimsey the year before. He kept his voice even. "How were they doing financially?"

She stared at him over her glass. "I don't remember."

A lie. It showed in her eyes and voice. He tried another approach. "Why aren't you doing their books any longer?"

She shrugged. "Earl likes shuffling store assignments to keep us on our toes."

And let him unobtrusively take over target stores, Cole reflected. Slick. "Were you keeping their books when they were burglarized?"

She finished off her drink. "Will you order me another of these?"

Another question she preferred to duck. He waved over the waitress.

Sara crunched a piece of ice. "Earl would never do anything detrimental to the company. He's devoted to it and Mr. Flaxx. You can almost hear him saying 'Master' when he talks to or about Mr. Flaxx."

Oh, yeah. Playing Igor to Flaxx's Frankenstein. "You don't have to convince me of his devotion."

The waitress brought the new drink. Sara sipped it. Cole watched wheels turn behind her eyes. "If you think there's something criminal in the books, why haven't you audited them?"

He wished he could read her mind. What she found in Lamper's files disturbed her enough to call him, but now she was backing off. Maybe to protect Lamper? He hunted for a soothing answer. "I don't *know* there's evidence of anything criminal, and we can't go on fishing expeditions." His gut feelings being insufficient probable cause for a warrant.

Their sandwiches arrived. Sara took a big bite of her Reuben. Cole saw the wheels still turning as she chewed. She swallowed, then said, "If you *could* go fishing, what would you be looking for?"

His neck prickled. "Why do you ask?"

She leaned toward him. "Because I can have a look if you want."

Current shot through Cole. Shit, yes, he wanted! But the opportunity sat in the middle of a frigging mine field. "Why would you do that?"

"Maybe to prove you're wrong about Earl."

Who did she really want to convince? He stared in frustration at the mine field. He said slowly, "If I asked you to look, you'd be acting as an agent of the SFPD, which needs a warrant or it becomes an illegal search. In which case, no evidence you found, or any growing out of what you found, would be admissible in court." Not to mention how deep in shit he would be.

Her brows rose. "What if I never asked you and went looking on my own?"

Smart lady. Beyond the mines, looming ever larger, the *Flaxx Goes to Jail* sign flashed brightly...irresistibly. Carefully Cole said, "If we never discussed this topic and in the natural course of performing your job you happened to come across information you felt we should know about, reporting it could provide probable cause for a forensic examination of the books."

"Never discussed what topic?" she said without a blink. "I believe I was telling you how sorry I am about Earl's appendicitis. If he hadn't had surgery, Kenisha and I would be taking off this Friday and Monday in a long week end, cruising down to Baja on the yacht of a friend. Now we can't go." She grimaced and sighed heavily...then smiled across the table at him. "Maybe you can suggest something for me to do instead? Maybe some indoor activity?"

A bare foot suddenly on his shin, sliding upward, said she already had an activity in mind. Suspicion and anger flared in him. Was this the real reason she wanted to meet? Not because anything in the books concerned her, but to give her an opportunity to come on to him?

He kept his voice level as he reached down to move her foot. "I'm married."

Her smile only broadened. "I do see your wedding ring. I also remember how you flirted with us at lunch." The foot came back up his leg, this time climbing to the inside of his thigh. "Don't tell me women haven't hit on you before."

He removed her foot again. "Why are *you*?" As if her offer to look in Flaxx's files were not dangerous enough— if she really meant it—add sex and the situation became a professionally and personally lethal explosive.

Her brows rose. "Why not? I like older men, especially when they're good-looking, have their hair, and are interesting company. At lunch you were all charm and guileless blue eyes, but I knew there had to be more to you. You're a cop. You're trained to use deadly force. You carry a gun and handcuffs— not that I'm into bondage."

No...she appeared to be into power. That was what most older men represented...status, influence, material possessions. Like her friend with the yacht. And a gun and handcuffs certainly represented power.

"I was right." She sipped her drink. "Tonight you feel dangerous. You're strung tight and your eyes have been dissecting me." She smiled. "Don't you find me attractive?"

A new surge of anger went through him at the manipulative subtext of the question. *You don't want me; fine; we're quits. I guess you're not interested in me looking in the books.* But even as that made him want to walk away...and reason said he should...he knew she had his number. He could not make himself give up this chance at Flaxx. The trick was to play the game, too...hold her off without losing her. "Yes, you're very attractive." Just not his type. She lacked wild red hair and breasts that strained bras and blouses.

Her smile broadened. "Then when we've finished, will you drive me home?" He almost heard her purr. "I'll fix coffee for us."

He nodded. "Sounds good." But his mind was racing. He needed a way out. Razor could provide one by calling his cell phone and pretending to be Communications wanting him at a burglary scene. She was unlikely to know that Night Investigations handled all burglary calls between six p.m. and six a.m. He slid out of the booth. "Excuse me for a minute. I need to hit the men's room."

"Jesus, Cole!" Razor shook his head. "There's rule bending and there's twisting them into pretzels. You may have blown anyone's chances of nailing Flaxx."

"Right now I'm more worried about Sara." He gave Razor a rundown on Wednesday night, from leaving the office to the explosive finale.

Listening, Razor's brows first hopped, hearing about the phone messages and calls, then rose toward his hairline as Cole described being killed. At the end, he grunted. "Damn. Where does my brain come up with this stuff?"

Cole's stomach plunged. Of course in thinking this was a dream, Razor considered it *just* a dream, unconnected to reality. Somehow he had to persuade Razor to act on the information anyway. He leaned toward Razor. "This isn't 'stuff.' Your subconscious is putting things together from things you've seen and heard without being aware of it."

"How would I hear or see anything about Wednesday night?"

Talk faster, numbnuts, Cole hissed at himself. Or this whole visit went down the toilet. "Inference and deduction. Putting together bits you know...my lunch with the women from Bookkeeping; my Monday meeting with a horny informant I strung along; my willingness to make a long Wednesday even longer in response to a phone call from a woman named Benay; my obsession with nailing Flaxx. You know if I were alive I'd have contacted Sherrie. This is your subconscious talking. Don't ignore it. Do you know who in Homicide has my case?"

Razor shook his head.

"It ought to be Andy Willner and Neil Galentree." He eyed Razor. "I don't suppose you'd go in and suggest that to Lieutenant Madrid."

Razor snorted. "You suppose right. Why Willner and Galentree?"

"Because they're working the firefighter's death. Somehow that has to be what's behind—"

"Jesus, here we go again." Razor sighed. "Are you still convinced that Flaxx—But what am I thinking." He banged his forehead with the heel of his hand. "Of *course* you still think Flaxx torched his stores. You don't believe in the suspect they have for those fires."

And obviously Razor remained unconvinced that Luther Thomas Kijurian existed only on paper. "Flaxx knows the building owner is always the prime suspect in arson. He's created Kijurian to draw suspicion away from himself. Kijurian is like the Man Who Never Was that the Brits used—"

"Used in World War II to feed misinformation to the Nazis. Yes, yes, I know. You've told me." Razor sighed. "Okay…let's go through this one more time." He ticked off points on his fingers. "You've told me Flaxx has a personnel file for the man. Their maintenance log and work orders say he unplugged toilets, worked on locks, and changed light bulbs. There's the payroll record with his salary on it."

"Flaxx went to a lot of trouble to set this up. But Kijurian's name is on the payroll for just three months before he was fired, allegedly for giving them a false Social Security number." Cole ticked off points of his own. "But where did all those records come from? The computer. And who's Flaxx's IT guru? Faithful henchman and cooker of books Earl Lamper. It's a snap for him to fake a personnel file. The work orders? Who pays much attention to who comes and changes the light bulbs? Someone went to those stores and did it, but the staff there can't remember who." He raised his brows at Razor. "I've asked them."

"Even though investigating arson isn't your job." Razor shook his head. "Damn it, the personnel file has a *photo*, a copy of which you've shown me, you remember. He's been described by witnesses who saw him throw the Molotov cocktails, as well as photographed in the crowd at a couple of the fires. People saw him at the residence hotel where he lived."

"Where he was never seen in good light or for very long and which he left the night of the first fire. Except for the fire photos, he hasn't been seen since. And doesn't he look just *like* someone who'd be throwing Molotov cocktails?" When Razor grunted in exasperation, Cole punched his shoulder. "Come on...think about it. Stocky, jowly, thick eyebrows and a mustache. An anarchist type straight out of Central Casting. Kijurian is a *costume*. That's why no one can find a trace of him now."

Razor set his glasses back on the end table and pressed his fingers to his eyes. "Cole..."

What did it take to convince him? "Damn it, Razor...it's too big a coincidence for Flaxx to be burglarizing his own stores then for someone else to come along and start torching them. And you've read the reports. Breaking the front window to throw in the Molotov cocktail set off the security alarms so the fire department arrived before more than contents burned. The buildings themselves sustained very little damage. Except at Woodworks. And notice there were no more fires after that. If Kijurian were real, do you suppose a firefighter's death would have scared him off?"

Razor looked up. "Okay, I can agree with that, but—"

"But it's Kijurian's name that's the final giveaway."

Razor blinked. "His name?"

Cole nodded. "Remember how I told you it sounded familiar but couldn't place it? The night after Woodworks burned I was doing the crossword puzzle in the paper and Kyle, who was hanging over my shoulder kibitzing, asked if Burglary was getting a new lieutenant. I said no, why, and he pointed to the margin of the paper. I saw I'd doodled Kijurian's name over and over—*L.T. Kijurian*. The initials did look like the abbreviation for lieutenant. That made something click. Music started running in my head."

"Music." Razor shook his head. "Where *am* I getting this stuff?"

Cole swore silently. He kept forgetting Razor thought this was a dream. "It's been cooking down in your subconscious, like it did in mine. When I hummed the tune for Renee, she identified it as Prokofiev's *Lieutenant Kijé Suite*. She showed me the CD. Then I remembered hearing her play it."

Razor grunted. "And of course you don't believe the similarity in names is a coincidence."

Cole shook his head. "Not after reading the liner notes. The music is from a Russian movie about another man who never was...a fictional army officer created by a clerical error."

Razor sat silent for a minute, staring at him. "I wonder if the real you came up with this, too. It sounds like something Cole would. But there hasn't been any change in the Alert for Kijurian. So if Cole did think that, and mentioned the idea to anyone, I guess they weren't convinced."

Cole grimaced. "Willner and Galentree weren't, no." If they had been, would he be alive today? Would Sara be just grumbling about missing the cruise to Baja? Not that Willner or Galentree were to blame for his current mess. Launching Operation Hello Dollies out of frustration with them had been his own doing. So were the consequences. "Razor, I need—there's something *you* need to do." *He thinks this is a dream, remember.*

Razor frowned. "What?"

"After you've taken Holly to school, you need to go to Homicide—"

"I'm already planning to drop in and see what's happening."

Cole nodded. "I'd expect that. But...you need to tell whoever has my case about Sara, especially about her working for Flaxx and what she might have seen. I never met her on Wednesday. She didn't kill me. But she needs to be found for her own safety. See that they read my case files on Flaxx so they have a real motive for my murder instead of Leach's lovers quarrel shit."

Razor's expression went wry. "Tell them how to run their case? They'll certainly appreciate that."

"They have to be told about Sara." Cole stared hard into Razor's eyes. "Her life could depend on it." But he could see another thought forming in Razor's head that set him swearing silently: Importance in the dream did not make it important in reality.

Razor said, "And how do I explain having knowledge of Wednesday night, and why I've said nothing before? I sure as hell can't tell them it came to me in a dream."

Cole clapped his shoulder. "Sure you can. We've all waked up with answers to problems that were bothering us when we went to sleep. This is more of that." But he could not leave Sara's safety solely to Razor and his fellow officers. He'd caused the problem; he had to do what he could to resolve it. "Now ...before I let you go on to another dream, will you do me one more favor? Look up phone listings for Joy Quon and Kenisha Hayes. I'll give them a chance to dream about me and tell me if they have any thoughts on where Sara is."

Razor blinked. "You want me to look them up in a dream phone book?"

"Please." He stood and stepped back from the futon.

Razor peered dubiously at him, then sighed and threw off the covers. He pulled the phone book from under the end table and opened it on his knees. "How do you spell Joy's last name...K-W-A-N or Q-U-O-N?"

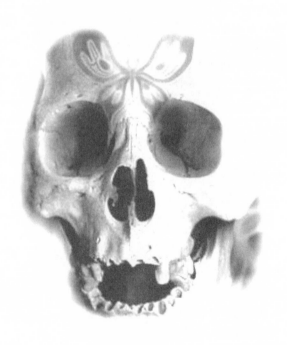

— 10 —

COLE LEFT RAZOR falling back into bed and headed across town again, reciting addresses in his head. Lucky he had a good memory, he reflected. He had automatically reached inside his suit coat before remembering he had no notebook. The addresses were all for K. Hayes. The Quon listings did not included a Joy Quon. Being single, she might still live at home. Now he just had to hope Kenisha was really Hayes's first name. With luck, she would also be at the closest address, in the Western Addition. The address lay outside the familiar Northern District streets, but, in reviewing a mental map, he estimated it was no more than six or eight blocks from the Northern Station. If a ziptrip would take him—

The street blurred, solidified...and Cole blinked in astonishment. He stood in the middle of the intersection outside the station. *Damn* it, how did this work! He had to concentrate like hell to reach Razor's place, but zipped here in mid—

His train of thought derailed as a car barreled out the front of his body. He stared after it, startled. That was amazing. The rapid staccato of jolts from the engine felt...wonderful. A hundred times better than Danny the Prick's body heat. Invigorating. Something he wanted to try again. As he jogged for the Hayes address, he stayed in the street and let himself be run through by other vehicles, savoring the energy jolt of each pass. He almost regretted arriving at the Hayes address. Before going in, maybe he would let a few more cars run through him.

That thought brought him up short. Cole hurriedly moved to the sidewalk. He had enough problems without becoming addicted to internal combustion.

The seedy Victorian in front of him had been divided into flats, with the mailboxes indicating that K. G. Hayes lived on the second floor. But a tricycle and some toy trucks on the floor of the apartment's livingroom made Cole doubt the Hayes he wanted lived here. One look at the very pregnant female half of the couple he found asleep in one bedroom confirmed that.

Cole returned to the street. One K. Hayes down, two to go. Maybe she was the one in Haight-Ashbury. Did he know a location near the address well enough to try ziptripping there? Nothing closer than he was right now, he decided…and broke into a jog.

The Haight address brought him to another divided Victorian, this time partitioned into studio apartments. K. T. Hayes occupied the rear of the ground floor. Opening his eyes after passing through the door, Cole found one woman asleep on the sofa bed. She lay on her stomach, face hidden in the crook of her arm, but photographs on the top shelf of an entertainment center told him he had the right Hayes. One showed Kenisha Hayes and Sara skiing, while in another they lounged on a sunny beach with a fit-looking man in his fifties.

Cole sat on the side of the bed and ran his hand along the exposed arm. "Miss Hayes."

Without waking, she shivered and pulled the arm under her quilt.

But a shoulder remained exposed. He rubbed it. "Kenisha …Ke-*neee*-sha, baby."

Squirming farther under the quilt, she mumbled, "What?"

Still not awake, he judged. But as long as she answered coherently, staying asleep was fine. "I need to ask you some questions about Sara."

"Sara?" Hayes's breathing paused. Her eyes cracked open. Her squint abruptly turned wide-eyed. "Inspector Dunavan?"

"Not in the flesh." He kept his voice low and soothing. "The chain and deadbolts on your door are still secure. I'm just a dream." He walked up to the ceiling, then back down and sat on a virtual chair beside the bed, propping one ankle on his other knee. "See?"

Her eyes drifted closed. "What about Sara?"

"Do you know where she is?"

Hayes grunted. "In the dream I was just having, we were cruising down to Baja. The sea was calm; the sun was warm. In real life, the last I heard she was planning to spend the weekend in the sack with you." Her eyes opened again. She frowned. "I wonder why I'm dreaming about you being here?"

"Maybe you're unconsciously worried about the questions she was asking around the office. Maybe Mrs. Gao was watching her in some threatening way?" He leaned back with his hands behind his head and propped his feet up on the edge of the bed. "And if you're worried, how better to deal with that than calling up a minion of the law?"

"Why would I be worried?" She scooted semi-upright against the back of the sofa. "Sara was just asking who used to have the books for certain stores, and all Gao said was if Sara worked on her accounts instead of gossiping, she'd finish up in the regular business hours."

Cole returned his feet to the floor and leaned toward her, elbows propped on his knees. "Did you have any of the stores she was asking about?"

She nodded. "A Different Country."

It had been burglarized three years ago. "How was it doing financially before the account was reassigned?"

"I don't remember."

After three years, possibly not. "Do you know where Sara might go if she wanted to hide?

Hayes's eyes widened. "Hide? Why would she need to hide?"

"She didn't come asking you for help?"

"No. If she's in trouble, maybe she went home. That's what I'd do. Her parents are in Bloomington, Indiana."

A logical choice that needed checking out...though if the threat to Sara came from Gao, the personnel files would tell anyone looking for Sara where to go. "How about the man you were supposed to cruise with this weekend?"

Hayes shook her head. "She just met him last week and I expect he's off on his yacht right now."

"What about other male friends?"

She shook her head again. "Most are only weekend flings...like you. I don't know any names. When she's telling Joy and me the juicy details, she just uses first names or nicknames. The few guys she sees semi-regularly, she doesn't talk about at all."

"You must know the dude in the bathing suit." Cole pointed at the photographs on the entertainment center. "Or was he just a fling, too?"

Her gaze followed the direction of his finger. "Jerry? I forgot about him. He's gay. He can't bring himself to come out publically, though, so he calls Sara when he needs a female on his arm. But he'll take her places just for fun, too, because they like each other. A few times he's let her bring me along. He has a great flat in London and a house in Belize that's to die for."

Belize. What a sweet place to lie low. But the man must have a place here in town, too. It was definitely worth checking out. "And Jerry's full name and address are...what."

"Gerald Lockhart. I'm not sure of the address, but it's in Seacliff."

Donald Flaxx's neighborhood. It would be interesting if Sara turned out to be hiding almost next door. "Do you have Miss Quon's address?"

"Joy?" Hayes shook her head. "She keeps her family life separate from the office and us. We've never been to her house."

Razor could locate the address and talk to Quon. Cole stood. "Thank you for your time." He could not resist adding: "I now return you to your regularly scheduled dream." Then he headed for the door. Rear vision spotted Hayes shaking her head and closing her eyes even before he passed into the hall.

Leaving the house, he felt satisfied. She had given him several leads to follow. Now he needed a computer. He headed for the Park District station a few blocks away.

Outside the holding cells there, Cole found one computer in use. The single occupant of their holding cells, a woman, lay sleeping on her bench, an arm across her eyes. No one paid attention to the other computer.

But using it was a bitch. The chair pushed under the desk forced Cole to operate the computer standing up. And experience on the Southern Station and Braff's computers did not make working with this one any less tedious. Hunting and pecking, he kept global vision watching the officer at the other computer and the rest of the room, hoping no one noticed the action on this screen. Luck seemed with him so far. Even when another officer joined the first and they turned to gather the pages collecting in the printer tray, neither looked in his computer's direction.

A commotion in the hall became officers hauling in a young black male.

He struggled between them. "You got the wrong man! That bitch is *lyin'!*"

Cole kept plugging away, forcing himself not to rush so he made no wrong key-strokes.

The officers unlocked a holding cell and shoved their prisoner in, leaving him cuffed. He swung back to the door, voice rising into soprano. "I done tole you, I never even *seen* the bitch before."

Before shutting the door, one of the officers shook his head. "Jerome, Jerome. You might get away with the innocent act if you'd learn to lie better."

Cole mentally pleaded with his fingers and the computer to work faster.

"You know how we know you're lying? Because when you do, your left eye starts winking."

Jerome immediately turned the left side of his face away.

All the officers grinned. Even Cole, as he tried to stay focused on the computer. He almost had the data on Lockhart.

If Jerome could keep them occupied just a minute longer now. But while one officer locked the holding cell door, the other headed in Cole's direction.

Cole swore silently.

The officer reached through Cole and pulled out the chair.

"Come on, come on," Cole whispered at the computer.

The officer paused, feeling along the back of the chair.

"Something the matter?" another officer asked.

"It feels like it's had an ice pack on it."

Lockhart's address and telephone number came up on the screen.

Cole hurriedly memorized them and glanced at the clock. If he wanted to catch Lockhart asleep, he'd better head for Seacliff. The idea of trekking across the city was more aggravating all the time, though. He *had* to figure out ziptripping! In the interim, it suddenly occurred to him, could he imagine himself a virtual car, or better yet, a virtual flying car?

Outside the station he sat down at the height of a car seat, lifted his feet clear of the ground, and visualized himself in a vehicle like the Weasleys' in *Harry Potter*. Then he stepped on a gas pedal, pulled his hands back as if holding the yoke of a plane, and pictured his vehicle moving forward and up.

Nothing happened. He remained sitting in mid-air.

"Shit."

Cole stood up. So much for that. Apparently travel required physical motion on his part. But while the flying car was out, there was no reason not to go one better than his previous walkway and make it an aerial route. Call it the Dunavan Diagonal.

Virtual stairs took him high enough to clear all the surrounding buildings, so nothing lay between him and Seacliff's lights to the northwest. He aimed for them and launched into a run.

He'd started racing flat out, but minutes later, as he crossed a corner of Golden Gate Park into the Richmond area, he stopped short, goosebumps running down his spine and arms.

He had an aerial view without the obstruction of a plane beneath him. The city spread out below like something under a glass ceiling...ablaze with light—street lights, headlights of vehicles moving through the streets, lights on the Bay Bridge behind him strung like a necklace across the bay. Ahead of him beyond the Presidio, the Golden Gate Bridge towers rose out of fog. More fog, puffy billows set aglow by the lights inside it, blanketed the northeast portion of the city from the Marina and Fisherman's Wharf toward the Financial District. Climb higher and he would see the whole Bay Area, he mused. That should be even more spectacular. And he did not have to stop there. Looking up, it occurred to him that he could climb high enough to see the whole planet...or even visit the moon. It would just be a really long walk.

Flashing lights broke into the thought. Below him, a police unit raced up one of the avenues. That jerked him back to reality with a quick stab of guilt for forgetting why he was here...Sara.

Cole re-focused on Seacliff and resumed running.

At Gerald Lockhart's address, the low, Spanish-style house looked modest behind gates that were more sculpture than security, iron wrought into elaborate trees with copper leaves. Inside the house, Cole found that the gates indicated where Lockhart preferred to spend his money. He had enough paintings and sculpture for an art gallery. He had also paid for location. Beyond the wall of glass and shallow terrace at the rear of the house stretched a spectacular view of the Pacific and Golden Gate Bridge.

Searching for Lockhart's bedroom, Cole hoped the man lived alone, or least slept by himself. So far he had been lucky in that respect with Razor and Hayes. Making the dream visit work with a lover there would be...probably impossible.

But fortune still smiled. Only one of the house's bedrooms was occupied, and it had just a single sleeper burrowed into the massive four-poster. Like the front rooms, the bedroom had an exterior wall of glass and the bed had been placed to take advantage of the view. For this house, Cole decided, he could envy Lockhart's money. Sherrie would love waking up in such a bed with that view.

Nothing of Lockhart showed except an ear and salt and pepper hair. Cole leaned over the bed and grabbed hold of the ear. "Jerry."

It brought no response. Cole grimaced. Damn. Was Lockhart going to turn out to be ghost blind? He rubbed the ear. "Jerry. Hello-ho. Talk to me."

To his relief, Lockhart grunted and turned over. As Lockhart opened his eyes and squinted up, Cole waded through him and the bed to the windows. With luck, that would sell this as a dream without him saying so. He passed through the windows onto the terrace. And Lockhart saw him. Rear vision watched the man sit up and stare sleepily after him.

After a few moments, Cole returned inside. "You have a great view. Sara said I'd like it."

Lockhart's forehead crinkled in puzzled furrows. "Sara?"

"Benay."

Lockhart's expression cleared. "Oh…yes…Sara. And who are you?"

"Just a dream figure." Cole waded far enough into the bed to lounge back against the post at the foot of the bed. "Have you talked to her lately?"

Lockhart shook his head. "I haven't seen her for a couple of months."

That could be considered an evasive answer. Hope rose in Cole. "But have you *talked* to her? Did she call here Wednesday night asking for your help…maybe asking to use your place in Belize for a while?"

Lockhart blinked. "What? No on both counts."

A thought struck Cole. Sara might not necessarily have called, just run. "Do you have permanent staff down there, or is it closed up when you're gone?"

"There's a caretaker couple." Lockhart smiled wryly. "If someone doesn't keep the jungle beaten back, it takes over."

"Has Sara visited often enough that they'd know her on sight?"

Lockhart considered. "Probably. Why?"

"Then might they let her in if she just showed up and said you'd given her permission to stay there?"

"I can't see Sara doing that. Why would she?"

"She could be in trouble and need a place to hide."

"Hide?" Lockhart stiffened. The last of sleep disappeared from his face. He ran his hands back through his hair, smoothing it. "Why—"

"Would the caretakers let her in?"

Lockhart eyed him a moment. "Not without checking with me. I always let them know when I've authorized someone to use the house. If they recognized Sara, they'd call me and ask about her. Otherwise they'd call the police and then let me know what happened."

So Sara had probably not gone to Belize. The matter of visas probably prevented any spur of the moment trip there anyway. But he had that flat in London, too. "Do you have staff at the London flat? Or does she have a key to it?"

"There's no staff and Sara doesn't have a key. She isn't that good a friend."

It might be worth checking anyway. Cole straightened and stepped out of the bed. "If you do happen to hear from her, you ought to let Inspector Kevin Rasgorshek know. He's in Night Investigations at the Central Police Station."

Leaving the house, Cole reflected that the chances of Lockhart acting on dream instructions were nil. The department would have to contact *him*. Which meant letting Razor know about Lockhart and where Sara's parents lived so he could pass the information on to Homicide.

But the question was, how to tell Razor. Not with another dream visit. He had to make the information real and credible this time. Could he do that with a note on Razor's computer? Cole jammed his hands in his coat pockets. So much of this ghost business was like banging his head against a wall. Too damn much. Did he have any hope of working it out in time to help Sara?

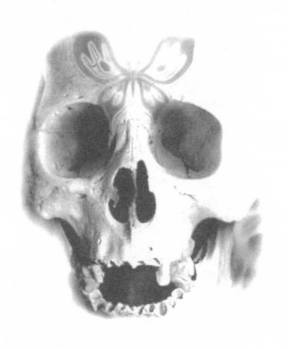

— 11 —

IT TOOK TWO tries, but Cole managed another ziptrip to Razor's place. For whatever reason, it did not work without thinking about the Coit Tower when he visualized the apartment.

But the fact it finally did work let him arrive while Razor and Holly still slept. Razor kept the computer in his bedroom, so Cole hoped Holly slept soundly. She appeared to be doing so when he slipped into the bedroom.

Once he had the computer booting, Cole realized he had no idea of the sound scheme, but to his relief, the desktop activated with only a modest *ta-da*. A quick check backward found Holly continuing to sleep undisturbed.

Watching the time on the bottom of the screen, he laboriously opened Razor's word processor and started typing. This time he gave up on perfection in favor of speed. The process still went glacially slow. And while he was working on just the first sentence, the sound of Holly's breathing suddenly changed.

Rear vision found her sitting up, blinking sleepily. Damn! What if he told her to go back to sleep? Would she hear him as a subliminal suggestion?

Too late. She stared toward the computer, eyes widening, then slid out of bed and padded over. He moved aside.

"Daddy!"

Razor arrived as fast as if *he* had ziptripped. "What's the matter?"

She pointed at the screen.

Razor had left his glasses in the front room. He squinted at the screen. "'Tell Homicide Sara's friend Gerald Lockhart owns...'" He looked down at Holly. "Do you know how that got there?"

Her forehead furrowed. "Well, when I first woke up I thought I saw Uncle Cole over here."

Cole saw goosebumps rise on Razor's neck. Belying the cheerful smile he gave Holly. "How about that? We both dreamed about him."

Too bad Holly was there. With Razor thinking about him, this had to be an ideal time to make a consciously awake Razor see him.

"Then who turned the computer on?" Holly asked.

Razor kept lying. "Me, probably. I dreamed about using the computer, too, and must have sleep-walked." After peering at the time on the screen, he shut down the computer, then ruffled Holly's hair. "I don't think there's any point in going back to sleep, do you? What say we get dressed and have waffles at Denny's?"

That gave Cole the urge to go home and watch Sherrie and the kids have breakfast. Reluctantly, he decided against it. He needed to keep track of Razor and hope for another chance to make the man see him. So he stayed with Razor, riding in the Cavalier's back seat, while Razor and Holly went first to Denny's and then on to Holly's school.

Cheerful Daddy Razor vanished as soon as the car pulled away from the school. He frowned. Every few breaths he took a deeper one, or grimaced. He drummed on the steering wheel. He ran a hand back through his hair and fiddled with his tie as though it were choking him.

Cole slid through to the front seat. "I hope you're trying to think how that message could have gotten on the computer. The answer's easy if you'll just accept that Holly *did* see me there. I know I claimed my oh-dark-hundred visit was a dream, but I lied. I was really there. That was a genuine conversation. Hey, amigo!" He waved his hand in front of Razor's eyes. "Give me some reaction!"

Razor stared fixedly ahead.

Cole slouched in disgust. "You're one hard-headed bastard. I think you can see and hear me, just like you did last night, but the idea's so crazy, your brain is pretending I'm invisible."

Razor had no reaction to that, either. Probably how *he* would be reacting in Razor's place, Cole had to admit.

"But I *am* here. Somehow I have to make you recognize that." And the sooner the better.

Following Razor into Homicide a short time later, Cole had no trouble seeing who had his case. Across the room, Norman Leach handed papers to Rafael Hamada, who sat with a hip propped on the edge of his desk. After a glance through the pages, Hamada passed them over to Charlie Dennis, sitting at *his* desk.

Razor threaded his way between desks their direction. Cole climbed virtual steps and trotted across the room above the desks.

Dennis wore half glasses to read the papers, but laid both glasses and papers on his desk as Cole arrived above him, then sat back watching Hamada and Leach. Dennis had seniority, but Hamada likely had the lead in the investigation. After twenty-three years in Homicide, Dennis was burned out and just marking time until retirement. He looked it, with slacks a bad match for the sport coat draped over the back of his chair and his tie, loosened even this early in the morning, as wrinkled as a Goodwill rescue.

Looking down, Cole recognized the page under the glasses as a phone record. But not his, he realized after stepping back to floor level. The list included his own cell phone number...two calls to it at 19:04 and 19:29, one received from it at 19:39. This was Sara's record.

Sweet. Maybe her latest calls could point the direction she had gone. He scanned the list...and started in surprise. At 23:03, the next entry, she called the Flaxx Enterprises number! Why would she call there?

"Well now...what brings Night Investigations here at this time of day?"

He looked up to find Hamada quirking a brow at Razor. While Hamada's six-five height surprised people who expected Japanese to be small, no one expected that Texas drawl.

"He and Dunavan are buddies," Leach said. His mustache twitched. "How's the fake bullet hole business these days?"

Behind his glasses, Razor went wide-eyed. "You still think Cole and I did that? Why couldn't it have been the joker who kept putting fake spiders in my locker and patrol unit and on the sun visor in my car, where they'd fall in my lap?"

Maybe messages that matched the one at home would get through to Razor. Cole looked around for an idle computer. Homicide's was already in use. Neil Galentree had a laptop, though...and the way he kept pausing to leaf through file folders and his notebook made Cole hope he might have to leave in search of missing information. Cole headed for Galentree's desk. At the same time, he continued watching and listening behind him.

Leach said, "I hope you're here just to ask how the investigation is going, not thinking of trying to get involved in it."

Cole leaned down to Galentree's ear. "Don't you have to go look through files or take a leak or something?"

Razor gave Leach a bland smile. "You mean you're not interested in information I might have on the Benay woman?"

Hamada sat up straighter. "*I'd* like to hear it...if you boys can finish the pissing contest some other time."

Razor hesitated.

"Go on," Cole called. "Even if you had only dreamed the information, you can see it fits together."

Frowning at a page in his notebook, Galentree stood. Hope rose in Cole...only to evaporate as Galentree dropped back into his chair and picked up his phone. He punched in a number Cole recognized as the crime lab's.

Razor took a breath. "This is an educated guess, but...I think Benay is an informant of Cole's who works for Flaxx Enterprises. I know he had an informant he expected to help him crack a big case. And the case he's been obsessed with is the Flaxx Enterprises burglaries."

Cole smiled. Nice logic chain.

"An informant." The twitch of Leach's mustache looked as skeptical as his voice sounded. "And you're just now mentioning it?"

Razor shrugged. "Cole never told me her name. The connections didn't hit me until last night."

Hamada glanced over at Dennis. "Look up the Flaxx number. See if it matches anything on Benay's phone records."

Galentree hung up the phone and pushed back from his desk. "Andy, I'm going to the crime lab. They have our gun ready to test fire."

At the next desk, Willner nodded.

Cole cheered silently. Finally. "Go, go. Take your time about coming back." As soon as Galentree turned his back, Cole sat down on a virtual chair and went to work, typing letter by laborious letter.

Over at Hamada's desk, Leach remained looking skeptical. "Why would Dunavan kill an informant?"

"I don't think he did. Maybe that's his blood in the car."

Leach shook his head. "It's on the passenger side."

"I know Cole," Razor said evenly. "If he were alive, no matter what he'd done, by this time he'd have contacted his wife or me, if only to explain himself."

Even dead, *I'm trying to do that*, Cole reflected wryly.

"Tex. There's a match." Dennis tapped the phone record. "This eleven o'clock call."

Hamada's brows went up. "She called there at night?" He turned toward Razor, expression going thoughtful. "Tell me what you know about these Flaxx burglaries."

Razor gave them a run-down, and included the fires.

Hamada whistled at Willner and waved him over. "Y'all're working that firefighter's death. Come hear this."

Cole winced. He could guess Willner's reaction.

And after listening to Hamada repeat what Razor said about the fires, Willner was as underwhelmed as Cole feared. "Jesus, Rasgorshek. Don't tell me Dunavan sold you that cockamamie theory." He outlined the evidence against Luther Kijurian.

To Cole's disgust, Hamada and the others started nodding as they listened.

"But Dunavan doesn't believe the evidence?" Dennis said.

Leach grunted. "It's typical. He can't give up a chase or an idea he's got his teeth into. I don't see how any of this is connected to Dunavan killing the Benay woman, though. Go home, Rasgorshek." He turned away. "I'll leave you to it, Hamada. Keep me informed of developments."

Cole caught the collective sigh of relief as Leach disappeared out the door.

Willner started back for his desk. "If you come across other information on Kijurian, let me know." Passing Galentree's desk, he stopped short. "What the..."

He had seen the laptop, Cole realized in disgust. Interrupted again!

Hamada turned. "Something wrong?"

"Something crazy. This thing typed a letter by itself."

Razor started. Hamada's brows went up. Dennis's expression said: *Yeah, right.*

Cole sidestepped clear of the laptop. If only he could type faster.

Coming closer to the screen, Willner stared. "Holy shit. Listen to this. 'Benay possibly witnessed Dunavan's shooting—"

The rush toward the desk interrupted him. In seconds he was surrounded. Cole backed through the desk to its far side.

Hamada read the rest of the message over Willner's shoulder. "'Dunavan's shooting in the 2EC garage."

His phone rang.

"Charlie, get that for me, will you?"

Dennis lumbered back to Hamada's desk.

Hamada pursed his lips. "Two EC garage?"

Razor's shoulders hunched as though against the cold. "The Flaxx offices are in Two EC."

"Interesting." Hamada continued reading. "'See Gerald Lockhart, Seacliff, re Benay's 10-10 or...'" His eyes narrowed.

"See Lockhart about her location or…what, do you reckon? Do you have any ideas, Razor?"

"No." He eyed the laptop as if it might bite.

"But you know the name," Cole said. "It's the same Lockhart in the message on *your* computer, old buddy."

Razor's eyes flicked in Cole's direction. He sucked in his breath.

Electricity shot through Cole. "Razor? You see me?"

Hamada glanced down at Razor. "Something wrong?"

Razor pulled his glasses off and polished them on his tie. "No. It's nothing."

Cole grinned across the desk in triumph. "Like hell it was nothing! Admit it, you son of a bitch…you saw me! You know you're awake and you *saw* me." He came around beside Razor and punched his shoulder. "Come on, look at me."

Razor stiffened but kept polishing the glasses.

Hamada eyed the screen thoughtfully. "Where's Galentree?"

"Gone to the crime lab." Willner's forehead furrowed. "But if he came across this information, why didn't he mention it to me, or tell you?"

"Just what I'd like to know." Hamada picked up Galentree's phone.

As he started punching in the crime lab's number, Dennis trotted over, face grim. "That was the lab about Dunavan's car." He handed Hamada a memo pad filled with notes.

Razor froze.

A mask slid over Hamada's face as he read. He looked up from the notes to Razor. "You might be right about Dunavan being the victim. They've typed the blood. It's the same as his."

Their faces all went grim.

"We don't know Benay's blood type, though," Hamada said. "Did Dunavan carry a backup gun?"

Razor put back on his glasses. "Just his issued weapon."

"Does he own a handgun of his own?"

"A .22 revolver for target shooting." Razor frowned. "Why?"

"They found a 9mm bullet embedded in the carpet of the foot well, possibly from a Glock."

And the department issued Beretta .40's.

Hamada hefted the memo pad. "So it looks like someone else brought their own weapon to the party." He flipped to a new page and copied down the computer message. "Andy, can I get you to ask your partner about this? I need to contact Flaxx Enterprises." He checked his wrist watch. "They ought to be in the office by this time."

Cole gave a thumbs up. Yes! Start hunting Sara. And work fast. The foreboding in him felt even darker.

Back at their desks, Dennis handed Hamada the phone records. Hamada punched the Flaxx number into his phone and handed the records back. "Try this number and see who she called after Flaxx, will you? And look up a phone number for Gerald Lockhart."

"Is there anything I can do?" Razor asked.

Hamada pointed at the chair beside his desk. "Guests are always welcome to sit down and—Hello, this is the San Francisco Police Department." He shoved a stack of Polaroids toward the edge of the desk, tore the page of lab notes off his memo pad, and laid it on the Polaroids. "May I speak to your personnel director, please."

Earl Lamper. Lamper had that job as well as being IT director and head of Bookkeeping. Flaxx wanted just one person having complete access to the computers, Cole suspected. Except, was Lamper there today?

Razor picked up the crime lab notes and the Polaroids. Cole read the notes over Razor's shoulder. The car had not been dusted for prints yet, but in going over the seats, they found blonde and black hairs on both the passenger and driver headrests, and—what? Fragments of clear plastic tape and sticky residue on the back of the passenger seat and headrest?

Cole frowned. Had the shooter left them? He could not remember the kids messing around with tape in the car.

Hamada introduced himself to someone else before asking: "Do you have a Sara Benay employed there?...Will you transfer me to Bookkeeping, then? I need to speak with her." His brows rose. "Well, that's handy." His brows climbed higher. "She's where?...Do you have a number where we can reach her?...Yes, sir, I can hold."

Razor laid down the memo sheet and began shuffling through the Polaroids.

Covering the mouthpiece of the phone, Hamada said, "No surprise...Benay isn't there, but this fellow says she flew home for a family emergency. He's checking to see if she left a number."

The Polaroids showed the Taurus...the blood-spattered dash, a blood-soaked headrest. Why blood-soaked, Cole wondered. Blowback blood would not do that.

Then he thought of the tape pieces and had a vision of his body, too difficult for the shooter to move to the trunk, taped upright in the seat. Had the shooter really risked driving like that? Cole whistled soundlessly. Even at night and with the windows rolled up, it was ballsy. Give the shooter credit for good nerves.

Another photo showed the front license tag. Which had a different number from his. The shooter must have switched plates. No, not switched plates, Cole realized moments later. A photo of the rear tag showed smeared numbers. In a third photo, some of the smeared numbers were gone, revealing his tag numbers. The shooter printed a fake number on label paper—before or after killing him?—and stuck it over the real one.

Cute. No wonder the ATL failed to locate the car for so long. The fakes would never stand up to a close inspection, but the shooter had gambled on no one looking closely. More evidence of his nerves...though he also probably drove conservatively until he dumped the car. And the gamble paid off. Without the tag getting wet and smearing, the car might have sat undiscovered for weeks.

"Tex," Dennis said. "I've got Lockhart's number. The number Benay called is the American Airways desk at SFO. Maybe she did fly home."

Willner strolled over. "Neil says he doesn't know anything about the message on the computer. He swears he didn't write it. I wonder who could have. There wasn't anyone near his desk after he left."

Razor rubbed his neck.

Cole grinned at the goosebumps there. "Yeah...no one material. Just the same individual using your computer. And Holly told you who that was."

Razor kept staring at the Polaroids, shuffling through them again.

"Go ahead," Hamada said into the phone. He jotted a name and number on the memo sheet under his transcription of the computer message. "Thank you, Mr. Lamper." He jiggled the switch hook and punched in the new number.

Cole leaned close to hear the other end of the conversation. The warm-voiced woman who answered identified herself as Sara's mother. No, Sara was not there...nor expected. Nor did her mother know of any family emergency.

Anxiety crept into the distant voice. "Where did you hear there's one?"

Hamada's drawl thickened. "I wouldn't worry if I were you, ma'am. It was third-hand information and I reckon I misunderstood."

Top that for soothing an anxious citizen, Cole reflected, and backed off to sit against the edge of the desk. His best Jimmy Stewart imitation never came even close.

He expected Hamada to hang up, but Hamada went on, his voice going lazily casual, "Oh, one more thing, ma'am...do you happen to know your daughter's blood type?"

Of course he needed to see if the blood could be Sara's.

The question must have worried the mother. Apology filled Hamada's voice. "Oh, I didn't mean to, ma'am. It's just that the party who asked us to locate your daughter thinks, or maybe that's hopes, she's type AB?"

Dennis gave the lie a thumbs up.

Hamada listened…shook his head. "Well then maybe I won't worry about finding her. I thank you very much for your time." He hung up and sat back in his chair, looking around at them. "Mom doesn't know her blood type but it can't be AB. Mom is type O and Dad type B." He pushed to his feet. "Charlie, contact this Lockhart fellow and see if he has any idea where Benay is. I'd better tell Madrid that instead of a killer cop, we've got a cop killer. We'll need to change the ATL on Benay to an Alert." He headed for the lieutenant's office.

Even though he knew this would happen, dismay shot through Cole. "No! Damn it, Hamada, *she* didn't kill me!"

Being a suspect did have the benefit of ensuring a concerted hunt for Sara. But remembering her mother's voice, Cole felt another shot of guilt at the idea of her parents being told their daughter was a cop killer. He had to prevent that. By the time they found Sara, he'd better be able to prove who really killed him.

He slapped Razor's shoulder. "Start seeing me! We've got work to do!"

Razor's hand tightened on the Polaroids. After a moment, he returned them to the desk. The one showing the bloody headrest sat on top, Cole saw. Looking from the Polaroids to the phone, Razor sighed.

Cole felt his chest tighten. Was Razor thinking of calling Sherrie?

"Dennis, mind if I use the phone?"

"Help yourself."

Definitely calling Sherrie. When Razor punched in the number, Cole recognized the tone sequence for his home phone. "She won't be home. She'll be at work." Staying busy to keep from going crazy. Joanna would tell Razor that. Was the delay going give him the chance to reach Sherrie and be there with her when she heard?

Cole sprinted through the outside wall and up high enough to see San Francisco General off to the south. But even with a Dunavan Diagonal, he still had to cover the distance. He could see the roof area over the ER. If only he could *be* there.

Almost before the thought finished, he *was*.

Cole stared around in exasperation—he was never going to understand this—then ran for the edge of the roof and down the building. Still, by the time his search of the ER located Sherrie in the orthopedic room, she was already on the phone there. With her face frozen and her fingers bloodless from their grip on the phone. A male nurse hovered anxiously at the door.

In a choked voice, she said, "There's no chance it's… someone else's?"

Cole's heart lurched at the mixed hope and fear in her tone. He moved close to hear Razor's end of the conversation.

"It definitely isn't Benay's. We'll need to check the DNA, of course, but my gut says…" Razor let the sentence trail off. He cleared his throat. "We have a bullet, too. I don't know what shape it's in but let's hope good enough to match it to the gun it came from."

Sherrie's mouth trembled. "I—" Her voice broke. She spun to lean her forehead against the wall. She raised a clenched fist as though to pound the wall, then let the hand fall limp. "I just want *him* back."

A strangling hand closed around Cole's throat.

A brunette nurse passing by stopped in the doorway to listen.

"Razor…please find his body." It came out as little more than a whisper.

Whether she felt it or not, he wrapped his arms around her. If only he could really hold her…make her pain go away. "Sherrie…" How did he apologize enough for putting her through this.

She hung up with a shaking hand and, shivering, turned away from the phone. Slipping out through his arms. Knowing she would did not stop the bleak ache it brought.

The male nurse said, "I'm so sorry. I've been praying he turns up alive. Do they have any idea who did it?"

She stared blindly at him, face so tight it looked ready to shatter. "Not yet. Excuse me; I'd better get this room cleaned." She turned and looked around, but Cole doubted she saw the jumbled casting cart or the crumpled sheets on the exam bed.

"I can do it," the male nurse said. "You go sit down for a few minutes."

"Thanks, no." She fumbled toward the bed. "I don't want time to think."

The nurse watched while she started stripping off the sheets, his face creased in concern, then left the room.

The brunette moved close to him. "So her husband's dead?" she murmured.

"It looks like it," he whispered back. "Earlier she told me they found his car with blood in it, and I guess they've identified the blood as his."

The pair of them started away. The brunette stopped whispering. "Well...if they're looking for who someone with a motive to kill him, they ought to see if that blonde hanging on him in Bon Vivre Monday night has a jealous husband or boyfriend."

Cole winced. Just his luck that someone who knew him was there, though her face rang no bells for him. But Sara had not been "hanging" on him!

Arriving half an hour late and breathless, Sara had tucked an arm through his, yes, and leaned her forehead against his shoulder as she heaved a huge sigh. *"Here I am, finally...no thanks to Tyrannosaurus Regina. God what a day!"* But he'd peeled her off even before asking what she wanted to drink.

The male nurse halted. "Are you sure it was her husband?"

The brunette cocked an eyebrow at him. "Tall guy... lanky...looks a little like Jimmy Stewart, right?" When the other nurse nodded, she went on, "So anyway, this blonde was all over him when she came in. Then they snuggled up together in a back booth, making out over a cozy dinner."

What! Cole glared at her. How the hell did she make snuggling out of sitting on opposites of the booth? And no one could have seen Sara's foot crawling up his leg later. He peered at her name badge. *Debra Brewer.* That rang no bell, either. Why was she—

In the orthopedic room, breath caught sharply. Horror shot through Cole. Oh no. No! Running back inside, he found Sherrie standing with her arms full of sheets and her face bloodless. She had heard. And in her stricken face he saw the demons from her childhood sinking claws and fangs into her.

"Sherrie, no! What she said isn't true! It didn't happen like that!" Damn! If only she would hear him. "Babe, listen to me. Brewer doesn't remember how it really was, or else she's trying to make it a juicy story!"

Sherrie turned away and stumbled to the laundry hamper. Cole followed her for a step, then halted, staring after her in despair. How much deeper and darker could this hole he'd dug for himself go?

— 12 —

HE HAD TO find Sara! Once she was safe, her name cleared, and Gao dealt with for assaulting her…then Sara could set the record straight with Sherrie, give her the true story. But first, he had to find her.

Cole shut out the anguish from Sherrie's pain and his anger at Brewer to try returning straight to Homicide. Concentrating, he visualized the room from the perspective of Hamada's desk, feeling himself standing there. Nothing happened.

Cole ground his teeth in frustration. Why could he go to *Burglary* with no trouble, but not Homicide, just a few hundred feet away? It made no sense. But, fine…he would ziptrip to Burglary and walk on down to…

…Homicide, the thought finished lamely as he found himself standing at its inner door. Cole fought an urge to bang his head against the door jam. Son of a bitch. This had no rhyme or reason. It was going to drive him bonkers.

"Someone's playing games with me, aren't they?" he said to the ceiling. "Well screw you."

He stalked across the room to Hamada's desk…straight through other desks, a typewriter, and the legs of the detective at the typewriter. Sending the typewriter ball into a brief spinning frenzy and Darrell Wineright starting in consternation.

Hamada and Razor glanced curiously toward Wineright. Willner and Galentree looked around from muttering together over Galentree's laptop.

Dennis seemed oblivious. "…no trouble finding the guy," he said. "He claims he doesn't have any idea where Benay could be. He's a flake, though. When I asked him about her I got this long silence at first, and then he said I wouldn't believe it but he woke up this morning thinking about where she might go to get away from everything…because—get this—last night he dreamed Jimmy Stewart asked him about her." Dennis rolled his eyes.

Hamada's brows rose. "Interesting coincidence."

Cole frowned. Lockhart never mentioned that "Stewart"— did he look more like the actor in the dark?—gave him Razor's name to call in case he remembered anything? That would have given them, and especially Razor, real "coincidence" to chew on.

But maybe Razor was already struck by Lockhart's dream. He had straightened in the chair, eyes narrowing. A moment later, though, he shook his head.

Cole elbowed him. "No, don't you write it off as coincidence! I visited him. And Kenisha Hayes. Remember *her* name coming up last night?"

Razor's only response was a flinch.

"Lockhart did have one suggestion." Dennis handed Hamada a sheet of the memo pad. "Talk to a girlfriend named Kenisha Hayes."

Razor started.

Hamada looked over at him. "You know the woman?"

Cole heard mental wheels race. Razor shrugged. "I remember Cole mentioning the name one time when he was talking about Flaxx Enterprises."

Dennis nodded. "Lockhart said Hayes works with Benay."

"Well, then…" Hamada straightened his tie. "I think a personal visit to the folks at Flaxx Enterprises is in order."

Cole hoped Hayes could give them more information than she had given him. But if not, the visit would still be good for seeing Gao's reaction to Hamada's questions.

Dennis sighed and started to heave out of his chair.

Hamada flicked him a glance. "I think I can handle it alone."

Dennis relaxed, clearly relieved.

Cole grimaced. *Before I get that burned out, please someone shoot me.*

Oh yeah, somebody already had.

"Why don't you run Benay through the computer?" Hamada pulled his gun out of a desk drawer and shoved it in the holster on his belt. "See if she owns a handgun. Then since the car ended up in San Jose, contact the airline desks there to see if she bought a ticket. And let's get Dunavan's case file on the Flaxx burglaries so we can go through it." He headed over to the radio rack, then out the door.

As soon as Hamada disappeared, Razor casually stood up. "I think I need a cigarette." He strolled for the door, too.

Cigarette? Following him, Cole thought not. Hoped not. He intended to be there at Flaxx Enterprises with Hamada, but if Razor were, too, the better the two of them could discuss things...once Razor started seeing him.

Sure enough, in the hallway, Razor's stroll abruptly became a running walk. He caught up with Hamada at the elevator. Cole halted behind them.

Hamada glanced sideways at Razor. "If you're wanting what I think...it's a bad idea."

"I just want to ride along."

Hamada shook his head. "You have too big an emotional stake."

Razor's jaw squared. "When a fellow officer's been killed, are any of us objective? Look, I can't sit and do nothing."

"There's a phone on my desk and a whole lot of airlines to check in San Jose."

The elevator opened. Razor followed Hamada in.

The car already held some uniformed officers, a trio Cole recognized as Public Defenders, and a suit who looked like a private attorney. Cole walked up the side of the car and stood horizontal to the ceiling with his head above Razor's.

Hamada lowered his voice. "You wouldn't be thinking this Hayes woman can point you to Benay ahead of everyone else."

Razor shook his head emphatically. "If she's guilty, she's all yours."

He put some emphasis on *if*, Cole noted with satisfaction. So Razor was reserving judgement on her guilt. Maybe he had not dismissed the night's conversation as just a dream. That was progress.

The uniformed officers and lawyers left at the ground floor. Razor stayed on for the ride to the basement. "Cole and I discussed Flaxx Enterprises extensively. Wouldn't you like information on the local fauna before you walk into their jungle?"

The elevator halted. Cole stepped down to the floor and followed Razor and Hamada out into the garage.

Hamada raised his brows. "How long does the wildlife orientation take?"

Razor's face went deadpan. "Too long to give you here."

Hamada snorted. "That figures. But you can fit it into a drive to Embarcadero Center, I suppose."

Cole heard Razor's heart rate jump. "No problem."

Hamada's mouth quirked. He walked away. "Start talking."

Cole had no interest in hearing facts and gossip he gave Razor in the first place. He might as well go on to the Flaxx offices and do a little surveillance. "Don't forget to tell him how Flaxx and Lamper hooked up," he called after Razor. So Hamada could understand that relationship.

According to Gina Galechas, it had happened during their sophomore year in high school, when Flaxx rescued Lamper from jocks who were stuffing him into a locker. Cole wondered what the real story was. He had trouble seeing Donald Flaxx as a defender of the underdog. However it went down, the deed had won Flaxx slavish devotion.

Cole brought up a mental image of the reception area. Could he parlay the last successful ziptrips into another one?

Apparently not. Despite hard concentration, to his frustration he remained in the garage. Well, there was always the Dunavan Diagonal. He walked out of the garage and trotted skyward. On the way up, he glanced south toward San Francisco General, recalling that trip. Maybe it made sense after all. He had to know what a destination looked like. Any place he saw, he certainly knew. So maybe he could zip line-of-sight.

When he had a clear view of the Financial District sky-scrapers, he sighted on the dark bulk of the Bank of America building and visualized himself there. Seconds later he stood on the building roof. Sweet! This was going to make travel much easier...though multiple jumps were still not as fast as a direct shot. He still wanted to work that out.

The Financial District spread below him, letting him spot and ziptrip to the roof of the 2EC tower, and from there, lope down the side of the building to a window he recognized. Bookkeeping.

He passed through the window and crossed toward the door. Everyone looked busy at their work stations, including Mrs. Gao. Cole paused beside Sara's computer, the only one not turned on, and glanced toward Gao's back. Even when he replayed Sara's frightened voice in his head, Gao failed to look dangerous. What if he rattled her cage a little?

He closed his eyes and worked a finger on the power button until he felt the tickle of connection. Then he stepped up against Sara's shelves to watch the computer boot and check out staff reactions.

No one noticed.

Cole smiled. Okay, then he would play some more.

He brought up a notepad program and started typing.

At the desk behind Sara's, Joy Quon glanced past her own monitor, then in a double-take, leaned sideways for a better view around it. Her jaw dropped. "Kenisha, look."

Hayes turned around at her desk in front of Sara's. When Quon pointed at the monitor, Hayes reached over and swivelled it toward her. After a hop of her brows, she read the message aloud. "'Gao, Sara told me about Wed nite.'"

That attracted everyone else's attention, including Gao's. She bustled back to the desk. "What's going on?" Seeing the monitor, she frowned. "What's this about? Who wrote it?"

Cole studied her closely, but detected nothing in her face or voice except annoyance.

"I don't know," Quon said. "I didn't see anyone there."

Lamper turned his chair to watch through the window of his office. With his narrow shoulders and eyes magnified by his glasses, Lamper looked the epitome of a nerd to Cole. His drawn face today accentuated that look. Aviator style glasses and the turtleneck he wore with his suit just made him look like a nerd trying to seem cool.

Disbelief filled Gao's sniff. She held down the power button until the computer shut off, then headed back for her desk.

Cole fished around in the power button once more.

Quon gaped. "The computer's booting again!"

Gao wheeled in mid-stride. After turning the computer off this time, she stood watching it. As seconds dragged on and the computer remained off, Gao's lips thinned. She raked Quon and Hayes with a scowl.

Lamper's phone rang. When he answered, his voice carried to Cole.

Gao turned her scowl on the rest of the staff, all standing and craning their necks to see Sara's monitor. "If you ladies have had your fun, there's *work* to do."

Cole started to reach for the power button, only to halt at Lamper's voice. "He's *here* to see me?" Lamper's expression struggled between annoyance and concern. "Tell him I'll see him in a couple of minutes." Then he turned back to his computer.

Like boss, like flunky. Shaking his head, Cole trotted out of Bookkeeping and up to the reception area. "Welcome, boys. Lamper will be with you when he thinks it appears he's squeezing time for you into his very busy schedule."

Hamada and Razor had taken seats where he always sat, ones that offered a good view of Gina's legs. Gina gave them her brilliant smile but her attention was clearly on a phone call. Though she spoke rapid Spanish, Cole caught enough to gather that this was the middle of a conversation to a girlfriend—interrupted by Hamada's entrance and now resumed—about a date on Saturday. Hung like a what, did she say?

Hamada understood better. He grinned.

Gina saw. She started and quickly ended the call, cheeks reddening.

"I'm sorry," Hamada said. "I couldn't help hearing."

The blush spread from her hairline into the deep vee of her blouse. "You speak Spanish?"

Better than he did Japanese. Few people expected that, which Hamada used to his advantage. But few outside of friends and fellow officers knew that because of the friendship forged in an internment camp between Hamada's grandfather and a guard named Rafael Navarro, Hamada had grown up in San Antonio with his family close to the Hispanic community.

Gina's phone rang. After answering, she nodded at Hamada. "Mr. Lamper can see you now. It's down the hall on the right."

In his office minutes later, Lamper looked across his desk at the seated detectives and regarded Hamada with a politeness that did not quite mask concern...or the usual surprise at the difference between Hamada's appearance and his voice. "I don't understand. If Miss Benay can't be reached through the number I gave you, I fail to see what more I can do. I'm sorry. It must be important if Homicide needs to reach her?"

Standing at the office door, Cole watched Gao. While her eyes remained fixed on her computer monitor, she was leaning toward the door, her head cocked...clearly straining to hear. He read no anxiety in her face, though.

Hamada gave Lamper a bland smile. "It would help us to know when Miss Benay told you about her family emergency."

"She left a voice mail message for my assistant Wednesday night."

That would be the call to this number. Cole caught Hamada and Razor exchanging glances that only another cop would notice. "May I speak with your assistant?" Hamada said.

Lamper raised his voice. "Mrs. Gao, will you please come in."

She came eagerly...and settled in the chair Hamada gave up for her, folding her hands in her lap.

Hamada sat on the corner of the desk that put his back toward the wall. "I'm interested in the voice-mail message Miss Benay left. Is it still on your phone?"

"I erased it." Her voice took on a defensive edge. "There was no reason to save it."

And every reason to erase it, if Gao was lying about the message.

Hamada said, "How did Miss Benay sound?"

Gao looked puzzled by the question. "Sound?"

"Was she anxious?"

As if she had shot a cop?

Gao considered. "Yes. Which is perfectly normal, I'd think, with a family crisis."

Cole frowned. If Gao was lying, she was damn good at it.

"When did you last see her?" Hamada asked.

"When she locked the front doors after me at a quarter to six."

Cole blinked. Gao left? Then she must have come back later. The security camera up front would have recorded it. Was there any chance they still had that footage after four days?

He walked out to Gao's computer. With luck, no one would notice the activity. He opened a notepad and started work on the message. At the same time, laboring over the keystrokes, he listened to the voices in the office.

"Locked up *after* you?" Hamada asked.

"Miss Benay worked late."

Rear vision caught Razor sitting up straighter. "Was anyone else here?"

Thank you, amigo! Cole thought. *Check out the dream story.* When those facts were corroborated, Razor would have to accept that the two of them had really talked.

"Not to my knowledge." Gao said. "What's this about? Is Miss Benay in some kind of trouble?"

Cole listened closely to her tone. Was she concerned for Sara...or anxious to determine what the police knew?

Hamada's face gave away nothing. "She may have witnessed an incident that evening."

"Then why are you talking to us? Ask Miss Benay. Didn't Mr. Lamper give you her family's phone number?"

"Apparently she didn't go home," Lamper said.

Cole halted typing to watch Gao.

She sniffed. "So this time she's been caught."

Hamada and Lamper's brows went up. Though Cole could not see, he imagined Razor's did, too.

Gao looked at Lamper, her lips tight. "I've often suspected that Miss Benay has claimed time off for family concerns as a pretext to give her long weekends for partying. I'm just surprised she did it in the middle of the week. No doubt Miss Hayes knows where she is. Excuse me."

She marched out into the main office.

"Miss Hayes," she began, and broke off to stare at her computer, going rigid with outrage. "Miss *Hayes*! How dare you play your games with *my* computer!"

That brought the men to Lamper's office door, Lamper moving more slowly than the others.

Hayes's chin snapped up. "I never touched it!"

"She's telling the truth," Lamper said. "She was sitting at her desk the whole time you've been in my office."

"*Somebody's* used it." Gao stabbed a finger at the monitor. "Computers don't write messages by themselves."

Hamada started. Razor froze.

"And this is like the one you denied writing on Miss Benay's computer."

Hamada shouldered past Lamper to come and peer over Gao's head at the monitor. "It's the same message, you mean?"

"No, but it's the same *kind* of thing."

Hamada read: "'Ck security tape for Gao and Sara's departure times.'"

Cole slid out from behind Gao's desk through Hayes's. As he did, he saw Razor's eyes follow the movement, widening in shock. Cole waved. "Yo, amigo!"

Razor squeezed his eyes shut.

Cole rushed over to grab his shoulder. "Don't do that and block me out!"

"Razor, are you all right?" Hamada asked.

Razor opened his eyes but looked away from Cole. "Just short of caffeine is all."

"Short of belief in your own eyes and ears you mean, you bastard." Cole bared his teeth. "Come on, man! I need your help."

Hamada turned to Lamper. "Does everyone leave through the front door?"

Lamper hesitated, then nodded. "It's the only door."

"Then may we look at the tape for that camera?"

Lamper frowned. Cole almost saw the word "warrant" in his eyes.

Hamada must have, too. His expression went earnest. "If we knew when Miss Benay left that night, it would help us determine if she could have witnessed the incident in question."

Lamper glanced toward his phone. "Excuse me for a minute."

He went in the office and closed the door. Cole debated following and listening to the call, but based on previous conversations with Flaxx, he imagined Flaxx saying something like: "Let them see the tape. This is no different than giving them a peek at a store account. We have nothing to hide, remember? We always cooperate with the law enforcement—as long as it's convenient."

And sure enough, when Lamper came out of the office, he smiled and, moving gingerly, led the way across the hallway to the Security office. Cole noted with interest that Gao included herself in the group.

In the Security office, Cole slid around everyone to the far wall, clear of the group.

The guard—Antoine Farrell according to his company name tag—was young and husky enough to deal with most trouble. He swivelled his chair from the bank of recorders and monitors. "You want to see a tape from Wednesday?" The overhead light gleamed on his shaved scalp as he shook his head. "I'm sorry, Mr. Lamper. We don't have those any-more. We record over them every forty-eight hours."

Cole swore. He had been afraid of something like that. Hamada sent Razor an *oh, well* glance.

Lamper shrugged at Hamada. "I guess there's no way to know when Sara left that evening."

Farrell twitched. "You mean you want to see the reception area tape?"

Cole felt his scalp prickle.

Lamper nodded. "Yes, but what difference does that make?"

"I think it means he has that tape," Hamada said. "Right?"

Farrell took a breath and looked up at Lamper. "Well… see…the machine for that camera ate the tape that night … after I left. I got the tape out and wound back in the cassette but when I tried playing it, it jammed at the crumpled part." As Lamper frowned impatiently, Farrell talked faster and faster. His tone went defensive. "So I was going to throw it away…and then I thought, it was running fine when I left, so it was the machine that messed up…so I kept the tape, so the next time the machine jams there's proof it's done it be—"

Lamper cut him off with a sigh. "Just show us the tape, please."

"Yes, sir." Farrell was light-skinned enough that his flush showed.

He opened a drawer and pulled out a cassette. After push-ing it into the slot of a TV/VCR unit sitting at one end of the counter, he punched Rewind and visibly held his breath. When the tape made no sounds of self-destruction, he let the breath out. "How much do you want to see?"

Lamper glanced questioningly at Hamada, who said, "Let's go from fifteen minutes before the office closes."

Cole climbed up to stand on the counter and look over Farrell's head at the TV.

With occasional pauses to check the time imprint, Farrell rewound to 16:45, then punched Play.

The camera's position above Gina's desk let it catch all the reception area except for the desk itself. Cole watched employees file out around five o'clock. The last one, Gina, wiggled her fingers in farewell at Farrell as he knelt to turn his key in the lock at the bottom of the doors. Minutes later, a middle-aged Hispanic woman appeared with a vacuum cleaner and ran it over the carpet. At five-thirty, she reappeared with a coat and purse. Farrell let her and himself out, locking the doors from the outside.

The time read 17:43:03 when Mrs. Gao appeared, accompanied as far as the front doors by Sara. Gao's frown and moving mouth suggested she was leaving Sara with strict instructions. The roll of Sara's eyes when she turned away indicated her opinion of those orders.

Watching the tape, Gao's mouth pressed into a tight line.

"I take it Miss Benay has a key to let herself out?" Hamada said.

"Not a personal one." Lamper shook his head. "When one of my staff wants to work late, they check out a key from Mrs. Gao or me. After they lock up behind themselves, they drop the key through a slot outside. It goes into the box there to the left of the doors."

"Fast forward until we see Miss Benay leave," Hamada said.

Farrell did so in short, cautious spurts. Donald Flaxx left just before six, letting himself out with his own key. The time imprint rolled on...18:15...18:30...18:45. No one else left or came in.

As the time passed seven o'clock, uneasiness stirred in Cole. Where was Gao? To catch Sara phoning him at seven-oh-one, she had to be back by now. Did she have any other way in?

He heard Razor sigh. The sound punched him. In it, Cole heard Razor's awareness of the doubt that threw on his information from the dream.

Cole swore. He needed to kick this around with Razor. The emergency exit was the only other way in that he knew. To use it, Gao would have had to tape the lock and climb all those stairs, an incredible effort he saw no reason for her to make. But why would Sara lie about who caught her?

Suddenly, with a crackle inside the player, the image on the screen froze. Farrell hit Stop.

"Nineteen-fifty." Hamada turned away from the player. "So Miss Benay had to leave after that."

"Does that make it possible for her to be your witness?" Lamper asked.

"She could have used the emergency stairs," Razor said.

Lamper frowned. "Why would she do that?"

"She had to go out the front door," Mrs. Gao said. "The key was in the box the next morning."

And the tape jammed just minutes before she left. The coincidence bothered Cole. *Was* it a coincidence? But why would Sara jam it, assuming she had access to the Security office? It prevented a record of when she left, yes. Why would she want that?

The more disturbing question was why Sara lied about Gao catching her. That chilled him. He wanted to find an excuse for it. Otherwise, what else might be lies?

"If we're finished here," Lamper said, "let's go back to my office and you can ask Kenisha about Sara's whereabouts."

"You should ask Inspector Dunavan, too," Gao said.

Cole stared at her. If Gao thought he was alive, then she could not have been part of what happened Wednesday night.

Lamper stared at her, too. "Why would Dunavan know?"

Her lips thinned. "Because they're sleeping together."

Hamada shot a deadpan glance at Razor. Cole swore. Shit! Leach's theory just got a boost in Hamada's book.

Lamper stiffened. "Why—" He glanced at Farrell. "Let's go back to my office. Thank you, Mr. Farrell." And he shuffled out.

Before following him, Hamada told Farrell, "Don't let anything happen to that tape."

Crossing toward Bookkeeping, Lamper glared at Gao. Dropping his voice did nothing to diminish the fury in it. "Why the *hell* didn't you tell me about Sara and Dunavan before!"

"Well, I—" Gao flushed. "I was going to make Miss Hayes tell you, but then there was the thing with the computer and we came over to see the tape and..." Her hands fluttered.

Lamper exhaled in a hiss.

Cole spotted Katherine Maldonado watching them curiously from her desk down the hall.

"What makes you so sure Benay had an affair with Dunavan?" Razor asked.

"Because Miss Hayes and Miss Benay talked about it in the restroom on Tuesday. I couldn't help overhearing." Gao's mouth thinned in distaste. "They came in while I was...well, in a booth. Miss Hayes asked how it had gone with Inspector Dunavan the evening before and did handcuffs and a gun on the bed table enhance sex the way Miss Benay thought. And Miss Benay said it was an evening she'd never forget."

Cole eyed Hamada's poker face and groaned. "Good going, Sara. Tell the truth and make it sound like something else." Though who could blame Sara for not wanting to admit how humiliatingly the evening had ended? "Good going, *Dunavan*, you stupid shit."

They reached Bookkeeping. Lamper stabbed a finger toward Hayes. "Kenisha! Joy, too. In my office!" He shuffled in and lowered himself into his chair.

Around the room jaws dropped. Had Lamper never raised his voice before? Cole wondered. Maybe not, considering how Sara talked about him. Hayes and Quon hurried into the office, faces baffled but wary. Cole leaned against the windows where he could watch everyone.

As soon as they sat down and Gao closed the door, Lamper said icily, "How is it Sara is having an affair with a police officer who has been *hounding* Mr. Flaxx for *years* with *slanderous* insinuations!"

Hayes and Quon exchanged quick glances. Hayes licked her lips. "It wasn't an affair. We'd met him for lunch a few times and she just wanted a fling with him…to make up for missing the cruise to Baja."

Razor started.

Cole circled behind the women to join him. "Yes…Baja. The cruise was real. So is everything else I told you."

Razor's heart rate jumped.

"Fling. Affair." Lamper clenched a fist. "It was *still*—"

"Excuse me," Hamada interrupted. "If I might please have a minute before you ream the young ladies?" Without waiting for Lamper's permission, he stepped forward to look down at Hayes. "It's very important I speak with Miss Benay and she isn't in Indiana. Do y'all know where I can reach her?"

Hayes blinked. "That's weird. Last night I dreamed Inspector Dunavan asked me the same thing."

Razor's heart jumped again. Abruptly, he reached inside his jacket and pulled out his cell phone, as though it had rung. Holding it up to show Hamada, he hurried out of the office and Bookkeeping. Cole followed.

In the hallway, Razor thrust away the phone and paced in tight circles, shaking his head. His heart raced. Cole saw goosebumps on his neck.

"Hey, take it easy!" Cole longed to grab his shoulders and shake him. "You're not going wacko. Let yourself admit that I'm around and you see me."

But Razor looked everywhere except at him. Cole swore. What did it take to crack his resistance?

A minute later Hamada strode out of Bookkeeping. He raised his brows. "What's going on, man?"

Razor pulled off his glasses and began polishing them on his tie. "Nothing's going on."

Hamada grunted. "Right. That's why you keep acting like someone's goosed you."

Razor shrugged. "It's just spooky…the computer thing… Lockhart and the Hayes woman both dreaming about Cole."

"Yeah." Hamada raised a brow. "You have any ideas about that?"

Razor shook his head. "Not a clue."

"But you knew about Dunavan banging Benay."

Razor jammed back on his glasses. "No! And I don't believe he was, in spite of what Hayes says."

After a long stare at him, Hamada sighed and headed up the hallway for the reception area. "I appreciate loyalty but...Benay had some reason to shoot him. Let's go see if Dennis is having any luck with the airlines, and start a search warrant for her place."

— 13 —

COLE WATCHED THEM leave. As much as he needed to keep working on Razor, he also wanted to see what happened here after Lamper reported to Flaxx. A glance into Bookkeeping caught Lamper shooing the women out of his office—Hayes and Quon looking relieved, Gao disapproving—and reaching for his phone. Cole hurried in, moving close enough to the phone to catch Flaxx's side of the conversation.

Lamper blurted, "Donald, I just found out that Sara—"

"Who?" Flaxx sounded distracted. Cole pictured him signing letters or checking e-mail while he listened.

Lamper frowned. "Sara Benay, one of my girls here in Bookkeeping...the one those Homicide detectives are looking for. She was having an affair with Inspector Dunavan!"

"What!"

Flaxx's surprise disturbed Cole. If Sara were forced to talk the way she claimed, Flaxx should know all about Sara and him.

"Tell me about this affair."

Lamper gave Flaxx a detailed report of Hamada's visit.

Impatient sighs came over the wire, but Flaxx never interrupted. And at the end, Cole was even more surprised to hear a chuckle.

So, clearly, was Lamper. He stared at the phone. "Didn't you hear me? Sara's sleeping with Dunavan and she worked on my account files last week!"

"Earl, Earl." Flaxx's voice oozed like honey. "I understand your concern, but there's no need for it. I have every confidence in your accounting passing muster with someone like her. And if she did stumble on..."

Cole mentally held his breath. *Come on, come on. Make an incriminating admission.*

"…irregularities…"

Irregularities? Oh, very cute. No help at all. Cole grimaced.

"…that gadfly *Dunavan* would be bugging us again, not Homicide. And last, since she's shacking up with him, no so-called evidence she thinks she's found for him is any good in court."

Cole blinked. Interesting. Flaxx talked about him in the present tense. Was that for Lamper's benefit? Or was it possible Flaxx knew nothing about his shooting?

"Whatever the story is with this Bennet woman…" Flaxx said.

Lamper frowned. "Her name's Benay."

"Whatever. It has nothing to do with us. So you forget about it and enjoy the day. You've certainly made mine, Earl my man! Way to go!"

Lamper sat up straighter, beaming.

If he had a tail, it would be wagging in ecstacy, Cole reflected. He patted Lamper on the head. "Good dog, Earl."

Then leaving Lamper reaching up to his hair with a startled look, Cole raced for Flaxx's office. He wanted to see Flaxx's real reaction to Lamper's report. Bursting through Flaxx's wall, he felt a *zing* down his spine. The cheerful voice on the phone had been replaced by a grim-faced Flaxx punching an in-house number into his phone.

"Get in here."

Cole sat on a corner of the desk to see who came.

When the door opened a minute later, he straightened in surprise. A woman strolled in—mid to late twenties, wiry, a model's bones, short-cropped blonde hair, junior exec skirt and jacket. She seemed familiar, although he could not remember seeing her around here before. Maybe her long, thin hands reminded him of his daughter Renee's? No…it was something about her face.

She settled into a chair, crossing her legs. "So…what's giving you a wedgie this morning?"

Cole cocked a brow. Interesting. A junior exec with attitude, and Flaxx just frowned. Someone else had been less tolerant, though. Bruises on her left cheekbone and jaw showed under her makeup. Recognition clicked. She had the same jaw line as Flaxx, and similar eyes...despite hers being baby blue and his an improbable aqua. How were they related? Both his daughters were younger.

Then Cole remembered that when he went to Razor's ex-wife Jessie at the *Chronicle* for dirt on Flaxx, her information included a half-sister twenty years Flaxx's junior, the product of Papa Flaxx's trophy marriage. Cole dug into his memory for the name. Iris? Irene? No, *Irah*...named, according to gossip Jessie had, for the trophy wife's own dear Daddy because they thought she was going to be a boy.

"My *headache*," Flaxx said, "is cops! This place is starting to crawl with them. It was bad enough with that bastard Dunavan hounding me. But then we got the arson cops, then homicide cops because of that firefighter. Now..." His nostrils flared. "Well, I've just had to sooth Earl because today he had a *new* set of homicide cops asking questions." He gave her a terse version of Lamper's report on Hamada's visit.

Cole listened with growing dismay. Listening to Flaxx, it was clear he knew nothing about Sara disappearing or the supposed affair until Lamper told him. Making it unlikely he knew about the hit, either. Which meant he never ordered it.

So who did?

A rising heart rate caught his ear. He stared at Irah. She appeared to be listening calmly, not even surprised at the story about Sara and him. But mention of the security tape had sent her heart into a jog.

Mental flags shot up, bells jangling. Cole came off the desk and over to the chair. "Were you here?" He did not remember seeing her among the group leaving, but the only faces of interest at the time were Gao's and Sara's. "Did you sabotage the tape?"

He bent down for a close look at Irah's bruises. One advantage to being a ghost, he reflected. It let him come inches from her face while she remained oblivious.

The bruises looked recent, no more than a few days old. The bells started clanging. She also had scratches on her wrists, just visible under the edges of her jacket cuffs. Sara's message said: *"The bitch tortured me into telling her everything. She held my—"* Remembering the anger mixing with Sara's fear, Cole expected she had clawed at the restraining hands.

He jerked back upright. Damn. He needed another look at that tape.

Irah's lack of reaction finally registered on Flaxx. "Is this old news to you?"

"No." Her heart slowed. "I'm just not surprised about Benay and Dunavan. I've overheard her and her cronies in the break room. A cop is someone she'd go for. I'm disappointed at her lack of company loyalty, though."

Flaxx's eyes narrowed. "So you didn't know she was shacking up with Dunavan?"

Hers went wide. "Not until now."

Cole frowned down at her. Could he be wrong? If she caught Sara, surely she would have told Flaxx.

Irah pursed her lips. "It must have been great sex to turn her. Maybe Dunavan has the same staying power in bed as he does for trying to pin burglary and arson on you."

Flaxx sucked in a sharp breath...only to release it as an exasperated sigh when a corner of her mouth twitched. "Damn it! Why are you always yanking my chain?"

She shrugged. "A girl's got to have some fun."

"Didn't you have enough for a lifetime in L.A.?" Flaxx grimaced. "I keep hoping you'll grow up."

What was it Jessie told him about Irah? *Mommy wanted to make her a beauty queen like herself, but the trophy daughter ended up with more appearances in juvenile court than pageants.* Due to stunts like taking off in Daddy's Ferrari at age twelve and leading the CHP and assorted other law enforcement agencies on a forty mile chase down Highway 280 at speeds nearing 200 miles an hour. According to Jessie, at sixteen she ran away with a waiter at the country club. Daddy Flaxx finally said to hell with her after he spent a small fortune having private detectives locate and bring her home, only to have her run off again to the boyfriend.

But now the prodigal had returned. Not necessarily as penitent as the Biblical one. Cole wanted to know a lot more about her.

Her expression went contrite. "I'm trying, Donald...really. Is that all you want with me?"

"Not quite. I want you to find this bookkeeper. I want to know how much she found out...and just to be safe, how much it will cost to give her amnesia."

Irah nodded.

"And..." Flaxx's voice turned to a snarl. "...think of a way to get rid of these cops...especially Dunavan. I want him the hell out of my life!"

Cole turned back to the desk and leaned across it toward him. "Ain't gonna happen, dogshit. I'm out of *my* life, but you're unfinished business, too, so while the first job is finding Sara and putting that situation right, I'll also keep working on taking you down."

"Dunavan may not be a problem anymore," Irah said. "I hear he's disappeared."

Cole listened for her heartbeat. It remained steady.

Flaxx blinked. "Heard how?"

She lounged back in her chair. "It was a big topic Saturday night in my favorite cop bar."

Flaxx's neck reddened. "What the hell were you doing in a cop bar!"

That interested Cole, too.

"Spending a..." Her eye brows wiggled. "...stimulating evening checking out the shortarms of the law. It isn't fair for you to have all the fun screwing the cops."

Flaxx closed his eyes and breathed deeply.

Cole grinned. She knew just how to yank that chain.

By the time Flaxx opened his eyes again, however, she had wiped her expression clear of amusement and sat straight and sober in the chair. "If Dunavan does show up again, I'll make sure he's in too much trouble to bother you. I'll file an assault complaint against him...pretend to be Benay and say he attacked me."

Flaxx perked up. "Will they buy it?"

"Me as Benay?" She snorted. "No sweat. As for the cops turning up here...you know you don't have to see them unless they have a warrant. I'll tell Gina to notify you, no matter who they ask for, and you can decide if they're welcome."

Flaxx considered that for a few moments, then nodded. "Do it."

Cole walked out with her and up the hallway to Gina's desk...where she included herself in the instructions—"Notify both Mr. Flaxx and me."

Now where? She headed back down toward Flaxx's office, but turned at the side hallway leading to the emergency exit. Cole knew where she had to be headed. Now the stepchild office made sense. Flaxx created a job for her and shoe-horned in an office where he could until he arranged something better.

"Where he could," Cole found on following Irah into Asset Management, looked like a converted storeroom...windowless, steel shelving along one wall, neutral walls, utilitarian carpet, stock office chairs, and a steel-and-laminate desk like those in Bookkeeping. A stepchild office indeed. What did Flaxx expect his asset manager to do in here?

While Irah sat down at her desk, Cole checked out magazine file boxes and stacks of brochures on the shelving. A buzz ran through him. The visible brochures were all for security systems. One of the magazine files had security equipment catalogs. The rest held six years' issues of *Security Management*. Flaxx had her doing something with security. Well, well.

He glanced toward her. "So I bet you have a key to—"

Then the magazine dates registered. Six years. He stared around in disbelief. Nothing better than this...cell had been found in *six years*? And she lived with it this way, just hanging a few certificates and photographs?

She might be resigned to it now. There had been no sign of irritation or discontent when she came in. She was even smiling as she swivelled to her computer. Ignoring the keyboard, she picked up a game control. A punch of a button resumed a game that Flaxx's call must have interrupted. She began blasting her way through city streets filled with thugs.

Maybe she was just happy to have a job, he reflected as he looked over the certificates. She had no high school or college diploma. These were all certifications that Irah Lorraine Carrasco had completed courses in race driving, survival, marksmanship, and self-defense. And, surprisingly, the SFPD's Citizens' Police Academy seven years ago.

Cole grunted. "*That* must have thrilled big brother." He glanced back at her. "Is it when you started going to cop bars?"

She thumbed her controls. "Die, rat breath," she spat, and grinned at an explosion.

Or maybe she just wanted a place to play games and, despite what she said to Flaxx, avoid growing up. While he had read the certificates, she had been feverishly working the game controls and talking back to threats muttered by the thugs. She must play this game often enough to know the various villains' dialog. Her exchanges with them sounded almost like real conversations.

That never-never-land attitude went with the largest of the photographs. Poster-sized, it showed a teen-age Irah on a beach with a slightly older male...their arms around each other and their surf boards, dental floss bikinis showing off beautiful tans, sun-bleached hair blowing in the wind. Golden children with no cares except perfecting the tan and catching a good wave.

The male must be her waiter. He had a *rules are for suckers* look in his eyes that raised Cole's hackles. If anyone like that came sniffing around Renee he would—

Cole caught himself and grimaced bitterly. He would do nothing, of course…because he was not going to be there. *Don't think about it, man.* Brooding over what could happen without him would just drive him crazy. He had to trust Sherrie to protect the girls. She ought to do fine, since, thank God, she would be seeing their boyfriends through the shadow of Eddie Trask.

He concentrated on the rest of the photographs to force his mind away from the subject. The line of 8 x 10's all showed Irah at play…bungee jumping, clinging like a spider to a sheer rock face, working a half-pipe on in-line skates, riding a bucking bull, showing off a target with the shots all in the ten circle.

The hair rose on his neck. He stared at the photograph. Not at the target demonstrating her marksmanship but at her other hand, the left one. It still held the target pistol, her thin fingers wrapped around the grip in an echo of an image burned into his memory—the shooter with his hand partially backed out of the plastic bag to display his gun.

"Son of a bitch!"

A jolt of astonishment and anger spun him toward the desk. Amid that roar, images from the shooting played in his head in machine-gun flashes. He circled the desk, comparing them to Irah. Height and weight looked right. Ditto the hands. The shooter had longer, dark hair, though, and a different voice…male…adolescent. Cole stopped behind the computer to look her in the face. It was amazing how killers, if she were one, rarely looked like monsters. He needed to see her ears. The shooter's had no lobes. But disk earrings covered Ira's lobe area. Maybe he could tell something from behind.

He started around for the other end of the desk…but jerked to a halt as the raspy voice he recognized as one of the game character's came out of her mouth. While he watched, she answered in her own voice, then without a hiccup, went back to the raspy voice.

Cole mentally kicked himself. The game characters had not been talking; *she* was. *And if you'd been paying attention, numbnuts, instead of getting your back up over the boyfriend and checking out her photos, you'd have figured that out fifteen minutes ago.* Being shot in the head had indeed blown his brains out.

She did voices. The three words reverberated through him to his toes and hands. He raced through the desk to behind Irah's chair and crouched to peer at the back of her ears. When he called Sara...who answered? Someone who accused Gao of catching her. Someone who begged him to come after her but insisted he wait in the garage rather come up for her.

The posts going through her ears barely cleared the lower edge of the cartilage. If she had lobes, they were minimal.

A jammed tape, it occurred to him, not only prevented a record of when someone left, but how many left...and in what condition.

Terror hung down in the garage.

Ice slid along Cole's spine and surged into his gut in a new, sharper burst of fear for Sara. If he was right about Irah, there was no reason to think she would stop at killing just him. Despair and fury at himself seared him. Was he too late to save Sara from the mess he'd created? Had he screwed up not just by encouraging her on Monday and by missing her phone calls Wednesday but failed her by now never being able to put things right?

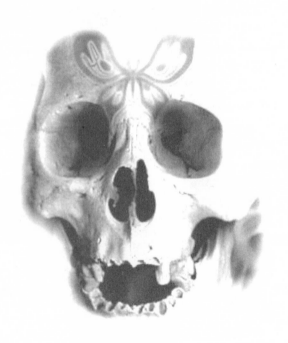

— 14 —

COLE SLAMMED A fist down on the desk, but the frustration of the silence and marshmallow feel only made him angrier. Shit, shit, shit. He scowled at the back of Irah's neck. If he was too late to save Sara, he reflected savagely, at least he could make Irah pay. What would happen if he put his hand through her spinal cord? He affected electrical current. Would that short-circuit nerves…stop Irah's heart?

The thought jerked him up short. He recoiled from it, appalled at himself. Killing Irah was no answer. Besides being murder, making him as cold-blooded as she was, it denied Sara justice. And if he could do nothing else, he owed her that…cleared of being his killer, then her killer arrested—

Cole caught at himself again. "Hey…whoa, man!" He was letting an emotional rush to judgement trample what brains he had left. "You need to step back and take a breath."

Despite his gut feeling and the circumstantial evidence, Sara might not be dead. Alone or accompanied, whatever her general condition, she had to leave the office under her own power. With several inches and a good fifteen pounds on Irah, she could not have been carried out. And certainly not carried anywhere without attracting attention. Ditto if her physical condition was noticeably bad. For the terror in the garage to be hers, she had to reach there alive. And she reached home.

Not necessarily, came a thought. Irah could have been there to make it appear that Sara fled.

He circled through the desk and around behind her computer. Leaning his forearms on the monitor, he frowned down at her. "Was it you?"

The voice mail message for Gao made more sense if Irah left it. He did not see absence excuses even occurring to someone running for her life. But...he needed to find out for certain about Sara.

He *was* certain Irah had shot him. But he knew nothing right now that would make Hamada consider her a suspect. He had zip for motive. That disappeared with the magic words "fruit of the poisoned tree." Nothing would have come of Sara's distress call, either, if Irah turned his call into a dismissal...telling him she was all right but fired and anxious to forget ever meeting him. He would have happily forgotten ever meeting Sara Benay.

There was one possibility to check out. Anyone might suddenly kill out of overwhelming anger or fear, but stone killers did not come out of the blue. There had to be indications elsewhere in her life of a capacity to kill. And not in target shooting or even her enthusiasm for video carnage.

Maybe something would turn up running her through the computer.

"See you in Hell, punk," Irah said to the computer, and in a voice that sound like some British actor, went on, "Too right, Captain Carrasco. Prepare to clear sector D-9."

Her glee made Cole want to spoil her fun. What would he do to a regular computer screen? He spread a hand across the screen and looked away long enough to sink through the surface. A pleasant buzz ran up from his hand. To his satisfaction, the area within the outline of his hand swirled in chaotic color.

Irah started. "What the..."

"Enjoy your game." Leaning down toward her, he intoned, "I'll...be...back."

Then he pulled his hand back and concentrated on a mental image of Homicide. Could he repeat his ziptrip there?

Apparently not. To his frustration, after three tries, he still remained in Irah's office. Well, he could always go to Burglary first. Which had been what he intended last time, he remembered, then ended up in Homicide.

He tried picturing Burglary. And found himself in Burglary. Shaking his head, Cole stumped out into the corridor. Was he *ever* going to figure this out!

Wait…including the view out Razor's window finally made that ziptrip work. Maybe it would work for Homicide, too?

They had a view of the Bay Bridge. Though just down the hall, he pictured that along with Homicide and gave the ziptrip a try. The corridor morphed into Homicide. Cole knocked on Hamada's desk for luck. Maybe there was hope for him yet.

The computer gods were smiling anyway. Homicide's computer sat idle. He hoped it stayed unneeded long enough for him to work.

Standing up at the keyboard, he struggled through menus to the search program. Though it cost him time and the aggravation of extra effort, he ran Irah first as Irah Flaxx. That came up negative. A disappointment, but not really surprising. If she had been using Carrasco since returning to San Francisco, all the records in the Flaxx name were from her juvie days.

He typed in the Carrasco name. Only to be disappointed again. She came up clean…local, state, and NCIC. He had expected no felony or misdemeanor convictions prior to her Citizens' Academy course. They would not have accepted her application otherwise. But something later pointing to a homicidal personality would have been nice to find. There was nothing…not even a speeding ticket. She had passed the firearms safety course required for gun ownership, which he expected, but of course the permit did not specify *what* firearms she owned.

The computer did produce one surprise, a hit on her name as the *victim* of a felony. Seven years ago…a burglary, ironically. The items lost, an antique string of pearls valued at fifteen thousand dollars and a trophy for an amateur stock car race, marked it as one of the Old Spice Burglar's jobs.

Cole always counted himself lucky that Old Spice ignored the Mission. The bastard had been driving Gayle Harris and Stan Fontaine crazy for almost eight years now. Their only description of him aside from his choice of aftershave—a muscular male of below average height—

came from a homeowner who lost a brief wrestling match with him. He typically entered Richmond, Pacific Heights, and Seacliff homes at night. The family woke in the morning to find their security systems defeated, home safes open, and valuables laid out in a display of what could have been stolen if the burglar wished. But he took only a few of the most valuable articles that could be easily carried—and easily fenced—and one item at the other end of the spectrum, with little or no value. Presumably as a souvenir.

Rear vision spotted Ellen Bredeson, Homicide's lone female inspector, heading for the computer. He tracked her progress while working to exit the program, and as it closed, noticed Charlie Dennis across the room beyond her, grinning triumphantly into his phone.

Dennis jiggled the switch hook and punched in a new number, then leaned back in his chair. "Tex, how's it going?"

Cole stepped out of Bredeson's way and hurried toward Dennis.

"Shit." Dennis grimaced. "So maybe it *was* a lover's quarrel. You'll be interested in what I came up with on Benay, then." He gave Hamada the same information Cole had found on the Narco bust. "But here's the interesting part. This Tony Novello's name rang a bell so I ran him, too, and guess what?"

Cole winced at the satisfaction in Dennis's voice. He obviously thought that an acquaintance who killed her boyfriend made for a case of Sara doing the same.

At the end of his recitation, Dennis listened, then said, "If she does, it isn't legal. There's no gun permit for her."

Cole moved around the desk close to the receiver.

At the other end of the line, Hamada grunted. "Too bad. That would give us probable cause for searching her apartment. With the manager following us around, we couldn't do more than walk through."

"'We', huh." Dennis smiled. "How'd you talk your way into her apartment? Welfare check?"

"Well of course," Hamada said righteously. "Young woman says she's flying home and doesn't make it. No one's heard from her for days. She could've had an accident and be lying unconscious in there." Hamada paused. "The manager was real understanding."

Dennis and Cole both grinned. If the manager had not been there, Hamada might have checked to see if Sara were lying in a desk drawer. Anything significant he found would be left untouched, of course, until he had a warrant that let him "discover" it legally.

"She took out of here in one hell of a hurry."

Dennis propped his feet up on the desk. "Would you like to know where *to?*"

Hope tightened Cole's chest. Maybe she *was* who packed?

"That would be helpful, yes," came Hamada's dry reply.

"How about Key West...first class ticket on American, one way..."

Cole grinned in relief.

"...Friday morning out of San Jose."

San Jose! Dismay rocked Cole back. No way could it be coincidence that she flew out of the same airport where his car was found. Shit. Instead of being a victim, she was involved in his death. But then, why the terror? Maybe she was not involved but witnessed his murder and somehow struck a deal with Irah. Irah drove her to San Jose and put her on a plane for the other end of the country.

"With her Mastercard," Dennis said. He listened, then sighed. "I'll get on it. Just for the Mastercard, right, until we know what other credit cards she has?"

Another possibility hit Cole. Irah told Flaxx she could pass herself off as Sara. Maybe she was so confident because she had done it once already? If she produced Sara's driver's license and credit card at the airline counter, would the ticket agent question her identity or take a close look at the driver's license to read the height and weight? Both were attractive blondes, and attractive women tended to look similar...as the cookie cutter babes in TV shows demonstrated. Most civilians erroneously focused on details like hair color and style in identifying people.

Had Dennis determined whether "Sara Benay" had actually *taken* the flight? Damn it, he wished he could ask! If she had boarded, it could be Sara, but if not...if Irah had Sara's ID and credit cards...His gut knotted. Foreboding beat at him.

He had Irah's address from the computer. Time to see what her home told him about her. He headed for the outside wall and through it.

A small voice in him started to murmur about due process and civil rights, but he stamped it into silence. What did a dead man care about those? Besides, he reflected, running up to the roof...if Irah killed Sara and him, she had certainly violated *their* civil rights.

He sighted west on the Sutro Tower. It stood well south of Irah's Richmond address, but as the highest point in the city, he ought to be able to go line-of-sight almost anywhere from there.

And seconds later, standing on the topmost crossbar of the tower, he contemplated landmarks in the vicinity of her address. Spreckels Lake in Golden Gate Park lay even with avenue numbers in the mid-thirties, which put it just blocks from her. He aimed for the lake. After jogging across its surface dodging boats, then out of the park, he had clear line-of-sight...down along the park on Fulton, then up the avenues.

Like the other houses around it, Irah's...sunny yellow with darker front and garage doors...consisted of two floors stacked over a garage. A more expensive house than when municipal employees first populated the area, but modest compared to Flaxx's pile of architecture. The entry hall had a keypad for a top home security system—a result of her burglary, no doubt—but her living and dining rooms looked as though she were as indifferent to her surroundings here as she was at the office. The livingroom had a small furniture suite by the front windows, but no pictures on the walls, no plants, and none of the personal clutter that accumulated in his own livingroom. Not a home, Cole mused, but a bivouac. Instead of a table, the dining room had a treadmill and a Bowflex. Dishes in a drainer on the kitchen counter indicated she did use the kitchen. Hoping she did not sleep in a bivouac, too, he headed upstairs.

To his relief, it was where she really lived.

Pulling down walls had turned the entire floor into one large master suite. Hassocks, reading lamps, and big, deep chairs furnished the sitting area up by the windows. Down one wall, bookshelves flanked both sides of a plasma screen TV/media center. Against the opposite wall sat an antique rolltop desk—closed—and curio cabinet crammed with kitsch. Between them a table held a printer, with a shredder-topped wastebasket beneath it. Cole peered down past the shredder into the wastebasket. Damn. If only he could pick things up.

To forget that frustration he went to check out the bookshelves…and blinked in amazement. He would not have taken her for a reader…and even less as someone likely to choose heavy reading. Aside from some mystery novels, college level texts filled one section of shelves…covering literature, history, psychology, and general science. Judging by the multiple book-marks sticking out of the tops, she had read at least portions of them all. Making up for not finishing high school, it appeared. A framed G.E.D. certificate stood on one shelf.

But he stared in amazement at the other section of shelves. The books and video tapes—both commercially produced and home-recorded—looked straight out of a police library…true-crime studies, profiles of American and British police departments, the California Criminal Code, texts on locksmithing and safes, on security systems, autopsies, firearms and ballistics, crime scene investigation, the art of interrogation, arson investigation. *He* did not own that much law enforcement related material. Her interest in law enforcement had not stopped with the Citizens' Academy.

At the bedroom end, the wall opposite her bed had been turned into a photo gallery. The photographs hung above a table displaying a large model of a classic Mustang GT...dark green, like the one Steve McQueen drove in *Bullitt.* He headed down to check out the photos.

And found a shrine. The "model car" was actually a custom funeral urn...flanked by a memorial book and a framed service program with the name Scott Ledonald Carrasco. Dates on the program cover indicated Carrasco had died eight years ago at age twenty-four.

Which probably explained Irah's return to San Francisco.

All the photographs featured the man in the surfboard photo. At first glance they appeared to be 8 x 10 enlargements of ordinary snapshots...showing Carrasco standing beside or sitting behind the wheel of various cars, and Carrasco drinking with Irah and buddies in bars or around a fire on the beach. Goosebumps rose on Cole's neck. Tattoos on the buddies screamed *jailhouse*...and the vehicles looked like a shopping list for *Gone In Sixty Seconds*...a BMW Z8, Mercedes SL, Porsche 911, Lamborghini Diablo, series E Jaguar, Dodge Viper, and a Mustang GT.

Cole itched to run Carrasco through the computer. Not that being married to someone with a record and felonious friends made a case for Irah being a killer. He grimaced. Unfortunately nothing he had seen so far indicated anything criminal. Not even her library.

Cole turned away to check her closet.

Once it had been of ordinary size, he guessed, but taking out the back wall of it gained access to an adjoining bedroom and gave her a huge walk-in. Clothes racks ran the length of one wall, opposite a bank of drawers and shelves. One shelf had medium and long-hair wigs on mannequin heads. At the far end stood a big armoire and a theater-type makeup table with lights around the mirror.

Looking the two pieces over, he felt the goosebumps come up again. Furniture like this usually had rim locks, the kind operated with a skeleton-type key. These had been fitted with cylinder locks. What did she want to protect...or hide?

Closing his eyes, he walked into the armoire. When he opened his eyes again, he stood in the dark and almost up to his knees in the drawer section. But he saw just fine. Not that there was much to see…just a gun safe on the floor at one end and frayed jeans and a battered leather bomber jacket on hangers at the other end, with equally battered work boots sitting under them. What made this worth extra security? True, there was the gun safe, but it had its own lock, operated with a key pad like his at home.

He waded toward the clothing. The jacket hung with a bulkiness that suggested the presence of something under it on the hanger. To check that out, he passed through to the far side.

Opening his eyes again, Cole found himself looking at a faded Kansas City Royals baseball cap hanging on a hook. His scalp prickled. He had seen a cap like that in photographs taken of onlookers at Flaxx fires…and the desk clerk and other guests at the Kijurian's hotel described him as wearing a Royals cap. A Royals cap, plaid shirt, and…a leather bomber jacket.

Cole spun around to the jacket. A plaid shirt hung draped over the lower bar of the hanger. This had to be the Kijurian costume. Who wore it? Irah had the clothes…but everyone who claimed to have seen Kijurian described him as stocky, which Irah definitely was not. Then he spotted the reason for the jacket's bulk…body armor hanging under it…not the bullet proof type law enforcement wore but the bulkier protective vest he had seen on bull riders. Like the one Irah wore in her bull-riding photograph. That vest under the jacket could make her appear stocky. What a tidy way for Flaxx to torch his stores…keep it all in the family.

Irah's face, though, looked nothing like the individual photographed in the fire crowd or that described at the hotel. Even discounting the bristling mustache and eyebrows, the Kijurian face was broad, Slavic, jowly.

Cole backed out of the armoire and eyed the makeup table. What was the movie where bit-part characters came on screen at the end and pulled off false faces to reveal themselves as famous actors? *The List of Adrian Messenger.* Could Irah create herself a different face like that? Were her supplies what she had carefully locked up?

Too bad he had no true sense of feel. Then he'd reach into the drawers of the makeup table and explore—

He smacked himself in the forehead. "Numbnuts! Why don't you *look* in the frigging drawers?"

Cole bent over and pushed his face through tabletop. The shallowness of the upper drawers limited his range of sight. To check contents took side-to-side sweeps, making him feel like someone reading a book through a loupe. But passing from cosmetics in the middle drawer to one of the side drawers, he found a salt-and-pepper mustache in a plastic box, and more hair the same color in another box. Yes! Those could be Kijurian's mustache and eyebrows.

Cole knelt to lean into the large lower drawer. It contained a stack of round boxes...containing hair, he found as he pressed down through them. Wigs? Excitement mounting in him, he shuffled over to the big drawer on the opposite side. Among the boxes, cans, and bottles there, one word leaped out: latex! The material movie makeup artists used to create false faces.

He jumped to his feet and raced out to check the bookshelves and confirm that Irah had books on theater makeup. There was also a videotape labeled *Ex-spy/secrets of disguises.* Which meant she had the knowledge and materials to make herself into Kijurian. He would love to see a face recognition program compare her to Kijurian.

Staring at some books on locks and security systems, it occurred to him...maybe Flaxx kept more than arson in the family. One of the problems in making the burglary case against him was the total silence on the street about him looking for men to pull the jobs. No wonder, if little sister could do it. Who knew the store security systems better? She was slim enough to fit through the small rear windows of stores broken into that way, and limber enough to hide in a small space waiting for closing time, as happened in some other stores.

Cole hurried back into the closet and stuck his head into the drawer portion of the armoire. Some rolls of electrical wire and electrical tape lay in it, along with a can of polyurethane foam and a black, child-sized backpack. The jumble of items in the small space of the backpack played hell with trying to see what was there. Going down through it, eyeball to item, he did make out needle-nose pliers, a small roll of electrical wire, more tape, another can of polyurethane foam, and a rolled bundle that could be lock picks.

Grinning, he sat back on his heels. The pack's contents needed to be spread out for a good examination, but it sure as hell looked like a burglar kit to him. What a piece of work Irah was...big brother's own personal in-house department of dirty tricks. No wonder Flaxx tolerated some attitude. It made for a tight, secure conspiracy...brother, sister, and devoted henchman.

Cole's satisfaction faded. The only murder the Kijurian outfit and burglar tools pointed to was the firefighter's. He needed evidence that Irah had killed him, and maybe Sara.

The murder weapon would be a start. He leaned into the armoire once more, this time into the gun safe. To his disappointment, all he could see were four zippered gun pouches. Seeing whether one of them held a Glock had to wait for a search. He stood and headed out through the bedroom, fighting uneasiness. In Irah's place, he would have thrown that Glock in the bay. He could only hope she'd hung on to it. He needed that gun. Right now, it looked like all the evidence he had against her.

As he crossed the sitting area, the curio cabinet caught Cole's eye. She had a cylinder lock on it, too.

Connections crackled in his brain. Cross-dressing...burglary ...kitsch. Cole ran to the cabinet and peered at the jumble on the shelves. He had barely glanced at the collection before ...registered the Mardi Gras beads, a scruffy Princess Leia action figure, and a prancing model horse with a long pink mane and tail...and classified the stuff as childhood treasures and

accumulated tchotchkes. Now he took a closer look and bells
clanged. He had seen such items on Gayle Harris and Phil
Braff's list of Old Spice's souvenir picks. An armless Barbie
doll, flat stones glued together and painted to look like a frog,
a snow globe with the Olympic rings and a pagoda, a letter
opener in the shape of a miniature samurai sword, a cast metal
figure of a jumping horse and rider.

It appeared Irah did not confine burglary to the Flaxx stores.

No wonder Gayle and Braff were chasing their tails.
Struggling in the dark with an athletic opponent who bested
him really screwed up that homeowner's perception of his
opponent. And Irah burglarized herself for, what…cover?
Or maybe to study the investigation process, the better to—

Another thought cut across that one, reverberating in him.
Irah takes souvenirs.

Feverishly, Cole began studying the shelves even more
closely. *That* was how to tie her to murder, find a personal
article of his here. Or of Sara's. He hoped there was nothing of Sara's, but while looking for something of his, he tried
not to overlook anything that might be hers. The problem
was guessing what that might be. Except for her butterfly
passion, he knew so little about her. None of the shelves
had a butterfly item.

None of the shelves had anything he recognized as
his, either.

He frowned irritably at the cabinet and started the search
over. She must have something of his here! Not those handcuffs on the bottom shelf. They were hinged and his had a
chain. Item by item, shelf by shelf, he examined the contents
of the cabinet a second time. And a third time. When that
found nothing either, Cole backed off and looked around the
room. Where else could she be keeping souvenirs?

Maybe the rolltop desk?

He put his head into it. One drawer contained a pair of
handcuffs with a chain, but he had no way to identify them as
his. His had no personalizing marks. Nothing else visible to

him in the drawers looked significant or incriminating. A laptop in the rolltop section was closed and inaccessible.

Backing away, he took one more look around. Frustration hissed through him. "I guess you won this round, Irah." For everything here, there was still no proof whether Sara was dead or alive, and no hard evidence against Irah for murder. He gritted his teeth. "But you've left evidence somewhere... and I *will* find it!"

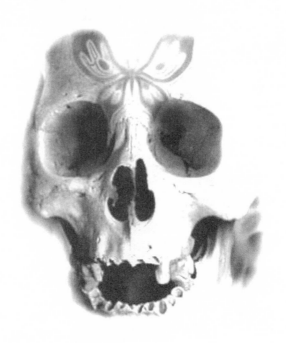

— 15 —

COLE EYED THE Mustang urn. Dear hubby was a good place to start. While running Carrasco on Homicide's computer, he also could hook up with Razor again and keep working on him. Assuming Razor had managed to stick with Hamada.

Before trying to ziptrip, Cole memorized details of the room and the view out the window…just in case he wanted to zip back for another look around. Then he concentrated… Homicide office, Hamada's desk, Bay Bridge view. *Be kind, travel gods.*

Irah's bedroom gave way to Charlie Dennis hunched over a typewriter, muttering to himself, but his fingers flying. Even burned out, he typed faster than anyone else in the Bureau. In this instance, Cole saw on peering over Dennis's shoulder, he was working on a search warrant for Sara's credit cards. An affidavit for the warrant already lay on his desk along with the affidavit and search warrant for the apartment…waiting for a judge's signature. So Hamada ought to be coming back to find a judge.

Across the room, Tom Padilla sat using the computer. Cole walked over to wait. He doubted there was much on Carrasco locally, but since Flaxx talked about Irah having fun enough for a lifetime in L.A., Cole hoped Sacramento and NCIC could give him something.

Padilla hit Print. While the printer worked, he rubbed a spot off the monitor with his thumb. The action reminded Cole of what his touch did to Irah's computer. Could he leave a message even without a digitized screen like Braff's laptop?

Padilla collected his printout and headed back for his desk.

Cole touched one finger to the screen and averted his eyes long enough to sink the tip into it. The image distorted where he touched…but to his disappointment, when he moved the finger, the only effect was a shift in the point of distortion. No trail remained. Bummer. He was stuck with using the keyboard.

Once he managed to access the records program, he found that, as he suspected, Carrasco was fairly clean locally…a couple of arrests for suspicion of burglary, one for passing stolen checks…the charges dismissed in each case. The lack of convictions explained how he had landed the country club job. Sacramento, though, listed several convictions in L.A., the last being for burglary eight years ago. The date of the conviction, Cole noticed, was three months prior to the date on the memorial service program. So Carrasco probably died in jail.

Exiting the program, Cole saw that Hamada had still not come in. No problem. That might give him time for a couple of messages.

He was finishing the first—*Did Benay TAKE her flight?*—when Hamada and Razor walked in. Hamada picked up the affidavits and warrants on Dennis's desk. Cole thought fast. He wanted them to see this, so he better attract their attention now. Once Hamada had the warrants signed, he would probably head straight back for Sara's apartment.

Cole yelled, "Razor…come look at the computer!"

As he hoped, caught unaware, Razor heard…and automatically turned before freezing.

Hamada glanced around from reading. "Something wrong?"

Razor turned away. "No."

Damn it! Cole stepped up on the nearest desk. "You son of a bitch! How much longer are you going to stay in denial!"

Hamada stared Cole's direction, but obviously saw nothing. Then his eyes shifted toward the computer. He strolled over. Dennis and Razor followed…Razor looking as though he were being dragged by his tie. Cole heard his heart racing.

Studying the monitor, Hamada shook his head. "It's a real epidemic."

"Padilla was the last one I saw over here," Dennis said.

"Padilla wasn't near Galentree's computer, though, and sure not at the Flaxx offices." Hamada raised a brow at Razor. "You positive you don't have any ideas about this?"

Razor shook his head. "I haven't touched the computers either."

Touched the computers! Inspiration hit Cole. Maybe *that* would do the trick!

Once when he and Razor had broken up a fight and chased one of the combatants to his house, the glass panel in the door had triggered an idea. He had nudged Razor and shined his flashlight at the glass. "Make a shadow dog." Razor had understood immediately. Grinning, he'd put his hands in the light beam, creating the silhouette of a dog's head on the glass. While Razor made deep barking sounds, wiggling his little fingers to work the dog's jaw, Cole had called, "Don't make us send in the dog!"

Incredibly, the subject had slunk out and surrendered. The phrase "sending in the dog" had been a running joke with them ever since.

Cole jumped off the desk and thrust his hands into the computer screen from the side. The screen went crazy, creating a dog head-shaped area of chaos. "Don't make me send in the dog, Razor!"

Dennis and Hamada blinked. "What the *hell*..." Dennis began.

Razor stopped breathing. "Oh, shit." He stumbled backward. Hamada and Dennis turned to stare at him, but he left the office walking as fast as someone could without running.

Cole chased after him. "Razor..."

Razor began running. At the elevators he almost collided with a pair of waiting Robbery detectives as he pushed past them to the stairwell.

Swearing silently, Cole followed but said nothing until Razor reached the ground floor and bolted out through the rear entrance into the parking lot. Then he raced ahead and planted himself in Razor's path. "Damn it, stop running away!"

Razor halted, squeezing his eyes shut. "This isn't happening."

Which meant Razor still saw him! Cole grinned at him. "Yes it is, old buddy. Dennis and Hamada saw what happened to the computer screen, too, so you know you're not flipping out. Admit it. I'm here and you see me. Now let's talk."

Razor dug out his cigarettes and lit one, hands shaking so much the lighter flame scorched the middle of the cigarette before connecting with the end. Even while taking a deep drag, he shook his head. "I need a drink."

"That won't make me disappear." Cole slugged Razor's shoulder in exasperation. "Why are you being so damn pig-headed!"

Razor reeled back, though Cole doubted he felt the blow.

A trio from the decoy squad eyed him as they headed for the rear entrance. "You okay?" asked one with a two-day stubble and the grimy clothes of a vagrant.

"Fine." Razor dropped the cigarette and crushed it under his heel. "I need to quit these things."

The three exchanged raised eyebrows as they went on inside.

Razor frowned after them, hunching his shoulders. "Even if I'm not nuts, I look it."

"So pretend to be talking on your cell phone."

Razor glanced at him, then quickly away. He fumbled the cigarettes out again and lit another. "This is *crazy*."

It was maddening, all right. "Terrific. What a welcome. You moan and groan and want me to go away. I thought you'd be glad to see me."

Razor took a shaky drag on the cigarette before answering. "Alive, yes. But..." He grimaced.

"So till death us do part applies to friendship, too?"

Razor stiffened and flushed. "It's just..." He shook his head.

"Impossible? But...ta-da..." Cole spread his arms wide. "Here I am. What's that Shakespeare quote you use, about Heaven and Earth being full of weirder things than we ever expect."

"I never expected anything like *this*." Razor took another long drag. "But maybe that *is* really you." The wry tone steadied his voice. "If you were my imagination, I'd have the quote

correct." He paused. "So that *wasn't* a dream last night? Even
walking on the ceiling?"

Cole quashed his impatience. Of course Razor needed time
to accept this. Except…if Sara was still alive, how much time
did they have to pull her out of danger? "I wasn't a dream. And
now there's more to tell you. But first…the guys from the decoy squad are coming back. Pretend to be on the phone."

"So they won't think I'm talking to myself? But hell, I
probably am." Still, he pulled out the phone, and as the trio
passed him, held it to his ear. "What more?"

Cole filled him in about Irah, the conversation with Flaxx,
her house, Carrasco's record, and Sherrie overhearing Brewer
at the hospital.

Razor listened without interruption, though he punctuated
the recitation with grimaces and twitches suggesting a continued internal struggle to revise his concept of reality. When
Cole finished, he shook his head. "I don't know. Even if
you're right about Flaxx's sister, we can't get into her place
without probable cause."

Cole snorted. "I *know* that. So help me find some."

"You have any ideas?"

"Call one of your Pig Bowl friends in L.A. and have him
run Irah's name. Maybe she's had arrests without charges. I'd
also like a copy of hubby's record, including known associates." Cole lifted his brows. "Maybe she keeps in touch with
old friends. She could be fencing the stuff from the burglaries
through one of them."

"Okay." Razor pitched his cigarette butt and brought up
the names list on his phone. After calling one and identifying
himself several times to individuals on the other end he finally
said, "Yo, Pascullo. This is Kevin Rasgorshek in San Francisco. How they hangin', man. Are you still working on that
Cobra replica?…Great. How'd you do?…That isn't bad. Say,
I wonder if you can help me out."

Minutes later he had his notebook open on the hood of a
car, taking down what the L.A. officer read off his computer.

Cole read as Razor wrote. They had nothing on Irah, except as Scott Carrasco's wife, but plenty on Carrasco himself. Suspicion of auto theft, burglary, suspicion of burglary, suspicion of receiving stolen property, passing stolen checks, forged checks. All his sentences were served in the L.A. county jail. Where his cellmate shanked him for a carton of cigarettes.

Then one comment from Pascullo pleased Cole. They suspected Carrasco of having an accomplice, possibly a small, thin male. Carrasco denied it, however, and they were never able to make him give up the name. Small and thin. Cole grinned. Irah. Carrasco might well have played the gallant knight and taken the fall by himself to protect her.

According to Pascullo, Carrasco gave his profession as a stunt driver and movie extra. Working as an extra would have given Irah experience with makeup and disguises.

"Got it. Can you fax me all that?" Razor gave a number. "Just mark it for my attention. Thanks. I owe you one."

"Where's it going?" Cole asked when Razor disconnected.

Razor flinched. Still spooked by his presence, Cole guessed. "The Central Station. It should be waiting when we get there."

"You're thinking of going now?" Cole raised his brows. "What about shadowing Hamada?"

"After the way I bolted out of there?" Razor grimaced. "He'll expect an explanation."

Cole grinned. "You could always tell him the truth. He won't believe you."

Razor grunted. "Right. Then he'll have me hauled away to the funny farm." He sighed. "And maybe I should be."

Give him time, Cole reminded himself. "So make him think about something else. Tell him you've had a tip that Flaxx's sister has criminal connections. Say your CI—which I am—heard she did burglaries and auto theft with her husband, though she never got caught because hubby always took the fall alone."

Razor shook his head. "He'll be interested for maybe five minutes...until I tell him Carrasco is dead and that I don't have anything more than rumor about Irah."

"That's fine. The point is…" Cole slung an arm across Razor's shoulders. "…you'll be back there. By this time Hamada could be ready to have the warrants signed. But when he goes to the apartment, he won't be looking for evidence that someone besides Sara packed."

Razor eyed him for a long minute. "I need my head examined, taking suggestions from a ghost." Still, he headed back for the Hall.

Falling into step with him, Cole grunted in mock disappointment. "You make me feel so appreciated."

After a glance at a pair of uniformed officers engrossed in their own conversation and cigarettes, Razor raised a brow. "How do I know whether you're right…or should I say, how do I know whether you're dead right or dead wrong?"

Cole grinned. They were making progress.

Inside, a group including uniformed officers and a pair of public defenders also waited for the elevator. To avoid one of them intruding into his space, Cole walked up the wall until abreast of the doors' top. Razor started, then pulled off his glasses and concentrated on polishing them on his tie.

Cole strolled on up to the ceiling. "Look, Razor, I'm Dracula." He grabbed the edges of his suit coat and wrapped it around him as though folding bat wings.

Razor polished his glasses harder.

The elevator doors opened. Cole hurried inside, keeping against the overhead panels. Razor put his glasses back on and stared at his feet.

When the doors opened on the Bureau floor, however, Razor lifted his head. Hamada stood outside. Cole reached down to walk his fingers across Razor's neck. "The gods are kind today." He slipped out of the elevator.

Razor followed, halting beside Hamada. "I was just coming back to see you."

Hamada's gaze searched him. "To talk about computers freaking you out?"

Razor flushed. "To let you know about an interesting call from an informant. If you're headed down to have the warrants signed, let me walk along and tell you on the way."

The down elevator looked crowded. Cole opted for the stairs and rejoined Razor as he and Hamada walked around to the judges' chambers. They halted outside Judge Barbour's door. A good choice. Barbour wanted the ducks lined up and she could smell creative probable cause from across the room, but she tended to give officers the benefit of the doubt on iffy points.

"Interesting," Hamada said when Razor finished, "but...don't you reckon Dunavan would have heard any rumors about the sister? He never said anything to you, did he?"

Razor hesitated. "No. But a buddy of mine in the LAPD is faxing me a list of Carrasco's known associates. Even though he never gave up the name of his accomplice, I'm thinking maybe a former pal will tell us if it was Carrasco's wife."

Hamada grunted skeptically. "We'll see. It doesn't sound like there's any more evidence of her involvement in the burglaries, though, than there is for Flaxx." He knocked on the chamber door.

It opened almost immediately. Judge Barbour smiled at them, a rawboned horse of a woman that rumor liked to whisper had been born male, despite three children proving the contrary. "Come in, Inspectors."

Just Hamada went.

Razor leaned against the wall outside to wait. "How can I tell whether she packed or someone else did?"

He had a point, Cole realized. Like Sherrie, Sara must have favorites for trips and others she always left behind. But only someone who knew her well would recognize whether the "right" clothes were gone.

"Kenisha Hayes might be able to tell," Cole said. "I'll go on to the apartment and see if I can spot anything that will justify you suggesting Hayes have a look. Catch you there."

— 16 —

AFTER TWO TRIES, he managed to ziptrip to the street outside Sara's building again. Hunting a reason to bring in Hayes frustrated him, however. How did he make Hamada care about which clothes had been packed? As far as he could tell, the choices were appropriate for a warm climate. The shoe racks had gaps in the section of casual shoes and sandals. One of the partially open drawers still held a few shorts, t-shirts, and tank tops.

Cole leaned on the dresser, drumming his fingers while he peered around. There must be *something* here they could use to—

A woman's distant scream broke into the thought. A scream that kept repeating.

He rushed into the front room and through the window to where he could see down the street. A block and a half away, people gathered in the street. The posture of one indicated she was screaming. And into the air rose trails of smoke.

For a moment, it took him back to 1989, settling in to watch the World Series at Razor's apartment while Sherrie and Razor's first wife Jessie fussed over the five-week-old twins. Only to have the world suddenly wrench beneath them. As the boards and cinderblock bookcase collapsed, dishes spilled from the kitchen cupboard, and beer cans toppled over on the coffee table, they'd stared at each other, sharing the same terrified thought: Was this the Big One? With no memory of having moved, he'd found himself in the street, leaning against a parked car for support, an arm around Sherrie and each of them holding one twin. The ground had continued its spasms for what seemed an eternity. When it went still, for a few moments the world felt eerily silent. Then he'd heard screams and seen smoke rising into the afternoon sky. Exchanging one glance with Razor, he had thrust Travis at Jessie and the two of them had run toward the screams.

Reflex set Cole running toward today's screams, too... angling down to the street. Though he wondered what he could do for the woman.

As he came nearer, the screaming resolved into a man's name. "Steve! Steve! No! Come back!"

The smoke poured from the doorway and a second floor window of a three-story apartment building. This Steve must be playing hero, going back inside to rescue something.

"Has anyone called 911?" Cole shouted.

Distant sirens, one paired with the air horn of a fire truck, answered that question. Moments later a man staggered out of the smoke with a yowling pet carrier. Bleeding scratches covered his hands. In the middle of the street he set down the carrier and collapsed to his knees, coughing.

The woman went down beside him, bursting into tears. "That was crazy!" But she embraced both him and the carrier.

"Is anyone else still inside?" Cole called toward the bystanders. He thought he heard pounding and a faint voice.

He ran to the door, straining to hear. He did hear someone inside. A thumping came from an upper floor along with a muffled cry for help. He hesitated, staring into the smoke, then laughed at himself. What was he afraid of? Smoke inhalation? Burning to death?

He charged through the smoke into the hallway and up the stairs two at a time toward the second floor. The pounding and cries for help sounded higher, on the third floor. A woman's voice. Flames ate at the upper steps and the hallway carpet. Shaking away the reflex that said to run away from fire, he plunged into it.

And halted in amazement. With flames surrounding him, a tremendous surge of energy filled him...even more than a vehicle running through him. And the flames died in the space he occupied...as if he had sucked them in.

A faint cry upstairs abruptly reminded Cole of the reason he'd come in. He raced on up to the third floor stairs. Maybe he could use the fire suppression thing to help the woman.

Or maybe not. Smoke filled the hall.

The pounding came from a spot toward the rear of the building. Cole passed through the wall by the sound and found himself in a bathroom. An elderly woman with one arm in a cast used her good arm to slap the handle of a toilet plunger against the wall in time with her calls for help. She had filled the bathtub and soaked herself in it. Water dripped from her slacks, blouse, and hair. But maybe after preparing herself to run for safety she found the smoke too thick, or the fire had reached the stairs by the time she was aware of it. So instead, she'd retreated in here. Wet towels filled the gap under the door. That kept the smoke out but now she had trapped herself. The bathroom had no window.

Her only hope was to leave her sanctuary and go to the front window, where she would be seen by the firefighters on the trucks he heard arriving. Could he make her hear him so he could give her instructions?

Passing into the bedroom, however, he found it full of smoke, too. She had to be physically fit to live on the third floor with no elevator, but there was so much smoke. To stay under it and reach the front window, she would need to belly crawl. Could she manage that?

"Hello. Hello in there!" Oh for the ability to knock on the door! But energy filled him. His voice even felt more robust. "Ma'am, can you hear me?"

A gasp of relief came through the door. "Oh, thank God. Yes! I hear you."

Hallelujah!

"Please...help me."

"We need to get you to the front window. But you'll have to crawl to stay under the smoke. Can you do that with your broken arm?" And could he remain audible to her? Maybe...if he obscured her vision, had her keep a towel over her head so she never realized no body went with the voice.

She hesitated before answering. "I don't know. It'd be slow. Don't you have oxygen or something so I can walk to the window?"

Slow would be bad. Though he saw no smoldering around the floor to indicate the fire was breaking through up here, the floor could be hot and he had no way to know. She needed to move fast. "I'll go for a rescue team. You keep pounding on the wall."

She paused again. "Keep pounding? Why, when you've found me?"

Cole kicked himself. He should have expected that. "To...tell me you're still all right. I'm going now but we'll be back shortly."

Not if he left it to her pounding, though. It sounded half-hearted compared to before. Her life depended on him telling someone about her.

He ran to the front window. Below, he saw uniformed officers pushing onlookers to the far sidewalk and, with the pumper truck hooked up to the hydrant down the block, a hose team coming in the front door. Could he make them hear him?

He ran down to the second floor and stood in the flames at the top of the stairs, again feeling the incredible flow of energy into him. "Hey!" he shouted. "There's a woman trapped upstairs!"

To his dismay, no one in the team spraying water up the stairs reacted.

"HELP!"

Still no one responded. Hearing him would be tough even if he were alive. Damn! If only they could *see* him. Red said a ghost back home could make herself visible for short periods. Urgency wracked Cole. He had to do so, too...or the woman up there would die.

In a foot chase, when his legs began feeling leaden and his throat and lungs burned, he'd dug for emotion to keep himself going…anger at the perpetrator he chased, hatred of losing a race, whatever lay handy. Now Cole grabbed at his sense of urgency, at his worry and the guilt over what might have happened to Sara…funneling it all into the will to be seen. *See me*!

Suddenly he felt…different, heavier.

"Holy shit!" yelled the firefighter holding the hose nozzle. "Is that someone up there in the hall?"

They saw him! "Get the ladder!" Cole shouted. "There's a woman trapped in her bathroom on the third floor!"

"Sir—!"

Cole lost the rest as he raced up to the apartment. At the front window, he waved his arms vigorously. To his dismay, the weight sensation started fading. No! Not yet.

Then someone outside pointed up. Okay! They saw him. The firefighter breaking out the second floor window signaled to the man on the ladder controls. The ladder began lifting.

Cole headed for the bathroom, feeling lighter by the moment. He gritted his teeth, trying to hang on long enough to make sure they found the woman.

Behind him, glass shattered.

"Back here!" he called, and through the door: "Ma'am …we're coming for you."

The firefighter appeared out of the smoke. Behind his face shield and above his breathing apparatus, he gaped in disbelief and alarm. Naturally, seeing a man standing there apparently breathing smoke. *"Hey—"*

"Don't mind about me. Get the woman in the bathroom." To give him no choice, Cole let go. As if a plug had been pulled, the last of the weight drained away.

On the ground a short while later, watching the old woman being checked out by a paramedic, he listened to the firefighter recount the incident. "…and he disappeared. I swear to God. One minute he was standing in front of me, and then he…dissolved."

Another firefighter snickered and tapped his respirator. "You sure it was air you were breathing there?"

The woman wrapped herself tighter in the blanket they had thrown around her. "I'd been praying to be found. Maybe he was an angel."

The firefighters' faces went politely blank. "This guy had a suit and tie, not wings."

She sniffed. "Who says they have to have wings?"

An angel. Cole smiled wryly. That was the last thing he deserved to be called. "But I thank you very much, ma'am." And at least he had finally done something constructive.

The question was…how he managed to make himself material enough for everyone to see him? Being able to pull that off at will would be a huge help.

Cole turned back to the burning building, where a firefighter on the ladder shot water in through the second floor window. Red said that when the ghost back home appeared, the room ended up a deep freeze. So…materializing needed beaucoup heat. Which the fire gave him. He remembered the energy pouring into him.

Did he need a fire's worth for materializing? He hoped not. Fires were not something he could find on demand. What about using ovens and boilers? A possibility, but hunting for one of those when he needed it would also be a drag. Cole shook his head. He needed something readily available anywhere 24/7.

The rumble of the pumper truck's engine caught his ear. He moved toward the truck, remembering the invigorating sensation of vehicles running through him last night. Could internal combustion be his answer?

Closing his eyes, he waded into the pumper's engine compartment. The staccato jolts of firing cylinders felt even better than he remembered…not the flood of heat the fire brought but an exhilarating riff like a string of firecrackers going off in him.

Then the engine began missing.

Cole leaped free, swearing at himself. *Way to go, numbnuts… kill the engine and shut down the hoses.* He should have realized that would happen after the way the flames died in his space. In assessing himself, though, he found a respectable level of energy, considering how little time he'd spent in the engine. This might work.

There was just the question of *how* he used the heat to materialize. But before working on that, he ought to touch base with Razor.

Line-of-sight took him to Sara's window, where he passed inside and found Hamada in latex gloves, going through the middle drawer of the desk.

Hamada pulled out a spiral-bound book with index tabs. After flipping through it, he laid it on the laptop. "Got her address book."

Since he doubted Hamada meant the comment for him, Cole checked the bedroom for Razor. And found him...laying boxes from the closet shelf on the bed.

Cole waved at him from the doorway. "I'm baaack."

To his dismay, Razor showed no reaction, not even a flicker in his eyes, as he brought the last couple of boxes to the bed.

Cole moved over to the bed and ran a hand front of Razor's eyes. "Hey, partner. Have you stopped seeing me?"

Apparently. Razor opened the first box and lifted out a wool shawl.

Oh-kay...reminder time. Cole walked through Razor. "Heads up!" And grinned at Razor's intake of breath and jump in heart rate. "Can you see me now?"

"That was cute." Razor stuffed the shawl back in its box.

Cole sat down on a corner of the bed. "It could have been worse. I thought about grabbing your nuts."

"Not a good way to stay friends." Razor opened another box. It had a vaquero-style hat. "Have you been lurking since we came in? Do you see anything suggesting Sara didn't pack?"

"No and no. But..." Cole told him about the fire and materializing. "Now I need to see if I can pull it off again. Do we know yet whether this alleged Sara Benay boarded the plane?"

"She did."

Then it really *was* Sara? Cole felt torn between relief she was alive and worry over her possible involvement in his death.

Hamada called, "Are you talking to me?"

Razor grimaced. "Just myself," he called back. "There's no sign of a gun or ammunition so far." He opened another box, whispering, "Dennis called Hamada about it a few minutes ago."

A thought struck Cole. "Did we check to see if she went all the way to Key West?"

"She missed the connecting flight in Chicago."

Relief evaporated. Shit. "Then it could be Irah. She went as far as Chicago and flew back on another airline."

Razor cocked a brow at him. "You realize Chicago's only a few hours from Bloomington by bus or car."

That was a thought, too. If Sara gave her family a convincing story about needing her whereabouts kept secret, they might lie about here being there. "Is Hamada having the Bloomington PD check for her?"

Razor nodded.

But Cole's gut feeling doubted they would find her. The mother had not sounded like someone lying. "I think it was Irah on the plane." His stomach knotted around lead and ice. "I'm afraid she killed Sara. We need to check flights from Chicago to SFO."

"We're not going to talk Hamada into that without probable cause."

The perpetual problem in dealing with the Flaxx clan. "Maybe I can find out if Irah was at the office on Thursday." He turned toward the door. "Catch you later."

"Where and when?"

Cole stopped. "Where will you be in, say…" He checked the clock on bed table. "…two hours?"

"Oh…" Razor opened another box. "…I thought I might talk to Sherrie and tell her what that nurse, Brewer, really saw."

Cole felt his chest tighten. "Thanks, amigo." He hoped she listened. Without Sara, Razor was all he had to speak for him. "You're the best. I'll try to catch you there."

He left through the front windows again, trying not to think about Sherrie. Right now he had other business. The easiest way to find out where Irah was on Thursday might be to ask. But for that he needed to be visible. The sensations from the fire remained vivid...energy pouring into him, his fear for the trapped woman, the driving urgency to make the firefighters see him. What baffled him was how, exactly, that had made him materialize.

To work it out, first he needed heat. If he wanted that to come from internal combustion, he also needed a busy inter-section. Letting cars run through him last night had been exhilarating, but collecting heat from groups of stationary vehicles would be more efficient.

After climbing high enough to go line-of-sight to a street of choice, Cole chose O'Farrell. It not only had busy intersections, its proximity to the Tenderloin gave him test subjects...hotel and store clerks who had seen too much weirdness there to freak out if his first tries were only partially successful.

After checking out several hotels and stores around O'Farrell, Cole found the perfect subject...a clerk in an adult book and video store, whose purple-sheened hair and implants under the skin on her forehead and bridge of her nose made her look like one of Star Trek's aliens. Stepping into the inter-section near the store, he reflected that she would probably be thrilled if someone seemed to beam down in front of her.

Beam down! The words echoed in Cole's head. He lis-tened, stunned. Yes! That explained ziptripping! It was like beaming. Beaming needed coordinates. He must, too...knowing not only what his destination looked like, but *where* it was. He moved forward again, stepping into the motor of a delivery truck, but felt the excitement in his racing mind more than he did the machine gun blasts from the engine cylinders. That explained why he went home and to Burglary so easily. He felt their location while picturing them.

The truck's engine coughed. Cole hurriedly moved to the car in the next lane.

Location also accounted for the Coit Tower and Bay Bridge helping ziptrip to Razor's and Homicide.

The car's engine missed. Cole moved on, zig-zagging between lanes. He shoved aside the excitement over ziptripping, and the urge to check right now whether he finally had it nailed, to think about materialization. Trolling traffic was working well. While not the blast of energy the fire gave him, the little blasts, each more intense than the fire, added up. When he had enough heat energy to try it, he'd better have some idea how to go about it.

Cole replayed memories of the fire while continuing to work his way through the idling vehicles. To his frustration, he remembered nothing except sucking in heat and desperately wanting the firefighters to see him. So much of this ghost stuff was mental. Maybe willing himself visible was all it took once he had plenty of energy. Which felt about now.

He trotted down the block to the porno shop. As he approached the clerk, who stood reading a magazine spread open on the counter, Cole willed himself visible, driving it with a sense of urgency. Visibility had been a life or death situation for the old woman. This time he pictured Irah running away, a distant figure on a vast plain, dragging Sara with her. Whether Sara was alive or dead, he could not tell...just that they were disappearing, and with them, the chance of catching Irah. He needed the clerk so see him. She *had* to see him.

But the sense of weight he felt at the fire never came.

He slapped the counter. Shit. He had the energy...though it was being used up standing here...and he certainly had the desire to be visible. What the hell else did he need for materializing? Some extra mental trick, no doubt...like everything else in this damn ghost business.

Cole thought about that. Maybe it did take a mental trick. For ziptrips he had to picture himself at his destination. Materializing might need something like that, too. Not just the desire to be visible but imagining himself being seen. At the fire, he might have done that and imagined himself through the firefighters' eyes.

Much of the collected energy had dissipated but he might as well try again with what he had left. He built a mental image of himself, feeling almost as if he molded it from the energy in him, and saw the clerk seeing him.

And...yes! He felt heavier. Not as weighty as before but a little beefed-up. "Excuse me."

The clerk looked up from her magazine. "Yeah?" She blinked. It became a puzzled stare. She reached a hand toward him.

However he looked...she *saw* him! "I'm sorry." He shrugged at her, and could not resist saying, "The transporter's having problems today." He slapped his lapel. "Scotty, this isn't working. Beam me back up."

He relaxed, letting the last bit of weight drain away. The clerk's jaw dropped. Grinning, Cole left the store. Not bad. He almost had it on the first try. The next try...

No, he decided...forget another practice run. Go for broke. If Sara was still alive, every minute counted.

Back at the intersection, he waded impatiently through the stopped vehicles, sucking in as much heat as possible by lingering in each engine to the point of stalling it. He did stall a four-cylinder Toyota...yet he kept pushing, trying to stoke up as fast as possible. As he did, he also mentally reviewed his semi-successful materialization for the clerk...and went over the new plan for ziptripping.

Finally Cole felt charged up and ready to roll the dice. Ziptripping to the Flaxx offices had failed before. But he had been thinking just about how the reception area looked, not the office location. If he had this figured out, now the jump ought to work, right? He unrolled a mental map, pinpointed

2EC on it and visualized the Flaxx offices in the tower, including elevation...saw himself there. "Scotty, beam me over."

The intersection blurred...and became Gina Galechas' desk. Cole blew her a kiss. Never had her legs looked better.

He backed out the front door. Now came the roll for all the marbles. He concentrated on the energy in him, in feeling shaped into himself...visualized Gina seeing him. Yes, he needed to be careful about letting people he knew see him walking around apparently alive. That would screw up the investigation. But he doubted anyone was likely to ask Gina when she last saw him. The sense of weight filled him. Quickly, still picturing Gina seeing him...and hoping the magazine in her lap engrossed her so much that she failed to notice that the door never opened...he walked back into the reception area.

Moments too late, he thought of the security camera. Shit! Would he show up on tape? Rear vision spotted some kind of reflection in the doors. Not like Gina and her desk reflected, though...just a misty patch. Then maybe he was safe.

"Good afternoon, Gina."

She looked up, and smiled as though seeing him made her day. It certainly made *his*. "Inspector Dunavan. What can I do for you today?"

"Give me some information, I hope. Can you tell me if Irah Carrasco was here in the office on Thursday?"

She frowned thoughtfully. "You know, I don't know. I don't remember seeing her, but lots of days I don't. She comes early and leaves late, and stays back in her office all day. Like today, I didn't even see her go out for lunch."

Disappointment bit into Cole. He had to find another way to learn whether Irah could have boarded the plane.

"Would you like me to call Miss Carrasco and you can ask her?"

He would love to see her reaction to him...but not around Gina. "It isn't that important. In fact, since she and Mr. Flaxx keep accusing me of harassing them, I'd appreciate it if you don't mention to anyone that I was here."

Gina put a finger across her lips and nodded. She whispered, "Have a nice afternoon."

That went well, Cole reflected with satisfaction, turning away...and he still had enough energy for a clean getaway. Then he realized he had a new problem—leaving while she looked at him.

When he reached the doors, he turned back toward her, then abruptly shifted his gaze to the hallway and leaned sideways, as though looking at something beyond the screening plants. As he hoped, curiosity made Gina swivel her chair and peer through the plants. Cole let go.

Gina turned around. "What did you..." she began, and broke off when she found him gone. After a moment, she went back to her magazine.

Cole headed down the hallway. What were Flaxx and company up to this afternoon? He looked into Bookkeeping first. It looked quiet. Everyone was working at their computers, with Hayes and Quon looking particularly industrious, eyes intent on their monitors whenever Gao glanced back across the room.

Cole circled Lamper's office and passed through the wall behind the desk to peer over Lamper's shoulder. Interesting. Lamper was approving a request for ordering new stock and Cole recognized the store name as one in the Russian Hill area, burglarized last year.

"I take it the store's doing better since its infusion of insurance money?" Cole said.

To his surprise, Lamper glanced around.

Lamper heard him? Cole leaned down to Lamper's other ear. "Now look this direction."

While not turning, Lamper cocked his head for a moment before continuing to type.

Cole backed off. It might be just a whisper, but Lamper heard something. That could be useful. Now if Flaxx and Irah heard, too...

But being *seen* offered more potential for rattling them. After all, as a ghost, his job description started with "haunt." Let

Irah come face to face with her victim. Maybe she would make fatal mistakes.

Continuing down the hallway, Cole eyed Security's door, wishing there were a way to have another look at the security tape and see for certain whether Irah showed up on it. Materializing gave him the ability to walk in and ask to see the tape, but he doubted Farrell would cooperate with Cole Dunavan. The effort of materialization probably ought to be saved for confronting Irah anyway.

Before leaving to collect heat, he checked to be sure she was in her office. She was...sitting at her computer. But not playing games this time. She had gone online to a security system manufacturer's web site. Keeping up-to-date on the latest developments Old Spice needed to watch out for?

What materialization would shake her up the most, Cole wondered. Just walking in and presenting himself as if nothing had happened? Or maybe taking a more spectral approach by coming out of the computer at her. Even better, of course, would be appearing as he most likely looked the last time she saw him...a bloody body with bullet holes in his head. Too bad he could not—

The thought stopped short. What kept him from doing the horror movie bit? He had to create a mental image for materialization. So he should be able to imagine himself in any shape he wanted.

He leaned close to her ear. "Don't go away."

Unlike Lamper, she did not react. On his next visit he would change that.

He looked around the office, feeling its place in the world so he could come straight back here. Then he walked out through the wall and around the corner of the building to where he had a line-of-sight to the Embarcadero. After picking an intersection and taking the feel of it so he could ziptrip back *there* as needed, he began his zig-zag stroll between lanes and stopped vehicles. He *ought* to be able to appear as anything he visualized, but *could* he? There was only one way to find out.

What shape did he want to use?

Judging by the successes in travel and materializations so far, he had to visualize it clearly. That should be no problem with real subjects he knew well. But a bloody body and other apparitions had to come out of his imagination. So he might as well go for something imaginary to see if it was do-able.

Nothing too weird, though. The light changed and he moved over to the halted southbound traffic. It should be something people accepted as real or they might still manage to block him out. Suddenly he knew just the form he wanted …not out of *his* imagination, but believable…and a natural for him.

After several more light changes, Cole crossed his fingers and went line-of-sight to Justin Herman Plaza and on into 4EC's mall. Then in a quiet corner, with no one looking in his direction, he stiffened into a mechanical posture. He concentrated, shaping energy into his target shape. When he felt weight, he checked himself out. And grinned. Yes! He looked covered in metal.

Robocop strode into the mall courtyard.

Around him, heads turned. Some brows went up. He spotted a couple of double takes…also rolled eyes. Again, he noticed that he reflected in store windows as a faint haze.

Even this way, not everyone saw him, he noticed. One woman said to her girlfriend, "What's everyone looking at?" A man's eyes, too, slid past with no indication of registering his presence. But otherwise Robocop appeared successful. Now on to haunting Irah.

Looking around for a spot to inconspicuously pull the plug, he spotted a security guard coming up behind him. Young, husky, a hint of swagger in his stride.

"Hi, there. That's a cool costume." The guard smiled, but above it, his eyes were wary. "It looks just the movie."

Cole smiled back. "Thank you. I built it myself."

"And you're wearing it this afternoon because..?" The friendly tone did not quite hide the edge on the question, nor the direction his eyes drifted...down toward the holster on Cole's hip.

Maybe an armed shape had been a poor choice. Cole kept smiling and stood as relaxed as the Robocop form could manage. "A friend bet I wouldn't have the nerve to walk clear through the mall in it. I stand to win fifty bucks."

"Is that a real Desert Eagle?"

"Nah...just a plastic replica." Cole felt himself starting to run out of steam. Holding his shape was harder than materializing as himself. Worse, another guard, female, strolled toward them. Trying to look casual but no doubt coming in response to the first guard's call for backup.

"It certainly looks real. May I see it?"

Meaning: hand it over. With that being impossible, the time had definitely come to pull the plug. The male guard's eyes had narrowed and his partner eased into a position off to Cole's side, her thumbs hooked over her duty belt near the pepper-spray. He would have to let go of Robocop here in front of them, too, since running for somewhere more private would create a situation that could endanger bystanders. Well, this ought to be interesting.

"Scotty, beam me up." And he let go.

The guards, and bystanders who had been watching them, started, then gaped in disbelief. "What the hell? Where did he go?"

The female guard frowned. "It must have been some kind of projected image."

"No way." The male guard shook his head. "He was as solid and three dimensional as you are...and we talked." He glanced around. "Where would a projection come from?"

Cole left them peering up at the promenade and lobby levels above. However much it bugged them trying to explain what happened, with luck, that was just a taste of how much he could mess with Irah's mind. Grinning in anticipation, he zipped back to the Embarcadero.

— 17 —

THE ANTICIPATION TURNED to frustration back in Irah's office. She had gone. Rather than waste the collection effort, he headed for Flaxx's office. She might be there and he could confront both of them at once. Or if Flaxx was alone, use the opportunity to rat Irah out and tell big brother what little sister had been up to on her own.

As Cole approached Flaxx's door, however, he thought of the security tape and realized that now he had a way to see it. Let the haunting wait a few more minutes. He changed direction for the Security office.

When Cole passed through the door, Farrell had his back to it, sitting relaxed with his hands behind his head while he watched the monitors. In particular, he appeared to be watching the reception area. On the monitor Gina bent over, straightening magazines on a side table, an action that raised her skirt in back, displaying the entire length of her legs. Cole made himself block out the show and concentrated on visualizing himself as Earl Lamper and his voice as Lamper's.

As soon he felt substance, he cleared his throat. "Mr. Farrell."

Farrell jerked upright and whipped his chair around. "Mr. Lamper! I didn't hear you come in."

It worked! And being Lamper felt easier than doing Robocop. Cole gave him one of Lamper's thin smiles, though he felt like pounding Farrell's back in celebration. "I'd like another look at that tape we showed the detectives."

"Yes, sir." Farrell pulled the cassette out of the drawer and pushed it into the TV/VCR. "How much of it?"

"Run it from noon until seven-thirty." That probably gave him a race between the tape and holding on to the materialization, but he needed to be sure Irah had not left earlier than the time period they checked before. Maybe the less he moved, the longer he could last.

Farrell started the tape. Images flickered for a second or two, then disappeared into static, followed by a partial image and more static.

"What the hell?" Farrell's scalp furrowed. "I don't understand. This was fine when I showed it to Miss Carrasco."

Irah! Cole swore silently. "When was that?"

"A couple of hours ago."

Hearing about the tape's existence would have startled Irah. She no doubt expected it to have been thrown away. And wanted it thrown away. If she was not seen leaving, it indicated she had been here to catch Sara and lure Cole to the garage. "Have you been out of the office since then?"

Farrell's tone went anxious. "Just to take a leak and get my lunch from the break room. And I locked the office."

No defense against Irah. She would have seen where Farrell kept the tape, and running a magnet over it enough to mess it up would not take long.

"This isn't your fault. You might as well stop the tape. There's no point trying to watch any more." Which was just as well. He could not hold the materialization much longer. "Still keep the tape, though." Experts might be able to salvage something.

He eased toward the door. While Farrell ejected the tape and returned it to the drawer, Cole said, "Thank you," and let go.

Farrell glanced around, and blinked. "Mr. Lamper?" Then he shrugged and turned back to his monitors.

Cole zipped back to his Embarcadero intersection and stalked angrily through the vehicles. Now he had no proof Irah had stayed late and—

A raucous outburst from gulls pulled his attention upward ...and bringing the clock on the Ferry Building tower into his line of sight. The time! This was about when Razor planned to see Sherrie! For all the time spent at SF General, Cole wondered, did he have enough sense of its location for a ziptrip? He opened his internal map and put a mental finger on the hospital...next to the James Lick Freeway, tucked between the Mission and Potrero Hill...then pictured the ER's location inside the hospital.

The Embarcadero turned into the ER reception desk. Yes! Maybe he finally had ziptripping nailed. Giving the oblivious clerk a thumbs up, he hurried past the desk into the ER.

Finding Sherrie and Razor might take time. They had a choice of places to talk, including outside, if Razor wanted to smoke. Cole had barely started hunting them, however, when he spotted Razor coming out of the nurse's lounge ...alone. Face deadpan, Razor headed for the exit. Cole's stomach knotted. The meeting appeared to be over, and must not have gone well. He angled to intercept Razor and ask what happened.

Before he said a word, Razor muttered, "Outside."

Razor saw him without being prompted? That was real progress. But in the parking lot, Razor did not look at him again until he had lit a cigarette and taken a long drag.

The meeting had not gone at *all* well, Cole reflected bleakly. "It was that bad?"

Razor exhaled. "Well it's sure as hell creeping me out."

Cole's stared at him in dismay. "What *happened* with Sherrie?"

"Sherrie?" Razor blinked. "I'm not talking about her. I'm talking about the other ghosts in there."

Now it was Cole's turn to blink. "You've seen other ghosts?"

"Oh, yeah." Razor took another deep drag. "Not like I do you. They're on the edge of my vision and when I turn to look, they disappear. And I didn't just *see* them. One kept saying a woman's name over and over."

"Why is that worse than seeing me?"

Razor grunted. "How would you like having things come at you in your peripheral vision?"

Okay, that would be unnerving to a cop. "I'm sorry. Were there many?" An ER could be awash in the spirits of the recently departed.

"Any is too many for me, but...." Razor shrugged. "...I guess I saw just four or five."

An idea hit Cole. A way to learn if Sara was alive or not. "Can I talk you into deliberately looking for another one?"

Razor winced. "Where?"

"The 2EC parking garage, for Sara's ghost. I hope you don't see it but if you do...we'll know she's dead."

"Yeah." Razor sighed heavily. "I'll give it a shot." He ground the cigarette out underfoot. "The car's that way."

Once they were in it and headed north, Cole came back to his other concern. "How did things go with Sherrie?"

Razor hesitated. "Well..."

"She didn't believe you about Sara?" Cole's gut felt like lead.

"She wants to, but...come on." Razor sighed. "I'm your good buddy swearing that nothing happened when you played along with a young, leggy blonde hitting on you. She didn't call me a liar but—how did she put it? She can understand how my affection for you both makes me want to protect your reputation and her memories of you." He shook his head. "It isn't like there's evidence to back me up...just my word against what the Brewer woman claims she saw, Sherrie knowing how bad you want Flaxx, and how nervous you acted between meeting Benay and disappearing. Which I have to say, amigo, even makes *me* wonder what happened in her apartment. You never said exactly." He paused. "Not that I don't believe you escaped with your pants still zipped."

Cole told him about Sara stripping down to her butterflies.

Razor sighed. "Now why couldn't that have happened to me? Okay, okay," he said when Cole glared at him. "I understand why you wouldn't want to mention that to Sherrie, but you should have told her *something*...given your version of the story before she heard Benay's."

Cole shook his head. "She'd have known I wasn't telling her everything." And imagined worse than the truth. Like she was doing right now. He grimaced. "I should have just come clean and trusted that my cold sweat would convince her I was being truthful and regretting my stupidity. Her father never sweated, and never regretted, either."

"Ain't hindsight wonderful?" Razor halted for a stoplight. "Anyway, it's going to take more than my word to make your case."

The thought brought a wash of despair. Cole fought it. He would think of something to do. Meanwhile, the idea of making cases reminded him…"I started to take another look at the security tape to check whether it showed Irah leaving for the night."

Razor blinked. "How did you manage that?"

"By materializing as Lamper, only—"

"Materializing as Lamper?" Razor's brows went up. "You can do that? Sweet. There's your answer for Sherrie. Show up as Benay and have a girl-to-girl chat."

Cole considered it for about a second. "No. Even if she can see me materialized, that's like lying to her." Sherrie deserved better than being conned, even when everything he told her was true. "And it wouldn't work if we determine Sara's dead. But I was trying to tell you about the security tape." Now he did.

Listening, Razor grimaced, then shrugged. "Well, it does make Irah look guiltier when we're able to put together a case against her."

If they could do so with evidence destroyed.

A parking space close to where his car had been was too much to hope for, but at least they found one on the same level. Before climbing out, Razor sat with his hand on the door handle. "If I spend the rest of my life seeing dead people, like the kid in that Bruce Willis movie, I'm blaming you, old buddy. How much of the garage are you going to want checked?"

"Just the area where I felt the terror."

Razor sucked in a breath and pushed open the door. "Let's do it."

Cole led the way back through the garage.

Razor said, "By the way, when Hamada and I got to the Hall, we ran into Leach in the elevator."

Shit. "And…?"

Razor gave a wry shrug. "He looked at me for a couple of seconds, then told Hamada, 'I trust you'll make sure Benay doesn't "resist arrest.""

Almost a blessing. Who would have thought?

They turned down the row where he'd parked to meet Sara. The terror washed over him again. "This is the place."

Razor glanced to both sides from the corners of his eyes. Halfway toward the other end he said, "I'm not seeing anything. Are you sure you remember where you parked?"

"Yes. Right down there." He pointed. "Where that VW is now." With his longer legs, Cole reached it first. "Do you see anything down here?"

"Not so far." Razor came toward the VW. "Still no. No." He started past, then abruptly halted. "Wait." He grimaced. "Damn."

A mixture of excitement and dread rose in Cole. "You see something?"

"I thought so, but now it's gone." He walked beyond the next vehicle, turned around, and came back. Behind the VW he halted again…glanced quickly sideways…shook his head. "Shit. There's something near you, but I can't get a good look at it."

Cole turned the direction Razor pointed. He saw nothing. Moving into the space did not change the strength of the fear he sensed. "You can look straight at me. Why not other ghosts?"

Razor shrugged. "Hell, *I* don't know. This one is jerking around and hard to keep in sight but beyond that…you tell me. It's one of your people."

Cole backed over beside the neighboring vehicle, eyeing the space behind the VW. They had something...but was it the source of the terror? And was it Sara? What could they do to see it better? "Keep your eyes straight ahead and walk past the car until the thing comes into sight, then try to look at it without moving your eyes."

Razor started behind the next vehicle...only to move hurriedly aside at the honk of a horn.

"Get out of the road!" A PT Cruiser rolled past, the blue-haired driver glaring out her window at Razor.

Cole flipped her off.

Razor moved over behind the vehicle on the other side of the VW, where he faced approaching cars. Gaze fixed ahead, he eased forward. Halfway past the VW's parking space he halted for a couple of seconds, backed up, frowned, eased forward again and halted once more. After a good portion of a minute, he reached up under his glasses to rub his eyes, then joined Cole beside the neighboring vehicle just as another car passed.

"Well?" Cole said.

Razor smiled wryly. "I feel like I'm in the Twilight Zone. I can't really be standing in a parking garage talking to one ghost and looking for another."

"Did you see Sara?"

The smile vanished. "Maybe."

Cold spread through Cole. "What did you see?"

Razor jammed his hands in his pockets and hunched his shoulders. "A female-ish shape, clawing at its mouth area. I say area because the only detail was the eyes. They were huge, and bulging like they were going to pop out. Like Schwarzenegger's eyes in that movie where he was caught out on the surface of Mars. And there's this muffled scream that's pure terror. 'No, no, please don't.'" He shuddered.

So was it Sara? Cole stared at the space behind the VW, where the trunk of his car had been. It had to be Sara. How could it be anyone else in this location? Certainty of it reverberated in him. Despite no blood being found in his trunk—

Cole felt a click in his head. No blood but bulging, terrified eyes; muffled scream; clawing at the mouth. Now the fear around him seemed to intensify. The cold bit deeper into him. "Could the lower face be blank because something covered the nose and mouth?"

Razor sucked in a breath. "You're thinking suffocation? But why go that route? Irah had a gun."

A much faster way to kill Sara. Unless Irah *wanted* her to suffer and was willing to risk someone hearing Sara thrash as she struggled to breathe. Cole imagined Sara experiencing the terror he had felt, only multiplied by the five or so interminable minutes it took to deplete the oxygen in her blood and her brain finally to shut down. Horror and rage flooded him. "Sara, I'm so sorry! I promise you Irah's going to pay for this!"

"If you can prove she did it," Razor said. "I still don't see a motive for killing either of you."

Cole did not, either. He set his jaw. "We'll ask her when we nail her. Now that I can appear as anything I want, I'll come up with the proof."

Razor eyed him warily. "You're not thinking of some ghost stunt like confession by impersonation, I hope."

Cole stared at him, inspired. "I was thinking of haunting them as Sara's and my dead bodies until they cracked, but you've given me a better idea."

Razor went even more leery. "Like what?"

"How about a whole new level of create-mutual-suspicion-by-telling-each-suspect-the-other-has-rolled-over."

Razor's eyes lighted. "Cute. But do you think it can work?"

"Piece of cake." Cole snapped his fingers.

Razor snorted. "Bull. There's a million things that can go wrong. Is there anything you'd like me to do?"

Nothing that Cole could think of right now. "I'll let you know. Until then, cross your fingers."

They both glanced toward the space imprinted with Sara's dying terror. Razor said, "On both my hands."

— 18 —

RAZOR WAS RIGHT, of course. Pitfalls and obstacles littered the plan. Foremost, he had no control over his subjects' access to each other. Unlike suspects in custody, they were free to communicate and straighten out conflicts and misunderstandings he tried to set up. And anything that betrayed his immateriality—running out of steam and evaporating before one of them, letting them try touching him—would shoot him down. Ditto if the original walked in on one of his impersonations. This needed careful planning.

He knew where to start, though. With Irah. He doubted she would crack easily. But coming eyeball to bloody eyeball with her victims ought to shake her up.

He made a trial run to locate Irah and found her working at her computer. Quickly, Cole sent himself to the Embarcadero…and while collecting heat from the vehicles there, kept his fingers crossed that Irah stayed put.

When he returned to her office, to his relief, she had gone no farther than the shelving, where she stood thumbing through a stack of *Security Management* issues. Cole grinned. Perfect.

Quickly, he moved through the desk and arranged himself in the chair with arms dangling limp, head thrown back with jaw gaping slack and eyes fixed blindly on the ceiling. The right eye anyway. Guessing at the bullet trajectory, he visualized the exit wound as a gaping hole taking out his left eye and surrounding bone, with blood covering his face and running down the side of his head to soak the backrest of her chair. Imagining his body like this felt creepy. He hoped it hit her that way, too.

As he drew on the accumulated heat energy, willing materialization of the bloody body, global vision let him watch her without taking his gaze off the ceiling. The feel of weight came just in time. She pulled one magazine out of the stack and turned around. Cole waited with grim glee for her reaction.

But her attention was fixed on the magazine. She flipped pages on her way back to the desk, never looking up.

He gave a long, quavering moan. "Iraaah…"

She turned a page.

He swore. Shades of that parking attendant. "Irah, you bitch, look at me!"

She neither glanced at him nor broke her stride in coming around the desk. Where, as he sat frozen in disbelief, she dropped into the chair.

The static buzz of their contact shattered Cole's paralysis. "Son of a bitch!" Shuddering with revulsion, he sprang free of her and through the desk.

Behind him, he saw her start, too, then shiver and run her hands down the arms of the chair. After a few moments, though, she shrugged and pulled her chair up to the desk, where she spread the magazine open on her blotter.

Cole swore in dismay. He needed her to see him, not be ghost blind! That meant he had to work everything through Flaxx and Lamper. Were they going to be enough?

He set his jaw. If they saw him, he would make them enough! If they saw him.

He needed more energy to check that out. Before zipping down to the Embarcadero, though, he better make sure Flaxx was there, and absorb the feel of the office's location. And why not take a shortcut there? Considering the suite floor plan, Cole guessed that the wall behind Irah's shelving separated her from Flaxx's private washroom and his built-in bar.

Closing his eyes, Cole walked forward into the shelving and kept going until he estimated he had cleared the washroom. A good guess, he found on opening his eyes. He stood about four feet from the washroom door. But he had done less well staying level. The carpet lay nearly two feet below his shoes.

While looking around, adding the office to his internal map, he stepped back down to the floor. At the same time, he frowned at Flaxx, who sat at the desk reading some papers and looking smug. The expression hit Cole like fingernails scraping a blackboard. What a pleasure it would be to shatter that self-satisfaction. But first Flaxx had to know Cole Dunavan was dead.

Cole eyed Flaxx thoughtfully. The question was how to go about it. Was there a credible way for "Irah" to come in and announce: "Hey, big brother; guess what I've been up to?" To carry off impersonations of these people, the behavior he gave them must be believable.

Flaxx pushed away from the desk headed into the washroom, closing the door behind him.

Cole stared at it, reminded of his fire rescue. The old woman heard him through her own bathroom door before he ever materialized. If Flaxx did, too, then the materializations certainly ought to work on him. And if Flaxx heard him, why not start the show right now? With a psychological flash-bang.

Mind racing, he stepped over to the door and listened. Sweet. He had caught Flaxx with his pants down. He pulled in some room heat to give his voice more substance. "Yo, Donald! How are things moving today?"

Inside, Flaxx called back, "Who's that?"

He heard! Cole grinned. Let the fun begin. He had no trouble putting acid in his voice. "It's Specter Dunavan, asshole. I'm hurt that as long as we've known each other, you don't recognize my voice."

"How the hell did you get in here?" Cole almost heard blood pressure rising. "I'm calling Security."

Excellent. "Yeah, I guess you would have a phone in there. Got to stay in touch 24/7, right?" He listened to Flaxx pick up the receiver. "But you're not as in touch as you think. You need to keep a closer eye on your Asset Manager. Little sister has been up to more than burglary and torching stores in her Kijurian disguise, and more murder than the firefighter's death."

The phone banged into its cradle. That meant he had just seconds before Farrell arrived.

"Thank you, Dunavan. I'm taking those accusations to Citizens Complaints...and you'll be hearing from my lawyers. You're finished...in such deep shit you'll never get out!"

Cole grinned. "Oh, I'm finished all right, but you're the one in deep shit. Irah murdered the bookkeeper, Sara Benay. Suffocated her down in the parking garage. And we can make you an accessory. Have a nice day."

From inside came a satisfyingly shocked gasp, but before Flaxx could respond further, the door of the office crashed open and Antoine Farrell rushed in, followed by Flaxx's secretary.

The two plowed to a halt, eyes scanning the office. Farrell's shaved scalp furrowed. "Where'd he go, Mr. Flaxx?"

Flaxx called back, "What do you mean, where'd he go?"

Farrell came over to the door. "There's no one here."

Flaxx barreled out, still buckling his belt. He stared around. "That's impossible. He was talking to me just a second before I heard you come in." His eyes narrowed as he eyed the office door. "Dunavan must have heard you coming, too, and stepped behind the door when it opened. Then he left while your attention was on this door."

Farrell ran from the office.

Flaxx scowled at Katherine Maldonado. "How did he get in here?"

She stiffened at the accusation in his voice. "I don't know. No one's come past me."

His scowl deepened. "He had to. You must have turned your back."

"But not for more than a moment, not long enough to—"

Flaxx stalked out of the office and up the hallway.

She followed as far as her desk and dropped into her chair with a hiss of exasperation.

Cole trailed along while Flaxx peered into one office after another, asking, "Did any of you see a tall, lanky guy heading toward my office or running away from it?"

Blank looks and head shakes answered him.

When they reached the reception area, they found Farrell there with Gina...who glanced up anxiously toward the security camera. "Have I seen Inspector Dunavan today?"

Cole kicked himself for that materialization. *Good job, numbnuts.* No one was likely to ask her about seeing him, huh? Now he either had a credible witness saying he seemed alive and well, or she lied, as he'd asked her to, and risked losing her job. He was making trouble for one woman after another.

"It's a simple question," Flaxx snapped. "He was in my office. I want to know how he got in."

Gina stiffened. "Not past me, Mr. Flaxx. I would have called you if he tried that. You can see for yourself on the tape."

Cole blew her a kiss. "Great answer." Of course she thought the tape would show him come in and leave.

Flaxx and Farrell headed back down the hallway. Flaxx said, "Yes, check your tapes. Maybe he found a way to come in by the emergency exit. Then save the tape that has him on it so I can use it to file a complaint against him. I'll check back with you in a few minutes."

Flaxx left him and strode back down the hallway. Angling toward the side away from his office door. Did that mean he was headed for the Irah's office? Yes. They turned into the side hall.

Flaxx pushed open the door without knocking and slammed it behind him. "So much for your claims of Dunavan never being a problem again."

She turned from her computer, eyebrows arching. "What do you mean?"

He planted his hands on her desk. "I mean he was just in my office."

"*Dunavan?*" Irah snorted. "That's impossible."

If Cole needed more proof that she'd killed him, the flat certainty in her voice gave it to him. *Now give me something for Hamada.*

"I wish." Flaxx leaned over the desk. "This time he wasn't even bothering to just insinuate things. He accused us outright of the burglaries and arson, and you of murdering what's-her-name, the bookkeeper he was screwing...and claimed I'm an accessory."

She froze for a moment and her heart jumped, then her eyes narrowed. "Dunavan was in your office." *Are you sure,* her tone said.

Big brother should love being doubted, Cole mused.

Flaxx's voice hardened. "I know his voice."

Irah sat up straighter. "Voice. You didn't *see* him?"

"He came in while I was in the washroom," Flaxx snapped. "I had the door closed. He mouthed off at me through it."

"Oh." Irah settled back in her chair. "But you're sure it was him...even though he'd have to get past Gina and Katherine, and Gina has orders to call you when any cop shows up?"

Flaxx flushed. "I'm thinking he found a way in through the emergency exit, and left that way, too. Farrell's checking the tape now."

"I promise you it wasn't Dunavan," Irah said. "So we don't know who we're looking for." She picked up the phone and punched an in-house number. "Antoine, what are you seeing on the security tapes?...Is there *anyone* unknown on them who's left in the last few minutes?...Terrific, but before you run that one, check all your monitors for an intruder. Check the supply room." She waited, drumming her fingers, and a minute later she said, "I see. Well, you keep watching and I'll get back to you." Hanging up, she stood. "Donald, do me a favor. Stand in the doorway and watch for anyone trying to reach the emergency exit. I'll be right back."

Cole followed while she looked into the break room and marched into both the men and women's restrooms and checked each stall. After leaving the men's room, she leaned into the Security office. "Any sign of someone hiding or trying to sneak out?"

Farrell shook his head. "Nope."

She smiled. "I thought not. Thanks. You can relax now. You're not going to see any intruders."

Back at her office, Flaxx still stood in the doorway. "Well?"

"The tapes don't show anyone leaving." She closed the door. "And there's no outsider visible in the suite."

Flaxx frowned. "Then what the hell happened to him?"

She sat down, looking thoughtful. "That's obvious enough. The question is *who* he is. There's one possibility that comes to mind."

"Who!"

Irah shook her head. "I can't imagine why he'd do it, or how he knew...Don't worry," she said as Flaxx's mouth thinned, "once I know for certain, I'll give him to you."

Flaxx eyed her for a few more moments, then grunted. "Make it quick." He turned toward the door.

What a piece of work Irah was, Cole reflected. She had completely sidetracked him from the subject of Sara's murder.

He moved up to Flaxx's ear. Could he make himself seem like an inner voice? "Why should this character accuse Irah of killing that bookkeeper?" he whispered.

Flaxx hesitated just a second before he continued reaching for the doorknob.

But the hesitation indicated he had heard. Cole tried again. "Why is she ignoring that and not denying it? That's suspicious."

Flaxx paused with his hand on the knob.

Cole kept whispering. "Is it possible the guy outside the washroom *wasn't* lying? I have to know. I can't afford more cops digging around if that bookkeeper turns up dead."

The shot hit home. Flaxx wheeled and walked back to the desk. "Why did Dunavan accuse you of killing the bookkeeper? Aren't you upset by that?"

She looked up wide-eyed. "An accusation delivered anonymously through a door? No."

A lie. It did worry her, Cole noted with satisfaction. He heard tension in her voice. Flaxx was relaxing, though. He obviously bought the innocent stare.

Education time, asshole. "Shouldn't she have said she isn't upset because she's not guilty? Damn. She's dodging my question." Cole whispered. "I can't let her get away with that! Let's see how she reacts to hearing how he said she killed the woman."

Flaxx scowled at her. "He said you suffocated the woman in the parking garage."

Irah's pupils dilated and her heart rate jumped. For a split second Cole also saw shock in her face. Then she regained control. Her expression turned mocking. "Suffocated in the garage by Colonel Mustard using the velvet pillow? I can't believe you're buying this guy."

Cole whispered, "Why won't you give me a straight answer? Is what Dunavan said bullshit or the truth...yes or no?"

Flaxx parroted the words, then slapped a hand on the desk and finished on his own. "That woman's linked to this company and if she turns up dead, Dunavan will—"

"He won't do anything," Irah said. "He's history. And Benay isn't going to turn up dead. Trust me."

"Trust you." Flaxx grimaced. "Trusting you has gotten me involved in burglary and arson. I don't want it to be murder, too."

Cole ground his teeth. Shit! If only he could be wearing a wire!

"I don't know why I listened to you."

Her smile was thin as a blade. "Because I offered you a chance to make more money and you love waving profit figures in front of Daddy. I've delivered what I promised, right? So listen to me again. Neither Dunavan nor Benay is going to pop up. I guarantee it."

"How can you be so certain?"

"Never mind. Per your often stated preference, you have results without being bothered about the details of execution."

She drew out the final word, her inflection savoring it.

Flaxx stiffened. He stepped back from the desk, staring at her in disbelief. "Oh my God. You *did* kill the woman."

Irah's eyes measured him for a moment, then she shrugged. "Yes."

Rage hit Cole in an incandescent bolt. A rage fueled in part, he realized, by his own guilt. One word, delivered so casually, as if it meant nothing, had just destroyed the last hope that he might redeem himself by finding Sara still alive somewhere… and indicted him for sacrificing her to his obsession.

He bared his teeth. Now taking down Sara's killer was all he could do for her. "And I will take you down for it, Irah, if it's the last thing I do."

"And as long as you insist on being given knowledge of a capital crime," Irah added, "you might as well know I killed Dunavan, too…also down in the garage." She fired a finger gun at Flaxx.

Cole swore. If only he could be recording this!

Flaxx choked. He stared at Irah in horror…then took a deep breath and asked casually, "What made you decide to do that?"

Despite his apparent calm, the air felt supercharged. Goosebumps ran down Cole's spine. Irah eyed her brother warily.

Before she could answer, he continued, "Did you ever consider…" His voice suddenly hardened. "…first discussing it with *me*?" His fist slammed down on the desk.

Irah jumped. "There wasn't time to ask."

New fury boiled up in Cole. Irah had killed two people, but what upset Flaxx was not having the chance to *approve* it? "You're as twisted as she is." He was going to love working them over!

"But Dunavan's a cop." Flaxx leaned on the desk toward her. "A fucking *cop*."

She gave him wide eyes again. "I didn't have a choice. Dunavan had Benay checking all of Earl's accounts that Gao assigned her and she saw the correlation between Earl taking over accounts and stores being burglarized. And my spy cameras caught—"

"What spy cameras?" Flaxx asked.

Something Cole wanted to know, too.

Irah smiled. "Little self-contained units I planted. They broadcast to a TV type receiver. Installation just takes a ladder and a few minutes. They've been very useful for checking out target stores in setting up the jobs." She settled back in her chair. "I thought we'd be smart to watch whoever worked on Earl's accounts. So when Benay stayed late, I did, too…which is how I caught her leaving a phone message saying she'd found incriminating evidence in the files. After a little scuffle to take away the phone…" She touched the bruise on her cheek. "…I found out she called Dunavan. When I hit Redial, the number offered to connect me to his voice mail."

"Jesus H. Christ." Flaxx straightened, shaking his head in disgust. "So she found something. That's no reason to *kill* anyone. You should have called me. Screwing around with Dunavan makes all that inadmissible in court. Plus we could have bought her off and made things very hot for Dunavan. Maybe lost him his badge."

Exactly what Cole would expect of Flaxx.

Irah sighed. "Unfortunately, by the time I learned what she knew, and about her relationship with Dunavan, there was no way to buy her off at any price."

Cole heard no regret in her voice. But he remembered the fear in Sara's.

Flaxx frowned. "Why not?"

Irah shrugged. "Persuading her to talk got…intense. I had to hold the bitch's head in a toilet until she almost drowned."

Which she enjoyed doing, it sounded like to Cole. Guilt choked him, imagining how Sara must have felt, the panic, tearing at Irah's wrists as she fought to come up for air…panic that was just a prelude to her later terror, when cloth or tape replaced water to suffocate her. Without him, Sara would never have been in that position.

"The toilet!" Flaxx recoiled. "That's disgusting!"

Irah smiled. "Not at all. You know how a sharp deal makes you feel? That's *nothing* compared to the rush of—"

She shook head. "Never mind. The point is she took the dunking personally. I made the mistake of turning my back on her to call you—because I *did* suggest compensation, after explaining why her information would never make it to court— and the bitch grabbed me from behind in a choke hold. 'Let's call the police instead,' she said. 'I'll bet I can take assault and battery to court. And don't even *dream* you can "compensate" me enough to drop the charges. Nothing will give me more pleasure than telling Inspector Dunavan and your insurance companies all about why you attacked me. Don't forget that firefighter's death is considered murder.'"

Cole groaned. He admired Sara's guts...but it would have been smarter to play along with Irah until she got clear. Irah obviously took the situation personally, too. Killing Sara the way she did now sounded like retaliation.

"Breaking the choke hold was no problem, of course, but it did mean roughing her up some more, which only made her attitude shittier. When I took her to your office—"

"My office!" Flaxx stiffened in indignation. "Wasn't it locked?"

Irah rolled her eyes.

He grimaced. "Of course...how stupid of me. You picked the lock."

Not likely, Cole reflected. That took two hands and she had to hang on to Sara. She must have a key. More knowledge she withheld from big brother. Well, well.

"But why take her to my office?"

"Because you have a bar. I needed your Jack Daniels—and don't have a cow; I've already replaced the bottle and you never noticed. I needed to calm her down and slow any attempt at escape while I decided what to do with her. Though of course I told *her* I was getting her drunk so if she tried calling the police after I took her home, they weren't going to believe someone they could practically breathalyze over the phone."

No wonder Sara sounded drunk. And in spite of that, when Irah stepped out of the room for some reason, Sara used the chance to call him again. A gutsy, gutsy lady. A wave of regret joined the anger and guilt in Cole. Too bad he never had the chance to really know her.

"I said that in the morning she'd see it was more profitable to deal with you than the police and court and our lawyers."

Flaxx nodded. "That's reasonable, and she might—"

"No, Donald." Irah spoke in the measured tone of someone explaining to a child. "She'd have done exactly what I would, called the police as soon as she got home, drunk or not. And..." Irah's eyes flashed. "...there's no way in hell that am I going to jail!"

Flaxx eyed her for several seconds, then shook his head. "But why kill Dunavan, too?"

"Let's say it's because he's been a royal pain in the ass! Even though he couldn't use anything Benay found, knowing for sure that evidence was there, he'd find a way to get it. I told you, there's no way I'm going to jail."

Flaxx groaned. "A *cop*. Fuck!"

She shrugged. "It couldn't have gone slicker. He thought he was coming to Benay's rescue. I made sure no one seeing me could identify me later. Between the liquor hitting Benay and her believing I planned to drive her home...as soon as I went back to the office for a minute...it was safe to leave her sitting in my car. I put on some thrift store clothes I keep in my trunk for quick disguises and went and did Dunavan." She fired the finger gun at Flaxx again. "Then I drove my car over by Dunavan's, put Benay in his trunk, and did her. After that, I drove their bodies away...to where..." she finished, with a ta-da spread of her hands, "...they will never be found."

Did him, did Sara. As though, Cole reflected bitterly, she were talking about making phone calls. But the gleam in her eyes and savoring tone in her voice belied the casual words. She enjoyed killing them. Her photographs screamed *adrenaline junkie*. And the rush from murder had to surpass all others. Risk enhanced it...leaving Sara in her car, shooting him without a silencer, taking the chance of someone hearing Sara's agonal struggles in his trunk, not to mention driving across town with a dead body taped upright in the passenger seat.

Flaxx's lips thinned. "Maybe they'll never be found, but the other cops are going to keep digging, looking for him. What's funny?"

Irah bit off her smile. "Nothing. Chill out. We aren't going to be suspects. Dunavan won't have told anyone about Benay. He couldn't afford to if he hoped to use her information in court."

"He damn well talked to *someone*. You said you have an idea who was outside the washroom. Tell me...right now."

She leaned back in her chair. "Be careful what you ask. You might not like the answer."

His lips thinned still more. "I'm not in the mood for fucking games. If you know a name, I want it!"

She hesitated, then sat forward, lacing her hands on top of her desk. "I don't *know*, not for certain. But I do know your joker works here."

"What!" Flaxx scowled at her.

Her brows rose. "How else could he disappear so fast? It's because he's someone we expect to see around. It also has to be someone who knows about the burglaries and Kijurian."

"But that's only—" Flaxx broke off, his eyes narrowing. "You're thinking of Earl? Ridiculous!"

Cole grinned. Things might shake up more than he thought.

Flaxx snorted. "That voice was nothing like his and Earl doesn't take a dump without asking for my approval. I *own* him."

She shrugged. "Maybe arranging to save a nerd's butt and let him hang out with your A-list clique doesn't buy you a worshiper for life after all."

"Arranging!" Flaxx flushed. "I *never*—"

"Oh, of course." She sat back in her chair. "My mistake. Forgive me."

The rescue had been a setup? Cole felt his ears prick. Then it made sense. He filed the information away under "Ammunition."

"Even without our friendship, what I pay him in salary and bonuses earns a *lot* of loyalty."

"Maybe Earl's losing his nerve. He did freak out about the firefighter being killed."

Really. Cole filed that fact away, too.

"But he was in the hospital on Wednesday!" Flaxx said. "There's no way he could know about anything that happened then."

She nodded. "You'd think so. But...who else fits?"

Flaxx's jaw tightened. "Stick up your little spy cameras and find out." He straightened and moved toward the door. "But...when you do learn who it was, you will come and tell me immediately, is that clear? Then *I* will decide what to do about him!"

Irah smiled. "Right. Absolutely."

Once the door closed behind Flaxx, the smile became a grimace. "'*I* will decide what to do about him,'" she said mockingly. Dragging a legal pad on the desk to her, she wrote Lamper's name...circled it...glanced across the room at the surfboard photograph. "It's got to be Earl, lover...but...how? Did Dunavan get to him as well as Benay? Does Earl have a stooge of his own watching me? And *why* would he pull that stunt? What is he figuring to get out of it?" She circled the name one more time and threw down the pen. "If it's him, I expect he'll let us know soon enough."

Cole grinned. This just might work. "Irah, I can't take your twisted ass off the street fast enough but, honey, I certainly appreciate the help you've given the cause here." He blew her a kiss. "Happy paranoia."

— **19** —

WALKING AWAY FROM Irah's office, Cole mulled over
what he wanted to do. Being devious and underhanded was
no problem. Cops were allowed to lie in pursuit of a confession. But he had to avoid anything that would screw up the
eventual prosecution. And of all the possible problems in
execution, nothing was more critical than timing…the time it
took to charge up for materialization, catching each subject at
the right moment. But…he had to gamble, and he did have a
few things going for him. Irah's suspicions of Lamper. Differ-
ences between her and big brother on how to solve business
problems. And he had Earl Lamper.

So let the games begin.

Most of the afternoon had gone, but he still had time for
an opening round that would tell him if he could work on
Lamper. Shuttling back and forth between Lamper and Irah's
offices, he waited for the chance to catch Lamper alone when
Irah was also alone.

To his frustration, Lamper seemed glued to his desk and
computer. But as five o'clock approached and the Bookkeeping staff began closing down their work stations while Lamper
kept working, hope rose. Once they cleared out, he was in
business. But hope died again when he saw that Mrs. Gao and
Kenisha Hayes showed no sign of quitting, either.

Cole scowled at them as the last of the others left. "Damn
it, go home, ladies."

He was considering trying subliminal whispers, when
Lamper shoved back from his desk and walked out of the
department. Cole followed. And cheered silently when
Lamper headed into the men's room…and into a stall. A lucky
break. He should be able to pull this off without materializing.

A quick check on Irah found her alone. Back in the men's room, Lamper remained the only occupant.

Cole leaned up against the stall door at the height of Irah's head, pulled in some room heat, just in case, and imagined his voice as Irah's. "So…had a good day, Earl?"

Stepping up high enough to see over the stall door, he found Lamper frozen on the john. The magnifying effect of Lamper's glasses made him look twice as startled. "Irah?" His hands clapped together over his lap, as though he thought she could see through the door. "What are you doing in here?"

Good. He heard. And the voice was right. Cole ducked back down. "I just wanted a word. Don't let me interrupt you."

"I'll be back in my office in a minute."

"No, this is better." Cole put an edge on his voice. "It's more private."

Another look over the door confirmed that Lamper heard it. His expression went baffled and wary. "What?"

"I never realized that you had any sense of humor but now that I see you do, I have to say your idea of a joke is in poor taste."

Lamper blinked. "What joke?"

"Standing outside Donald's washroom this afternoon…pretending to be Inspector Dunavan and making accusations about me."

"Standing—" Lamper's jaw dropped. "I did no such thing! What accusations?"

"About Wednesday night." Cole turned Irah's voice into a snarl. "About Dunavan and Sara Benay. Who's been talking to you?"

An angry flush rose in Lamper's face. "I don't have any idea what you're talking about. What do you have to do with Dunavan and Sara? Will you please leave? If you want to talk to me, do it in my office."

He was recovering his composure. That needed to change. Cole ducked down. "Don't make me an enemy like…others have, Earl. That would be a big mistake." He backed away to the screen wall and around it. "A *very* big mistake."

Lamper called Irah's name. Moments later, trousers rose from around Lamper's ankles and the toilet flushed. Lamper peered cautiously out of the stall, then into the hallway. Then he beelined for Flaxx's office. Cole followed.

Maldonado had gone and Flaxx's door stood open. Lamper knocked on the frame. "Donald, I'm sorry to bother you. May I come in?"

Flaxx waved him in with a hearty smile. "You're always welcome. You know that." He eyed Lamper. "Is something wrong?"

Perching stiffly on a chair, Lamper licked his lips. "I—I just had a...bizarre encounter with Irah."

Flaxx's smile turned into lipless displeasure as Lamper described the incident.

"She's wrong, Donald." Lamper leaned close to the desk. "I wasn't outside your washroom. I swear. What kind of accusation could there be about her and Inspector Dunavan and Sara? And saying I shouldn't make her an enemy sounded, well, like a threat. Why would she think I'd make her my enemy?"

Cole listened in satisfaction. Lamper's bafflement and concern must reassure Flaxx of Lamper's innocence and his control of his flunky.

The smile came back, even heartier than before...reassuring. "I think Irah was indulging in a little twisted humor of her own. I'll talk to her and straighten it out." He walked Lamper to the door, an arm across his shoulders. "Don't you give it another thought. Worrying won't help your recovery, you know."

Lamper still looked uneasy as he returned to his office. Behind Lamper's back. Flaxx's smile vanished. He stalked down the side hallway toward Irah's office. Cole short-cut through the wall to be there when Flaxx banged in.

Irah stood at her desk pulling sun glasses out of her purse, clearly preparing to leave. Her brows rose. "Barging in without knocking is becoming—"

"What the hell did you think you were you doing!" Flaxx slammed the door closed. "Need I remind you how important

Earl Lamper is to this operation? Where do you get off threatening and upsetting him?"

She set the sun glasses on top of her head. "What are you talking about?"

He folded his arms. "Don't try playing innocent! Did you think he wouldn't come straight and tell me?"

She zipped the purse closed, laid it down, and sat on the edge of the desk. "I wouldn't expect anything else from Earl, but...what did he have to tell this time? You'll have to enlighten me."

Cool and controlled, Cole noted. Her pulse had not changed by a beat.

Flaxx enlightened in terse sentences.

Her eyes narrowed as she listened. Cole watched wheels turn behind them. When Flaxx finished, she shook her head. "That never happened. I haven't left this office since our last chat."

"Can you prove that?"

She glanced toward the door. "Is Katherine still here?"

"No."

"Then I can't prove it. But can Earl prove I was in the men's room?"

Flaxx's nostrils flared. "You think Earl would *lie*...to *me*?"

Cole smiled. *Unthinkable, right? But your opinion of old Earl may have to change.*

Irah said, "Since I never did what he's claiming, what else would you call it? Why he's doing it, I don't know, but it goes along with him being the one outside the washroom. He's definitely up to something."

"No." Flaxx shook his head emphatically. "I could tell he doesn't know anything about the washroom incident or Wednesday night. So lay off him! Have you put up any spy cameras yet?"

"I can't with people in the office."

"Then stick around until everyone's gone. I want you set up *tonight* to start hunting the bastard who *did* pull that stunt." He wheeled and stalked out.

She caught the door to keep it from slamming again. "Nobody knows better than you, Donald, right?" She closed the door. "You want spy cameras, you got 'em. And they're going to prove you're a fool."

Cole grinned. The opening round had scored some hits.

Then he sobered. He needed to pass Irah's admissions on to Razor. And he had Round Two coming up...the first real test of his ability to pull off an impersonation. It would make or break of his game plan. If he screwed up, it went down the tubes, leaving him no way to prove Sara innocent of killing him. And Irah and Flaxx would walk.

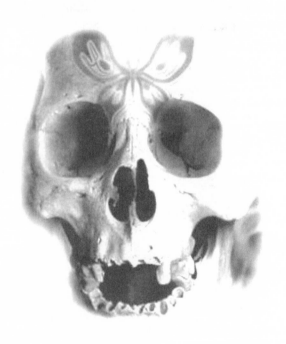

— **20** —

FINDING RAZOR WAS no problem. At six he came on duty at the Central Division Station. Cole just needed to intercept him.

Cole tried for a ziptrip...pinpointing the station on his mental map, concentrating on feeling the location as he pictured it, Vallejo Street outside, and Columbus and Broadway within sight east and south.

The mental image became reality. He stood in the middle of Vallejo. In celebration, he let several vehicles run through him before trotting around to the rear entrance. Minutes later, Razor came toward the door, too. Unfortunately a uniformed officer followed him from the parking area and two more came out the rear entrance.

Razor flicked Cole an acknowledging glance and tipped his head toward the door. Cole followed him inside to the bullpen.

The fax from L.A. lay on Razor's desk. Razor carried it to an interview room and spread it on the table. "It looks like Carrasco had a fair number of buddies." He kept his voice low. "If we had probable cause for getting Irah's phone records, I could cross-reference it with these. Have you come across anything interesting?"

"Oh, yeah...but nothing you can use yet." Cole reported Irah's confession.

Razor swore softly. "This is like standing in front of a candy store with the damn door locked."

"I'm working on the lock." He gave Razor a rundown on all of Round One.

Razor grinned. "That sounds like a good start. It just might work. Now what?"

"I'm off to Round Two."

Or Round One-B, Cole reflected a short time later, after reaching Seacliff via Dunavan Diagonal and line-of-sight. Standing on the arc of Flaxx's driveway, he stared up at the Mediterranean wedding cake...white stucco, red tile roof, arched windows with embellished casings, main floor windows opening onto mini-terrace balconies. He had no idea how freely Earl Lamper visited here. Presumably Flaxx invited him from time to time to maintain the appearance of a friendship, but was Lamper welcome to show up uninvited?

Cole climbed to the front door but before trying the bell— if a TV remote and computer worked for him, the bell should, too—he passed through the door to scope out the house. Without surprise, he found that in the entry hall, Flaxx had gone for the most ostentation he could afford...black and white marble floor, a grand sweep of staircase, an elaborate chandelier hanging from a soaring ceiling.

Cole turned toward the broad arched entrance of the nearest room, then heard voices farther back in the house. The sound led him to the dining room, where he found Flaxx— business suit traded for casual slacks and a turtleneck sweater—eating dinner with his wife and one daughter. The older one attended an exclusive women's college in Virginia, Cole remembered Jessie telling him...the same one her mother had graduated from. Always the one to cut corners, Flaxx had picked a trophy wife for his first marriage...Virginia aristocracy and a reputed descendant of General Robert E. Lee. Though Maitland Flaxx was not his type, Cole admired her classic beauty. She could counter any threat to her marriage from some twenty-something arm candy by making them look like mere glossy plastic. The question, he mused as he turned away, was what Maitland had seen in Flaxx worth marrying.

While Flaxx ate, Cole explored the house. If Lamper knew his way around, a counterfeit Lamper could not afford to stand with no idea where to go. He took time to absorb the feel of location, too...orienting himself for future ziptrips.

Back in the dining room, the meal wore on…nearly silent. What a difference from the mealtime circus at home, he reflected. They always had several conversations crossing each other amid wisecracks and occasional disputes. Tiger sat like a sphinx in the arch between livingroom and dining room, gaze zeroed on Sherrie and him, poised for a "hoover" command that would let him charge in to clean up bits of food Hannah dropped. Cole ached to be there tonight.

But maybe the mood of this dinner came from Flaxx. He wore the frown and inward-focused expression of someone lost in unpleasant thoughts, discouraging chit-chat. Thinking about the conversations with Irah and Lamper this afternoon? Cole hoped so.

A trip out to the kitchen found the cook cutting a cake. He hurried back to the front hall. If they were coming up on dessert, he needed to get ready. After one more glance around to be sure he had his coordinates here, he trotted outside and ran a Dunavan Diagonal to China Beach, where he had a line-of-sight to the Golden Gate Bridge.

Cole grinned. Feast time. Northbound lanes, already clogged with outbound traffic, slowed still more with reduced visibility from fog coming in across the middle of the bridge. Southbound lanes backed up at the toll booths.

Working both north lanes and toll booth traffic, he counted time in his head, trying to estimate when Flaxx would finish dinner. After sucking up heat for as long as he could, not sure how long he might have to maintain the materialization, he finally decided to head back. If Flaxx became involved in something for the evening, he might be impatient with a visitor.

Cole zipped to the front hall and walked on back to the dining room. Empty. So where might Flaxx have gone? He checked the library. Which actually deserved the name, though the tidy shelves and rows of matched bindings suggested some decorator had provided the books, buying them by the yard.

Pay dirt. Flaxx stood at a section of bookcase that had been turned into a liquor cabinet, pouring himself a glass of Jack Daniels. He carried his drink to one of the big leather chairs that faced each other in front of the fireplace, sat down, and took a cigar from a humidor on the side table.

Watching Flaxx clip off the cigar's end in a miniature guillotine beside the humidor, Cole frowned. Even if Flaxx heard the doorbell, he would expect the maid to answer it. Was there a way to make Flaxx answer it? The fewer witnesses to the materializations, the less chance of including someone who was ghost blind, but *no* witnesses meant no corroboration for these encounters.

Flaxx picked up a big silver-cased lighter beside the humidor and flicked it on. Cole closed his hand over the flame. It snuffed out. Flaxx flicked it on again, and again, Cole killed it. After three more tries, and growing more irritated with each failure, Flaxx slapped the lighter back on the table and jerked open a drawer. Pocket-sized boxes of matches lay inside. Flaxx struck a match from one of them.

After three matches failed to stay lit, he tried matches from a second box, and then from the third.

"Son of a bitch!"

He stalked out of the library and turned down the hall. Maybe headed for the kitchen in hope of finding a match there that worked.

Cole raced out through the front door and put his finger through the doorbell button. When the bell sounded inside, he concentrated on shaping himself into Lamper. Now if only he had not irritated Flaxx *too* much.

A frowning Flaxx jerked the door open. The frown turned into astonishment. "Earl? What are you doing here?"

So he looked believable. And Flaxx's tone answered Cole's question about Lamper showing up uninvited. That would be no. So he needed to explain this behavior.

"I...I'm sorry." Cole hunched his shoulders as he had seen Lamper do. "But I need to talk to you."

"Why didn't you just call...or wait until morning?" Irritation ran under the polite tone.

Cole licked his lips. "Well...it—it just seemed like something I ought to talk to you about right away, in person and not on the phone." He paused as though gathering himself, then blurted, "Irah called me at home."

Flaxx eyed him a moment, then stepped aside. "Come on in."

Cole backed against the balustrade. "I won't take long. I'm fine out here." Safe from meeting Maitland or the daughter.

Flaxx forced a smile. "Whatever you like." He clamped the unlit cigar between his teeth and sat down on the top step. "Now, what about Irah's call?"

Cole sat down at the far end of the step, where he ran no danger of Flaxx touching him. "It didn't make sense. She said that pretending innocence and whining to you about her coming after me in the men's room wasn't going to save me. She said you both believe I pulled that stunt outside the washroom ...because it couldn't be anyone else...and now you think I'm scheming against you." He leaned toward Flaxx. "Donald, you don't believe that, do you? You know this company is my life, the way it's yours."

Flaxx, listening deadpan, chewed on the cigar for a moment before replying. "I know how loyal you are."

"And then she talked about how since I have knowledge of..." He lowered his voice. "...of certainly burglaries and fires—that's why I didn't want to say anything on the phone—I'd better not be losing my nerve. That it's so easy for someone to disappear and never be seen again." He hunched his shoulders. "That sounded threatening again."

The real Lamper could not have heard Flaxx swear under his breath, but Cole did. Aloud, Flaxx used a reassuring tone. "Relax." He stood up. "I'll put a stop to it. I won't let her do anything to you."

Remembering the arm across the shoulders at the office, Cole moved down a step as he stood. "Thank you. You've always taken good care of me."

Flaxx looked past him at the drive and street. "I don't see a cab. Don't tell me you came over by bus."

Oops. He'd forgotten about transportation for Lamper. The bus trip would have been a long one, with several transfers. Cole shook his head. "I took a cab. But I'll catch the bus back. The stop isn't too far from here." Even as he said it he winced inwardly. Right, a man who had abdominal surgery a week ago was willing to walk two or three blocks to a bus stop.

Flaxx stared at him. "That's ridiculous. I'll call you a cab."

There was no way to maintain the materialization even long enough for the cab to arrive. "No, really, that isn't necessary. I've been recovering very fast. The doctor said mild exercise is good." He headed down the steps.

Flaxx frowned after him until he reached the bottom, then wheeled and went inside.

Cole let go of Lamper and raced after Flaxx.

Inside, Flaxx headed to the library and the cordless phone on the desk. After punching in a number, he carried the receiver to the side table and picked up his drink.

An answering machine clicked on at the other end. A voice that sounded like Jack Nicholson said, "*You have reached the Carrasco residence. We're unavailable at the moment so you'll have to leave a message. If your call is urgent, don't have a cow. Try our cell phone.*"

It was a great imitation, Cole mused. Since Irah did not give the cell phone number, presumably anyone who mattered was supposed to know it already.

Flaxx did. He punched in another number without looking it up...took a swallow of his drink while it rang.

This time Irah herself answered...shouting to be audible above juke box music and a roar of voices.

Flaxx wasted no time on pleasantries. "I thought I told you to leave Earl alone!"

In the pause before she answered, Cole pictured Irah's brows lifting. He expected her to ask for an explanation. Instead, she said, "All this yelling can't be good for your blood pressure."

A male voice close to her said, "I hope that isn't a husband or boyfriend."

"No, just my brother."

"Who's that?" Flaxx demanded.

"Oh…a gorgeous motor officer who's offering to let me play with his throttle and ride his machine."

Motor officer! Ice shot through Cole. Could she be out to repeat the thrill of cop killing? "Where are you?" Cole whispered in Flaxx's ear.

"Are you at the same cop bar you were before!"

Shit. Not the question he wanted Flaxx to ask. He needed more than a yes or no answer.

"What is it with you…threatening Earl again, then playing with cops! Are you *trying*—"

Irah broke in. "Wait! Let me go somewhere I can hear you better. Guys, if you'll let me out, please. Oooh, is that your backup weapon? Don't lose it. I'll be right back."

The quality of the sounds coming through the phone changed shortly, reducing to quieter street noises. None of them distinctive enough to pinpoint the bar's location.

"That's better," Irah said. "First of all, playing with cops is as much business as pleasure. I've learned that a certain detective's car has been found…with his blood type in it…and the number one suspect is our own Sara Benay. A lover's quarrel gone bad. So sad. Now…" Her voice sharpened. "What's this about threatening Earl again?"

Flaxx reported the visit. While he did, he picked up the lighter and flicked it…shook his head irritably as it worked…lit the cigar.

"That's a flat out lie," she said when he finished. "I came here from the office about five-thirty, which Officer Mazzucco can verify, if you want me to put him on."

Mazzucco. The name rang no bells.

"And I certainly wouldn't have called Earl while sitting in the booth with Mazzucco and his buddies."

Flaxx chewed the cigar. "You could have done what you're doing now, step outside for a minute."

"But I didn't." Cole heard her breath hiss. "Look, Earl's lying... just like he's lying about the men's room incident."

Flaxx scowled. "*You* look. Earl has no reason to—"

"No *apparent* one, maybe, but...something's going on. Why else would he come to your place, out of the blue, to tell you something it would be a hell of a lot more convenient, and easier on him, to call you about?"

"He explained that he wanted to avoid mentioning certain business strategies on the phone."

"When you were just able to do so without naming them?"

Flaxx's expression went uncertain.

Cole eyed him with satisfaction. *Are we starting to wonder about good dog Earl?* He hoped so.

"You still there? Maybe considering that worms do turn?"

Cole grinned. Very good. He leaned close to Flaxx's ear. "She might have a point."

Flaxx stiffened. "Not Earl!"

Was it arrogance, or stubbornness, refusing to believe he might be losing control of Lamper?

"So keep away from him! Is that clear!"

As Flaxx broke the connection, Cole pictured Irah mockingly mimicking her brother's words. Damn! Where was she? "If she kills another cop, I'm holding you responsible."

Frowning, Flaxx returned the phone to its base station.

Cole wished he could read Flaxx's thoughts. But maybe he could add something more to think about. He moved up to Flaxx's ear again. "She's crazy. Earl turning on me? Impossible. Still, it won't hurt to keep an eye on him. For damn sure I need to watch Irah. Did she even bother listening to me just now? She's never listened to anyone...except maybe her precious Scott. Maybe I better call her back and find out exactly where she is, to make sure she isn't on her way right now to confront Earl again."

But to Cole's frustration, this time Flaxx gave no sign of hearing. He turned away from the phone and threw himself in a chair, where he finished his cigar and drink, then shaking his head like someone trying to clear away fog, left the library.

Cole stared after him, thinking about Irah. Was it possible she might confront Lamper? In her place, he would be upset at being lied about twice. Going after Lamper would certainly help *his* cause. And mean that the motor cop was safe.

Lamper's address put him in Potrero. Cole ziptripped to the nearest location there he knew, San Francisco General, then worked his way to Lamper's house. Staring up the steps from the street, he appreciated being a ghost. Any living person climbing those needed to be part mountain goat, and carry oxygen.

Inside, the house surprised him, yet seemed right for Lamper...a mixture of art deco and oriental, almost monastic in its simplicity and tidiness. Judging by the classic Eames chair, though, no expense had been spared on individual pieces. Or on his hobby. Cole counted eighteen chess sets on the glass shelves of a large art deco étagère. And Lamper obviously did more than look at them. The top shelf of the étagère displayed numerous chess trophies with dates ranging back to when he would have been in high school.

Cole found Lamper by himself in the one lighted room in the house, a spare bedroom turned into an office, where a custom desk stretched along most of one wall to accommodate two computers and their peripherals. A chess board graphic filled the monitor of one computer. Lamper, now wearing a Mr. Rogers cardigan over his turtleneck, gripped the mouse. Whether he played against the machine or someone online, Cole could not tell...but he saw that Lamper had more on his mind than the game. His eyes kept wandering from the monitor to a cordless phone lying beside it. Was he waiting for a call or debating calling someone? Whichever it was affected Lamper's concentration. After agonizing over a move, he made it, then groaned almost immediately...and groaned again at the answering move.

The phone warbled. Lamper jumped. He reached for it, then hesitated. The phone rang a second time, then a third, while Lamper's hand hovered over it.

Then as it started to ring a fourth time, he snatched it up. "Hello? Oh, hello, Inspector."

Inspector? Cole moved closer.

On the other end Hamada's voice said, "You left a message saying you have a question?"

Well, well. Cole's ears pricked. Interesting.

Lamper took a breath. "Yes. Have you located Miss Benay yet?"

"I'm afraid not."

"Inspector Dunavan doesn't know where she is?"

Hamada's voice remained even. "No. Have you thought of something that might help us?"

Wheels turned visibly behind the magnified eyes. Cole held his mental breath. Could Lamper be about to say something connecting Sara to Irah?

To his disappointment, Lamper shook his head. "I'm sorry, no. I just—I just wanted to see if you'd learned anything. It worries me that she'd go off and not tell someone where she is...Kenisha Hayes, at least. You—you don't suppose something's ...happened to her?"

Great question, Earl. Thank you. He had hoped the men's room conversation would start Lamper thinking about darker possibilities in Sara's disappearance.

Hamada paused before answering. "We have no evidence of that."

Lamper sighed. "That's a relief. Thank you for calling back."

Cole pictured Hamada hanging up the phone and thinking that Lamper knew something he was not ready to talk about yet. At this end, now would be a perfect time for Irah to show up and wipe out that relief by dropping more dark hints about Sara. Perfect as long as the real Irah did not arrive or call.

He checked the time on the computer. It had been nearly half an hour since Flaxx talked to Irah. Cole decided that if she made no move in this direction by the time he could materialize, he would risk it.

After walking out onto Lamper's front porch and orienting it on his internal map, he zipped to the Embarcadero intersection he used this afternoon. It should still have enough traffic to let him accumulate the heat he needed in a reasonable time.

It did, and since Lamper's place was a new destination, he crossed his fingers before ziptripping there. But it worked without a hitch.

Now the question was whether Irah had made contact in the meantime. In the office, the chess board remained on the one monitor, but Lamper had moved to the other computer, typing e-mail. Nothing in his expression or body language showed distress that might be attributable to a call from Irah. Great.

Cole returned to the porch and prepared to materialize and hit the door bell. Then rear vision caught a Mustang GT cruising by in the street below.

His antenna shot up. Not just because of the car's suspiciously slow speed. The vehicle itself rang a bell. Scott Carrasco's funeral urn was a model Mustang GT...and Irah had a photograph of that model and color car on her shrine wall.

He zipped line-of-sight to the street ahead of the car, where he could check out the driver as the car passed him. Irah sat behind the wheel...wearing a black turtleneck and with her hair covered by a black watch cap. Cole leaped to the roof of the car and slid down through it into the passenger seat to study her. She also wore black running tights, the thin-soled shoes of rock climbers, and a black fanny pack. He smiled. This looked very interesting.

It became even more so. She drove around the block and parked one street over from Lamper's. Cole followed as she slipped between two houses there and over the back fence into Lamper's postage stamp yard.

Did she intend to burgle Lamper? He grinned. Perfect! Once she was inside, he would head for the Bayview Station. Materialized as Joe Citizen, he could report that a friend he was just talking to on his cell phone saw someone breaking into a house. They would catch Irah in the act. With her under arrest for burglary, they would have probable cause for searching her house and car. Razor needed to be alerted so he could be on hand to recognize the Kijurian clothing and the items they found in the makeup table as evidence of another crime.

Except…the house had evidence of only arson and burglary. Even if they found the tweaker clothing and Elvis mask in her car, only Razor would recognize them as evidence, and he had no way to explain that knowledge. Nor did the presence of a Glock in her gun safe—assuming they were allowed to open the safe and find such a weapon—give them grounds to compare bullets from it to the one that killed him.

Angrily he abandoned the idea of having her arrested at Lamper's place. If she walked on the murders, what good was nailing her for burglary and arson? Nothing else mattered if Sara went without justice.

But maybe he could still make use of the burglary.

— 21 —

LAMPER WAS CLEARLY visible between the vertical blinds of the office window, pausing frequently as he typed. Irah must see him, too, but she still tried the French doors opening onto the patio. Standing close behind, Cole heard her heart racing. When the handle failed to turn, she pulled a mini flashlight from her fanny pack and shone it around the door casing. Either that revealed something or she believed the security system notice on the door, because she backed away. She also ignored an unlighted window that probably opened into the kitchen. Instead, she moved along the house in the other direction, crouching to pass below the office window.

Her target had to be a small horizontal window high up near the eaves, the only other one on this side of the house. Experience had taught Cole that because of the height and size, homeowners with such windows could be careless about locking them. She must know that, too. But how did she intend to reach the window?

Irah bent her knees, then leaped upward in a spring that would have done credit to an NBA player going for a slam dunk. The fingers of one hand hooked on the sill. The slope and narrowness of the sill made it look impossible to grip, but Irah hung on. With toes braced against the side of the house, she even raised up enough to push at the window with her other hand. Playing the odds worked. The window pivoted inward. She reached over the sill to clamp that hand on the inside, followed it with the other, and worked both sideways until they were hard against the vertical jamb. Then, spider-like, she walked her feet sideways up the house until she could slide a leg over the sill. The other leg quickly followed and she eeled her way backward through the window.

Cole ducked under her through the wall and watched her drop soundlessly into the tiled shower stall. From jump to landing, breaking in had taken no more than thirty seconds. He wondered whether she took up rock climbing to train for burglary or at some point had seen the other applications of those skills.

The bathroom door stood open. A click of computer keys came up the hallway. After pausing to peer out before leaving the bathroom, she padded silently toward the livingroom. The sound of the computer stopped. Just short of the door, Irah crouched with her head nearly to the carpet. Fishing a dental mirror from the fanny pack, she extended it past the door jamb. Inside the room, Lamper sat staring thoughtfully at the ceiling.

How did she plan to pass the door? No matter how deep in thought Lamper was, motion in his peripheral vision was going to attract his attention.

Irah made no attempt to pass, however...just continued crouching, watching the mirror. When, eventually, Lamper turned his back to the door for a moment, she exploded into action. In a second she had rolled past the opening. Using momentum to carry her onto her feet again, she slipped on to the livingroom. Behind her, typing resumed.

The mirror went back in the fanny pack as she glanced around. Cole guessed that the light coming in through the front window from the porch and up the hall from the study, faint as it was, let her see well enough. The ètagére caught her attention immediately. She headed straight for it. The mini light came out and its pinpoint beam moved from one trophy inscription to another.

All right...time to spoil all Irah's stealth. Now he was happy for her ghost blindness. He coughed loudly.

The click of computer keys stopped. Irah's heart rate jumped and she held her breath. But she also kept reading trophy inscriptions. Computer keys resumed clicking...stopped again...resumed once more. Irah let out her breath, though her heart rate remained high. Cole trotted to the study door to see if there were any indications Lamper had heard him.

Lamper had. He stared at the door. He tapped a few keys, then broke off and sat with his head tilted, listening...tapped a few more keys...listened again.

Cole stepped over to him and leaned down to his ear. "Did I hear something? I ought to get up and take a look."

But if Lamper heard, that action did not appeal to him. He stayed put.

Cole returned to the livingroom. He found Irah taking trophies off the shelf and setting them on the floor. Moving quickly. She had the trophy shelf almost cleared. What did they have here, one of Old Spice's signature displays? Proof she *was* Old Spice. Sweet. *Don't forget to take a souvenir.*

He coughed again...as loud as he could this time. Then he raced to the study to see Lamper's reaction, and prod him some more if necessary.

The door slammed in Cole's face. Passing through it, he also found himself passing through Lamper, who stood inside pressing the lock on the doorknob with one hand while punching 911 on the phone in his other hand...so tense he did not even react to the walk-through.

Cole snarled at him. "No, damn it! Don't call the police! I just want a confrontation between you and Irah."

Lamper said into the phone, "There's someone in my house. I hear him in my livingroom."

This might still work if he acted fast. Cole dived back through the door and willed his voice into Irah's. "Don't have a cow, Earl," he called. "I'm just making a little social call."

The door jerked open. As it did, however, Cole saw that Irah had disappeared from the livingroom. Damn. He ran up the hall, reaching the bathroom in time to see her feet disappear out the window. Ducking through the wall, he found her somersaulting, catlike, in mid-air, and landing on her feet. She sprinted for the back fence. In seconds she was through the adjoining yard and between houses, back on the street where she parked.

There, between one stride and the next, she pulled off the watch cap and went from a dead run to strolling. As casual as though finishing a leisurely evening walk, Irah sauntered to the Mustang, started it, and drove away at a decorous speed.

Cole raced back to the house. Lamper had the livingroom lights on now and stood staring at the trophies on the carpet. He still held the phone. "No, it won't be necessary to send an officer. Whoever it was is gone."

Lamper began returning the trophies to their shelf. As he did, Cole saw that one had lost the chess piece topping it. Only bare threads remained, where the figure screwed on. Lamper saw, too. Dropping to his knees, he peered under the étagère and nearby furniture.

Cole leaned down to him. "It isn't here. Irah took it."

Lamper sat up on his knees. He reached for the vandalized trophy, frowning. "Damn her," he muttered.

For future reference, Cole wanted to see exactly what Irah took, and where she put it. He left Lamper fingering the bare threads and called up the image of Irah's place, feeling its relationship to Spreckles Lake. Lamper's front room morphed into Irah's bedroom.

Now he had to wait for her, hoping she came straight home. He used the time to double-check the evidence in the armoire and makeup table, then look over the contents of the curio cabinet again. But he still found nothing on the shelves that he identified as his or Sara's.

He drummed his fingers on the glass. "Come on, Irah. Get home."

Finally he heard a garage door rumble up, then down. An interior door opened. A minute later, near-soundless footsteps raced up the stairs and Irah whirled into the room, flushed, eyes glittering. She saluted the shrine wall. "I wish you could have been there, lover. Whooo!" She grinned. "What a squeaker...out by the skin of my teeth!"

Cole bared his teeth. "What a rush, right?"

She unclipped the fanny pack and toed off her shoes. "But I didn't leave empty-handed. I found an interesting fact for Donald to chew over in the morning and of course..." She dug in the fanny pack and held up the metal figure of a rook. "...a new keepsake."

Hefting it in her hand, she crossed to her desk and rolled open the top. From a drawer at the back, she pulled out a key to unlock the curio cabinet. Then, humming, she stood at the open door rolling the rook back and forth in her hand while she contemplated the shelves. Presently she leaned down to a lower shelf and set the rook next to the jumping horse figure.

After giving the rook a pat on its crenellated top, she straightened, skipping her fingers up the shelves as she did so...and pausing occasionally to fondle an object. Her hum gave way to a dreamy smile.

Anger flared in Cole. "Remembering the fun we had collecting those, are we?" Each of those objects represented people left feeling violated...and never able to feel safe at home again.

With his anger, though, came a spark of hope. Killing Sara and him had to rank tops on her "fun" scale. Would she go to the objects that let her relive the experience?

She took a small carved red lacquered box from the top shelf and stood turning it over in her hands, her fingers tracing the carving. Could it be Sara's?

Probably not, he decided as he realized she was pressing on parts of the carving. It was a puzzle box and must be hers if she knew how to open it. But puzzle boxes could hide things. Maybe something she could not afford to leave in plain sight? Hope jumping in him, Cole watched her hands intently, memorizing the movements.

After another minute of pressing here and sliding a piece of carving there, a drawer slid out the side. Irah pulled out a cloisonne butterfly pendant. A pendant that he remembered from Bon Vivre, dangling into Sara's cleavage.

Cole bared his teeth. "Gotcha!" But triumph gave way to anger and revulsion at the near ecstasy in Irah's expression. "You really enjoyed shoving Sara's head into that toilet, didn't you? Or are you remembering the *big* fun...seeing the terror in her eyes down in the garage, when she was fighting to breathe but realized she was going to die!"

Though he had never been a hothead, Cole knew that if he were able to touch Irah right now, he would be fighting the urge to beat the shit out of her. That would be way too easy on her. To give Sara justice, Irah had to be booked, jailed, tried, and convicted…with every twisted detail laid out in the newspapers and court for public viewing. And for whatever comfort his and Sara's families could take from it.

After letting the butterfly swing on its chain for a minute, Irah hung the chain on the top of cabinet door and pulled the drawer out farther. A feeling like a deep sigh of contentment spread through Cole. Oh, yes…this was definitely a *gotcha*! Inside lay an inspector's star with his number on it.

Razor had to know about this!

He shot back to the Central Station. Only to find Razor out.

Rather than try to locate him, Cole waited for the chance to use a computer. In this division, the machines in the holding cell area never stayed idle for long, he knew, so he tried to work fast, keeping the message short: *Razor: sis has a souvenir from me! specter.*

He barely finished before an officer headed toward him. Hopefully the officer would pass the message on to Razor, but rather than wait through where-did-this-come-from-what's-it-about, he went back to work. He had suspicion, paranoia, and nightmares to create.

First stop, a quick jog to the Columbus/Broadway intersection to suck up heat, then a ziptrip to Lamper's house again.

He found Lamper at the microwave in his kitchen, removing a large mug with the tag of a tea bag hanging over the side. Cole waited while he discarded the tea bag and carried the mug out to the livingroom. A book lay open on the ottoman of the Eames chair. Lamper sat down but did not pick up the book. Nor did he more than sip the tea before setting the mug on a side table. He glanced at front door, then at the front windows—which had the drapes closed now—and past his table and chairs to the French doors. Clearly on edge.

Cole smiled. Good. Opportunity knocked.

He backed into the hallway and visualized himself as Irah. Then stepped out into the livingroom.

Lamper's start lifted him almost out of the chair. Continuing the motion, he stood the rest of the way. "I don't know how you got in here this time since I locked the bathroom window, but you could have come to the front door."

Cole shook his head. "That would have been too easy."

Lamper's mouth thinned. "At least you got my message."

Message? Cole remembered the phone ringing while he waited for Irah. Her machine answered it somewhere downstairs, but he had not bothered trying to hear the message the caller left.

"I don't know why you took that piece of my trophy, but I'll thank you to return it." Lamper held out his hand.

Cole kept smiling. "I prefer to keep it."

Lamper's lips thinned still more. "I'd hoped to straighten this out without going to Donald."

"Good idea." Cole put knife edges on the words. "He's already annoyed about you whining to him about me. And you don't want to piss me off, too. I've already warned you that's a bad idea. That's why I'm keeping your trophy piece, to remind you not to screw with me."

Lamper flushed. "Don't threaten me. Donald won't stand for it. And since you're not going to return the rook, I don't know why you bothered coming back. Get out."

He had more nerve than Cole had expected. Too angry to be intimidated, or that much belief in Flaxx?

Belief in Flaxx, Cole decided. Changing that was going to take some work. Or maybe, it occurred to him, change it was the last thing he wanted. His mind raced. He could use the loyalty against them.

Was it possible to change shapes in the middle of a materialization? How much energy would that use? Only one way to find out.

"Irah didn't come back," he said. "You fell asleep there in your chair and this is a dream." He visualized himself...and with downward vision watched himself morph.

Lamper's jaw dropped.

Cole said, "Why don't you sit down and make yourself comfortable. Because I have things to say. This is a cautionary dream."

Questions leaped in his eyes, but Lamper seemed unable to make his voice work. He dropped into the chair.

Cole sat on a virtual chair facing him. The morph used a chunk of energy. He needed to move as little as possible now. "Yes, cautionary dream. Today was very upsetting, so your subconscious has cooked up this dream to sort things out. Because Dunavan's a cop, he's being used as the voice of order and warnings. Irah represents disorder. You're on the money there. She's lethal."

Lamper blinked. "Lethal!"

"Yes." Cole leaned toward Lamper. "Burglaries and setting fires aren't enough of a thrill for her anymore. She's moved on to murder."

"Murder?" Lamper's expression went skeptical. "That's—"

"Ridiculous? No. Your subconscious wouldn't be talking like this if you didn't suspect something like that." He paused. "She killed that firefighter."

He stiffened. "That was terrible, but...it was an accident."

"In the eyes of the law it's murder. And you know there's more. The remarks she's made about people disappearing have you worried that there's a connection to Sara dropping out of sight. That's what made you call Hamada, even though you wouldn't tell him. Or maybe you don't realize it consciously. Listen. You need to pay attention to your gut feeling. For some reason she wants Donald to mistrust you. *She* could have been there outside the washroom. You know what a good mimic she is. What if her plan is working?"

Lamper came up stiffly in the chair. "No. Donald wouldn't—"

"Can't you sense the danger?" Cole pulled in room heat. "Aren't you feeling a little cold?"

For answer, Lamper shivered.

"Don't forget that despite all the years you and Donald have been buddies, Irah is family. She has influence. She talked him into the burglaries and arson, remember."

Cole debated saying something to the effect of Flaxx being less a buddy than Lamper thought, and revealing the truth about the "rescue" in high school. No, he needed to wrap this up quickly and save that news for a better time.

"He should never have listened to her." Lamper huddled in the chair. "We were doing just fine without her ideas...and it wasn't illegal. At least he listened to me and stopped the fires."

"But he does listen to her, and she's whispering poison in his ears about you." Cole let go of the materialization except for his voice. "From now on, watch your back."

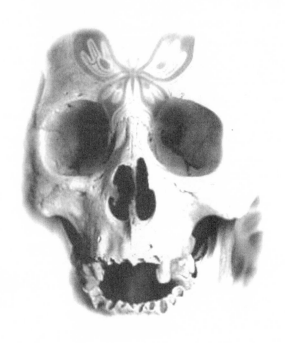

— 22 —

THE BIG WORRY about working on Flaxx was Maitland Flaxx. To pass himself off as Flaxx's dream, he had to keep her from seeing him. His earlier exploration of the house showed him that Flaxx and his wife had separate bedrooms, but those connected through a large bathroom and presumably they slept together at least once in a while. Cole hoped not tonight.

Luckily, no, not tonight. His ziptrip to the house found Maitland asleep in her bed and Flaxx looking over a spread sheet at a desk in his room. But yawning as he did so. They had both doors into the bathroom closed. Good enough.

Cole charged up at the Golden Gate Bridge, then zipped back to Flaxx's bedroom. The yawns had given way to nodding over the spreadsheet. Cole grinned. Now he could use the apparition that had failed with Irah. He carefully visualized a big exit wound, a bloody gaping hole in place of his left eye and a chunk of forehead, then materialized and ran his fingers across the back of Flaxx's neck. "Hey...wake up, asshole."

Flaxx jerked awake. And recoiled, scrambling backward out of the chair and up against the wall behind it. "Jesus!"

"No, you prick." Cole walked through the chair and within inches of Flaxx's cringing face. "I'm what's left of Dunavan after Irah put a bullet through my head."

Flaxx squeezed his eyes shut. "This can't be happening. I'm dreaming."

"Of course you are."

Flaxx hesitantly opened his eyes again.

Cole backed off to the edge of the desk. "That's the only way what's left of your conscience has a chance to express itself. So take a look at what you've done. This is me...and this is how Sara Benay looked the last minutes of her life."

He had planned the image, accurate or not, while charging up. Now he morphed into it...Sara's figure upright but with her wrists behind her and bound in clear package sealing tape; ankles bound, too; the shirt the shooter wore folded up and taped tight over her nose and mouth; her eyes bulging in terror above it.

Flaxx recoiled again. "I didn't kill her...or you!"

The phantom gag did not interfere with talking. "But you're willing to let Irah get away with it. Which is really stupid." Cole put a sneer in his voice. "She likes killing. It's a rush. Couldn't you tell when she told you about it? Who knows who'll end up in her sights next? It could even be...you." And with that, he let go.

Flaxx stared at the space where he had been...glanced around and looked astonished at finding himself standing, then shook his head. "Crazy dream." He headed for the bathroom.

Cole smiled grimly. "That's just the beginning, too."

Flaxx had climbed into bed and fallen asleep while Cole charged up again. No problem. Cole materialized on the far side of the bed as Lamper in his Mr. Rogers sweater, but glowing brightly in the dark. "Donald? Donald!"

Flaxx roused, blinking. "What the hell..."

"I'm sorry to disturb you." Cole waded into the middle of the bed. "But you said I'm always welcome and..." He ran his hands back through his hair. "...I'm too upset to sleep. I've been worrying and worrying, trying to understand why Irah is accusing me of pulling that stunt outside your washroom. And then...I had this thought." He paced on out of the bed on Flaxx's side, then back into the middle. "I guess it's actually your thought since this is your dream, but maybe she's accusing me to distract you from remembering what a good mimic she is and that she's the one person who could know what happened Wednesday night."

Flaxx blinked irritably at him. "You think it was Irah? What possible reason would she have for the stunt?"

Cole shrugged. "I don't know. You're right. What personal agenda could she have?" He backed out of the bed and visualized himself fading…until by the final words of his last sentence, only Lamper's voice remained, plaintive, apologetic. "I'll go. I'm sorry to have disturbed you."

Flaxx fell back against the pillow, shaking his head. A minute or so later he rolled over on his side and closed his eyes.

Cole charged up again and zipped back to materialize as Lamper again, standing at the foot of the bed. "Donald! I'm sorry to disturb you."

"Not again," Flaxx groaned.

"But I've been worrying and worrying, trying to understand what's happening. We had a good thing going that wasn't supposed to hurt anyone except the insurance companies, but now…"

Flaxx grimaced and closed his eyes. Thinking to escape this dream? No way.

Cole waded up the middle of the bed almost to the pillows. "Donald, you know I'll do anything for you, but…I knew Sara. I liked her. I don't know if I can live with murder."

That brought Flaxx sitting upright, alarm in his face, dream or not. "Earl, get a grip. I didn't want it but it happened. You just keep cool. I'll get us through this."

Cole shook his head. "Not without doing something about Irah. She's out of control, acting on her own. She can destroy us."

Flaxx's voice went soothing. "Don't worry. I'll handle her."

Oh, great opening. Cole concentrated and abruptly morphed into Irah, sitting cross-legged on the bed. "You'll handle me, will you?" He laughed. "Just try. But I'm not the one you need to watch out for, brother dear. Earl's the weak sister. If anyone's going to bring us down, it'll be him. Say the word and—or on second thought, maybe I should just go ahead and waste him preemptively. I can make it look like an accident."

"Irah…" Flaxx began in alarm.

But Cole let go.

Flaxx rubbed his face, heaving a deep sigh. "Enough is enough." He swung out of bed and padded to the bathroom.

Following, Cole watched him take a medicine bottle out of a drawer. He read the label over Flaxx's shoulder. So Flaxx thought a sleeping pill would end the dreams, did he?

"The problem with those, Flaxx, is they don't really put you to sleep. They just relax you so you can fall asleep. I don't intend to let you relax."

But he had made the points he needed to. Now he just wanted to reinforce them...and give Flaxx the most miserable night of his life—until Flaxx's first night in jail anyway—to put him in a good mood for tomorrow.

Charging up took longer as the streets quieted, but to keep the sessions as brief as possible, Cole settled for collecting less heat and making each of the night's succession of materializations brief. Just enough to interrupt Flaxx's sleep again. Deciding he might as well have fun at it, Cole made it a parade of monsters from the movies the kids and Sherrie loved: Robocop, the Creature from the Black Lagoon, Wolfman, Dracula, Freddie from Elm Street, the alien from the *Predator* movies, the alien from the *Alien* movies, a scythe-carrying figure of Death, a seven-foot version of Godzilla, and not least, the Mummy, with Sara's eyes...all interspersed with appearances by himself—the exit wound in his face increasingly larger and more hideous until he had no face. Everyone muttered warnings about Irah's homicidal tendencies and Earl Lamper's failing nerve.

At breakfast in the morning, Maitland stared across the table at Flaxx in concern. "Donald, are you ill? You look terrible."

Flaxx grunted. "Thank you very much for the encouragement. I *feel* terrible...like I didn't get any sleep." He reached for coffee. "I had stupid dreams all night."

Cole nodded in satisfaction and went in search of Razor.

— 23 —

EENIE, MEENIE, MEINIE, mo…where to go? Cole tried Razor's apartment first. And was rewarded by the sound of running water. He headed for the bathroom, where steam rolled out over the shower curtain.

He leaned against the counter. "Did you get my message?"

On the other side of the shower curtain, Razor chuckled. "Oh, yeah. And you had the whole Central Station scratching their heads over this mysterious Specter. Because as usual, no one was near the computer when the message appeared." He paused. "So what did she take?"

Cole told him about Lamper's rook first, then the puzzle box.

The water went off. Jerking back the shower curtain, Razor reached for a towel. "Christ, this is driving me nuts. Knowing the where, how, and who of yours and Sara's murders and where to find what evidence…with nothing I can do about it!" He dried himself with a vigor that threatened to peel off his skin. "I can't get near the evidence. I can't even tell anyone because there's no way I should be able to know about it." He yawned. "And I'm OD'ing on caffeine to stay on my feet so I can hang out with Hamada. Going without sleep is harder than it used to be." He yawned again. "So how did the night go?"

Cole gave him a rundown.

During the recitation, Razor dressed and filled a travel mug with coffee. "I think dying has found an untapped sadist in you. You're really getting into this haunting business."

Cole considered. Tormenting Flaxx *had* been a pleasure. "It has its moments. Now I'll go ruin their day."

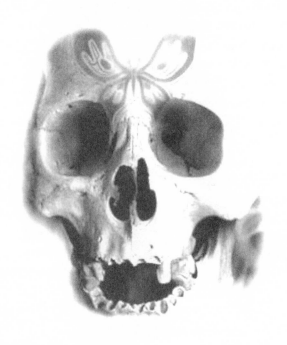

— 24 —

NOT KNOWING WHICH people were going to arrive when, what opportunities he would have for working on everyone, or how much time he would have for zipping out to recharge along the way, Cole worked traffic on the Embarcadero three times longer than he had before. Fortunately, there seemed no limit to how much heat he could pull in. How long he could store it remained to be seen.

From the intersection, he zipped to the Flaxx reception area to wait...using as little energy as possible and hoping it was going to be a short wait.

He had his wish. Irah arrived in minutes. From his seat against Gina's desk, Cole watched her lean down to unlock the doors. And he watched the appreciation on the face of Antoine Farrell coming up behind her. The skirt of her suit today was short enough to rival any Gina wore. She spotted Farrell but made no attempt to pull her skirt down behind, apparently unconcerned about how much underwear she might be showing off.

"Have a good day, Antoine," she said as they came in and, leaving him in the reception area, headed down the hallway.

Cole wanted to catch Lamper coming in, but after a moment of debate, followed Irah. Behind him, Farrell grinned as he uncapped the coffee he had brought with him and murmured, "It's starting pretty good."

Irah headed to her office, where she dumped her shoulder bag in a desk drawer, then pulled a little portable TV from the file drawer in the desk. The receiver for her spy cameras? She confirmed that by turning it on and running through the channels. Each one showed an overhead view of an office. Lamper's he expected, but seeing Flaxx's surprised him.

So she was spying on big brother, too. Sweet. He would make sure Flaxx knew. The cameras had to be eliminated since it would be bad if she caught Flaxx and Lamper talking to thin air. But the cameras gave him good ammunition again her and ratting Irah out would be such a pleasure.

Returning up front, he found Farrell sitting at Gina's desk. Probably he did that every morning until Gina came in, so the doors could remain unlocked for arriving employees. While Farrell sipped his coffee, Cole studied him, memorizing his appearance from all angles. Now, if Gina would just arrive before Lamper, so Farrell would be out of sight in the Security office.

No such luck. Lamper walked in with Farrell still watching the doors. To Cole's satisfaction, Lamper showed strain around his eyes and wore a preoccupied expression. He barely nodded to Farrell as he came through the reception area.

Cole followed him. He would just have to go ahead and do this. When Lamper unlocked Bookkeeping's door and went in, Cole materialized as Farrell. "Mr. Lamper, excuse me."

Lamper turned in surprise. "Yes?"

Cole lowered his voice. "I need to tell you about something I saw in Miss Carrasco's office yesterday when I carried some stuff there for her."

Lamper frowned. "What was that?"

"Promise you won't say anything to her. She'll know where you heard it and I don't want her for an enemy." His conscience did not need Farrell suffering for this impersonation.

Lamper's frown went wary. "What did you see?"

"Well...she had this little portable TV on her desk, and...your office was showing on it."

Lamper sent a startled glance toward his office. "My office?"

Cole edged closer and lowered his voice still more. "I don't know why, but she's got a spy camera in there."

Lamper's eyes widened. "Really," he said in a flat voice. "Thank you for telling me."

"What are you going to do about it?"

"Nothing." Lamper gave him a thin smile. "I have nothing to hide."

Walking out and letting go, Cole grimaced. That was a surprise. He had expected...hoped for...outrage that would sent Lamper storming to Flaxx. He had to do a better job of reading Flaxx and Irah if he wanted to pull this off.

And he'd better read Flaxx correctly right now, he saw, looking up toward the reception area. Flaxx had just walked in. But Gina had not arrived and Farrell still manned the reception desk.

Cole took stock of the energy in himself. Did he still have enough to go again? Maybe.

He let Flaxx almost reach his office door before materializing behind him as Farrell again. "Mr. Flaxx, can I talk to you?"

Flaxx turned, frowning. "Shouldn't you be up front?"

His mood had not improved since breakfast. Excellent. "Do you know there's a spy camera in your office?"

Flaxx stiffened. "What!"

Cole gave him the same story he had Lamper, repeating the plea not to give away who revealed about the camera. "I thought at first maybe you set it up in case that motherfucker from yesterday comes back, but it's aimed at your desk, not the office door or washroom, and Miss Carrasco acted like she didn't want me to see. So I thought I'd better tell you."

Flaxx scowled down the side hall. "You did the right thing." The next moment he was stalking toward Irah's office.

Cole let go of Farrell and followed.

Flaxx cranked the knob and looked shocked when it failed to turn. He pounded the door. "Irah! I want to talk to you!"

Seconds later she opened the door and eyed him. "Something wrong?"

He pushed past her into the room and wheeled on her. "Where the *hell* do you get off putting one of your damn spy cameras in *my* office!"

Her brows rose. She closed the door. "A camera in your office?"

He reddened. "Don't play innocent! I want it *out!*"

She smiled. "Then it's gone."

Cole blinked. What? Instant capitulation?

It astonished Flaxx, too, deflating him. His mouth opened and hung there.

"I'll be right there. Let me get a ladder from the custodian's closet."

Five minutes later she was up on the ladder unhooking the grid over the lights. "You know, I'm just following your orders, looking for whoever was outside the washroom yesterday."

"By spying on *me?*" But the indignation lacked the force of his earlier outburst.

"To learn what Earl is up to." She picked at tape securing the tiny camera in the light fixture. "You trust him too much. I planted cameras on both of you so I could monitor the bullshit he's feeding you."

Talk about bullshit. Despite how busy her hands looked, suspicion scratched at Cole. Climbing up beside her on a virtual ladder confirmed his doubts. She was only pretending to remove the camera. No wonder she agreed to Flaxx's demand so readily. In a movement hidden from Flaxx, behind and below her, she fished another tiny camera from the breast pocket of her suit jacket and palmed it.

After snapping the grid back in place and backing down the ladder, she waved the palmed camera in front of Flaxx's face. "Here. Okay? You want to have a happy face for the store manager meetings today."

If not happy, he looked at least mollified…unaware that he had been conned.

Cole noticed Irah did not ask if Flaxx wanted her to remove the one in Lamper's office. He noticed Flaxx never mentioned it either.

That left cameras still in both offices. Damn. Well, he would just have to work around them.

Then he realized he could also *use* them.

Irah hauled the ladder away. Cole followed her. After returning the ladder to the custodian's closet, she settled into her office and as he hoped, switched on her spy monitor.

The Lamper channel showed him talking to Mrs. Gao.

Irah switched to the Flaxx channel. He scowled across his desk at Maldonado. "My wife's already told me that. I had a rough night. Make my coffee strong today."

Now would be a perfect time for a materialization that made use of Irah's spying. He needed an energy charge first, though, and before he could zip to his intersection of choice, Irah was already switching channels to watch Lamper. How often did she switch back and forth?

A short wait told him that she focused most on Lamper, which was to be expected. But she did periodically check Flaxx. He could work with that, he decided, and zipped to the Embarcadero.

From the Embarcadero he came back to Irah's office, where he waited until she switched channels to Flaxx. Flaxx sat with his chin propped on one hand as he looked down at a brochure spread open on his desk. A bobble suggested the hand was holding up his head.

Quickly, Cole ran through Irah's office wall and the washroom to the door of Flaxx's office. He materialized as Irah. "Donald."

Flaxx looked up, scowling. "Try knocking before you come in."

Last night had really dented the urbane facade. "Are you this grumpy just over that camera?" Cole sat down across the desk from him, hoping Irah was still watching. "I told you I put it in to help you."

"Without bothering to ask first." Flaxx's mouth tightened. "But then, you're not bothering to ask about much of anything lately, are you? I think that gives me the right to be grumpy, as you put it. You may be my sister but..." He sat forward and stabbed a finger down on his desk. "...I own this company and you're an employee. If you can't remember that,

I'll fire your ass out of here just as fast as I would anyone else! Now what do you want."

Please let Irah be catching this. "To ask if you know Earl plays chess."

Flaxx grunted. "Of course I know Earl plays chess. Every time he won a trophy he'd come around waving the thing like a dog showing off a new toy. So what?"

Cole tented his fingers. "So...chess uses strategy and mind games." He paused, hoping to provoke a response that would let Irah follow the conversation.

"What of it?"

Not a helpful response. "Chess strategy doesn't necessarily focus on the next move. It may be more concerned with the next five or six moves. So the current move may not make sense. It may even involve a sacrifice. But it sets you up for a checkmate. I'm thinking it's occurred to good old Earl that between you thinking he's indispensable and what he's learned about events in the past week, he's in a position to better his position here...maybe demand to be made a partner."

Flaxx stared at him in exasperation for several moments, then reached for his phone. "Earl, will you please come to my office right away for a meeting with Irah and me?"

Shit. Cole's mind raced. He did not want Irah seeing both men talking to someone invisible to her. He needed out of this. He widened his eyes and stared past Flaxx out the window.

As he hoped, Flaxx swivelled his chair to see what was outside the window.

Cole let go of everything except Irah's voice. "I need to run to my office." And he still had energy to spare.

Flaxx turned. "Irah, don't—" His blink of disbelief turned to a sigh of exasperation. He started to stand but sat back down when the door opened and Lamper came in. "Earl." He produced a mechanical smile. "Have a seat."

Lamper sat on the edge of the chair, peering anxiously at him. "What's up?"

From the doorway, Irah said, "That's what I'd like to know."

Good, she came. Cole relaxed, and felt even better seeing the calculation in her eyes as she looked Flaxx over. After she sat down, he stood to the side where he could watch all three faces, keeping motionless to hang onto the spare energy.

Flaxx leaned against the desk in front of them. He sighed...a sound carrying weariness and sadness. A sigh intended to portray him as a burdened man? "Earl, Irah...we have a problem. Ever since the washroom incident yesterday each of you have been coming to me with suspicions and accusations of the other. But..." He paused as though searching for words. "...that's counter-productive. We have nothing to gain and everything to lose by turning on each other. So let's bring everything in the open and clear the air so we can get back to business."

Ah. Cole's lip curled. This was a pep rally. *Rah, rah go team.*

Lamper seemed to agree with the idea. He nodded at every sentence. Irah crossed her legs, folded her hands together in her lap, and eyed the others appraisingly.

Flaxx started to cross his arms over his chest, then must have decided that made his body language wrong. Instead, he slid his hands into his jacket pockets, thumbs hooked outside. "And the first problem we need to resolve is your belief, Irah, that Earl was outside the washroom."

"I swear I wasn't," Lamper said.

Flaxx nodded. "I believe you. If for no other reason than whoever it was had knowledge of...certain events that you don't."

"How do you know he doesn't?" Irah said. "And who else could it have been?"

"Well..." Now Flaxx folded his arms. "There's you."

Cole smiled. So last night's visit had planted at least one seed.

Irah arched her brows. "Really."

Lamper straightened, looking thoughtful. Remembering that coming up in *his* "dream" last night?

"You're familiar with the event mentioned and you're a great mimic," Flaxx said.

"But with no reason to pull such a stunt." She remained unruffled.

But Flaxx smirked as though he had scored points on her. "Earl doesn't have one either. So...I don't want any more men's room confrontations or accusing phone calls to him at home."

The beginnings of a grateful gleam in Lamper's eyes turned to bafflement. "Phone calls? She hasn't called me at home."

The smirk vanished. Flaxx frowned. "What the hell? When you showed up on my doorstep last night you said—"

Lamper gaped at him. "What are you talking about?"

Now it was Flaxx's turn to stare, his expression equal parts astonishment, disbelief, and anger. "You mean you deny coming to my house last night?"

If Lamper had been a dog, Cole reflected, he would have been cringing, ears and head down, tail tucked tight between his legs. "Donald...I—I was home all evening. I never left."

Irah peered at him, then at Flaxx. Cole wished he could read minds, because while her face went deadpan, a gleam in her eyes said her brain had gone into overdrive.

"Ask Irah if I wasn't sitting at the computer when she sneaked into my house."

While Irah's brain cooked on all cylinders, Cole gleefully watched Flaxx's trip and fall flat. Gears screamed almost audibly as he floundered through shifting. The Mister Rogers theme parodied itself in Cole's head. *It's a beautiful mess in the neighborhood...*

Flaxx almost sputtered. "Irah, you—"

"I wasn't going to say anything," Lamper said, "but you said get everything in the open...and I want back the rook she stole off my trophy."

Irah arched her brows. "What makes you think *I* was there?"

Lamper's mouth thinned. "Besides the fact that you came back later and admitted you had the rook? I recognized your voice through my computer room door. 'Don't have a cow,

Earl,' you said. 'I'm just making a social call.'" He looked up at Flaxx. "But when I opened the door, she'd gone. Just like you and your washroom, Donald."

Flaxx frowned thoughtfully at Irah.

She was eyeing Lamper and her baby blues had turned to ice. She opened her mouth to say something.

But Flaxx cut her off. "I don't give a shit if you were there or not or took a piece of trophy."

Lamper stiffened.

A glare from Flaxx deflated him. "I don't even give a shit who was outside the washroom...unless you can tell me, Irah, that it was someone outside of us three."

"No," she said.

"Then I just want all this crap *stopped*!" Flaxx glared at both Irah and Lamper. "We have a business to run. A *profitable* business...if we keep our minds on it. Let's make money, not war. Remember the old line about hanging together or hanging separately? Remember it! Now, let's get back to work."

Rah rah, go team go.

The two of them started to stand.

Flaxx pointed at Irah. "I need you to stay a few more minutes...to go over details of the manager's meetings."

Her brows rose but she settled back in her chair.

If the request surprised her, Cole wanted to know what Flaxx really had to say. He leaned against the desk to wait.

After Flaxx walked Lamper out, he closed the door. "I don't understand why Earl denies he came over last night. If it *is* like chess strategy, the way you were saying earlier, I don't see where it can possibly go."

"The way *I*—" Irah's eyes narrowed speculatively. "Tell me. How many people saw Earl at your place?"

Flaxx looked surprised by the question. "Just me. I happened to answer the door. Why?"

"Oh, I was thinking that it might be worth asking anyone else who talked to him what their impression was of his demeanor."

The frown deepened. "No one else talked to him. It wasn't a social occasion. *Did* you break into Earl's place last night?"

She hesitated a moment, then shrugged. "I wanted to look around…see if there was anything that might tell me what he's up to it. I didn't. But I was there just once. I didn't go back."

Cole hurried out and up the hallway to Bookkeeping. With her away from monitoring her spy cameras, this was a good time to work on Lamper. But it had to be a brief materialization.

After making sure no one was looking his direction, he materialized in the doorway as Irah. Eyes turned briefly his direction, but none with the start of someone registering the fact that he'd appeared out of nowhere. He stepped into Lamper's office.

Lamper eyed him warily. "Yes?"

Cole gave Irah's face a conciliatory smile. "I owe you an apology. I was wrong about you and the washroom." And he was wrong about how much energy he had. He gritted his teeth to hang on to the materialization.

Lamper's expression went skeptical. "You changed your mind in a hurry."

"I had the truth thrust on me. Meet me out by the elevators in fifteen minutes and I'll explain."

Of course Lamper wanted to know. That showed in his face. So did suspicion. "Why not tell me here, now?"

Cole thought fast. "You're in a fish bowl." He tipped his head toward the office windows. How much longer before Irah returned to her office? "And I don't want to risk being overheard."

"*You're* the one with—" Lamper caught himself just in time.

Cole smiled inwardly. *Good thing I'm not Irah; you slipped there, Earl.* He edged toward the door. "Meet me. You need to hear this."

After a moment of hesitation, his expression still suspicious, Lamper nodded.

As soon as he made it to the hallway, Cole let go and zipped to the Embarcadero.

Watching the clock on the Ferry Building tower, he worked through traffic the whole fifteen minutes. The materialization might not need this much energy, but he wanted to be sure he had enough.

From a ziptrip back to the reception area, he walked around to the elevators…checked to be sure he was alone, and materialized as Irah. Now if only Lamper were prompt.

He was…coming out of the office doors just seconds later.

"So who was outside the washroom that's going to shock me so much?" Lamper asked. Still skeptical, Cole noticed…and looking around as if he thought this was some kind of trap.

The elevator doors opened, letting off a couple who stood studying the floor directory.

Cole strolled down the corridor away from them and the Flaxx offices and lowered his voice. "The person outside the washroom was the same one Donald talked to at home last night. If you're telling the truth about not going to the house—"

"I am!"

"Then he hallucinated you being there. I think he hallucinated the washroom thing, too." Might the real Irah be wondering the same thing?

Lamper gaped at him. "Hallucinated! That's ridiculous." He wheeled away.

"Who did he talk to, then?" Cole said. "You know it wasn't you. It wasn't me. I'm good at voices and disguises, but I'd have to be a shape-shifter to pull off that visit last night."

Lamper halted and slowly came back. "Maybe he made up the story to see how you'd react…thinking you'd incriminate yourself about the washroom."

Cole arched his brows. "Did he look like someone making up a story? He *believes* you were there. And that isn't his only conversation with someone who wasn't there. When he came in this morning, I saw him standing by his office seeming to be talking to Farrell…only Farrell was at the reception desk the whole time."

"So you say." Lamper's frown clearly said he did not believe a word.

"Ask Farrell if he followed Donald back from the reception desk. I think Donald's cracking up."

Lamper snorted. "Bullshit!"

Cole heaved a deep sigh. "I'm afraid not. He's—" He pretended to struggle internally, then lowered his voice almost to a whisper. "Wednesday evening I got a frantic call from him asking me to come in, that there'd been an accident. When I got here Benay was lying dead on his office floor."

Lamper choked. "What!"

"It seems he came back to the office a little after eight for something and saw Benay working late, and he noticed, maybe for the first time, that she's attractive, and invited her into his office for a coffee break. During chit-chatting she flirted with him and one thing led to another and—"

"With Donald?" Lamper said in disbelief.

"Why not with Donald? He isn't so obsessed with making money that he's forgotten he's a man." Cole smirked. "A little sexual conquest now and then is good for the ego. And Benay liked entertaining alpha males." *Sorry for the cheap shot, Sara. But…it's true, isn't it?* "Only Donald got overeager and tore her blouse. That apparently killed the fun and made her mad, because she started fighting him. The next thing he knew she'd tripped and hit her head on the corner of the desk and stopped breathing."

The shock in Lamper's face faded. His mouth went grim. "Why call you? Why not his lawyer? It was an accident."

Cole nodded. "That's what I told him…but he was in a screaming panic and wouldn't listen. He just kept saying, 'Do something. Get rid of her.' Because of her torn clothes and bruises, he didn't think the police would believe it was an accident, and he was afraid how Miss Mint Julep would react." Having no idea of Maitland's views on sexcapades, Cole happily assigned her one. "Boys can be boys but they're supposed to keep their affairs out of the headlines."

"So you were the loyal sister and took away the body."

Cole grinned inwardly in satisfaction at the acid tone. "Wouldn't you have helped if he called you?"

For a moment Lamper hesitated, then nodded. "Of course...*if* something like that happened."

"If? Think about it. Doesn't that explain her not telling someone where she was going? *I* left that message for Gao, so people wouldn't miss her. Sometime this week I'm going to leave another message, quitting her job."

The beginnings of belief flickered in his eyes. But that should not last long.

Cole lowered his voice still more. "Unfortunately the trouble didn't stop with Benay. We'd taken the body down to my car on a dolly, folded up in a toilet paper carton from the supply room, and were about to cram the box in my trunk when who drives in but *Dunavan*. Of all the fucking bad luck!" He shook his head. "I suppose he and Benay were going to meet. He spotted us and when he'd parked, he came over and made a wisecrack about us hauling away incriminating records. He reached out like he was going to open the box. Donald went white. I didn't realize he'd picked up the folding shovel I keep in my trunk. The next thing I know, he's swung it like an axe, straight down on Dunavan's head. It killed him instantly."

Lamper's eyes ballooned behind his glasses.

"God, the blood!" Cole shuddered. "And Donald totally *lost* it! I had to slap him to snap him out of it before someone came to investigate the noise, and so he could help me put both bodies in Dunavan's trunk."

Lamper's belief snuffed out. "Bullshit." His jaw set. "I don't know why you're trying to feed me this crap, but I don't believe a word of it! Donald is cracking up?" He snorted. "Ridiculous. He's been acting perfectly normal."

Cole frowned at him. "You realize if he falls apart, he'll take us down with him. And no way in hell am I going to jail. I think we need to head off trouble. The two of us can run things without Donald if necessary."

Lamper went stone-faced. "Is that what this is about? I won't help you steal this company."

Cole narrowed his eyes. "True-blue Earl. Donald doesn't deserve so much loyalty, you know. That rescue in high school? It was a setup so he could use your gratitude to write papers for him and—"

"That's a *lie!*" Lamper's eyes flashed.

Cole shrugged. "Okay…stay blind if you want. Just don't get in my way."

He could hold the materialization a little longer, but this felt like the place to quit. He walked away. Around a corner and out of Lamper's sight, he let go. And hoped that this time he had played Lamper right.

— 25 —

LAMPER RETURNED TO his office, his forehead furrowed in the expression of someone holding a troubling mental debate. Lamper eyed his phone from the office doorway for a long minute before closing the door and picking it up. He punched an outside number.

"Hello, Maitland," Lamper said. "This is Earl Lamper."

Cole sidled close enough to hear the other end of the conversation.

"Why, good morning, Earl. What can I do for you?"

"This may sound like a strange question, but...did Donald come back here to the office last Wednesday evening?"

Cole hoped Lamper was just making sure Irah's story could not be true.

Maitland laughed. "I'm sure he wished he had. I dragged him to an evening of Stravinsky at the Civic Center. Why do you ask?"

"Oh...I'm just straightening out some questions about computer access times."

That satisfied her. And hanging up, Lamper wore a satisfied expression. But that lasted only a minute. Then he began looking even more troubled.

Cole cheered him on. *Worry, Earl, worry.*

After more indecisive hovering over the phone buttons, he punched Flaxx's extension number.

Flaxx answered. "Yes?" A terse greeting that was followed by a noticeably impatient sigh when Lamper announced himself. "What do you need? I have a group of store managers arriving here any minute."

On his end on the phone, Lamper grimaced in apology. "I'm sorry to bother you, but...Irah was just talking to me and—"

Flaxx's tone sharpened. "Just now?"

"Yes. She had me meet her out by the elevators. And I have to warn you." Lamper dropped his voice to a whisper. "She—she tried to convince me that you killed Sara Benay and Inspector Dunavan."

"What!"

"That's ridiculous of course. But what concerns me is she went on to say—"

"You say you were talking to Irah out by the elevator just now?"

Cole frowned. The phrasing sounded as though Flaxx wanted someone else to know what Lamper was saying.

He raced down to Flaxx's office…and found Flaxx gazing across his office at the conference table…where Irah was placing brochures and stapled pages in front of each chair. The bar stood open, with a coffee urn and box of pastries on the counter.

Flaxx's jaw tightened. "Thank you for telling—…Wait, Earl. I don't have time to hear the details now." Hanging up, he caught Irah's eye. "How long did it take you to bring that security upgrade information from your office?"

She considered. "Maybe three minutes."

Did that mean she had been here the rest of the time? Cole grimaced. He had expected her to go back to her office, not hang around where she had an alibi for the chat with Lamper. But maybe damaging Lamper's credibility was just as useful. He welcomed anything that created mutual suspicion.

Irah smiled at her brother. "If you think I saw Earl in that time, it would have been a meeting faster than a two-dollar whore's blow job."

Flaxx eyed the phone. "Is your spy camera still in Earl's office?"

"Yes." She drew the word out, eyeing him.

He frowned. "It doesn't make sense that Earl would lie to me, but with him denying that visit last night…I want you to watch him for me. Tell me what he says and does."

"You got it."

Cole grinned. *It's even more mess in the neighborhood.*

She carried unused brochures and papers to his desk. "These are for the group this afternoon."

Cole walked back to Lamper's office. The way Lamper's gaze kept wandering from the computer monitor suggested he was having trouble concentrating.

From behind the monitor, leaning his forearms on top of it, Cole frowned down at him. What now? Make another appearance as Irah, delivering more blatant threats? Except Lamper might know Irah was in this morning's meeting. So far, no one had realized individuals were in two places at once, but he could not expect that luck to last.

Suddenly that thought connected with two others: Lamper's blind loyalty and the managers' meetings. The click of interlocking pieces reverberated in Cole. He studied Lamper with growing excitement. Done right, revealing the existence of a duplicate might be *exactly* what he needed here.

"You stay here and stew," he said. "I'll be back as soon as I can."

He gave himself another long emersion in internal combustion. This had to see him through two materializations.

The first was as Gina. He materialized just outside the door of Bookkeeping and hurried inside into Lamper's office, putting excitement in his expression and whisper. "Mr. Lamper...you've got to see this. A man just came in to see Miss Carrasco and...he looks like he could be your twin!"

Lamper whipped around from his computer. "What!"

"Yes." Cole grinned. "I had to come tell you. He's gone down to her office."

Behind the glasses, Lamper's eyes narrowed. Cole watched the mental wheels whir. "A double for me...here to see Irah?" He came to his feet. "Thank you. I do want to see him."

Cole stuck behind him until out in the hallway, then let go and raced ahead to Irah's door, where he became Lamper. He stood with his hand on the doorknob when Lamper rounded the corner.

Lamper jerked to a halt, staring. When he started forward again he moved with the caution of someone approaching a bomb. Cole heard his heart pounding.

Cole pretended to give a guilty start. "Well…this is bizarre, isn't it? I didn't expect to meet you."

Lamper looked him over intently, and glanced from Cole's suit to his own, identical in every detail. "You're a friend of Irah's?"

"No, an actor she hired for this gig." Cole paused. "You know about it, don't you?"

Lamper never hesitated. "Of course. I just—ah—seeing you is startling."

"You can say that again." Cole grinned. "Charles Arthur's the name. The whole gig is strange, but…" He shrugged. "…for ten thou for two days' work, I can put up with whatever's in this security demo. Can you tell me what going to your boss's house as you last night was about, though?"

Triumph lit Lamper's eyes. "What did Irah tell you?"

"Squat. She just gave me my lines and dropped me off."

"It was…part of the setup." Lamper paused. "What are you—I mean, you're clear about what you do today, aren't you?"

Cole nodded. "Sure. I'm supposed to wait in her office. At noon I put on my makeup…"

"Makeup?" Lamper said in surprise.

"That's how I get into this meeting this afternoon. I go in as one of the store managers. In the middle of the meeting I jump up, pull out a gun loaded with blanks, and shoot at Flaxx." Cole felt a wash of enthusiasm…as if he *were* the actor, describing a real job. "He pretends to be hit. I run out and down to the emergency exit door, then take the stairs to the shopping arcade where I strip off my disguise and try to lose myself in the crowd.

"Some super-duper tracking device, a spray or a bug Carrasco shoots at me—she didn't really say what it is—is supposed to lead them to me. If it doesn't and I make it out of Embarcadero Center without being caught, I head for the airport and catch my flight back to L.A."

During the recitation, Lamper went ashen. His heart rate launched into overdrive, making his pulse throb visibly in his neck. "Don't," he said hoarsely.

Cole blinked. "Don't go back to L.A.? Why not?"

"Don't go through with the job." He reached out, clearly intending to grab Cole's arm for emphasis. "Go to the airport now."

Cole hastily backed beyond reach. "Are you crazy? Why should I do that?"

"There—there's—" Lamper floundered. "There's a...power struggle going on in the company and Irah is—I think she'll give you a gun with—ah—real bullets."

Cole retreated another step. "That's crazy, man. But even if she tried that, you think I'm not super careful about props like guns? No way am I taking a chance on walking in there with live ammo."

"She'll manage a switch somehow."

"Uh...well...I'll be even more careful." He kept backing away. "Excuse me. I want to check out the stairs."

Walking to the stair door, he watched Lamper with rear vision and ground his teeth. *Go, go! Don't hang around seeing I can't open the door.* To his relief, before he reached the exit, Lamper stumbled away. Cole let go and followed him.

Lamper went as far as Maldonado's desk, where he stood staring at the closed office door. "I need to talk to Donald. How soon will the meeting be over?"

Maldonado glanced around. "I don't know. Shall I have him call you when he's free?"

"Please. Tell him it's very important."

Back in his office, Lamper dropped into his desk chair, pulled off his glasses, and sat with his face in his hands.

Mrs. Gao came in from her desk. "Are you feeling ill? You don't look at all well."

Terrible, in fact. Lamper's face had gone so grey and tight, a death's head seemed to be looking out of it. Cole refused to let himself feel any sympathy.

Lamper put his glasses back on and gave her a weak smile. "I'm just a little tired today."

"Would you like some tea?"

"Thank you."

While sipping the tea, he watched the hallway door, heart rate still up. Obviously waiting for the meeting to end. And then he would try to call Flaxx and warn him. Flaxx must be kept from giving it any credibility.

Praying the meeting would run a while yet, Cole zipped down to fill up on heat again.

Coming back, he found Lamper still sitting staring at the door. Cole felt as if he had a racing heart, too. Now he *wanted* the meeting over...as soon as possible.

Ten minutes later a group of men and women passed in the direction of the reception area. Lamper almost dropped the mug in his eagerness to reach for the phone again.

Cole raced to Flaxx's office. Maldonado's chair was empty, so he materialized as he ran. And stepped inside the office just as the phone rang.

Shit. Irah was helping Maldonado pick up coffee cups.

He jumped out of her sight behind the half-open door. Peeking around the edge, he waved to attract Flaxx's attention.

Flaxx scowled, waving him away, and picked up the phone. But the scowl quickly became a startled stare. "This is who?" Then he smiled wryly and crooked a finger. "Come on in, Earl. You'll never guess who's on the phone."

Cole shook his head. "You're busy. I'll come back later." He backed out of sight and let go. Shit. He hoped that appearance was going to be enough.

He walked back in to see.

"Who is it?" Irah asked.

"Just a minute," Flaxx said into the phone and hit Mute. "Katherine, leave the rest of those cups for now, will you? And close the door on your way out." Once she left, he turned to Irah. "He says he's Earl Lamper."

"And?"

"Earl was just at the door." He took the phone off Mute. "I have bad news, whoever you are; your game won't work this time. A minute ago I was *looking* at Earl Lamper." His expression went incredulous and his voice furious. "Really. Fuck off." He slammed down the phone.

Irah eyed him. "What was that about?"

"The Earl on the phone said the one I saw at the door was an imposter." Flaxx drummed his fingers on the phone. "I wonder…"

This was probably going to be an interesting conversation but Cole left it to go back to Bookkeeping and see Lamper's reaction to the call.

He caught Lamper on the way out of Bookkeeping. Not going far, though…just to the men's room. Alone there, face bloodless, a pulse throbbing in his neck, Lamper paced in front of the basins. After several rounds he turned on the cold water in a basin, soaked paper towels in it, and pressed them to his face and neck. A man in torment, Cole judged. Pushed into a corner.

Cole still had enough energy to push some more. If he kept the materialization short. He turned himself into Irah and stepped from behind the screen wall. "I understand you met Charlie Arthur."

Lamper whipped around. He clutched the wet towels like a shield. "I don't know how you can even be thinking of doing this," he said hoarsely. "I'm not going to let you do it."

Cole leaned against the stalls, keeping Lamper facing away from the mirrors. "I don't know what you're talking about. Charlie's just here to demonstrate a security device."

"The hell he is!" Lamper threw the towels in the basin. "Why does he look like me?"

Cole hesitated, then shrugged. "That's insurance. If you're with me or don't interfere, he discards the store manager disguise on the way downstairs and no one knows what he really looks like. But if I don't feel you're with me, I'll have him pull it off before he goes through the exit door and

your face will be on the security tape as the man who shot
Donald. It's your choice."

He backed toward the screen wall. "But don't try seeing or calling Donald to warn him. I'll be monitoring a spy
camera in his office. Not that he's likely to believe your
story anyway."

Once around the screen wall, he let go, then came back to
find Lamper standing with his face twisted by a desperate internal debate. Cole wanted to shake him. *Come on, come on,
Lamper. You're such a faithful lapdog; don't just stand there! How
much do you want to save that bastard? You're not a violent man, so
haven't I pushed you to the point there's only one way to do it?*

"I've got to save Donald," Cole whispered at him. "I can't
let her kill him."

The mental torture raged on for another five minutes, however, before Lamper pushed away from the basins with a sigh.
It sounded despairing.

He stumbled out of the room and back to Bookkeeping.
There he went into his office long enough to dig a business
card out of his desk. "I have to step out for a few minutes," he
told Gao.

Lamper stepped out as far as the elevators, where he pulled
a cell phone from of his pocket and punched in a phone number on the card. "Inspector Hamada, this is Earl Lamper again.
I need you to keep Donald Flaxx from being murdered this
afternoon."

Cole groaned. "No, damn it; that's the wrong approach!"

Lamper frowned. "By arresting the killer, of course…
What!"

Cole had no trouble guessing that Hamada must be saying they could not arrest someone when no crime had been
committed.

Lamper's face twisted in angry desperation. "What if I tell
you the killer *has* committed crimes…two murders, one of them
Inspector Dunavan. Does that make you more interested?"

— 26 —

LAMPER PROBABLY FELT as if the question had sucked him into a tornado. In minutes, following instructions from Hamada, he had met a black-and-white at the Sacramento Street entrance and been whisked to the Hall of Justice and Homicide's interview room. Razor brought him coffee. Across the table, Hamada and Dennis gave him undivided attention.

Cole sidled up beside Razor. Glancing at him, Razor gave a thumbs up.

"Now Mr. Lamper..." Hamada's drawl oozed. "...tell us what you know about Inspector Dunavan's murder."

Lamper licked his lips. "I don't know the details, just that Irah Carrasco, Donald's sister, killed Dunavan and Sara Benay on Wednesday night and she's going to kill Donald this afternoon."

"Irah isn't," Cole whispered to Razor. "I just told Lamper that."

Razor winced.

"It got him in here, didn't it?"

Lamper twisted his hands together. "One of the store managers in the meeting this afternoon will be a ringer, an actor who thinks he's playing a part in a security demonstration, only the gun will have real bullets. I've tried to warn Donald but...I can't make him listen. Why are we wasting time here? Go to Embarcadero Center and arrest Irah!"

Hamada gave him an apologetic smile. "How do you know Miss Carrasco killed Inspector Dunavan?"

"Because she told me so this morning."

"She *told* you?" Dennis said.

"Well..." Lamper paused. "She said they were dead, but the person she claims killed them was at a concert Wednesday night, nowhere near our offices."

Hamada and Dennis exchanged glances. Hamada sat back in his chair. "So you don't *know* she killed Inspector Dunavan."

"I don't have proof, no, but I know the kind of person she is. She's—"

"Do you know of a motive for Miss Carrasco to kill Dunavan and Benay?" Hamada asked.

Lamper chewed his lower lip. "Well…Do you have to have a motive?""

Cole shook his head at Razor in disgust. "This is going nowhere. He can't bring himself to say anything that's going to implicate Flaxx in any crime."

Hamada sighed. "We need some evidence indicating she committed murder. Otherwise…" He spread his hands. "…there's nothing I can do."

"You have to do *something!*" Lamper clenched his fists. "Irah's crazy!"

Hamada shook his head. "I can tell that you genuinely believe Mr. Flaxx is in danger, but—"

"She broke into my house last night. Arrest her for that."

Hamada pushed to his feet. "That's a burglary. Our Burglary unit will need to handle the investigation. Inspector Dennis can take you down to them to file a complaint."

Cole frowned. Were they really kicking Lamper out…or playing him?

Lamper stared at Hamada in dismay. "Investigation! Complaint! You mean I'll have to tell everything all over again to another set of detectives? By the time we go through that, Donald will be dead!"

"I'm sorry. Charlie, if you'll take Mr. Lamper—"

Cole slipped around behind Lamper and leaned down to his ear. "The firefighter's death is murder. You know she started that fire. She can be arrested for that."

Lamper's fists clenched desperately. "Wait!"

Hamada sat back down.

Lamper pulled off his glasses, and buried his face in his hands.

Hamada waited. Lamper took several ragged breaths, as though about to speak, but just released them again. The silence stretched on.

Hamada let it last several minutes, then said, "What time is that meeting again when this murder is supposed to take place?"

Lamper lowered his hands and clasped them together tightly on the table in front of him. "I don't want to do this to Donald, but I don't know how else to stop her. It all needs to end anyway. It's gone too far. The burglaries were one thing, but then she wanted to do fires in the stores with merchandise too big for burglaries and came up with this Kijurian masquerade."

Hamada's expression never changed, but Cole saw the name Kijurian register and knew that inside Hamada, every nerve had come alert.

Lamper rushed on. "I never liked the idea of fires. I didn't even like the burglaries. Donald and I were doing fine without them, and nothing was illegal. But Irah talked Donald into it. No one would get hurt, she said. She'd throw the Molotov cocktails at night when the stores were empty. Except her fire at Woodworks killed the firefighter. You can arrest her for that, can't you?"

Hamada nodded. "Yes. If you have personal knowledge that she—"

"Yes, yes, I have it." Lamper grimaced. "I have personal knowledge she set fire to our stores. I have personal knowledge of it all...the fires, the burglaries, the insurance fraud. I'm a conspirator, accessory, or whatever. So arrest me. Read me my rights. But for God's sake...*go arrest Irah*! I think she killed Sara and Dunavan because Sara had access to my files and found evidence in them and told Dunavan. She wanted to keep anyone else from learning what Sara found. Irah swore to me that she would never go to jail."

Hamada glanced at his watch, scribbled *Search warrants for home, office, car* on a page of his notebook and handed it to Dennis, then stood. "Wait here."

Cole whispered to Razor, "Bring up souvenirs. You have to be able to look in that puzzle box."

"Do you know if Irah takes souvenirs from her crimes?" Razor asked.

Lamper chewed on his lower lip. "She took the rook off my trophy when she broke in."

Outside the interview room, Hamada told Dennis, "Include personal effects of Benay and Dunavan in the warrant."

He disappeared into Lieutenant Madrid's office while Dennis rolled a form into a typewriter and began typing furiously.

Cole realized that while he still had feelings of guilt and unfinished business, that of foreboding had gone. They knew Sara was a victim, not a killer. And her killer was a warrant away from arrest. *We've almost got her, Sara.* But they still needed to find the bodies. Even when they did, he wondered whether he could rest in peace with Sherrie's belief in him shattered.

— 27 —

HAMADA RANG THE bell at Irah's house, but Cole knew neither he, Razor, nor Darrell Wineright expected anyone to answer. One of the Richmond District uniforms with them carried a ram. Hamada stepped aside and was motioning to the officer with the ram when to all their surprise, the door opened.

A small oriental woman stood in the opening. "Miss Carrasco not home." She started to shut the door.

Hamada caught it and, holding up his ID, introduced himself. Then he pulled out the search warrant. "I have a warrant to search this house. Please stand aside."

She kept pushing against the door. "Not come in. Miss Carrasco don't like."

"This paper says we can."

She held on for another moment, then released the door and turned away. "I go call Miss Carrasco."

In one long stride, Hamada caught her upper arm. "No...you don't call Miss Carrasco." He led her into the livingroom. "What's your name?"

"Mrs. Dien."

"Mrs. Dien, why don't you just sit here while we work." He pointed at a chair. At the same time he sent a glance at Razor and Wineright that said: *Watch her.*

"I clean," she said, pointing at a vacuum cleaner sitting in the doorway to the dining room.

"Not today."

They pulled on latex gloves and fanned out through the house.

"Upstairs," Cole told Razor.

Razor tapped Hamada's shoulder. "Why don't we take upstairs? I think we're more likely to find goodies in her personal space."

Hamada nodded.

A uniformed officer came with them. Their brows went up at the books and tapes.

Even Razor blinked in surprise. "She *has* been studying us," he murmured to Cole.

Then they saw the curio cabinet. "Souvenirs?" Hamada said.

Cole told Razor where to look for the rook.

Razor pointed it out to Hamada. "There's the trophy piece Lamper mentioned."

"Bag it." Hamada tried the door. "Locked."

"Luckily I brought these." Razor pulled a lock pick set out of his pocket, and shrugged when Hamada's brows rose. "I figured there was a chance we'd find locked drawers."

Especially when a ghost reconnaissance warned him about it.

Razor ignored Cole's wink and went to work on the lock.

Cole peered into the wastebasket beside the desk. Mrs. Dien had not cleaned up here yet. Maybe good luck for them. Something new had been added since yesterday. "Razor, check out the green stuff here."

Once the cabinet door was open, Razor came over and lifted off the shredder. Reaching in, he pulled out a narrow strip of bright green paper with black lettering that formed the bottom three-quarters of *U.S. Postal Service Delivery Confirmation Receipt.* He held it up to Hamada. "Interesting. I wonder why she shredded this."

Hamada looked around from bagging the rook. "Let's piece it together and find out. Maybe she mails her burglary loot to her fence. One burglar back East used to do that. Bag the trash." He frowned back at the cabinet. "I wonder where all this other stuff comes from."

Razor put on a thoughtful expression. "You know, it looks to me like what the Old Spice Burglar's been taking. Don't you think?" he asked the uniformed officer.

The officer stared at the shelves. "Yeah. But I thought Old Spice was a man."

"Maybe we've been wrong." Hamada's frown deepened. "If she took souvenirs from Dunavan and Benay, it's going to be hell finding them. Let's check the desk and the rest of the room first."

"Puzzle box," Cole said.

"I wonder." Razor stepped back to the curio cabinet.

Hamada raised his brows. "Do you see something?"

"No, but...you know, if I killed a cop and wanted a souvenir, I'd take his badge. That can't be left out where Mrs. Dien might see it, though and this is a puzzle box." Razor lifted out the box and shook it. They all heard the rattle inside. "My sister had one of these things. She kept her diary in it, thinking no one would be able to read it. But she underestimated how determined a little brother can be. It took me three months, but I finally solved it."

Cole grinned. "You've always been a great liar."

"Let's just hope..." Razor began prodding. "...this one goes faster."

Pulling up the memory of Irah opening it, Cole described her actions to Razor. He thought he gave the directions clearly...but the box stayed closed. Razor tried again...again without luck.

"We could just smash it," the uniformed officer said.

Razor closed his eyes. "Wait. I think...There!"

The drawer slid out. They stared at the butterfly pendant and star.

"Son of a bitch," the uniformed officer breathed.

"Is that Dunavan's?" Hamada asked.

"That's his number. And Benay's apartment was full of butterfly stuff."

Hamada nodded. "We'll see if her girlfriends recognize the necklace."

While they bagged the box and its contents, Hamada pulled out his cell phone and called Lieutenant Madrid. After disconnecting, he gave Razor a grim smile. "It's quite a party downtown. Lamper's baring every corner of his mightily troubled soul, so now Willner, Burglary, an ADA, and Fraud are also hanging on every word. And Dennis is wearing a path to Judge Barbour's chambers. She just finished signing a search warrant for the Flaxx offices and computers. If we leave Wineright to finish searching here, Madrid will have Galentree meet us at Embarcadero Center with the Flaxx office search and arrest warrants." He paused. "So Dunavan was right about everything. Too bad he won't be there to put the cuffs on them."

Cole grinned.

Meeting his eyes, Razor said. "I think he'll be with us in spirit."

— 28 —

TO GINA, THE reception area must have seemed filled with cops...Hamada, flanked by Razor and Neil Galentree, followed by two pairs of uniformed officers. Her eyes went big as dinner plates.

Hamada's hand came down on hers as she started to take the weight off the switch hook of her phone. "Don't announce us." Then he marched on toward Flaxx's office.

Razor peeled off at Bookkeeping long enough to empty it. "I have to ask you to leave, ladies. Right now, please. Take your hands off your keyboards and don't touch them again. Just collect your purses and coats."

Mrs. Gao pulled herself to her full height. "We have to what? What's this about?"

"We're serving a search warrant."

While Razor ushered them out and slapped a seal on the door, Cole hurried after Hamada.

"Where is Miss Carrasco's office?" Hamada asked Maldonado. Eyes wide, she pointed down the side hall.

"Is Mr. Flaxx in?"

Maldonado frowned. "Yes, but he's in a meeting. What is—Wait! You can't go in there!"

But Hamada was already opening the office door and leading two uniforms in. Galentree took the other uniforms and headed down the side hall. Cole hesitated, torn which direction to go, and finally went with Hamada.

The men and women at the conference table turned, staring. Flaxx pushed back from the table and stood. "What's *this?*"

"Donald Flaxx, I have a warrant for your arrest." Hamada waved it in front of him. "Turn around and put your hands behind your back."

The jaws of the store managers and Maldonado, who had followed Hamada in, dropped.

Flaxx drew himself up. "Arrest? For what!"

"Let's see." Hamada pursed his lips. "Conspiracy to commit burglary, accessory to burglary, conspiracy to commit arson, accessory to arson, murder in the commission of a felony, fraud, conspiracy to commit—"

The jaws kept dropping.

Flaxx turned to Maldonado. "Katherine, call Wayne. Have him come to the Hall of Justice."

She scrambled for the phone on the desk.

Flaxx let Hamada cuff him, but his lip curled. "My lawyers will eat you alive. I don't know anything about any of this. That bully Dunavan's tried everything under the sun to pin something on me. He even slept with one of my bookkeepers. But you just try taking anything she told him to court."

Hamada smiled. "We're not arresting you on the basis of any information from Miss—"

"Hamada! Carrasco's gone!"

They whirled toward Galentree in the doorway.

Cole raced through the washroom and wall into Irah's office. And swore. On the desk sat her spy camera monitor… showing the main Bookkeeping office. The view from the spy camera she planted to watch Sara! Her jacket hung on the back of her chair, high heels lay on the floor beside it, and a bottom drawer of the desk stood open an inch, blocked from closing by blonde curls. The remains of an envelope with a strip of tape across each end lay beside the spy monitor.

He ran out into the hall to find Galentree leading a group his direction. Seeing Razor, too, he said, "She spotted you in Bookkeeping, and probably went out the emergency exit. There's a desk drawer with at least one wig in it so I'm betting she's put on another and rigged herself some kind of disguise. There's an envelope on the desk that looks like it was taped under the desk or a drawer. It could have had new ID or money in it. I'm going to try catching up with her on the stairs."

Through the exit door, he took the stairs in bounds... leaping to the middle of the flight then vaulting the center railing to land in the middle of the next flight, and vaulting that railing to the middle of the next flight. Could he overtake Irah? What a nightmare for containment if she reached the shopping arcade. Three levels interconnecting with all the other buildings in the complex. Numerous street level exits.

Even if they blocked all the exits, how did they spot her when they had no idea what she looked like now...not color or style of hair, not what clothing she was wearing. She'd left her jacket, so she must be planning to acquire new clothing. She might even dress male. And once out of Embarcadero Center, she could go anywhere. Damn, he was an idiot! He should have remembered the spy camera on Sara and warned Razor about it!

Above him, heavy running footsteps echoed in the stairwell. One of the uniformed officers giving chase? Below him he heard nothing. Maybe she was running barefooted.

As he dropped past level after level with no sign of Irah, his stomach began dropping even farther. By the time he reached the Promenade Level he was swearing in frustration. He made a quick survey of the area but saw no one who could be Irah. Ditto after rushing down escalators to the Lobby and Street Levels.

Son of a bitch! She'd managed to outrun him after all.

He zipped back to the Flaxx offices to give Razor the bad news. But of the group that arrived with Hamada, he saw only one uniformed officer...who stood outside the door of Bookkeeping watching Katherine Maldonado face the entire office staff. Half were talking at the same time, demanding to know what was going on and what would happen now. All of them looked frustrated, worried, and lost.

Maldonado tried raising her voice above theirs. Without luck.

Then Farrell, standing at the back of the group, put two fingers in his mouth and produced a piercing whistle. In the startled silence he said, "Give the lady a chance to talk."

In the silence Cole also heard voices in the direction of Irah's office. Hurrying there, he found Razor and Galentree searching it. The surfer photograph lay face down on the desk. Strips peeled from the surface of the cardboard backing indicated that the envelope had been taped there.

Razor looked around from checking behind other photographs.

"I lost her," Cole said.

Razor muttered under his breath, "Hamada alerted mall security before taking Flaxx away and we've got Central District officers on their way to sweep the surrounding area and search the mall."

"Let's hope they can recognize her."

"You say something?" Galentree asked.

"Just talking to myself." Razor dropped his voice more. "At least she can't use her car. The secretary told us where the company parking spaces are in the garage and we've got a man watching it until it's picked up for processing."

"I'm going back down to look for her."

But standing in the middle of the street level courtyard presently, he wondered where to look. He had to do more than just wander the shopping arcades and streets outside. The security officers and uniformed PD he saw were already doing that much. That stash behind the picture—whether new ID, cash, or credit cards—indicated she had planned for the possibility of flight. Maybe as far back as the day she became Asset Manager, deliberately choosing to have her office near the emergency stairs. If he could guess her plan, he might intercept her.

Cole put himself in Irah's place. With cops coming in the front door, she reached for her escape kit and bolted out the back. Her objective would be to reach the street and leave the area before they had time to surround it and trap her.

But...leave it for where? In her place, he would want out of the city. The fastest, nearest means for that was the Bay Area Rapid Transit. Make it to BART's Embarcadero Station and she could be on her way to Oakland.

Since he knew the Embarcadero Station, Cole ziptripped there. Even though unable to collar her himself, when he spotted her he could whisper her location in the ears of the uniformed officers scanning the ticket lines and platform. He searched among the waiting passengers, too...trying to ignore clothing and hair color and concentrate on just height and build, hands and ears. Two women and one young male raised his hopes, and officers stopped both of the women without his urging. But on closer inspection, neither the women nor the male were Irah.

Maybe she had not arrived here yet. Buying new clothes would take a little time. He moved to the street and worked his way back toward Embarcadero Center. But while he passed two patrol units and two bicycle officers, he reached the Sacramento Street entrances without seeing her. Had she taken another route? Or maybe chosen alternative transportation?

He zipped to the ferry terminal on Pier 1...then line-of-sight to a ferry churning its way toward Oakland. But the search among its passengers failed to turn her up. So did checking out passengers at the terminal when he zipped back there. Ditto checking the Sausalito-bound passengers at the terminal behind the Ferry Building.

Cole headed back across Justin Herman Plaza. On the way he spotted another possible candidate there. A bicycle officer saw her, too. Nearing the pair, though, Cole saw she was only another false alarm.

Cole shook his head as the bicycle officer let her go on her way. The false alarms indicated everyone was doing their best watching for Irah, but they were still missing her. Maybe *had* missed her. If only he could figure out her escape plan. If she had not tried for BART or the ferries before the police staked out those and other obvious transportation, maybe she intended to rent a car using new ID. That still required reaching a car rental office.

Or...since she knew they were expecting her to flee, what if she did just the opposite? Knowing the Tenderloin from playing Kijurian, her plan might be to go to ground there, hiding among the homeless or in cheap hotels until the heat died down. The risk of hiding in plain sight was unlikely to bother her. She might even get off on it.

Hiding in plain sight. He stared toward Embarcadero Center. What if she were already doing that? In a few hours hundreds of office workers would start heading home for the day. Avoid detection until then and she could lose herself in the exodus.

Cole rushed into Embarcadero Center to search it again. This time, though, he could use a system. Not that he felt a hundred per cent confident about anticipating her moves, but if *he* wanted to wait for quitting time without attracting attention, he would set himself up in a location where people sat for long periods. Starting at 4EC, he combed all three mall levels, peering closely at everyone sitting at a table. None of them were Irah. He moved on to 3EC.

And despite his careful scrutiny, he still almost missed her.

Maybe it was the long fingers spread across the back of her book that made him turn around, or the title on the book's spine, registering after he passed her. *Catch Me If You Can.* He walked around the table she shared with two other women...to all appearances oblivious to everything but her book. While the other women chatted with each other, Irah's eyes lifted from the page just to reach for her drink or eat a bite of salad.

She had gone quasi-Goth. Her blouse, black, had sleeves ending in long ruffles. A black skirt came down over black platform boots to her ankles. Hair the color of redwood hung around her shoulders, hiding her ears and some of her face. What showed had black lipstick and eyes like holes...heavily lined in black, with dark purple eye shadow. A black coat or cape lay folded over the table's fourth chair.

Cole circled her several times to satisfy himself this *was* Irah. Even on close examination she remained difficult to recognize. Then he zipped to the Flaxx offices to tell Razor.

The offices were empty, a seal on the front doors. Waiting for the forensic search of the computer.

Before checking Homicide to see if everyone had returned there, Cole went back to Irah. She still looked settled, and if he were right she would remain there as long as she could without attracting attention. But he found himself reluctant to let her out of his sight, afraid that if he did, she would disappear again.

Suddenly her heart rate jumped. He quickly spotted the reason, a pair of uniformed officers, strolling in her direction. Though looking everyone over, they did not appear to notice her. Should he leave them ignorant and go tell Razor? If he let them know, however, they could arrest her quietly. Not have half the PD come charging in here, led by Special Operations. But how did he communicate with them? He had no time to go soak up heat for a materialization. He had to act now.

Cole looked around. There was the way Red's hometown ghost made herself visible, of course. Not a solution he liked. Chilling things might drive everyone out of the area, including Irah. But he saw no other choice. And maybe the open space would spread the heat loss out enough to make it less severe.

Imagining himself as a sponge, or inhaling with his whole body, he began drawing in heat. But there was so much less of it than in a car engine. He sucked harder, deeper, scrambling to build enough for materialization as he moved past Irah and toward the officers.

As he used rear vision to keep track of Irah, he saw people at the table nearest him shiver, then those at tables farther away. They reached for jackets. A couple stood and walked away. One of the women at Irah's table did, too.

The Oriental officer of the pair hunched his shoulders. "Man, who opened the freezer door?"

Cole hoped he had enough heat. Time to see. He circled behind a tree and visualized himself as his sister Trish…with a star in his jacket pocket and his arm in a sling, so they would not expect assistance with the arrest. The moment he felt weight, he stepped from behind the tree into the officers' path, keeping voice low. "Yo, guys. Hold up a minute."

They halted, expressions polite...Silvela and Yee, according to their name tags. "Yes, ma'am. What can we do for you?"

He showed them the star. "I'm Lieutenant Trish Deckard, Ingleside District. I'm on sick leave but one of the security guards I know told me you're hunting Irah Carrasco? That she's suspected of killing an officer?"

Her name brought them on alert. "You sound like you know her," Yee said.

"Yes. And she's sitting at a table just down the concourse. Don't look! She's watching you. When I passed her I could tell." What Irah thought about two officers focused on thin air in front of them, he had no idea, but hoped it did not spook her. "She's the redhead."

Both officers glanced down the concourse from the corners of their eyes, heart rates picking up. Silvela said skeptically, "Are you sure? She's just sitting there reading."

Cole nodded. "I met her when one of their stores in our district was burglarized. And women know other women, no matter what they're wearing." Whether true or not, it sounded good. "Ah...I wouldn't do that," he said as one of the officers started to reach for his radio. "She'll know she's been made. I'm thinking you ought to arrest her now while you have the chance, then call it in."

The two exchanged glances. "How do we have a chance when she knows we're here?"

Cole explained his idea, prepared for skepticism, but they were young enough to feel the weight of the rank he had given himself. They agreed to do it. So he stepped aside and they continued on toward Irah. Back behind the tree again, he let go, then followed them.

They approached, seemingly ignoring her, discussing the Giants' chance at the World Series this year. Then as they started to pass, Silvela halted and looked down at her. "Say, is that a good book?"

Yee halted several steps later, putting him behind her.

Irah looked up with no outward indication of nervousness. Her heart rate, though, said adrenaline was pumping. "Yes. It's fascinating how he got away with all those impersonations."

"What's your name?" Silvela asked.

Her brows rose. Her heart rate went higher, too. "Fiona Brazaski." She smiled at him then back over her shoulder at Yee. "Are you trying to pick me up?"

"May I see some identification?"

"What's this about?" the other woman at the table asked.

Silvela gave her a bland smile. "Just routine. Miss Brazaski?"

Irah closed her book, pulled a billfold from the pocket of her skirt, and took out a driver's license.

"Fiona Brazaski, red hair, blue eyes," Silvela read. "Can you repeat your birth date for me?"

"June Fifth, 1977." She gave him an anxious frown. "Have I done something wrong?"

She had probably memorized the birth date, anticipating that she might be asked for it, but reeling it off with no hesitation impressed Cole.

Silvela glanced toward Yee. Cole groaned at the uncertainty in it. *Come on, come on. Don't give in to doubt! Check out the hair!*

Yee said, "Look at this, Irah."

She started to turn her head, then caught herself. But too late. And knew it. She breathed a curse.

Cole grinned. Good job!

"Why don't you take off the wig, Miss Carrasco," Silvela said.

Irah stared hard at him for a long moment, then smiling wryly, reached up and pulled off the wig. While the other woman gaped, she ran her hands back through her own hair and shook it out. "I guess I'm busted." She stood, and stepping clear of the chair, put her hands behind her back.

Cole's spine prickled. He had hoped they could take her without a struggle but this was too easy. After her statements to Flaxx about not going to jail…after killing Sara supposedly to prevent that…she was just giving up?

But she stood passive while Silvela cuffed her and patted her down for weapons, and while Yee, voice carefully neutral, informed Communications of the arrest. With one of them holding each of her arms, they led her down to the ground level and out to their patrol unit.

She smiled at them. "I thought my disguise was good. You guys are sharp. This ought to earn you a commendation."

Walking beside them, Cole could see them start thinking about that. He frowned. They needed to stay focused. While the officers' heart rates had returned to normal, Irah's continued racing, still pumped for action. She was planning something.

Yet they reached the car without incident and put her in the back.

Then as Silvela started the engine, she said, "Wait. I forgot my cape. It's still back there at the table."

Not forgot. Cole felt sure she had known very well they were leaving it. She probably intended to do so, stepping away from the table so it would be overlooked as they arrested her. Leaning down to the passenger window, he told Yee, "Forget about the cape. Take her straight to the Hall."

"You won't need it in jail," Silvela said.

"But my bag is under it, with a gun in it."

Cole's gut said it was a trick but…how could they afford to gamble on that?

Yee jumped out. "I'll be right back."

She shifted in the seat, grimacing. "These cuffs are hurting me," she said in a small voice.

"I'm not going to loosen them." Silvela drummed his fingers on the steering wheel.

"You don't have to. Tightening them will help more."

He glanced back through the cage in surprise. "What?"

She shifted position again. "It's a fact. Snugger cuffs cause less discomfort. Then double lock them. I learned that at the Citizen's Academy. So could you please tighten them?"

Alarms screamed in Cole. One officer disposed of temporarily, the other being asked to open the door. "Don't do it!"

But Silvela opened his door, no doubt disarmed by the word "tighten" and her passive behavior to this point.

Cole drew on heat in the air to pump substance into his voice, and yelled a warning at Silvela.

Too late. Silvela had already opened the rear door and was leaning down toward Irah.

Her left hand whipped from behind her back with the cuff that should have been around her right wrist gripped in her hand like brass knuckles. It smashed into Silvela's throat. As he reeled back and collapsed, choking, she leaped from the car. Blood dripped from her right hand, scraped raw by pulling it out of the cuff. Whooping, she ripped the badge from his shirt, then jumped into the front seat, slammed the car into gear, and floored the accelerator. Seconds later the lights and siren came on.

Cole overrode an impulse to zip into the car and stay with her. Instead, he tracked her visually as he knelt by the downed officer, cursing his inability to use the radio. "Someone call 911!" Trusting that no one would ask where the voice came from.

At least she remained in sight, heading straight up the street. He winced at a near collision as she shot through an intersection. A seeming eternity later, Yee appeared with the cape and handbag. Up the hill, brakes squealed as cross traffic at another intersection tried to avoid a collision.

Yee halted in shock. "Dom!"

Cole jumped to his feet. "She's got your unit. She just made a left...I think on Montgomery. Call it in. I'm going after her."

Yee stared around in confusion, looking for the voice, then gave that up to kneel by his partner and hit his radio switch..

Cole sprinted after the patrol unit...running through people and vehicles. One woman saw him as he came at her. Her eyes widened. Cole plunged through her with an apology. She yelped. Rear vision caught her whirling to stare after him in disbelief and bewilderment.

At the next intersection he raced through crossing traffic. With a clear vision of the Montgomery intersection, he zipped line-of-sight to it, then peered down Montgomery toward Market. But he saw no flashing light bar, heard no siren. Damn! Had she shut it down, or turned off Montgomery?

He zipped toward Market a block at a time, pausing at each intersection to look both ways down the cross street. The only police car he saw was coming up Post toward him, with two shapes visible through the windshield. Cole swore bitterly. Irah had given them the slip again!

— 29 —

ZIPPING TO HOMICIDE, Cole found that news of the assault and escape had reached there. Hamada stood outside the interview room in his shirt sleeves, a tower of frustration amid a cluster of detectives. "Son of a bitch! She's slipperier than a greased pig!"

Beyond the group, their television monitor on its tall stand had an image of Flaxx sitting at the table in the interview room. The man with him Cole guessed would be Wayne Kaslin, Flaxx's favorite attorney in the big law firm three floors below the Flaxx offices. Lieutenant Madrid's presence in the group told Cole that he pulled Hamada out of the interrogation to hear about Irah.

"Was there a gun in the purse?" Hamada asked.

Dennis shrugged. "The sergeant who called didn't say."

Hamada snapped, "Someone find out."

"Galentree and Willner," Lieutenant Madrid said. "If there's a gun, get it to the crime lab. And pick up that cape, too. She had to buy it in Embarcadero Center. Maybe she paid for it with a nice new credit card she'll use again so we can track her." As the detectives headed for the door, he turned to Razor. "How are you coming on the phone records and that delivery receipt?"

Razor had his coat off, too. He pointed to a desk near the TV monitor, where a Rolodex and phone company printout sat beside a bag of shredded paper and a partial reconstruction of a delivery confirmation receipt. "Thursday she made five calls to the L.A. area on her cell phone. They all match entries in her Rolodex. There's one to her *from* L.A. at 6:30, a different number that I can't find in the Rolodex."

L.A. area. Cole trailed a finger down the printout. Razor
had written names by five circled numbers. He bet if they
ran the names, the computer would spit back criminal records.
These had to be some of her old buddies, called to ask if
they knew anyone in this area who could help her with a
disposal problem.

Razor continued, "I've got three quarters of the receipt
pieced together, enough to know that she mailed the whatever
on Saturday but didn't fill out who it went to."

"Keep working on it."

Hamada also went back to work…disappearing into the
interview room. Madrid and a detective Cole recognized from
Fraud—Maurice Lima—stood watching the TV monitor. Razor kept glancing up at the monitor, too, while he dug through
the bag of shreds.

"How's it going with Flaxx?" Cole asked.

Razor grimaced. "Only the lawyer is talking, and of course,
according to him, Flaxx knows nothing about any burglaries or
arson, and is shocked, *shocked* to hear that his sister is suspected of murdering two people."

Lima looked around. "Do you always talk to yourself,
Razor?"

Razor shrugged. "That way I'm assured of an audience. I
won't worry unless it isn't my own voice I'm hearing."

"If you don't mind," Madrid said, "there are voices I'd like
to hear…those." He pointed at the monitor.

Hamada had rejoined the interview. Across the table from
him, beside Flaxx, the lawyer said, "Inspector, this has gone
far enough. I demand to know what alleged evidence you
think justifies these charges. Because you know that any seemingly incriminating information obtained from Inspector
Dunavan sleeping with one of Mr. Flaxx's Bookkeeping staff
is fruit of the poisoned tree."

Flaxx smirked.

Cole felt his ears burn. Anger at himself hissed through
him all over again.

Hamada drawled, "Counselor, any relationship between Miss Benay and Inspector Dunavan, if it existed, is irrelevant." The camera caught just the back of Hamada's head but Cole heard his thin smile in the words. "Because the charges are based on a statement made by Mr. Earl Lamper."

Flaxx came out of his chair. "What! That's bullshit. What would Earl have to tell you. Unless you coerced him, of course."

"Why don't we let y'all judge for yourselves." Hamada rose to his feet. "If y'all'll come with me?" He ushered them out into the office, to the TV monitor.

Lima pulled chairs over for them while Madrid stopped the recorder and ejected the tape that had been recording Flaxx's interview. They replaced it with another tape.

When he punched Play, the interview room came up on the monitor again. But this time Lamper sat behind the table, facing Willner.

Lamper shook his head. "It doesn't matter if I'm incriminating myself. This has to be stopped somehow. It's gone all too far."

"What has?" Willner asked.

"The burglaries, the arson, the fraud. Irah. Her especially. It was all her idea to start with. She talked Donald into it."

Flaxx froze.

"Now it's out of control. *She's* out of control." Lamper shook his head. "God. Poor Sara! I don't understand why—"

"When you say she 'talked Mr. Flaxx into it', what do you mean, exactly?"

Lamper hesitated and licked his lips, then sighed. "Irah talked him into burglarizing—that is, into letting *her* burglarize some of our businesses, and later set fire to others."

Flaxx stared. "I don't believe this! It's faked!" But as the tape rolled on and Lamper told about altering the books of faltering stores, ordered to do so by Flaxx, the color drained out of Flaxx's face. Then his face hardened. "I've seen enough! Shut it off. I can't believe it. After all I've done for him. That bastard. That lying, underhanded, sneaking son of a bitch!"

He scowled up at Hamada in righteous indignation. "It's all lies...from beginning to end."

"Donald," Kaslin said in a warning voice.

Flaxx seemed not to hear him. "Now I understand some things that didn't make sense before, why more and more of my stores have been burglarized...despite Irah's supposed security improvements. He and Irah were ripping me off!"

"Donald, be quiet."

Cole almost wanted him to. After all the years of encouraging crooks to give each other up, and despite working the Flaxx crew to make this happen, Flaxx's instant turn on his faithful dog disgusted him. Even though said dog had turned on Flaxx first.

"It must be terrible realizing you've lost control of your company like this," Hamada said.

Flaxx stiffened. Red boiled up his neck.

"Donald, *don't say another word, damn it!*"

This time Flaxx heard. His mouth snapped shut.

Kaslin stood up. "We're done here. Book Mr. Flaxx and let's see a judge about bail."

"Let me show you one more thing first," Hamada said. He ran the tape forward.

By this time the questions had turned to murder, and they watched Lamper repeat the conversation where Cole, as Irah, accused Flaxx of double murder.

Flaxx's expression went incredulous, then furious. "That bitch!" He turned to Hamada. "I don't know why she told him that story but she's lying! I don't know anything about it, and I couldn't have killed them. I have an alibi for Wednesday evening."

"Donald..." Kaslin's hand flexed as if he wanted to slap it over Flaxx's mouth. "For God's sake shut *up*! If you refuse to follow my advice, why the hell am I wasting my time here?"

Flaxx's jaw jutted. "I'm not going to let them pin a cop killing on me. I didn't shoot Dunavan!"

Kaslin swore.

Flaxx frowned. "What?" Then glanced up and noticed the deadpan faces around him. "What?"

"*Shoot* him, Mr. Flaxx?" Hamada drawled. "No one has said anything about how Inspector Dunavan died."

Flaxx stared at him, pupils dilating. He turned to Kaslin. "Conference."

They walked to a far corner of the room.

Hamada eyed them. "Flaxx reminds me of some dogs. They charge the fence barking and snarling like they'll tear you apart, but you walk on into the yard and they roll over on their backs peeing themselves in submission."

Lima wiggled his brows. "And guess who he's going to roll over on."

Thinking of Irah...Cole said, "I'd love to stick around for Flaxx peeing himself, Razor, but Irah's still running loose. I have to go find her."

"Wait!" Razor said. He laid down the last strip of the confirmation receipt. "I've got it."

After scribbling down the confirmation number on a message pad, he hurried to the computer. Everyone followed. Cole climbed a virtual ladder to peer down past them at the monitor while Razor brought up the Post Office internet site and typed the number into the tracking window.

Cole stared at the delivery results. Son of a bitch.

"Colma?" Dennis grinned. "Well, I'd wonder if she mailed the bodies, except they'd have to go parcel post instead of priority."

Colma. Where everyone in San Francisco went to be buried. "Razor, when Flaxx fretted about cops digging around the company for clues to my death, Irah treated it like a joke. She said they wouldn't know where to dig."

Razor sucked air through his teeth. "What's the area code there? The same as Daly City, right...650?"

He raced back to the desk where he had been working. Carefully, he set aside the report form with the assembled confirmation receipt on it and dumped the whole bag of shreds on the desk.

"What do you have?" Madrid asked.

"There was something handwritten, in a kind of purple ink...torn into pieces, not shredded." Razor pawed through the shred strips. "I saw a piece with the numbers 650."

Hamada, Dennis, and Lima joined him sorting the shreds. When they found a promising piece, however, no one touched it. Using the eraser ends of two pencils like chopsticks, Razor picked the piece up and transferred it to where he was assembling the note. Protecting any fingerprints on it. Slowly, pieces fit together, revealing the beginning of a phone number and the beginning and last letters of a name.

A throat cleared behind them. Kaslin said, "Although Mr. Flaxx had absolutely nothing to do with either murder, some time after the fact he came into possession of information about them. In return for that information, I want any charges relating to the murders dropped against Mr. Flaxx."

"Dream on," Hamada said.

Kaslin just smiled. "Get someone from the DA's office in here and he and I will talk."

Madrid picked up a phone. "Take your client into the interview room."

Waiting for the Assistant DA, they continued hunting pieces of the note in purple ink. Shortly after the ADA's arrival and her disappearance into the interview room with Hamada, Razor completed the note...giving them a phone number and single name: *Tankersley*.

While Razor checked Irah's phone records, Dennis grabbed a phone book. "Bingo," he said shortly. "There's just one Tankersley in Colma...Gilbert Tankersley." He headed for the computer. It gave him a hit. "Tankersley did a stretch for forgery." He took the news in to Madrid, who had returned to his office.

Irah had mailed something to an ex-con living in the cemetery city. Payment for services rendered? Cole's gut rippled. Could they be close to finding Sara and his bodies?

"But there's no record of a call from either Carrasco's home or cell phone to that number," Razor said.

She had to call it from somewhere. "Razor, if she didn't want to risk a link to that number by using her own phone, maybe she went to a—"

"Pay phone!" Razor finished. "Would you..."

"I'm on my way."

From a ziptrip to Irah's house, Cole hopped line-of-sight south to Golden Gate Park and north to Geary in search of pay phones. He brought Razor back numbers for two.

Razor pretended to learn them in a phone call and passed them on to Dennis, who rolled a form into his typewriter to start warrants for the pay phone records.

Razor lowered his voice. "Galentree called while you were gone. No gun in the purse. They did find where she bought the cape and the rest of her getup...with a credit card...but it was Benay's."

Cole gritted his teeth. "I've got to go find her."

"Looking where? Even as a ghost you can only be one place at a time. We'll get her eventually. Now that she's iden-tified as a cop killer, can't you leave her to us?"

Cole explored himself for an answer. The leaden discom-fort of guilt and unfinished business remained. "I think so I have to see her locked up. And find Sara's and my bodies...to give everyone closure."

And what about Sherrie? he wondered bleakly. The thought of leaving without getting straight with her wrenched him apart.

Madrid came out of his office smiling. "Good news. The cruiser Carrasco stole has been located at Union Square. Willner and Galentree are on there way over."

Union square! Cole groaned. "Dying's turned me stu-pid, Razor. I should have thought of that." What better place to go...the parking underground out of sight with every major department store in America around it. In fifteen minutes she could buy herself an entirely new appearance. Alternatively, from there she could just disappear into the

Tenderloin. But at least it gave him a place to try picking up her trail. "See you later."

"Wait," Razor whispered. "I'll come, too. Two sets of eyes are better than one, and I can carry a radio so you'll know if Irah's sighted."

A good point, Cole reflected. He had missed having communications.

Madrid called Hamada out of the interview room and told him about Tankersley. "I just talked to the Colma PD. He's kept his nose clean there but they know him. Get this. He operates heavy equipment for the Pacific Hills Memorial Gardens. That includes their backhoe."

Backhoe! Cole's skin prickled. It did look like Tankersley had to be involved in disposing of the bodies.

Razor shrugged into his coat. "Lieutenant, Hamada, I think I'll go give Willner and Galentree a hand at Union Square."

Nodding absently, Madrid asked Hamada, "How's it going with Flaxx?"

As he and Razor headed for the door, Cole listened to Hamada grunt. "The ADA is dropping all charges related to Dunavan and Benay's murders in return for Flaxx confessing to the burglaries and arson, and spilling everything Carrasco told him about the murders."

"Then let him spill to Lima and Dennis. You go down to Colma. The CPD is picking up Tankersley. Lean on him to get an admission that Carrasco brought him bodies to dispose of, and find out where they are."

Cole thought again of the ghost airmen movie. As their bodies were recovered, they faded away. Despite wanting his and Sara's bodies found, his gut knotted in anxiety. If this did work like that movie, catching up with Irah ASAP became more important than ever.

— 30 —

THE HUNT AT Union Square looked well under way when Cole and Razor arrived. Patrol units swept up and down every street in the area like a swarm of black and white bees. Officers on foot checked out pedestrians in the plaza and on the grass tiers along Geary. Down in the parking garage, they passed a cruiser parked behind another cruiser that had officers going through its interior and trunk. After Razor found a parking stall for his own car, they walked back to the unit.

Razor said, "I'm assisting Homicide."

"I don't know where the inspectors are. They left here ten minutes ago."

"What are you finding?" Razor pointed at Yee and Silvela's unit.

A sergeant smiled. "More than I expected to. Our cop killer trashed the unit...hoping to find a spare handcuff key, I'm thinking...but left all the weapons and locked up behind herself. She took the keys but since we have an old homeboy with us..." She nodded toward an officer by the trunk, who sighed at what was obviously an all-too-familiar joke. "...it didn't take us long to get in."

Cole saw what she meant by Irah trashing the unit. Up front, the glove box and clipboard holding citation and report forms had been emptied onto the seat and floor. In the trunk, the plastic case of the first aid kit lay on its side with its contents scattered across the jumble of other trunk items. On top of everything lay a pair of bloody handcuffs, surrounded by opened hand-wipe packs and the blood-stained wipes themselves...also half-used rolls of gauze and tape, and opened antibiotic ointment packets.

The sergeant said, "It looks like she gave herself a little first aid."

That might not be all she used the kit for, Cole reflected. The EMT shears had a black thread caught at the pivot. She needed a quick change of appearance before appearing on the street. He had a vision of her whacking the ruffles off her sleeves and shortening the long skirt. The hand wipes resembled what Sherrie used to clean off makeup. Since the Goth eyes changed Irah's looks so much, so would cleaning them off.

He pointed out the thread to Razor.

Razor lifted the shears up near the trunk light, and pulling the thread loose, twisted it between his fingers. "Do we know if anyone saw her leave the garage?"

The sergeant eyed the thread. "Not that I've heard. And no one's called in a sighting of her in the area."

Because Irah no longer fit the broadcast description. The portions of sleeves and skirt were probably in the nearest trash barrel, along with the wig and wipes she used to remove the eye makeup. "Let's see if the attendant remembers a blonde in a miniskirt and platform boots."

Razor handed the sergeant the thread. "I better catch up with Galentree and Willner."

When Razor gave the attendant in the booth the modified description, he got a nod. "Sure, I remember her."

"Did you see where she went?"

The attendant snorted. "Yeah, crazy broad. She was so anxious to get to Macy's she ran straight across the street through the traffic."

Razor, however, walked to the corner and crossed with the light.

When they came into Macy's minutes later, he peered around. "Now where? Ladies' Wear?"

Straight ahead lay the beauty salon. Cole eyed it. "Irah seems to like doing things with her hair for disguise. She has those wigs in her desk. She used a black one for her tweaker disguise. You remember how different Jessie looked when she changed her color or style."

"Jesus...don't remind me." Razor winced. "The hair de jour. And God help me when I didn't recognize her instantly. How is it something that seems quirky and cute when you're going together drives you crazy after you're married? But..." He frowned skeptically. "...I don't see a fugitive sitting around having her *hair* done. Besides, you can't just walk into these places. Jessie made her appointments days and weeks ahead of time."

"There's nothing to lose by asking."

A glossy young blonde behind the salon reception counter turned their direction with an inquiring smile.

Razor smiled back. "I think you're right. There's nothing to lose by asking."

In response to his questions, though, the blonde—Tiffany, according to her name badge—shook her head. "No, I haven't seen anyone of that description. We don't have walk-in clients."

But people did cancel appointments and someone calling in for an appointment could luck into a slot that opened that way. Sherrie had once. A computer sat on a lower side section of the reception desk, a schedule-looking grid on its monitor. Cole waded through the desk for a closer look. "Ask her about this S. Benet who's scheduled for a cut and color an hour from now."

Asked, Tiffany checked the monitor, then looked across at Razor in amazement. "How ever did you read that? As a matter of fact, she did just get the appointment. She called begging to know if we could work her in, that she's a last-minute bridesmaid substitute for a wedding this evening. Lucky for her we had a couple of cancellations this afternoon and will be able to fit her in."

Razor frowned as they walked away from the salon. "Do you think it's really Carrasco?"

"A name that can be pronounced Benay can't be just coincidence."

"Even if it is her…" Razor shook his head. "An hour. Is there any chance in hell she'll keep the appointment?"

"There's one way to find out."

Razor considered that, then, standing amid the cosmetics counters, he pulled out his cell phone. "This time there's going to be plenty of backup."

He might want backup, but when he called Communications and had Willner and Galentree come meet him, convincing them to call Madrid about setting up a stakeout proved another matter. They stared at him in disbelief. "Cops are swarming Union Square and you think she made and will wait around to keep a *hair appointment?*"

Razor nodded. "I think she's counting on us never expecting anything like that. What do we have to lose except an hour?"

"The ability to show our faces in the Bureau again if you're wrong," Galentree said.

"How long did she hang around Embarcadero Center with *that* area swarming with cops?"

The partners raised *what do you think?* eyebrows at each other but after a minute, Willner called Madrid on his cell phone.

"Now just pray we're not wrong," Razor muttered.

Amen. "I'll be back in time to see."

Razor blinked. "Where are you going?"

"Colma." A very high Dunavan Diagonal and line-of-sight ought to take him there in fair time. "I want to see how Hamada's doing."

— 31 —

GILBERT TANKERSLEY LOOKED to Cole as though he
wanted his body worthy of his name. His biceps bulged and
his shoulders strained at his t-shirt. Heart beating steadily, he
looked up in Zen-master serenity at Hamada, who sat with a
hip propped on the table in the Colma PD's interview room.
"Sure, I know Irah Carrasco. I wouldn't call her a friend, but
we've met, oh, maybe a dozen times at car shows. I run into a
lot of people at car shows, even the lieutenant there." He
glanced past Hamada to the uniformed lieutenant lounging in
a corner behind Hamada. "Why?"

"She called you Thursday evening."

Cole wondered whether Hamada knew that for certain or
was bluffing.

If a bluff, it worked. After a moment of hesitation, in
which his heart rate jumped, Tankersley said, "So?"

Hamada eased his tone from accusatory to casual. "What
did you talk about?"

"Cars." Tankersley's tone added: *of course.* "It's what we
always talk about when we run into each other."

The Hamada raised his brows. "She called you from a pay
phone to talk about cars."

Tankersley stared steadily back at him, heart rate a little
faster yet. "Was it a pay phone? She said she was at a book-
store where she'd seen a book that she thought I'd mentioned
wanting. She wanted to know if I'd like her to pick it up for
me. I made sure it was the right book, then called her back
and said sure, get it."

"And how is she getting it to you?"

He smiled. "She already did. It came in the mail yesterday
afternoon. If you want to see it, I'll have my wife bring it over."

Tankersley had the story down pat. He made it sound good. The lieutenant was beginning to give Hamada that *are you sure about this* look. Which made Cole wonder if practice had perfected this performance. How often had Tankersley provided disposal services?

"Yes, I would like to see it," Hamada said.

If he thought he was calling a bluff, Tankersley fooled him. "I need a phone." Tankersley took Hamada's and punched in the number Irah had written in purple ink. "Hey, it's me....Hell, I don't know. They're jerking me around. Now they want to see the book that came in the mail yesterday. Bring it over, will you? Thanks, hon." He hung up. "She's on her way."

Cole had no doubt that Irah had sent the book. A book raised no eyebrows if a corner of the package were damaged in route. But somehow she must also have included money. Tucked between the pages, maybe...hundred dollar bookmarks.

"You haven't asked what this is about," Hamada said.

Tankersley leaned back in his chair, hands behind his head. "I haven't done anything wrong and I don't figure you'd give me a straight answer, so why bother?"

"Then I'll surprise you." Hamada leaned down toward him. "This is about Irah Carrasco killing a cop."

That jolted Tankersley. He came stiffly upright in the chair. "A cop!" His heart galloped.

Hamada sat back again, folding his arms. "She then spent a portion of Thursday calling friends in L.A. One of them gave her your number."

"Wait, wait, wait. Hold it." Tankersley waved his hands back and forth in front of him. "*I* gave her my number, and that was several years ago."

Hamada paused. "You're not in her Rolodex."

Tankersley shrugged. "That isn't my fault. Anyway, what does—Oh, I see." His tone went bitter. "You think because I work in a cemetery, I did something with the body for her. Once you have a record, you're guilty of everything from then on, right? Well I did my time and I've gone straight since. You check with my parole officer. I make every appointment and meet all the conditions of my parole."

Give Tankersley credit. He put just the right amount of indignation and injured innocence into his performance. The lieutenant looked increasingly doubtful. Too bad the lieutenant could not hear Tankersley's heart thundering.

"So what…you think she brought me the cop's body Thursday night and I slipped it into a grave ahead of whoever was going in Friday? For your information," Tankersley said, "we didn't have any burials on Friday, or Saturday, and I couldn't have arranged a double occupancy even if I wanted to. Unless you think I could drop in a body in broad daylight in the middle of all the preparations for the graveside service. Because we dig the graves the day of the funeral. Check with the cemetery office."

Cole's stomach dropped. That had to be the truth, because he knew they would check. But with no burials, what happened to the bodies?

Maybe he could find something at the cemetery.

Cole oriented the interview room on his internal map, then jogged out of City Hall and down the southbound lane of the highway. This time he worked the moving traffic, but watched the vehicles coming up behind him, ready to jump aside if one of the drivers blew his horn or gave any other sign of seeing him. By the time he reached the Pacific Hills gates, he had amassed enough heat for a materialization.

The cemetery driveway forked, with a sign pointing toward the cemetery office…tucked up among trees out of sight with a small barn and several other out-buildings. A counter in the office ran halfway across the room. The wall behind it held a big dry-erase board marked off in calendar-like columns and rows. Two women sat at desks between the board and lateral files on the opposite wall. Cole waited until one of the women, middle-aged, walked into another room and the other looked occupied with her computer. Then, since no one here knew him, he materialized as himself.

"Excuse me."

The woman swivelled her chair…setting the beads braided into her cornrows clicking against each other. "I'm sorry. I didn't hear you come in." She stood and came to the counter. "May I help you?"

"I'm with the San Francisco police. I need to know if you had any burials on Friday or Saturday?"

Pencil thin brows rose. "No, we didn't. See?" She pointed to the dry erase board. "Like I just told an Inspector Hamada on the phone."

"Hamada." Cole pretended to sigh. "Why does he keep doing that…ask me to check on information and then do it himself." He paused. "May I look at the board?"

She shrugged. "If you want."

He came around the counter. In the Friday and Saturday columns, the squares of the row labeled *Services/burials* were empty.

Thursday had a service, he noticed, but listed for 3:00 pm, well before Irah had learned Tankersley's phone number. Could Tankersley have access to other cemeteries? The burial schedules of them all—what were there…fifteen or sixteen?—might have to be checked.

There was a burial on Monday. However, the service was at 11:00 am.

"The graves are dug the day of the burial?"

"Yes."

Then he noticed the row below the burials, labeled *Groundskeeping*. The Monday square said: *Backhoe and crane: PN x 4*.

"What's this notation mean?"

He stepped aside in case she came over, but she barely glanced where he pointed. "That we need to have four graves dug and vaults put in them."

"But you said the graves are dug the day of the burial and there was only one burial yesterday."

She frowned for a moment, then gave him an apologetic smile. "There was. Those four weren't for burials. They're pre-need graves. That's what the PN stands for. Some plot owners have us dig the grave now, put in a vault, then cover it up and sod it over. They'll put up a headstone, too…especially with a family plot…with all the names and birth dates on it. Then, when the grave's needed, we just have to uncover the vault."

He stared at the board notation, hope rising…then falling again. "I suppose the crane notation means the vault goes in immediately after the grave is dug?"

"That's right."

The older woman came back into the room. She halted, staring at him. Cole wondered what she saw. Maybe, like Red, she recognized ghosts? She squinted, tilting her head. "Do you know you don't have an aura? I've never seen any-one without an aura before."

The younger woman winced. She dropped her voice to a whisper. "It's okay. The sixties were just real good to her, is all." In a normal tone, she went on, "We can't leave an open hole. It's unsightly and dangerous. We'd be liable if someone fell in."

Damn. A grave could not be reopened inconspicuously in the middle of the night, either, not when lifting a vault lid needed several men or a crane.

Still squinting at him, the older woman said, "Except only one of those vaults went in yesterday. The rest had to wait until this morning."

The younger one looked around in surprise. "Why?"

The older woman broke off studying him to grimace at the younger. "The crane broke down again. You were out of the office when Mr. Daniels came in fussing about equipment maintenance and covering up the plywood over the holes to keep an 'esthetic appearance'. Gilbert was still in the shop working on the crane when I left last night."

So Tankersley stayed late in the cemetery and three graves stood open all night. Cole wanted to grab the ladies and kiss them. "Thank you. That's very helpful."

He strolled toward the door hoping they would go back to what they were doing before. And the younger woman did return to her desk. The older one, though, resumed staring at him. Oh well, what the hell. He went ahead and passed through the door.

From outside, he zipped back to Macy's.

A different young woman stood behind the reception counter of the salon...just as blonde as Tiffany, glossy in a silk slack suit, but presumably a policewoman. Willner sat in the waiting area, picking through the magazines as if fearing contamination, looking like a put-upon husband waiting for his wife. He called to the receptionist, "Is there anything to read that isn't about what my man *really* wants or how to lose weight while making delicious desserts?"

She grinned.

Galentree, nearby, wore work clothes with the Macy's logo and seemed to be fiddling with lights under a cosmetics counter.

But where was Razor? Finally Cole spotted him at the top of a ladder, his back to the salon area, fiddling with a vertical banner printed with autumn leaves. Oh, right. Tomorrow was the first day of September.

Cole climbed a virtual ladder to join him. "Are you four all that's waiting for Irah?"

"There are store security officers in plainclothes at all the doors. At this door, they're the window washers outside." Razor shook the banner, then began fussing with its attachment again. "How's it going in Colma?"

"Hamada needs help cracking Tankersley and I think you can give it to him." Cole briefly recounted the interrogation and his trip to Pacific Hills.

Razor stared at him. "You want me to pass that information on to Hamada? How am I supposed to explain knowing it?"

"You have many mysterious sources of information."

Razor snorted. But then he sighed and took out his cell phone. Punching in the number, he said, "You realize that after this everyone will definitely consider I'm a wack job. Yo, Hamada...a little bird tells me that yesterday Tankersley dug four pre-need graves and didn't put in three of the vaults until this morning." He paused. "Hamada?"

At the other end of the connection, Hamada said, "Are you down here, too?"

"Nope. I'm up a ladder in Macy's waiting for Carrasco to keep a hair appointment."

Another silence, much longer, came over the phone. "You're shitting me."

Razor grimaced. "No, I swear."

"A *hair* appointment? And you know what's what's happening down here in Colma? What the hell is going on?"

"Ask me again some night when this is over and we're both half smashed. Gotta go." He jammed the phone back in his work pants.

"How much time do we have?" Cole asked.

Razor checked his watch. "Ten to fifteen minutes."

"Then I want to see how Tankersley reacts."

He zipped to the interview room.

Hamada stood hefting his phone and shaking his head. Then he raised a brow at Tankersley. "What was that number for the Pacific Hills office?"

Tankersley recited it.

Hamada punched it in. "This is Inspector Hamada again. I need to verify some information I just received. Did you have three graves sitting open last night?"

Tankersley froze.

On the cemetery end of Hamada's phone, the voice of the younger woman in the office said, "Yes. Didn't the other detective tell you?"

Hamada's eyebrows rose. "What other detective?"

"The one just here, that we told about the pre-need graves."

Hamada frowned. "I think he told someone else. What was his name?"

"Come to think of it, he didn't say his name."

In the background, the older woman said, "He looked like Jimmy Stewart."

Hamada eyed the telephone as if it had turned into a bomb. Disconnecting, he gingerly dropped it back in his pocket, then shook himself hard and pinned Tankersley with a grim stare. "You think I'm jerking you around? Just keep lying to me, amigo, and see what I do. Which of those graves did you put Inspector Dunavan and the woman into?"

Tankersley yawned. "I don't know what you're talking about. Now either arrest me for something or I'm leaving."

Hamada bared his teeth. "If we have to pull all those vaults up, I'll charge you with everything I can think of, starting with being an accessory after the fact in the murder of a police officer. I will, in fact, make your life a living hell. So why don't you cooperate and not piss me off any more than I am already?"

Tankersley stared up at him for a long minute, then dropped his head. Despite his muscles, he seemed to shrivel in the chair. "She never told me he was a cop. She said they were her husband and a bimbo she'd caught him fooling around with. I—I never did anything like that before."

In a pig's eye, Cole reflected. He was lying through his teeth. But that hardly mattered at the moment.

"I needed the bread and a friend in L.A. knew that, so he suggested I help the lady out. She brought 'em down Thursday night and I stashed 'em in an old mausoleum until—"

"Cut to the chase, amigo," Hamada said. "Where do we dig?"

Tankersley sighed. "I'll show you."

— 32 —

A ZIPTRIP TO his virtual ladder at Macy's found Razor still on the real one fussing with fall banners. In the salon area, Willner continued playing the waiting husband.

"How's our time?" Cole asked.

"Almost there." Excitement ran under the quiet words. Cole heard Razor's heart speeding up. "What happened in Colma?"

"Tankersley's going to lead them to my body." Urgency beat at him. Lead Hamada, but not too quickly. Please let them capture Irah first.

Please let her show up.

He looked down, checking out all females near the salon, hoping he recognized her. She was bound to have changed her appearance again. He just hoped those model's bones gave her away.

His gaze started to slide past a stocky, butch woman carrying shopping bags and a suit bag, then jerked back, his neck prickling. Not stocky. Her baggy cargo pants and heavy knit turtleneck, with sleeves coming down her hands to her fingers, just made her look that way. So did her square jaw. But the ears revealed by hair slicked back and darkened by gel had no lobes.

Relief matched a chill at how easily she might have gone unrecognized. He had guessed right. She really was arrogant enough to keep her appointment.

"She's here!" he whispered, and scrambled to the floor.

Above him, Razor murmured into his radio. Willner peered over the top of his magazine, catching the eye of the policewoman at the reception desk.

She gave Irah a radiant smile. "Welcome. Are you Miss Benet?"

"Yes." Irah eyed her. "What happened to Tiffany?" Her voice sounded different, as if she were talking through clenched teeth.

But it was tension in her body that vibrated Cole's antenna. "Watch it," he called to Razor, backing down the ladder. "I think she smells the trap."

"Tiff had a doctor's appointment," the policewoman said easily. "I'm Lexie. You're having a cut and color, right? Michael will be taking care of you. This way."

"Will you take these, please?" Irah held her bags out toward Lexie.

At Lexie's momentary hesitation, of course reluctant to tie up both hands, Irah threw the bags in her face and spun away. Lexie fought free of the suit bag, clawing for the gun tucked in the small of her back under her suit jacket. Willner leaped to his feet and in front of Irah. Galentree and Razor closed on her from the sides...all with guns drawn. In the salon, customers in a position to see the scene gasped.

Irah stopped short, glanced around at them, then laughed. "Get real. You're not going to shoot in here, with a store full of civilians and all of you in each other's crossfire." Reaching into her mouth, she pulled a roll of gauze from between each lower gum and cheek. Her jaw shape returned to normal. She worked her lips. "I'm glad to get rid of those."

There was the deceptive passivity again. "Watch her, Razor!"

"Get down on your knees," Galentree said.

She went down, but not on her knees. Abruptly, she dived down and forward, arrowing between Galentree and Willner. They dropped to tackle her. Only to find her no longer stretched out but curled in a tight ball, somersaulting forward and onto her feet again. She sprinted for the doors.

Cole hurled himself through Willner and after her. He might not be able to stop her, but if she eluded the store security officers outside the doors and managed to pull off another escape, he would be with her every step. Then once she settled somewhere, he could report her location.

Behind, Razor yelled into his radio. Through the glass ahead Cole saw the two window washers drop their squeegees and move in front of the doors.

Irah swerved to a door in the set where a middle-aged woman had just entered. She grabbed the woman's arms, spun her around, and as the startled woman yelped in protest, slammed her forward...back out the door.

Alarm shot through Cole. Was she taking a hostage?

No...a weapon. Irah shoved the woman at the nearest security officer. While he scrambled to catch the woman, Irah dodged past. The other officer lunged for her. His fingers closed on the shoulder of her sweater. She instantly spun and rammed a foot into his knee. He reeled backward, yelling in pain.

The moment his hold released, Irah whirled again. She charged across the sidewalk and off the curb into the traffic of Geary Street.

Where she spun once more, this time to face them and raise both hands in one-finger salutes, smirking triumphantly.

The world froze.

Twice Cole had experienced the sensation of things happening in slow motion. The time a drug dealer shot at him, he swore he saw the bullet emerge from the muzzle flash and float toward him, moving so leisurely he could count its rotations. But never before had motion stopped altogether.

He was the only moving object in a world of statues...pedestrians petrified between one step and the next, birds immobile in midair. One security officer had congealed in mid-collapse of his leg. The other officer had his arms under those of the woman shoved at him, keeping her on her feet. Inside the store, Razor reached for the doors, Willner and Galentree just behind him. Irah stood planted in the street flipping them off. And fifteen feet away, a delivery truck sat in the same lane, its driver's face just starting to contort in horror. His foot, Cole knew, would be headed toward the brake.

Then he saw the driver's eyes widen a fraction more, and the truck shift forward slightly. Turning, he found Razor closer to the door. The officer with the woman had begun swinging his head Irah's direction. The world continued to move…just at a glacial crawl, in eerie silence.

Cole grabbed for Irah. "No! I won't let you get away this easy!"

He might as well have been catching fog. His hands passed right though her. He could only watch…furious, despairing, impotent…while the truck inched toward her.

In real time the brakes must be screaming, but the truck had no chance to stop. On both sides of the street, pedestrians oozed around in the direction of the sound. Horror spread across the faces of the security officers.

The engine passed through Cole in machine gun heat bursts. Then the truck hit Irah. Her body leisurely contorted, the near side of it moving forward under the impact with the grille and compressing against the far side. Her head tilted back toward the truck. She floated into the air and arced toward the sidewalk…where she landed like a rag doll, limbs sprawled unnatural directions.

Abruptly, time came unstuck. Normal motion exploded around him. Razor burst through the store doors. Cole scrambled clear of the truck, which finally skidded to a halt in a screech of brakes and tires. Around him everything seemed to be screeching—the woman Irah had used as a battering ram, pedestrians, the brakes of other vehicles. Metal screeched, too…shrieking and crumpling as another vehicle piled into the back of the delivery truck, and a third vehicle into that one.

One of the screams, Cole realized, was his own…a howl of pure rage. Irah had eluded them yet *again*…and this time escaped forever!

Razor dropped to his knees by the motionless form and felt her neck for a pulse. Looking up at Cole, he shook his head.

Cole cursed vehemently.

Then Razor's eyes widened. "Wait!" He looked over his shoulder at Willner and Galentree. "Call an ambulance! She's still alive."

— 33 —

COLE STOOD WITH everyone else clustered outside the exam room doors in SF General's ER...Razor, Willner, Galentree, Lexie, several uniformed officers...watching through the windows while doctors and nurses worked over Irah amid a web of IV and oxygen lines, ECG and blood pressure leads. The head of a portable x-ray machine darted in and out over her, recording the bony trauma.

"Isn't that a waste of medical resources?" one of the uniformed officers said.

A number of expressions agreed.

"Razor!"

Warmth flooded Cole at the voice. He turned happily. "Sherrie!"

She walked past him to Razor. "What are you doing here?" Her voice sharpened in concern. "Who's been hurt?"

"Not an officer," Razor reassured her.

"She's a cop killer," Willner said.

Sherrie caught her breath and looked quickly at Razor. "The Benay woman?"

"No." He reached out to put an arm around her. "Someone else, who really killed Cole."

He might as well have dropped a match into gasoline. Stiffening, she knocked the arm away. Her eyes flamed, and the heat of her fury crackled out through her hair. "And you brought her *here*? Trying to keep her *alive*?"

"You want her to stand trial for his murder, don't you?" Razor said.

Her hands clenched. "I want her *dead*!"

"Why don't you let us drive you to pick up the kids and take you all home?" Razor caught the eye of a uniformed officer, who nodded. "We know where Cole's body is and are going after it."

She froze. As if someone had thrown a switch, she went eerily calm. "Thank you. Will you call my mother and tell her I'm coming home?" And she walked out with the officer.

After calling Joanna, Razor called Lauren. At the other end, his ex-wife said, "I'm just about off duty. I'll pick up Holly and go over."

Cold trickled through Cole. The ritual had begun, family and friends gathering around the bereaved family. Lieutenant Lafferty and the chaplain would come to notify her when his body was found. Then there would be the funeral. He hated police funerals...the church full of officers in dress uniforms, eulogies about laying down one's life and giving the last full measure, the street full of vehicles topped by light bars. The long cortege of police cars down to Colma. Rather than think about it, he wandered into the exam room.

The doctor stood studying x-rays hanging up on the view boxes. He turned away, grimly shaking his head at a nurse. "Let's get a CT and MRI and see just how bad a prognosis we have."

What? Cole circled them to the view boxes. And stared. He had seen enough x-rays over the years to know what the human skeleton should look like. Irah's rads recorded disaster. Two cervical vertebrae had shattered. One fragment looked driven into the spinal cord itself.

On the exam bed, Irah groaned. The heart monitor beeped faster.

"She's regaining consciousness," another nurse said.

The doctor quickly stepped back to the bed. Cole moved to the foot of it.

Irah opened her eyes. She stared around with the dazed expression of the half-conscious, her mouth working. After several tries, she managed a weak, ragged: "Where..." The oxygen mask turned it into a whisper.

"You're at San Francisco General," the doctor said.

Irah stared up at him. "Alive?"

"Yes." He smiled at her. "You're alive."

Her face twisted. "No!" The whisper rasped, enraged. "*No!* Get away from me, all of you! Get those fucking needles *out* of me!" Her chin jerked toward the IV tubing. But a moment later her expression went baffled. She stared down at her arms. "My arm won't move." Horror spread across her face. "I can't feel it!" Her voice rose. "I can't feel *anything!*"

Cole smiled in grim satisfaction. "Hey, Irah...can you say quadriplegia?" Much of the lead in his gut dissolved. This time they had her for good.

The cervical collar prevented her from lifting her head, but Irah's eyes shifted to stare toward the foot of the bed. "You! How can you be here?"

He started. She *saw* him?

"I'm an ER doctor," the doctor said. "Dr. Anson."

Irah's eyes stayed focused on the foot of the bed, furious. "You're dead!"

Anson and the nurses exchanged puzzled glances.

Triumph warmed Cole. Maybe being so close to death herself broke down her blindness. "That's right. I'm dead. While you're still alive. That truck needed to be bigger or going faster to do the job you wanted. But you're alive just from the neck up." He gave her a knife-blade smile, savoring justice. "No matter what kind of defense your attorney mounts, you've got a life sentence in an escape-proof prison. With no possibility of parole. And since I can't see a jury sentencing a quadriplegic to death, on behalf of Sara and myself, I wish you a long, long life."

Staring at him, her glare turned to horror, and she began screaming...her voice rising higher and higher toward hysteria that was equal parts fury and despair.

But before Cole could enjoy it, weakness swept him. Suddenly he stood in evening light looking into a grave. A body was being lifted out of it in a canvas sling. In the bottom of the grave, next to a trenched section, part of another body showed through a layer of dirt...a female hand, blonde hair. Sara.

Cole swung into the grave and knelt to touch the hand. "We got Irah. She's going down for what she did to you. I only hope you can feel how sorry I am for what *I* did to you."

Did he see a stir in the air beside him, or only imagine it and a brush of warmth across one cheek?

Before he could decide, more weakness hit him. He looked up to see the sling being spread open. A camera flash went off several times. The Colma lieutenant said, "God...700 pounds of concrete vault did a job on him."

Cole climbed out of the grave and, feeling oddly detached, stared at his crushed body as Hamada went through the pockets. He thought of the dead airmen movie. Was he about to disappear? He checked himself and saw with relief that he still looked solid.

Then he realized the world had changed. Things looked... translucent. Instead of him fading, the world was. Protest rose in Cole. *No, not yet!* One piece of lead still lay in his gut, the one with Sherrie's name.

"Imagine that," the lieutenant said as Hamada found a billfold in one hip pocket and Cole's cell phone in the coat. "A killer too squeamish to clean out her victim's pockets."

Hamada grunted. "More like she reckoned he'd never be found."

Cole stared at the phone. It still looked in good shape. Hope sparked in him. He leaned down close to Hamada's ear and strained to put substance into his voice. "See if the phone still works!"

Hamada froze. Cole saw goosebumps rise on his neck.

"Try the phone."

Hamada just stared at it for several moments, then pushed the power button.

Hope surged higher as the screen lighted. "Play the voice mail messages. My password is 03686."

Hamada stood, hefting the phone, an inner struggle visible in his eyes.

"Something wrong?" the lieutenant said.

"I reckon I'll see." Hamada punched up the menu and went to voice mail. Playing the messages, his expression turned bemused.

"My wife needs to hear those messages," Cole said. "Call her up on your phone and play them for her. Please?"

Hamada looked around...and stared incredulously at him. "Please call her."

"What are you looking at?" the lieutenant asked.

Hamada quirked a brow. "Maybe the explanation for a lot of weirdness. Excuse me. I need to make a phone call."

Cole quickly zipped back to the hospital, to Razor, still standing outside the exam room.

Razor glanced at the others and sidled away from them, lowering his voice. "What's happened? You're fading."

So was Razor. His colors looked washed out and objects behind him showed through as shadows. Cole's throat tightened. "They've found my body. Sara's, too. And my phone. Hamada's going to play the voice mail messages for Sherrie. I don't have much longer here."

"Cole, I—" Razor's voice caught.

Cole's throat closed completely. Damn. How did the two of them say goodbye? "It's been fun, huh, partner?" He punched toward Razor's shoulder.

Razor punched back. "Always a blast."

Cole zipped home. It looked surreal, turned to layers of colored glass. It felt held-breath tense. Lauren and Holly had arrived. The kids sat together in the livingroom watching *Harry Potter*, but silent except for Hannah, who squealed at the flying car.

From the doorway, he said softly, "I love you, gang. Have a good life. I'm sorry I won't be there."

In the kitchen the women cut up vegetables and tossed them in Sherrie's big soup pot...working without talking, either. Tiger, lying by Sherrie's feet at the sink, looked up at him and whined.

Cole bent down to pet him, then stood and wrapped his arms around Sherrie, wishing she could feel him, even if only as a chill. But she showed no reaction.

His chest constricted. "I wish you'd hear me. I screwed up. Me and my obsessiveness screwed up royally. But I didn't screw around. Not with Sara, not with any other woman… despite what Debra Brewer thinks she saw. There's only been you. They've found—"

The phone rang.

Joanna answered it. "It's for you, Sherrie. An Inspector Hamada."

Sherrie slid out of his arms. But he followed her to the phone, chest tight. Not bothering to listen to Hamada's end of the call, he watched her face. She caught her breath and tension drained from her face. As it did, color faded faster from the glass layers around him.

Sherrie hung up and stood leaning her forehead against the phone.

He reached out to touch her hair, which still had color when almost nothing else did. "You know, I really wanted to grow old with you and watch this wild red hair turn to wild white hair."

Sherrie lifted her head. Her hand went to her hair…where his hand touched. "I would have liked that, too."

The constriction unwound in his chest. A sense of lightness filled him. Contented, Cole stepped back, watching her while the world went transparent and disappeared.

Author's Biography

Lee Killough has been storytelling almost as long as she can remember, starting somewhere around the age of four or five with making up her own bedtime stories. In grade school the stories became episodes of her favorite radio and TV shows: Straight Arrow, Wild Bill Hickock, Sergeant Preston of the Yukon, and Dragnet. Beating the episode-writing practice of Trek fans by almost two decades.

Then, in keeping with wisdom that says the golden age of science fiction is about age eleven, a pre-teen Lee discovered science fiction. Having read every horse book in the school and city libraries, and repelled by the "teenager" novels that seemed to be about nothing but high school and boyfriends, she began desperately hunting something new to read. And discovered science fiction. From her first SF novel, Leigh Brackett's The Starmen of Llyrdis, she was hooked. But along with the pleasure of devouring this marvelous literature came fear. She lived in a small Kansas town with a small library and she could see that as with the horse books, she would soon read the section dry.

So to keep from running out of science fiction, she began writing her own. And because the mystery section adjoined the SF section, leading her to discover mysteries about the same time as SF, her stories tended to combine SF with mystery.

They still do...with a noticeable fondness for cops (the influence of a childhood watching TV shows like Dragnet, Naked City, and Highway Patrol). Vampire cop Garreth Mikaelian hunts killers in Blood Hunt and Bloodlinks (published together by Meisha Merlin as BloodWalk) and in Blood Games. She has future cops Janna Brill and Mama Maxwell, space-going cops, werewolf cops in her novel Wilding Nights, and now a ghost cop in Killer Karma.

Lee lives and writes in Manhattan, Kansas, where she lives with a miniature Schnauzer in a house bursting with books and enjoys a committed relationship with, fittingly, a book dealer.